It seemed as though  beating and her mo... *knew* this woman! Jem was staring at the screen, unable to take his eyes from the degrading scenes. Daisy opened her mouth to speak but only a strangled sort of sound emerged. She poked her elbow into Roy's side and as he looked down, his forehead was creased as though he was wondering what the hell was the matter with her. Jem had begun stepping from one foot to the other. He was breathing fast. Daisy looked away and sought Vinnie's face across the room. He was watching both her and Jem. She could tell Vinnie knew something was very wrong.

June Hampson was born in Gosport, Hampshire, where she still lives. She has had a variety of jobs including waitress, fruit picker, barmaid, shop assistant and market trader selling second-hand books. *Fatal Cut* is her fourth novel. Her first three novels, *Trust Nobody*, *Broken Bodies* and *Damaged Goods* are also available in Orion paperback.

By June Hampson

Trust Nobody
Broken Bodies
Damaged Goods

FATAL CUT

JUNE HAMPSON

An Orion paperback

First published in Great Britain in 2009
by Orion
This paperback edition published in 2010
by Orion Books Ltd,
Orion House, 5 Upper St Martin's Lane
London WC2H 9EA

An Hachette UK company

1 3 5 7 9 10 8 6 4 2

A CIP catalogue record for this book is
available from the British Library.

ISBN 978-1-4091-0374-5

Typeset by Deltatype Ltd, Birkenhead, Merseyside

Printed and bound in Great Britain by Clays Ltd, St Ives plc

The Orion Publishing Group's policy is to use papers that
are natural, renewable and recyclable products and made
from wood grown in sustainable forests. The logging and
manufacturing processes are expected to conform to the
environmental regulations of the country of origin.

www.orionbooks.co.uk

This book is for my mother, Florence Ladysmith Pike,
and my father, Ernest Arthur Pike

Man is the cruelest animal

Friedrich Nietzsche 1844–1900

ACKNOWLEDGEMENTS

Grateful thanks to my editor, Sara O'Keeffe.

PROLOGUE

Her tongue emerged from her heavily painted lips like a small pink snake and her eyes closed in mock ecstasy as he entered her. From the radio in the kitchen David Cassidy was asking how he could be sure love was real. There was definitely no love in this act, she thought.

Her hair, black as jet, bounced about her face as she tried to steady herself by gripping the brass bedstead while he rode her hard. Remember to relax your muscles or the bastard will tear you apart, she told herself – and for fuck's sake smile for the bleedin' camera and *think about the money.*

'Yes, yes!' She mouthed the words she was primed to say.

His sausage-fingered hands with nails bitten to the quick were on her shoulders, fingers that were digging into her flesh as he thrust into her. On her back she could feel the scrape of the metal studs of his black leather belt and vest and knew she'd end up with bloody welts when he finally collapsed stinking and sweating on to the stained sheet.

'Yes, oh, yes,' she cried, 'I love it. You're so big.'

At least the partially zipped leather face mask camouflaged the kid's bad case of weeping acne so she didn't have to think about that. He couldn't be any more than seventeen and hadn't said two words to her before they started fucking, but then, she wasn't being paid to have a conversation with him, was she? He was hung like a donkey and she guessed that's why they hired him. She told herself, pretend he's Adam Faith who's so good looking and sexy in that TV programme *Budgie*.

And then she was making a mental shopping list of food she'd buy from the supermarket on the way home, and perhaps a soft toy for baby Rosie, maybe even a Tiny Tears, for hadn't Rosie cried when she'd had to give the doll back to Val's daughter? One thing was for sure, both she and her neighbour, Val, who never refused to look after her child, would be eating a slap-up meal tonight – the first decent meal either of them as unmarried mothers living on Assistance had eaten in a while. Maybe she'd even buy an Arctic Roll for pudding.

'Fuck me harder,' she cried.

The camera would be recording her every facial expression and every movement of the bloke riding her. Thank God it couldn't record her shame.

The room stank, it was windowless, airless and the three men filming were watching without emotion.

She thought back to how easy it had been to get into debt and for the worry to consume her. And then how quickly the interest on the debt had spiralled, and her terror at the man's threats and punishment.

The money she'd be paid for this one-off porn flick would set her free.

Free from the fear, free from the debt.

She could begin to live again. Maybe get a part-time job.

'Yes, I love your huge cock.' She repeated the memorised script that had been scribbled on a page from a grubby exercise book.

'I'm coming,' he yelled theatrically.

'Fill me with your cum,' she shouted.

With her eyes now closed to fake passion she saw nothing.

But she felt the sharp object rip into her throat, smelled the metallic tang of fresh blood. Opening her eyes and looking down she saw the red drops falling, splattering, and then gushing onto the grubby white sheet. The man, spent, sprawled by the side of her, his mouth a wide silver-zippered gash in the blackness of the leather. The pain swelled. Oh God, what was happening?

Then she saw the bloodied knife clutched in his fist.

She lifted her hand and felt the slipperiness of her slit throat. The blood was pouring through her fingers.

'Help me,' she croaked.

The three men were staring back at her.

Not one of them moved. Their faces were blank masks.

'Help me,' she tried once more.

And in that instant she knew she'd never see her child again.

'Help …'

Blackness was enfolding her in its arms. She was dying and the camera was still turning.

CHAPTER 1

Asfendiou, the Greek Island of Kos, April 1972

'Please God,' she whispered, her heart overflowing with love for her beautiful boys, 'don't ever let anything or anyone harm my sons. Not when for once in me bleedin' life everything is on the up an' I feel so happy I could burst!'

Daisy Lane bent over the bed and tenderly wiped the perspiration from Eddie's forehead. His dark hair was damp, causing it to curl even more tightly than it usually did. In sleep his breathing was deep, untroubled as only a ten-year-old's can be. In the next bed, six-year-old Jamie's sheet was wound so tightly around his perfect little body it seemed as though he wanted to hide from the world. He moaned quietly in his sleep. Daisy touched his blond hair and sighed. His downfall was his jealous nature, but why it should be directed towards his brother, Eddie, she couldn't fathom. Perhaps he'd grow out of it ... after all, didn't she treat both boys equally?

She shook her head, banishing her sudden negative thoughts.

Vinnie was in the next room. Lovely, lovely Vinnie! Jamie's father had come to Greece to see her, a surprise that definitely added to her happiness and would thrill the boys when they woke.

Daisy glanced in the long wall mirror. It seemed ages since she and Vinnie had shared time together. Smoothing her blonde bobbed hair back behind her ears she turned, weighing up her body, and decided on the black halter top and the black shorts that looked like a tiny skirt, enhanced her tan and showed off her slim figure.

If that didn't get him going then nothing would, she thought. God, but she'd missed him. That was just one of the downfalls of being involved with a copper, and a bloody straight one at that! Served her right, she supposed, for co-owning Daisychains, Gosport's premier nightclub, with the notorious London gangster Roy Kemp, friend of the Krays.

Coppers and gangsters just didn't mix socially. It didn't help either that she was looking after Roy's nefarious interests while he was banged up at Her Majesty's pleasure.

Negative thoughts again, Daisy, she scolded herself. Vinnie's come to see you, so bleeding well make the most of it! At least here in her little Greek house she was free from prying eyes.

The thin curtain fluttered at the window letting in a small breeze and the scent of flowers wafted into the room from her garden. Already Kos was about to excel itself with sunshine and colour in true Greek style. Daisy decided 1972 was turning into a very good year indeed. She winked at her mirrored reflection, closed the door behind her and went out to join her man.

'Why do I always forget how tall you are?' Her arms snaked around Vinnie's waist and she leaned her head against his broad back, breathing in the male scent of him, combined with the orangey cologne he always wore. She'd interrupted the conversation between Vinnie and her very pregnant friend Susie that was taking place on the stone-flagged garden terrace covered with trailing grape vines. 'Where we goin', Detective Inspector Vinnie Endersby?'

He twisted round to face her and she saw that his beautiful, different-coloured eyes were twinkling. Dark honey and chocolate, eyes that she wanted to drown in.

'You'll see when we get there.' Daisy wondered at the seriousness of his tone but quickly dismissed it. Wherever he was taking her, she thought, they'd be together.

'Jesus Christ, Daisy, let the bloke 'ave a shower an' freshen up,' said Susie. 'He's only just got 'ere.'

'It's only a piddly little trip from Gatwick, Suze. Besides if you 'adn't stayed gassing to 'im he'd 'ave had a bleedin' shower by now!' Daisy pulled a face at her friend.

She and Susie had rigged up a shower with a hose from the kitchen tap out into the garden and hung it from an olive tree. The kids thought it was great fun, and Daisy had reckoned it was one way of getting them clean without them making a fuss. A blanket strung across a branch served as a shower curtain.

'I think a quick shower outside would be in order,' said Vinnie, disentangling himself after kissing her chastely on the forehead. 'So would another cup of tea.'

Daisy rocked back on her heels. 'You're supposed to drink plenty of fluids when it's hot. Fancy a glass of retsina?' She'd grown quite fond of the dry white Greek wine.

'Tea's fine,' said Vinnie, unzipping a small holdall he'd hoisted onto the table. He searched through it and pulled out a folded and ironed light blue shirt. Daisy watched his movements. He wore no rings but his hands were well formed, his nails neatly clipped. She loved his hands. Hands were one of the first things she noticed about people. Hands and teeth. It didn't matter if a person had crooked teeth, if they were clean and white it showed a person looked after themselves.

Susie said, 'Well, you drinks the same bleedin' large amounts of tea at 'ome in Gosport when it's freezin' cold, so what's your answer to that?'

Daisy glared at her. 'If you're trying to pick a fight it won't bloody work!'

Susie shrugged and helped herself to some water from a blue and white jug on the table, splashing it into a sturdy tumbler. Daisy grinned at Vinnie, then nodded towards the garment he was holding.

'That shirt's been pressed well. I'll 'ave to get you to iron my stuff 'cause our Suze is getting very slapdash about her work now she's the size of a bleedin' 'ouse!'

Daisy saw Vinnie colour up. She'd embarrassed him. Her grin deepened into a smile.

His curly hair was shorter than the fashion of the moment dictated though he'd allowed his sideburns to grow a little. It must be difficult, she thought, being a copper and unable to follow fashion. She wondered what he'd look like with a droopy moustache. Probably ridiculous; he was too clean cut for facial hair.

'C'mon, you.' She hoisted Susie from the chair in which she'd wedged herself.

Vinnie asked, 'How long you got to go now, Suze?'

''Bout a couple of months.'

'You sure?' Daisy could see the doubt crossing Vinnie's face.

'She's got mixed up with 'er bleedin' dates, hasn't she? We got 'er booked into Blake's Maternity Home but she won't keep 'er appointments with the doctor.'

Daisy was still grumbling as she ushered Susie inside her whitewashed house. 'Get in the kitchen, Suze. Don't want you gettin' any bleedin' ideas if you sees my Vinnie in the nuddie.'

'I might be missin' my husband somethin' terrible but I think you can keep your copper to yourself.' Susie, with a big groan, plonked herself down on the sagging green velvet sofa.

'I don't know how you manage it,' said Daisy. 'In all the time the pair of you 'as been livin' with me I ain't never seen you cross with each other. You been married donkey's years but you're still like bleedin' newly weds.' Without waiting for Susie's reply Daisy carried on, 'You sure you don't mind me an' Vinnie poppin' out for a while an' leavin' you with the boys?'

'It's me job at 'ome in Gosport to be chief cook, bottlewasher and child minder, ain't it?' Susie put her hands beneath her belly as though supporting her unborn child. 'What's so different 'ere?'

Daisy busied herself plugging in the electric kettle. 'You could do with a bit of a kip yourself, take it while you can. Eddie an' Jamie'll sleep for ages.'

'I know you persuaded me to come away because we both needed a bleedin' break but I feel fine now, honest I do. A few days in the sun an' I soon gets me energy back. I'm a bit like you, Dais. I reckon the sun recharges me batteries.'

Daisy was peering into the dark recesses of the high cupboards looking for biscuits. 'Aah, gotcha,' she said, pulling out a packet of Bourbons. 'Your old man's one in a million, ain't he, to entrust you to me in your condition?'

'Why wouldn't he? He knows I'm all right with you. And 'e 'ad the offer from you to come 'ere an' all, didn't he? But he didn't want to spend time away from managing his bleedin' World's Stores. Anyone'd think it was the only grocery shop in Gosport's High Street. Anyway – ' Susie paused and took a deep breath. 'He'll be eatin' his dinner at 'is mother's every night an' they'll be decidin' all sorts of things about the baby.' She patted her stomach. 'But I miss 'im, Dais.'

'Why wouldn't you? You do know how 'appy I am for you? About the baby, I mean. I'll always be 'ere for you.' Daisy set out mugs on the draining board. She thought about Susie's first child, a little girl who had died in a terrible road accident. Si and Susie had waited a long time for this baby.

'I do know. If it wasn't for you taking me in when I was a kid ...'

'Don't start on that!' Daisy didn't want to be reminded of how hard she'd worked to make a living in the grubby cafe in North Street. Susie had turned up one night, an abused kid on the run from her stepfather, and had willingly helped Daisy further the success of the caff. 'We 'ad some good times as well though, didn't we?'

Susie nodded, her blonde curls bouncing around her face. Her blue eyes shone with happiness.

'I met my Si an' you fell in love with—'

Daisy interrupted Susie. 'A lot of water under the bridge since then, Suze.' She put a mug of thick dark tea and the sugar bowl on the coffee table by the side of her friend then stared hard at her. 'There are times, Suze, when I think I'll never get over Eddie Lane.' The words had come out of her mouth without her even thinking about them. She felt the touch of Susie's warm hand brush against her fingers.

'I know. No one will ever take 'is place. But he's dead and gone an' you got 'is son, who's like his bloody mirror image, an' you got a good relationship with Vinnie. Not to mention your pet gangster, Roy Kemp.'

Daisy pulled her hand away. 'How many times do I 'ave to tell you that my business with Roy Kemp is strictly that, a business relationship ...'

'Might be for you, Dais, but maybe not for 'im ...'

'I'm mindin' 'is interests, as well you know, because I owe him the bleedin' money he put up for Vera and me to open our business!' An image of Vera, the feisty ex-prossie who was at this very moment not only coping with the running of Daisychains but her own massage parlour in Gosport's High Street, brought warmth to Daisy's heart. Daisy trusted Vera with her life.

Susie smiled at her then raised her eyebrows. 'You knows that an' Vera knows that an' I knows that. An' we all knows you wants to run the club drug free. I just don't think Roy looks at things in the same way.'

Daisy was breathing heavily, watching as Susie stirred sugar into her tea. She was trying to think of a witty remark when Vinnie's shadow cut the bright sun from the doorway and she turned to see him watching her, his curly hair damp and glistening from his shower.

'Where's my tea then?'

'Just like a bloke, expectin' to be waited on 'and

and foot,' said Daisy, but she went over to the draining board and brought back his mug. Handing it to him, their fingers touched and as the fiery longing sprang to life inside her, Daisy mentally counted her blessings.

'I'll just take a quick look at the boys. I won't wake them.'

Vinnie quietly opened the door on the sleeping children. His Jamie looked like an angel. He wished he could spend more time with the lad instead of flitting in and out of his life. That's exactly what it felt like at times, he thought. That he was forever flitting between cop shops in London, Liss and Gosport, and juggling crimes he was working on while trying to put some stability in his two sons' lives. He couldn't walk away from his wife, Clare, because of his son Jack and he didn't want to walk away from Daisy because he loved her and Jamie. It also pained him that he was in Greece at Roy Kemp's request.

He stared at the wallpaper with its pictures of trains and planes and then his eyes dropped to a large wooden box in the corner where toys spilled across the woven carpet. The room smelled of blossom from Daisy's mad tangle of a flower garden outside, while inside you could almost touch the atmosphere of love that Daisy surrounded her boys with. She was a damn good mother, he'd give her that.

His eyes travelled to young Eddie. Jesus but he was the spit of his father at that age! A mental picture flashed through his mind of the two of them as kids, him and Eddie Lane, best friends, racing through the back alleyways of Gosport after scrumping apples and the fruit falling from their rolled-up jumpers, laughing at their crime yet terrified of getting caught.

He could sense Daisy hovering behind him and smell her perfume. He was growing hard. He turned, causing her to step backwards while he gently closed the bedroom door on the children.

He gathered her into his arms, nuzzling his face down into the enticing warmth of her neck. For a slim woman her breasts were large and luscious, just the way he liked them.

A quick thought slid into his mind. Why couldn't life always be easy? Why did bad people want to hurt the innocent? He pushed the thoughts away. He didn't want to upset Daisy here. Now was not the right time to tell her of his fears.

Instead he asked, 'Why do sleeping boys look like butter wouldn't melt in their mouths?'

'And little buggers when they're awake,' said Daisy. 'Jamie's still wettin' the bed, you know.'

'He'll grow out of it. Everyone knows little boys are worse for piddling than girls.' He stared hard at her. Her long-lashed green eyes were wide and trusting. 'I love you,' he said.

'I know,' she whispered back before her lips found his. With short tender kisses he then traced her cheeks, her nose, her forehead. He felt her shiver with excitement.

'You're beautiful,' he said and swept her hair off her face. She moved her arms to his shoulders and he let his hands wander over the warmth of her flesh while he breathed in the softness of her skin. It always amazed him that she fitted against him like she was supposed to be there and that such a small person could fill him with so much pleasure. He would have liked to wave a magic wand and make her small enough to fit in a matchbox that he'd carry with him everywhere. His palms found her breasts and he cupped them one in each hand. 'Perfect,' he whispered, delighted to feel her nipples harden and thrust themselves against the thin cotton of her top.

Susie's voice cut short his excitement.

'If you two don't bugger off, I'll not get a nap because the boys'll be awake!'

He heard Daisy's deflated sigh match his own.

The air was dry and warm as Vinnie led the way down to the road. Daisy's house was on an incline reached by stone steps that were garnished with terracotta pots of bright red geraniums. Vinnie knew that when Daisy was at home in Gosport her beloved pots were tended by the owners of the nearby Taverna Asfendiou. That was another thing he admired about Daisy. She got on with people. It was rare to hear her put someone down or say bad things about them, and people gravitated towards her.

At the bottom of the steps, parked on the road's grass verge, was the motorbike he'd hired at the airport. Vinnie climbed aboard and started up the engine.

'Get on,' he yelled, steadying the machine. He felt her arms around his body, felt her make herself comfortable on the pillion seat, and soon he was moving through the sleepy village. Some of the houses were still in ruins. He knew the earthquake of 1933 was to blame for this. After the desolation many families had relocated to the larger town of Kos, the island's port. It was a small island, barely thirty miles long, but the terrain changed from sandy beaches to pine forests and bare mountains. 'I'm going to whisk you away so I can have my wicked way with you without interruptions.' He had to shout, the warm wind was taking his words away.

'Thank God for that,' Daisy yelled back. He released one of his hands from the bike's handlebars and patted her clenched fingers that were gripping his waist.

The bike plunged through the Greek countryside and Vinnie loved the sensation of being at one with the machine, the sun and the speed. Smells of herbs, flowers, and the yellow whins that were whisky scented filled his nostrils and he wondered whether it was possible to get drunk on smells.

On the airport road he headed towards Kefalos. Here the land was uneven, with vegetation growing in gullies. The wind from the sea had torn away all but the strongest trees, which had bent themselves into strange shapes to survive. The sea, blue today as baby ribbon, bordered volcanic earth and outcrops of rock. And then ahead, like a thin yellow stripe, the road pushed upwards in a zigzag to the top of the mountain where the small village of Kefalos lay.

After a while Vinnie changed gear and slowed the bike to a standstill.

'Just look at that view.' He waved an arm expansively, taking in the panorama around them.

'Fuck the view, I thought I was never goin' to get you to meself,' Daisy said. She'd climbed off the seat and was rubbing at her bottom. He shook his head and smiled at her then switched off the bike's ignition, rose from his astride position and set the machine on its stand.

'Come here,' he said. 'It really is so good to see you.' He noticed her eyes travelling over his body, and the familiar hardening began at his groin. She reached for him.

He kissed her for a long time, tasting her sweetness, holding her head back so he could kiss her throat and her neck.

'Not here.' Daisy tugged away and led him from the road to the shelter of a group of trees. A grassy hillock gave them invisibility from the road.

He pulled her down on to the soft spring grass. The ever-present chirrup of the cicadas was in his ears. Kneeling before him, Daisy picked up his hand and raised it to her lips, kissing each finger in turn, then, with her eyes locked to his, she began undressing slowly. Mesmerised, Vinnie watched her every move, while the breeze sent tantalising wafts of her perfume and skin to inflame him. When she was completely naked she said, 'Your turn,' and began unbuttoning his shirt.

The pleasurable sensation of her fingers on his skin made the surfaces of his body tingle with anticipation. 'Let's get these off.' She unzipped his jeans and he wriggled out of them, looking down at his hardness, and the milky fluid glistening at the engorged head of his cock.

She was gazing at him with such tenderness.

And then he was inside her, pushing through the soft folds of her body, pushing and pulling back, pushing and pulling back until he could almost stand it no longer.

The fucking, he thought, was as soft as velvet yet as hard as stone. She grasped him tightly and thrust her pelvis at him as though wanting him to come yet willing him not to. Every movement was a discovery that made him want to cry out.

'Come now,' he commanded.

A jolt ran through him like wildfire, wave after wave.

Tears of happiness seemed to stream from every pore of Daisy's body.

'We came together,' she said.

Afterwards Vinnie clung to her. Held her tight and close. She had exhausted him, mentally and physically, and he felt marvellous!

'Daisy?'

'Yes?'

'I love you.'

'I know you do,' she said.

He, feeling the sun on his skin and the weight of the woman he loved at his side, closed his eyes. He was completely satisfied. Until he remembered why he had to come to Greece.

CHAPTER 2

They were in the village square, where sunbaked, white-painted houses nestled together between shops whose doorways were festooned with hanging plastic strips that were supposed to deter flying insects from entering. The bike was parked near the war memorial and Daisy could hear children playing. A taverna beckoned; sitting outside it were dusty men drinking liquorice-scented ouzo.

'You gonna tell me what this is all about?' Daisy felt Vinnie's arm tighten across her shoulder. 'You didn't come all this way just to make love to me, did you?'

'We'll go into that taverna and I'll explain.'

She looked into his eyes and saw they were troubled. She nodded, and her steps fell in with his as he loped across to the taverna.

Daisy practically threw herself on to the hard blue chair.

'Well?' she said, as soon as the waiter had deposited the large ouzos and glasses of water on the table and left. 'I can see you got somethin' on your mind, spit it out.' She wiped the back of her hand across her lips after downing a large mouthful of her drink. 'What's going on?'

She looked expectantly at Vinnie, but knew he wouldn't be rushed.

'Where do you want me to start?' He raised his glass to his lips.

'At the bleedin' beginning would be nice.'

He set his glass back on the table.

'I've watched your son Eddie grow close to Roy Kemp. I know he looks on him as a father figure, but I just don't want the boy to lose sight of who his real father was.'

Daisy opened her mouth to speak, ignoring Vinnie who tried to wave her words away.

'Eddie Lane was a villain,' she said. She nodded as Vinnie caught the waiter's eye to bring more drinks. She knew Eddie's father could be cruel, she knew he could be kind. But he'd loved her with a passion and never once had he involved her in anything sordid. And she'd loved him. And probably always would.

Daisy looked about her. At the dappling on the table as the sun shone through the leaves of the sheltering olive tree, at the bright white of the neatly clipped cloths on the tables. She picked up her drink and swallowed, feeling its warmth hit the back of her throat and soothe her jangled nerve ends.

'And the point of all this?' she asked.

'That you make sure young Eddie knows his father was nowhere near as ruthless as Roy Kemp is. Eddie Lane strived to protect the people he cared about.

Revenge for what he saw as unjust deeds came as natural to him as breathing. Roy Kemp isn't small time, he's an out-and-out bastard.'

'I do know that, Vinnie.' She thought of how she'd fallen under the spell of the gangster, Kemp, with his David Essex gypsy-like looks. And how he'd done the dirty on her by getting another woman pregnant and spoiling Daisy's dream of Daisychains by making the club a haven for drug deals.

'Didn't he have Eddie Lane killed for movin' in on 'is territory? That ain't somethin' I can bleedin' forget, is it? But I wish you'd believe me that I only work for the bloke to set meself free of debt.' Whether Vinnie believed her or not he was still looking at her strangely. Fear clutched at her heart. 'There's more, isn't there?'

He nodded.

One of the reasons she and Vinnie saw so little of each other nowadays was that Vinnie's job meant a great deal to him. Mixing socially with gangsters just wasn't a viable proposition for a copper.

But her profit from Daisychains would enable her to provide Vinnie's son, Jamie, with a good future. She tried to treat both boys the same and Eddie had a trust fund maturing for when he came of age. Vinnie's wages and the fact he wasn't a bent copper taking bribes meant his money was accounted for almost before he opened his wage packet.

'You're not worried that Jamie'll look up to Roy Kemp?'

He shook his head. 'Jamie's got a real father.' He paused. 'Me.' Then he drummed his fingers on the table. 'Look, Daisy, I knew with you I'd only be second best after Eddie and I never really minded that, but Roy Kemp snaps his fingers, I have to pass messages on, and you go running. I need you, all of you, permanently in my life.'

'I won't, *can't*, give up Daisychains,' she said quietly, 'and you can't abandon your career. The police force is your life, like Daisychains is mine, and if you gave it up, well, after a while you'd begin to resent me for that and we'd be at each other's throats quick as a flash.'

'But I want you.'

'You got me.'

He opened his mouth to protest but she put her finger across his lips.

'A detective living with Roy Kemp's woman ain't gonna go down too well with your superiors, is it? Even if I ain't his bleedin' woman no more. Anyway, you're still married to Clare.'

'Bugger my superiors. Bugger Clare.'

Daisy sometimes wondered if Vinnie had turned to her on the rebound after finding out that his wife was having an affair with Vinnie's boss. Daisy had been vulnerable after Eddie's death and she and Vinnie had gravitated towards each other, finding the comfort each craved. Clare's affair had disintegrated, so she'd taken the boy, Jack, and moved in with her mother and father at their country house in Liss. Promotion had taken Vinnie's boss to pastures new.

Daisy encouraged Vinnie to make the most of visiting his son. Vinnie had told Daisy that Clare's father was going into hospital soon for some routine checks.

'Thank Christ one of us has some sense, Vinnie. I won't ever let you give up your career for me.' She leaned across the table and kissed him. 'It's enough for me that you love me.'

It was as though he'd not listened to a word she'd said for he started on at her again. 'You could give up the club. We could go away together. Take the boys. Start a new life.'

'And 'ow far would I get before I get dragged back? Roy won't let me go without a struggle because I know too much about his business. I owe 'im money. He'd send someone to find us an' I don't want to live in fear.'

Vinnie looked at her like a kid who'd had his football stolen. The silence that followed could be cut with a knife.

Despite Roy being shut away in Parkhurst he still held the upper hand. A dark night, a knife in Vinnie's guts, a shot to the head. Roy had warned Vinnie off Daisy years ago, Roy had told her so. But that was before Roy had got Angel pregnant.

'When I've paid Roy back I'll be able to run the club how Vera an' me wants it run. There'll be no backhanders to coppers from the Gosport nick who let *him* do pretty much as *he* pleases because *he* won't be controllin' Daisychains no more.'

'He isn't supposed to be doing any business from prison.'

'You know that an' I know that, Vinnie. He's like the Krays. Their empire keeps on runnin'. Where d'you think the money comes from to soften life in prison? Favours don't come out of respect for the bleedin' big villains they are. Respect, my arse, it's money talkin' every time.'

Vinnie was looking at her with great sadness. 'The sooner you're out of his clutches, the better. How do you feel about him being released soon?'

Daisy shook her head. She doubted sometimes whether she'd ever be truly free of Roy Kemp. He wasn't serving the full term of his imprisonment because his sentence had been cut for 'good behaviour'.

'I don't care one way or the other. When he saddled Daisychains with drug dealers, any feelings I 'ad for 'im went straight out the window. Even when I found out he'd fucked Angel an' put 'er up the duff that didn't hurt me 'alf as much as him killing my dreams for the club. Money is his God. Oh, he loves 'is mum and Charles an' my Eddie, but it all 'as to be on his bleedin' terms. The only reason I ain't ever been busted by the coppers, as you well know, is because he greases their palms so well.'

Daisy knew Roy couldn't risk losing face if she upped and left the working relationship simply because she'd had enough. The timing had to be just right. Else she'd be the one to come off worst.

She also knew drugs were here to stay. But if she

could make Daisychains a drug-free area then she'd have peace of mind. Cannabis didn't stay recreational. She'd seen it lead to the hard stuff, cocaine and heroin. Dependence brought misery. She hated the new deals with the Turks and Africans set up by Roy's mum with Charles, Roy's one-time driver and now his father-in-law. She hated it that some club owners supplied drugs to their girls who prostituted themselves to keep their bosses and their habits fed. Daisy had witnessed the sad results of this so often.

She and Vera paid good wages to their girls, with no pressure other than to do the jobs they'd been hired for. Daisy and Vera's girls were well sought after because they were clean and had regular medical check-ups. This was how Vera had managed to get in on the London scene, supplying girls to government ministers for their parties. High-class whores for high-class people in high places.

'You know I mourn that our relationship has to be put on the bleedin' back burner, an' it ain't 'elped that you 'as to work in London as much as you do. But Vinnie, when we do spend time together, it is bloody lovely, ain't it?'

Vinnie didn't answer her. There was something about the look on his face that made fingers of ice grip the back of her neck.

'You didn't come 'ere just because you wanted to see me, did you?'

Vinnie reached across the table and enfolded her

hand in his. His lovely different-coloured eyes held hers.

'You've got to go back to Gosport sooner than you planned,' he said. 'Roy Kemp sent me to get you.'

Daisy rocked back on her chair.

'What the fuck do you mean?'

Vinnie narrowed his eyes before he answered her.

'Roy's got a bloke on his case in Parkhurst. Reckons he's the son of Jack McVitie. He's out for revenge, big time ...'

Daisy couldn't help herself. 'Then it's a bleedin' good job he's inside where Roy can 'andle 'im,' she broke in.

Vinnie sighed. 'McCloud's got contacts on the outside, Daisy. Because the bastard's in prison it doesn't mean you're safe ...'

'Me! What d'you mean?' Daisy's heart was thudding. 'I ain't done nothin' ...'

'The bloke's not thinking straight. He wants to hurt Roy for killing his father. And with Roy's release imminent ...'

'But it's Ronnie and Reggie Kray copped thirty years for the gangland killing of Jack the Hat. Roy was only implicated.' Daisy couldn't get her head around the insanity of it all.

'McCloud can't get near the twins, their protection's too dense. But he's sworn to come after you and yours because Roy cares about you. He's already had a go at Roy. Cut him with a knife.'

Daisy was shaking now, the horror of Vinnie's words chilling her to the bone.

'Cut him?'

'Oh, don't worry, he's fine.' Daisy caught the sarcasm in Vinnie's voice.

She didn't speak for a while, then she said, 'That fuckin' bastard shouts an' I 'ave to run? Everything I've worked for is back in England. Me 'ouse, me business, me friends. But more importantly, my boys need to be where Vera and me can keep 'em safe.'

She gave a long-drawn-out sigh as she digested all the information and its implications before she said, 'I got to get home to Gosport immediately.'

CHAPTER 3

'You've got yellow jaundice,' the Isle of Wight prison doctor flung at him.

'From your fuckin' dirty needles,' came Don McCloud's reply.

'Don't worry, you'll be out of here soon enough.'

McCloud gazed at the white-coated bespectacled man who stank of antiseptic and had now moved on to the other bed, where he spent even less time talking to the prison hospital patient. Next, the doctor would visit the four-bed ward across the corridor to check on the gypsy who McCloud had slashed with a razor-blade shiv. McCloud fingered his broken nose and winced as his hand brushed against the flap of skin where the knife had been forced back on him, and which had been sewn back on to his cheek.

'Cunt!' McCloud yelled down the ward. He thought about the fight that had landed him in the hospital. He'd put the nut on a guard in the corridor and when three more fuckers had arrived from nowhere he'd fought the lot of them. He was sedated, put in a straitjacket, and flung in a padded cell where he'd received a kicking. What did he care? Fuck all! The first guard had had eight stitches put in his chin.

McCloud laughed out loud. 'There was fuckin' blood all over him,' he said to Col in the next bed. Col didn't answer. He was attached to a drip, his eyes closed.

He'd get even with the bastard screws what had done him, McCloud thought. His food was being spat in and when one of the warders told him he'd pissed in his tea, he'd kicked the tray out of the fucker's hands.

If there was one thing his father had taught him it was never to let any bastard get the upper hand. He smiled: finally he'd been shifted to Parkhurst where he could exact his revenge on that bastard Roy Kemp. He'd do it slow, chip away at the fucker before he got out of the nick and leave him sweating about the day that pretty little blonde of his would get it. Kemp didn't know it yet, but there were those on the outside who wanted that fucker out of the way just as much as he did and would look favourably on McCloud if he got the deed done first. And who could possibly implicate him for any mishap to the girlie when he was banged up for the remaining five years, plus three hundred days added on for the assault?

He ran his hand through his hair and examined the blond strands that clung to his fingers. Took after his dad that way an' all. He'd started to lose his hair in his twenties, his dad had, only no one never really realised because of his bleeding hat that he wouldn't take off for no bugger. That trilby gave him his nickname, Jack 'The Hat' McVitie.

'They're scared shitless at what I'll do next,' he said, shaking his head at the still figure near him. 'Not that I should be in 'ere.' He looked at the silent Col, then around the sparse ward with its four beds, only two occupied. His eyes also travelled to the high barred windows that never seemed to let in light. 'Got fitted up, I did. I was goin' straight. Decent job as a bouncer at Duggan's in Soho. You know the place, got about fifty steps leadin' up to the fuckin' door. Me an' this Big Tony was doin' our job. A lot of people reckon bouncers are only there to take it out on the fuckin' customers but that's a load of bollocks. If there wasn't customers we wouldn't have a fuckin' job. A bouncer's job is to protect paying people from the stroppy cunts what throws their weight about.'

He stared hard at Col. 'You ain't dyin' on me, are you?'

McCloud swung himself out of the blankets and went and sat on the other man's bed. He put his face down against the man's blue-tinged lips.

'Thank Christ you're still breathin', Col, else the cunts might blame that on me as well. As I was saying, I reckon you'll be thinkin' how come a lanky bastard like me was a fuckin' bouncer? Well, I'll tell you. My old man put me to the fights when I was seven. First in a gym so's I could learn the moves, then he'd cart me round the gypo camps an' bet on me to win against their kids. Bare fuckin' knuckles it was. He got

31

me into it young, see? I ain't gonna say I never lost a fight but I went into it never expectin' to lose. I've 'ad hundreds of fights. Put a fair bit of cash in the old man's pocket. Kept me ma fed an' watered an' all. But I went inside for armed robbery when I was nineteen an' I didn't like fuckin' Durham prison one little bit so I reckoned on comin' out to gettin' the kind of job that keeps me in trim.

'This fat geezer starts actin' up before he gets inside Duggan's an' I tells 'im he can't go in. He throws a punch my way, then this tart is shoutin' to this geezer, "Finish him, Mike. Go on, kill 'im," an' the goadin' spurs 'im on an' he comes at me again. The first punch I ignores, because I likes me job an' I don't want to upset the boss. The second punch reaches me so I throws one in his guts and follows it with a really low-down one in his goolies. It can't have 'ad the desired effect because he plants one in me left eye. Fuckin' 'ell, that tosser could take it.

'The crowd is goin' fuckin' wild now, jeerin' and shoutin', an' you can smell they're out for blood. He staggers, an' I bend down an' plant two in 'is ribs. I finish 'im off with one to the side of his 'ead an' he falls and rolls, arse up in the air, down them fuckin' steps. I swear I heard 'is head hit every step.

'There ain't no cheering now, Col. He's lyin' at the bottom of them steps as still as you are now. Only he ain't been seen by no doctor. So that's how come I got eight years. Just doin' my job. He snuffed it, but it wasn't really my fault, was it? If it 'ad been me what'd thrown that first punch I'd be doing longer, wouldn't I?'

'Get back in your bed, McCloud.' The screw had returned with a mug of hot cocoa which he put on the floor at the side of his chair before collapsing into it. McCloud could smell its chocolate sweetness from across the room.

'Just checking on him, sir,' he said. But he climbed back into bed anyway. 'How's my mate Kemp?'

'If you got any fuckin' sense you'll keep away from him. He's not best pleased with you marking his face.' The guard searched for and found beneath his chair the gardening magazine he'd left there. 'You were lucky to get the punishment cell for that,' the screw said.

'The fuckin' needle, restraints and a kicking in the cell,' he reminded the screw.

'Thank your lucky stars you ain't like your bedmate there. So don't you think of trying to get out of here by starting a riot like he did.'

'I know you bastards after the fighting in the association room made Col run the gauntlet. He could 'ardly fuckin' walk when he was forced to sprint between two lines of guards in riot gear and all of 'em armed with bleedin' sticks an' iron bars. That fuckin' floor was slippery with 'is blood for days after.'

'You'd better watch your mouth and your back, McCloud. Roy Kemp ain't gonna forget you in a hurry for putting the gypsy in the ward opposite.'

'I sliced into his pet gorilla and gave him somethin'

33

to remember me by, didn't I? It ain't right. The twins got what they deserve for killin' my old man – Kemp should 'ave got thirty an' all. Fancy that silly fucker jumping in front of Kemp like that. Gypos are usually a bit more savvy, they don't like getting 'urt. Found out he used to fight like I did at the fairs and camp-grounds. Maybe the guv'nor can set up a fist fight between us, bit of entertainment like?'

'Reckon you could take him, then?'

'My ol' man would 'ave said so.'

'McVitie ain't around no more though, is he? That's if he really was kin to you. Why ain't you got his name?'

'Me ma wasn't *married* to 'im, but it don't mean he weren't me dad.'

He saw the guard shrug, pick up his mug of choco-late and take a deep satisfying swallow. McCloud thought about his father's easy smile. He'd been a big bloke, six foot two in his socks and like a fuckin' ox. Sure he took pills – they was to ease the pain in his hands caused by some gang that smashed his hands with crowbars. After that the pills and booze got to him. Didn't stop him playin' football in the street with all the kids, though. Barry Street that was, in Bethnal Green where McCloud was brought up.

He liked the women, Jack did. McCloud liked them too, as long as they didn't get clingy and whiny, but a few backhanders usually put 'em in their place.

Lauren was a nice girl. Her and her kiddie gave him a nice settled feel, until she wanted to know where he went and what he was doing when he wasn't tied to her apron strings.

Wasn't his fault the little bleeder kiddie cried all day and every night. It 'ad to go, didn't it? The kid ended up in a sack in the river.

Lauren changed after that. Got thin and scrawny. Half the time she didn't even listen to 'im any more. It was like fuckin' a bean pole. He liked women with a bit of meat on their bones. He wondered where she was now, then decided he didn't give a shit.

'I heard Jack would swallow anything that gave him a kick, that right?'

McCloud glared at the guard who had his feet up on the table and was lounging back on his chair.

He thought of the black bombers that fuelled his dad's temper. 'My father could fight anyone,' he said. 'He was afraid of no bugger.'

'He was a right bastard, I'll give you that,' said the guard.

'He operated on his own. He wasn't part of no firm or gang.'

'Way I heard it he was too unreliable for anyone to take him on. Caused trouble wherever he went, didn't finish a job he was supposed to do for the twins and generally pissed everyone off. Gave 'em so much aggravation they sorted him out at Blonde Carol's in Evering Road at Stoke Newington. That's it, ain't it?'

McCloud was shaking. He'd heard how his father had been lured there by the promise of a party with plenty of booze and women. Reg Kray had got him in the room and fired a gun at him. Only it hadn't fired. The .32 semi-automatic pistol had jammed. His dad had tried to escape, got as far as diving for the window and breaking the glass. Had his head and shoulders through when Reggie and Ronnie Kray, helped by Kemp, pulled him back inside the room again.

Reg Kray done him with a butcher's knife. Drove it into his face, then into his chest and stomach so many times that the knife finally stuck through his father's throat and bedded itself in the floor.

Then the place was cleaned up and the body got rid of. The body of his father, the man who'd taught him to fight, to play football. Jail sentences weren't enough for them bastards the Krays, nor for Roy Kemp. Kemp was getting out soon. That was a fucking laugh. Why should he walk around with that blonde tart on his arm when he helped kill McCloud's father?

An eye for an eye, a tooth for a tooth.

Roy Kemp deserved to die. So did that fucking blonde bint he was so fond of. McCloud had an ace up his sleeve though – Roy Kemp's days as king of his manor were drawing to a close. McCloud had mates on the outside who wanted rid of the bastard just as much as he did, but for a different reason.

Daisy Lane wouldn't be around much longer either, he'd already made arrangements on that score.

Meanwhile, McCloud's mother was dying her own death because the body of his father had never been found. Drinking herself into an early grave in that poxy council flat.

'My old mum took it bad, you know, an' I can't do fuck all about it because I'm in 'ere.'

The guard looked up from the magazine and yawned.

'They'll let you out for the burial,' he said.

CHAPTER 4

'That fuckin' Isle of Wight boat upsets me stomach every time!'

'Think yourself lucky, Daisy Lane, you ain't got so far to go as some of them wives visitin' their men in Parkhurst Prison. It's only a ferry-boat ride to Portsmouth before you gets on the big boat an' then it don't take *that* long to get there.'

'It ain't you what gets seasick, is it, Vera?' She looked out of the window at the empty crisp bags and bits of newspaper chasing about the Gosport pavement in the May wind. 'An' just 'ear them bleedin' words! "Tie A Yellow Ribbon Round The Old Oak Tree"!'

Vera cocked her head to one side and listened like a cheeky Gosport sparrow to the top hit Tony Orlando song coming from the radio at the back of the bar at Daisychains, then started laughing. Daisy couldn't help herself, she put her hand over her mouth but that didn't stop her giggles escaping.

'You always see the bleedin' funny side of everything, you do!'

'Laugh an' the world laughs with you, cry an' you cries alone, Dais. But it is a bit appropriate, ain't it? He'll soon be out, won't 'e?'

Daisy stopped giggling and grimaced, hauling herself as tall as her five foot three would allow. She put her hands on her hips, breathing in Vera's Californian Poppy perfume, which almost but not quite eclipsed the stale fag smoke in the bar of their club facing the Gosport ferry and the bus station. She stared down at the shining brass foot rail, then across the polished wooden bar top at the coloured bottles of liqueurs that were seldom asked for but gave the place a bit of class, to the rows of Babycham that seemed to fly out of the place. At the far end of the bar the morning barmaid was chatting to an elderly man whose eyes never seemed to leave the girl's breasts. He must have been leering at her for some time for his ashtray, next to his glass of Guinness, was overflowing.

Finally Daisy looked at her own serious face reflected in the mirror at the back of the bar. She glanced away quickly, attempting a smile, for Vera's words were the tonic she needed to face the journey to see Roy Kemp.

'He ain't me 'usband, never was an' never will be. I ain't no prison wife. I've been commanded to visit him but I wouldn't care if I never set eyes on that bleedin' gangster again as long as I live. Fancy him settin' up a meet between 'imself and Vinnie while he was out on an acclimatisation trip. That bloke's got the nerve of the devil!'

She'd tried to change the subject but she knew Vera wouldn't let the club business go, she'd have to have the last word. She was like a dog with a bone once she got hold of anything.

'The three of us sharing our club 'ere makes Roy a bedfellow, an' that's as good as bein' married, girl.'

Daisy eased off one of her black high-heeled shoes and rubbed her aching foot against her ankle, steadying herself by holding on to a bar stool.

'It's not often you're wrong and you're bleedin' right there! But it's such a drag, specially when the channel's rough. There'll be people puking up all over the place, and then when I get there I 'ave to board that prison bus—'

'Shut up moaning. You got nothin' to worry about 'ere. I'm keeping an eye on this place an' your boys are all right with Suze. Jesus, but she's a size now, ain't she, Dais?'

'I rue the day I ever got involved with that bastard,' Daisy went on, ignoring Vera. 'If I 'ad my way I'd cut 'im out of our lives altogether.'

'You and me couldn't 'ave opened this place without Roy's 'elp. Remember 'ow skint you was a few years ago?'

Daisy's full attention swung towards Vera. It was true, every word. She had taken Roy's money and the club had given her a good living, but the price had been high. Too late she'd discovered that Roy's network of drugs businesses, which she detested, went hand in hand with the loan. Even now there was a bloke in a suit, hunched over a half pint and sat in the corner booth. Every so often he'd hand over a small package and money would change hands.

Daisy hauled herself on to the bar stool and sighed deeply. Then she met Vera's steady gaze and in resignation said, 'You want the honest truth, Vera? I'm scared. It ain't normal for Roy to call me in to see 'im, and it certainly ain't right for 'im to make me cut short me 'oliday with Suze. Roy don't get worried if it ain't worth worryin' about so I'm scared …'

'Stop it!' Vera snapped Daisy back to her normal cheerful self and she shrugged.

'Will you phone the house and check on Suze later? I know she insists she's fine but …' Daisy watched as Vera nodded.

After a while Daisy started swinging her legs. Stop scaring Vera, she told herself, think about something else.

'Why is it always better when you get your shoes off?' Daisy saw Vera relax and pull up another bar stool so they could sit next to each other. The barmaid glanced their way and Daisy shook her head to her unspoken enquiry about drinks.

'Even better when you soaks your feet in a bowl of salt water, Daisy.'

Vera's feet had always bothered her. That came of standing around on street corners in all weathers in her ridiculously high heels, waiting for punters when she was on the game. Those days were long gone but Daisy was proud of Vera and the way she dressed to show off her neat figure. Today she wore a tight black skirt with a frilly red silk blouse cinched in at the waist, and a pair of lethal-looking peep-toed black high heels.

Vera was ageing well, she'd give her that. She looked as good now as she did when Daisychains had first opened its doors to the public of Gosport in 1966, the day of the World Cup. The pair of them had been anxious that the football match would keep the punters away but they needn't have worried. Who could forget England winning for the first time and the team carrying Bobby Moore from the field brandishing the cup? Celebrations had given Daisychains a great opening night and they'd done well ever since.

Daisy sighed as she looked at the gold scrolled clock on the wall at the back of the bar and checked her watch against it. Her eyes fell on the wide gold bangle the love of her life Eddie Lane had given her. Her thoughts slid easily to her children. Her boys were her life.

It wasn't long before Daisy was walking past the bus terminal opposite the club. Outside the public toilets, Alec the drunk was putting the finishing touches to his chalk pavement drawings and Daisy grinned at him and dropped some cash in his tin mug. After buying a ticket at the booth for the short trip across the water, she walked down the ferry gardens and then found a seat on one of the squat ferry boats that every few minutes sailed the strip of Solent water between Portsmouth and Gosport.

The chug-chug of the engines caused the sea to spew out a white frothy V shape behind the boat. The rest of the water was grey and choppy and the air salty sharp with spray. Daisy decided it would probably rain later. She clutched her leather handbag to her side and stared back across the water where Daisychains dominated the skyline and stood proudly at the entrance to the High Street.

The club was Gosport's premier nightspot. Punters came from all the surrounding areas to try their luck at the gaming tables and ogle the girls. Angel, with her fall of blonde hair, was a great draw. Daisy paid her well and Vera used her for her upmarket escort service. Besides Heavenly Bodies – her massage parlour in the High Street – Vera was now running a very exclusive line in call girls for known faces in government, both locally and up in the Smoke. Vera was an astute businesswoman.

Daisy knew her own success was due not only to hard work but also to her association with Roy and his mates, the Kray twins, even though they'd been banged up since 1969 for their parts in the Cornell and McVitie killings. Ron Kray was imprisoned for the George Cornell murder, with Reg as an accessory, and Reg for murdering Jack McVitie with Ron as an accessory. The twins were in for a thirty-year stretch and Roy went down for five years as an accessory for helping dispose of McVitie's body, even though it was never found.

Daisy knew her connections to the London mob helped to bring in named punters to the club but, because of those same connections, Daisy was forced to meet Vinnie Endersby in secret when she'd really rather have been tucked up with him in his little house in Alverstoke Village. Daisy was pissed off that even though she'd never so much as put a foot wrong in her life, for Vinnie to be openly living with her would do his career no good at all.

Thank God Jamie would always be a strong link between them. She knew the bond between father and son was powerful.

She was brought out of her thoughts by the bump of the ferry boat against the Portsmouth pontoon. She watched as the boatman flung the rope in figures of eight around the bollards to secure the craft before allowing the passengers to disembark. Workers and shoppers poured chattering from the boat and began the hike up the slope near the harbour railway station to the bus terminal.

Nelson's flagship, the *Victory*, was in dry dock and Daisy could see naval warships moored in the dock-yard. There was always something going on in the city of Portsmouth, she thought, but it was Gosport she loved: its rundown buildings, the smell of fish and chips and beer hovering over the town, the flurry of the market, the noisy pubs and colourful characters. She couldn't imagine living anywhere else in England,

and though she loved her little house in Greece, Gosport was her real home.

She climbed the steps of the Portsmouth harbour station and bought a ticket for the regular ferry to the island.

Once on board, Daisy settled up on deck, perched on one of the slatted wooden seats. A dose of salty air would do her good, she thought, and when she'd had enough she could go and sit in the boat's cafe. It wasn't long before they were heading out for the English Channel, and immediately the vessel met the rough open sea her head started thumping. If she didn't take a couple of Anadin soon the headache would turn to sickness and she'd throw up. Fancy coming from a seaport town, living with the sea all round, and not being able to sail on the water!

Yet Daisy knew she'd never like to live far from the sea. Its sights and smells held her spellbound. Gulls were diving and swirling, making noises like crying children. She looked around her. Not too many people had braved the upper deck, most were down below where it was warmer. It might have been spring, she thought, but on the water the wind hadn't lost its sharp edge. A couple of women were earnestly gossiping and a family were occupying a long bench further along.

The sounds of the sea crashing against the boat as it ploughed through the waves combined with the noise from the engines were beginning to work their black magic. Daisy descended the metal stairway into the public quarters.

'A cup of tea, please.'

Slopped in its saucer it was handed over.

'Milk and sugar over there.' The elderly scowling waitress wiped her wet hands on her off-white pinafore and then motioned to the end of the counter where a half-empty milk jug and a bowl of sugar with a wet spoon were anchored in a wooden well.

The air was stuffy with fag smoke but Daisy was used to that. She paid for her tea and carried it towards an empty table.

Sipping her tea after swallowing a couple of tablets she thought about how the time spent with Vinnie was so precious. Their last conversation in the tiny bedroom of his terraced house came to mind. They'd made love, tenderly, and in the afterglow they'd discussed the future again. But always Vinnie wanted more than she could give. Sometimes Daisy felt like she was spreading herself so thin she'd break.

She finished her tea, returned her cup and saucer to the miserable waitress, and climbed the metal staircase back up to the deck. The ship would be docking soon and passengers would disembark on the Isle of Wight, a place awash with high-security prisons.

Thank God this awful visiting lark would end soon, thought Daisy, as she slipped into the ladies' toilet to tidy herself. Once she was off the boat she'd take the bus that went to Parkhurst Prison. She brushed the blonde hair that framed her face and fell to her shoulders in a long bob. A dab of mascara, a light touch of green on her upper lids to enhance the green of her eyes and the tiniest smear of lipstick and she was satisfied. Daisy had never considered herself pretty but she knew she had something men liked. She was also aware that men felt safe enough to confide in her. She could keep their secrets. But she couldn't abide liars. You could believe a thief but you couldn't believe a liar.

The tea and the Anadin had worked wonders and she felt much better once the vessel had docked.

In the throng of jostling people leaving the boat Daisy thought she spotted one of the bar girls from Daisychains. She peered into the crowd pushing their way noisily down the gangway and saw the unmistakable flowing titian locks of Leah.

'Leah!'

The girl turned at the sound of her name but didn't stop. In fact, she ignored Daisy and swiftly made her way through the crowd.

It *was* Leah, Daisy hadn't been wrong. The gypsy-style clothes confirmed it. Leah's face was pale, distressed.

Daisy knew little about the girl, other than she did her job well at Daisychains and could be trusted. Leah kept her head down at work and Vera got on well with her. They knew Leah's husband was in prison – perhaps he'd been transferred to Parkhurst? Visiting times varied from prisoner to prisoner so it wasn't surprising Daisy had never noticed the girl on her previous trips. Daisy shrugged. If Leah didn't want to talk to her she probably had her reasons.

The prison bus was half full with women and noisy children when Daisy climbed inside and a quick glance told her Leah wasn't on it.

Daisy settled herself on a seat next to a window, took a deep breath and primed herself to meet her ex-lover.

CHAPTER 5

Roy sat on his bed, hands clasped, his fingers entwined, waiting.

Elton John was singing softly on the radio as Roy looked around his dismal cell with its blue-painted wooden floorboards, worn and ugly. Wood dominated the whole prison, which to him seemed like something out of a fairy tale by Grimm, and no wonder, he thought, with five hundred prisoners locked within the grey building.

He was well aware he was more fortunate than most as his small living space held luxury items other cons couldn't afford or weren't allowed. Backhanders to screws and officials had provided them. A record player jostled for space on the shelf with a tape recorder and his radio. A deeper blue shag-pile rug did its best to cover the floor space and he'd had dark blue curtains and a matching bedspread sent in to him from his Daisy.

Two pictures adorned one wall. One was his mother's wedding photograph, showing her and Charles smiling from ear to ear, and the other was of

Daisy and her son Eddie, taken in the garden of her house in Western Way. Both pictures were glassless.

A large vacuum flask, usually filled with hot water to enable him to make drinks when lockdown was in operation, stood empty on his table. He was banged up from nine at night until the cells were unlocked for breakfast at eight in the morning. Not that he really minded the solitude, since it gave him time to think, to plan and to read. He had more books in his cell than most prisoners. He remembered Daisy saying to him, 'You're never alone with a book.' Her words had proved true.

He also had a wardrobe. The usual issue per con for clothes was a small cupboard. Money again had greased palms so he could keep the suits he'd had brought in, his silk shirts and his Italian handmade shoes in good order. The small cupboard contained his prison garb and shoes, and a pair of trainers.

He looked at his gold watch and reckoned Daisy should be on the premises by now.

Roy had lost weight and gained muscle during his stint in prison. It wasn't from his work as a cleaner, one of the easiest and most sought-after jobs inside. He guessed his weight loss was due to making full use of the gym and the exercise yard. He liked to box and was glad he'd kept up with the sport from his early years when he and Reg and Ron Kray and their brother Charlie had practised together. He smiled, remembering the time Ron and Reg had fought each other in the ring. Their mother had shouted blue murder at the promoters when she found out.

The food in the prison was putrid and so backhanders were paid for special meals. He liked thick steaks and smoked salmon and fruit. He pitied the new inmates coming to this place from prisons where the grub was better. There'd been a few new faces around lately.

He twisted his chunky ring with its black onyx R set in the gold. The ring reminded him of more pleasurable times spent outside the dark walls of the island prison, and he knew those good times would soon be returning. He was allowed to wear his signet ring just as married men were permitted to keep their wedding rings.

Roy hated dirt and clutter and kept his cell immaculately clean. He despised the smell of his outer surroundings, the odour of piss and stale sweat combined with cheap disinfectant.

At night he'd lie awake, listening to the sounds of locks turning and keys jangling, of men crying, and of the screams and shouts of frustrated prisoners. It could have been worse – his five years was nothing compared to Reg Kray's stint of thirty in Category A. His twin, Ronnie, given a similar sentence, had recently been transferred from Durham. Sometimes he wondered how the poor buggers kept their sanity.

Soon, the screws would come to escort him to the visiting room. He unclasped his hands and tapped his fingers impatiently on one knee of his outstretched legs. He'd put on a dark blue Savile Row suit so that Daisy would see he still knew how to dress, and had splashed himself with cologne, the citrus one she preferred. His hand went to the scar healing above his left eye. That bastard McCloud would pay for what he'd done. If it hadn't been for the gypo stepping between him and the nutcase, he could be the one in the hospital – or worse. He'd show his thanks when Jem the gypsy got out, give him a job, make sure the bloke was all right. That's what he'd do.

He sighed. Possibly this might be Daisy's last visit to Parkhurst. Thirty days and ten hours and he would be out of this fucking place, heading to London to see his mother and Charles and check on his businesses there. Then it would be down to Gosport to see Daisy and her lad, after looking in on his businesses on the south coast.

Roy owed his relatively short sentence of five years to Reggie and Ronnie who both believed in the East End tradition of keeping their mouths shut. Since his activities weren't common knowledge to the rest of their firm, the ones who'd squealed on the twins could say nothing about him so he'd escaped the long sentences doled out at the Old Bailey that fateful day in 1969. That little shit of a copper, Nipper Read, had to be content with seeing the rest of the Kray firm go down for shit-long bird.

When he got out he was determined he'd keep his promise to Reg to look after the twins' beloved mum. That wasn't going to be hard, not when Violet Kray and his own mother were best mates. Both Violets were travelling together to the island next week. The twins' mum had been getting worn out what with Ronnie stuck in Durham and Reg here, so it was a little easier for her now. She'd visited both her boys every week while campaigning for them to be together.

Roy kept his head down in Parkhurst where there were too many villains willing to have a go at a name. The place was a hotbed of violence. Even the riots of 1970 hadn't cooled the inmates down. Only last week, Ian Brady, the moors murderer, had had a nasty fall down some stairs. It was only to be expected with so many frustrated no-hope villains caged together. That fucking McCloud …

Right out of the blue the bastard had come for him. Light on his feet and arms knotted with muscles. He'd whipped the made-up knife from his sleeve and slashed at him. Roy had felt the sudden sharp pain of the skin parting above his eye, and then he was momentarily blinded by the warm wetness of his own blood. Roy'd swung at him, missed, then sidestepped as the bastard had lunged forward again but, instead of the next cutting Roy was so sure was coming, Jem had pushed between them like a fucking charging bull.

Roy hadn't seen where the shiv had cut Jem but he heard a grunt then McCloud's cry of pain. Then the knife was flung to the floor. McCloud had fallen to his knees and Roy had kicked him in the face. Blood spurted from his nose and cheekbone quickly, dripping on to the blue painted wooden floor. Roy had wanted to destroy that fucker.

Jem was bleeding but he rose from the floor, staggering as though he were punch drunk. It was like a game of noughts and crosses had been started on his face, the cuts were so numerous.

'Get away now,' Jem had hissed, for now a crowd of cons were milling around them in the corridor. The stench and noise of their excitement was high in the stifling air. The knife had been grabbed up and hidden by an eager hand but the racket had already alerted the guards. Roy had to think quickly. Doors were opening, keys were rattling, uniforms were coming.

The gypo had done him a favour. Jem knew he was due to get out soon. For Roy to be found fighting, extra time would be added to his sentence. He did as Jem said, pushing his way through the cons and leaving the gypo giving McCloud a ball-kicking.

In the lavatory he stared at the mess above his eye in the metal mirror. But only for a second. Then he washed it, thankful the cut ended through his brow and hadn't reached the eye itself. It was a clean, straight wound that would hopefully heal with no more than a scar running down his forehead to his eye. He winced as he moved his skin but immediately felt ashamed. This scratch was nothing compared to the cuts and bruises the gypsy had received, and on his behalf!

Roy had run his wet hands through his hair and tucked in his shirt. He was presentable enough just to have been a bystander, he reckoned. He dragged his hair down over the sliced skin and left the lavatory to find screws running wild. The one thing he was sure of was that when questioned each man present at the scuffle would reply, 'I didn't see nothin', sir.'

Later, as he expected, Jem had been restrained and taken to the hospital wing. McCloud had messed up Jem's face and he had three cracked ribs and numerous bruises. But his eyes hadn't been gouged.

Roy was aware it should have been him in that hospital bed.

Across the corridor in another ward, McCloud – still in restraints – was sleeping off the injection.

Since then there'd been a stillness about the place that Roy could almost touch.

He'd made sure the gypsy didn't have to eat the shit the hospital provided and had paid to get him magazines and books brought in, even a radio to help while away the days.

Roy stretched his arms above his head. Why was it he couldn't shake off the feeling that there was more to all this than prison aggro? He was used to looking over his shoulder every moment, for he knew there was nowhere in the prison system he was safe. But why especially *now*?

He heard the footsteps before he saw the screw.

'Let's go.'

Roy got up and allowed himself to be escorted on the long walk to the visitors' room.

When she saw him, her eyes lit up and her mouth curved into a smile. He hoped it was genuine.

'You're a sight for sore eyes,' he said. She had on a black trouser suit that clung to her small frame like a second skin. She was sexy without being tarty. She always wore black, said it made her feel as though she was melting into the background, as if that were ever possible with Daisy Lane, he thought.

She leaned towards him for their customary kiss. Her scent wafted over him, Chanel Number 5, familiar and provocative.

Her lips were like velvet and he felt a stirring in his groin. He mentally cursed his mistake in finding himself in bed with Angel after a drunken bout. The rot had started in his and Daisy's relationship after that, and his landing her in the shit with drugs in Daisychains hadn't helped.

She wasn't to know the coppers had been closing in and time was running out for him after that fiasco with McVitie in Blonde Carol's flat. And it did, on 8 March 1969, when Reg and Ronnie went down. All the firm were rounded up after that, and he'd not escaped the net. Thank God Daisy had taken over the business down south where he'd left off.

'You look good,' Daisy said. 'Except for that bloody great cut. Do it shaving? Or did someone get a bit too close for comfort?'

Without thinking, he touched the long raised scar.

'Don't you worry about me, girl.'

'I'll 'ave to tell Vera it looks like you done it shark fishin' in bleedin' Africa. Bit sissy to let 'er know someone cut you up.'

Despite her flippant words he'd seen the concern in her eyes. It was almost as though she was appraising the severity of the wound and had decided there was no cause for alarm, for her next words were, 'Why did I 'ave to cut short me holiday to come and see you? Couldn't it 'ave waited?'

'How are the boys?' he asked, ignoring her question to him. He looked around the crowded room, a noisy, smelly gathering of convicts and visitors, and kids running riot with officers never taking their eyes away for a second.

'Fine. You gonna answer me questions?'

They both knew he only cared about her eldest son. When his own boy had been born and he'd witnessed what that fucking drug Thalidomide had done to the poor little sod, he knew he could never love him the way he cared for young Eddie.

He'd wanted a perfect child. Angel had had a sickly pregnancy, so to ease her symptoms her doctor had prescribed tablets. The tablets had contained Thalidomide. Too late, the drug was removed from the market. By then many children had developed the birth defects of shortened or missing limbs. His child had not escaped – he had been born without feet.

He didn't want to think about Michael. He stared into Daisy's green eyes, wishing the noise and smell of their sad surroundings could be erased.

'How's Vinnie?'

'You should know. You sent 'im to Greece to bring me back,' Daisy said, those green eyes flashing.

She couldn't be blamed for finding solace with that bastard of a detective, Roy supposed, especially as he wasn't around to put a stop to it. It had always been there, simmering away on the back burner, her and Vinnie Endersby.

At least with the hold Roy had over the bloody copper he knew full well the bastard would do his bidding. Straight-as-a-die Vinnie Endersby had helped him plant the boxer Valentine Waite, whose body was at this very moment mouldering away beneath the pet's grave marked 'Jock' in Gosport's Stanley Park.

Only three people knew of the boxer's final resting place, himself, Charles, and Vinnie. Vinnie had crossed the line between bad cop and good cop that night to avenge Daisy's treatment at the hands of that psycho. It had never been made public that Valentine Waite was a mass murderer but Vinnie had been given a leg up the ladder to inspector for solving the crimes. Now Vinnie and himself were bound together as securely as by an unseen umbilical cord.

'As long as you two don't flaunt yourselves in my face,' he smiled at her. 'Or ever turn the lad against me.'

Odd he should feel so much for the lad when he'd had his father, Eddie Lane, killed for moving in on his territory before Eddie junior was born. Eddie Lane was dead but he'd never lie down all the time his son was alive.

Even odder was Roy's plan, not that he'd told any-one, to pass his business to the boy when he retired, so in a droll way young Eddie would get on a plate what his father had strived and died for.

'Eddie'll make up his own mind about you when he gets older, mark my words.' She licked her lips and gazed at him thoughtfully. Her voice was caring as she said, 'I'm here ... what do you want?'

Roy put out a hand across the table and felt the warmth of Daisy's fingers. 'He's a bright lad, that one,' he said, 'as well as a looker.'

'If you're interested in my Jamie, he's a bright boy an' all.' She spat the words at him but didn't take her hand away. That was Daisy showing a bit of her fire. She was like that, always said what was on her mind. They knew each other so well, he thought. What a pity things had turned out the way they had.

'You going to ask after your own lad?' she said.

'I pay for his needs. I don't want a fucking update.' Why did she always have to hit a raw nerve?

'I'll tell you anyway. Michael's an intelligent boy too. It's his feet what's not proper, not his bleedin' brain. No one knew what that fuckin' drug was goin' to do – any more than you know what effects them drugs you peddle in Daisychains are 'aving on people. But then you don't want to know about that either, do you?'

'He reminds me of a seal with those flippers for feet.'

The words were out before he'd realised Daisy would jump on him.

'Bastard!' She snatched her hand away and noisily

made to stand up. Roy saw a screw eyeing them both, saw the agitation in the man's eyes.

Daisy knew how to behave in a prison, she wouldn't make a fuss, he told himself. He tried to make amends.

'Sit down,' he hissed. 'You know I speak without thinking sometimes.' She was glaring at him, breathing heavily, but she did as he asked and sat down again. 'It's not my fault I find the child unlovely and unlovable,' he said.

Her voice rose again. 'If you only took the time to get to know 'im. He's almost six, for Christ's sake ...'

Roy glared, willing her to end this heated conversation. He didn't want to panic the officers. Any trouble now and he might lose his remission, but Daisy was determined to make her point.

'That boy needs someone to take an interest in 'im, not just wash his bleedin' clothes. You pay that simpleton Malkie to look after him while Angel flaunts her fanny. You're a nasty bit of work, Roy Kemp.'

'I bought him a wheelchair so he can get out in the fresh air.'

'Big deal!' He could see her temper was simmering. 'I just don't believe you don't 'ave any feelings for him.'

'Enough!'

He wasn't really angry because Daisy was only stating the facts as she saw them. He'd always yearned for a child of his own and when Angel had confessed the kiddie she was expecting was his he'd been over the moon. It wasn't his fault he couldn't bear to look at the boy.

After a silence when he knew Daisy was rooting around for something different to talk about, she came out with, 'Susie's the size of a tank and Angel's doin' well.'

'I ain't seen that bitch Angel since I've been in here.'

'What d'you expect?'

'I expected, as I made sure you kept her on at Daisychains – because of the boy, I may add – that she might want to look me up ...'

'You expected wrong then, didn't you? Anyway, she's makin' good money for Vera. She's servicing exclusive London clients. Vera's got in with some woman called Nora or Maureen Levy or somethin'. Runs 'igh-class call girls, so Angel's dolled up to the nines an' eatin' in posh places. But that's 'er an' Vera's business, I don't ask. Anyway, you worried about her?'

'Am I fuck!'

'That's all right then. An' you don't 'ave to worry neither that I ain't keeping to my side of the bargain.'

He could hear the bitterness in her voice. Roy knew she was referring to looking after his interests. He thanked God for Daisy's honesty.

'An' your mum an' Charles 'ave got everythin' under control in the Smoke.'

Just then he heard Daisy's name being called. She turned towards the voice and he looked across the room in time to see Reg Kray blow Daisy a kiss. He was having a visit with a young dark-haired bloke Roy hadn't seen before. Roy acknowledged his mate and Daisy gave Reg a huge smile and returned the kiss.

'He looks tired,' she said, turning back to Roy.

'So would you, doin' a bleeding thirty-year sentence. He'll get out in twenty years or so if he's lucky. He's got a right to look tired and pissed off, don't you think?'

'Does Reg 'old it against you that you come off lighter than 'im?'

'Reg ain't like that, Dais. He could've dropped me in the shit if he'd wanted. 'Sides, the coppers had been waiting a long time to get the Krays. I was just a bonus to them.'

Daisy shrugged, she didn't judge people. That was another thing he liked about her.

'Mum says she ain't seen much of you lately?'

'I got two kids to look after, a club to run an' your fuckin' business to keep me eyes on. And I was happy in Greece until you made sure I come runnin' ...'

Daisy sat back in the chair and ran her fingers through her blonde hair. She had a high colour from the sun but there were dark patches beneath her pretty eyes. He knew she hated the winter and this year the spring had been a long time surfacing. It might be May but it still hadn't warmed up. He knew because he spent as much time as he was able out in the exercise yard. The Isle of Wight was supposed to be one of the warmest places in England but you could have fooled him, he thought.

'By the way, it also upsets me that your mum don't seem interested in little Michael either.'

'Don't start on that again. Mum thinks the world of you, that's all you need worry about. She just gets upset about the boy.'

He thought about Daisy in Greece. She was always happy when she was in that small blue and white painted stone house in the hills of Asfendiou. He thought she'd have been more responsive to him, not prickly like a fucking cactus plant.

He was brought out of his thoughts by Daisy's insistent voice.

'You do know Vera pushes your boy down the sea wall and out Stanley Park. She dotes on 'im like she does my two.'

'It was my money bought the wheelchair,' he snapped. 'Else she couldn't push 'im anywhere!'

'I just wanted to say, he might not be able to walk so good but the little bugger can't 'alf draw. He sits with a drawin' book and sketches the boats in the Solent. Makes Vera draw too. Only thing she was ever good at was drawing the bleedin' punters in when she was on the game. She don't know one end of a pencil from another but she sits and tries. They get on well together ...'

He glanced away and sighed.

'You want me to say I'll see 'im, don't you?'

Her long-lashed, gold-flecked Joan Collins eyes bored into him. When he got out he'd give her Daisychains, or rather he'd sign his third over to her, not that he'd tell her yet. He needed one last favour from her. And even if she wouldn't help him, he'd still give her his share of the bleedin' club. She'd done all she could to make sure he'd be on the up again. He looked at her. He wanted her.

'I'll think about it when I get out.'

'I'll take that as a yes, then?'

'Bloody bitch,' he said, shaking his head. 'You're so fuckin' pushy when you want to be. You never let up, do you? You'd steal a blind man's fuckin' eyes then come back for 'is bleedin' eyelashes, you would!'

She gave him a big smile.

'Thanks,' she said. And now he just knew any minute she'd start on about him and the drugs in the club again.

It was like he'd read her mind.

'You'll keep your promise that if I looked after your businesses while you was banged up you'd leave me to run the club 'ow I want when you got out? Once I've paid you back the money I owe, of course?'

'Does that mean you want nothing to do with me after all we've meant to each other?'

He was goading her.

'That ain't what I meant and you know it. Just stop supplying the Gosport area with drugs through the club.'

'If I step out some other fucker will step in …'

'But not in Daisychains.'

'Get real, woman. What are you worrying about? I promised you'd get no police harassment and you never get a rumble, do you?'

'I want it to stop.' He looked deep into her eyes once more and couldn't escape her anguish written there. She was a good person and she was pleading with him.

Sometimes he hated himself for the power he held over people.

But he still needed that one last favour from her.

Much as he loved her he had to reel her in like a heavy fish, give a bit of slack then tighten the line.

Instead he confided, 'Daisy, Mum an' Charles want out as well. They got their eye on a place in Spain, near my villa.' He laughed. 'The sun, the sangria, the Costa del Crime, everybody wants a bit of it in the end.'

His old lady needed a rest and Charles wasn't getting any younger. Roy knew that during the time he'd been banged up crime had moved on. The money wasn't in prostitution now, or in the protection rackets. It was in drugs. Drugs, pornography, and more drugs. Africa was opening its doors to the big bosses but the Kenyans liked to play it safe, liked to know the punters they dealt with weren't fly-by-nights. And the Colombians favoured the old villains to do business with. Names like him. Cocaine, once thought of as only a rich man's drug, had come into its own on the street. The Turks were fighting for control of the heroin market and, thanks to Daisy and Charles, he was ready to fight and expand his share of that market. The African market was where he was determined to be.

'I once told you I always pay my debts.' He had her full attention now, but he had to ignore the glitter of tears in her eyes. He needed to push her to the extreme edge of what she'd do for him, and then some. 'I owe you, Daisy, but I'll offer you more than you dreamed possible. Help me one last time and you can have your fuckin' club *and* your copper, no strings attached.'

Her forehead creased. He could see she was wondering how he was going to hand Vinnie on a plate to her and clear the club of drugs.

Then he saw relief. The promise of a smile began to light her face. He knew how much she wanted to live openly with the detective.

Once, her face had lit up like that for him, until he'd spoilt it all by not keeping his dick in his trousers.

She wanted the club and the freedom to love another man.

He'd lost her.

It was like a knife was being dragged through his heart, but even if she didn't want him, he had to protect her. He put his hand to the side of his head, bent forward and, in a voice he was sure only she could hear, said, 'The prison authorities have moved a bloke here from Winchester. This tosser, Don McCloud, reckons he's the son of Jack "The Hat" McVitie, one

66

of the scumbags I'm supposed to have helped the twins dispose of.'

'He ain't even got the same name ...'

'His old lady was some bint McVitie had on the side.'

'He cut you?'

Roy nodded. 'He cut a mate worse. This mate, a gypo, he stepped in and took what was meant for me. This McCloud's a nutter, Daisy, but I can't take any more chances. The bastard fashioned a knife from a toothbrush and razor blades.' The colour had drained from her face.

'When a bloke's got something in his head, heaven and earth won't shift it,' Roy went on. 'He reckoned there was some cover-up during my sentencing. According to him I should have got a similar sentence to Reg and Ronnie. Been trying for a long time to get near me, apparently ...'

'Out with it. That ain't all, is it?' He could see the questioning fear in Daisy's eyes. 'The sentencing was long ago,' she said. 'How come all this 'as surfaced now?'

'Because I'm due out. Or maybe because he couldn't get close enough before.'

'So?'

'So he's seen *you*.' Roy could see she was working things out in her mind. 'He knows where you live.' The little colour that had returned to her face quickly drained away again.

'But he's in 'ere! An' you said he's a nutter!'

'What if he's a clever nutter? What if he's made arrangements because of your connection to me and—'

'My boys?' Daisy gasped and put her hand to her mouth. 'You think he'd send someone to hurt my boys?'

'Or you.'

CHAPTER 6

'You clumsy cow!'

Vera bent and picked up the note Leah had let slip from her fingers and passed it back to her.

'Sorry, Vera.'

'You been dropping stuff left right and centre 'ere in the bar this morning. What's the bleedin' matter with you?'

With her left hand the girl awkwardly shut the till. Her red hair, that Vera knew didn't come from a bottle, fell across her face. Vera's eyes flew to Leah's right hand, held at an odd angle against her slim hip. Before she could protest Vera firmly but gently raised Leah's arm and stared at the grubby Elastoplast. The girl yelped.

Greeny-white slime showed at the base of the girl's palm. Leah tried to pull her hand away. 'Oh no you don't, young lady.' In a trice Vera'd ripped off the plaster.

'Jesus Christ! These are cigarette burns.'

She pushed the girl towards the bar flap without waiting for a reply, at the same time yelling, 'Jimmy, get 'ere!' The pot man appeared from the stage area where he had been half-heartedly cleaning ashtrays. 'Mind the bar for five minutes, I'll be through there with Daisy.' She nodded towards the office.

He looked at her, his eyes lighting up like beacons on a dark night. Vera knew he'd help himself to a pint of Brickwood's. She propelled the girl towards the office.

'Would you credit this, Dais?'

Daisy looked up from the stack of unpaid bills she was tallying up in a large red book.

'Don't talk to me about bleedin' credit. You come in to make me a cuppa?'

'Nah, I come to show you this.' Vera was standing over her trying to unclench Leah's fist. 'Don't say you did this to yourself.'

Daisy rose from her seat behind the desk. Leah turned her head away but Vera had already seen the brightness of tears. She had a soft spot for the girl. Leah, with her wild gypsy looks and floaty clothes that completely covered her body and left the men wondering exactly what was beneath those simple outfits, was a barmaid, and a damned good one.

Leah had an easy smile that lit up her face and showed a mouthful of white teeth and her skin held the olive sheen of a true gypsy.

And Leah was exactly that. One of the Hampshire clan and married to a bare-knuckle fighter named Jem O'Donnell.

Daisy said, 'What the fuck?' A sour smell came from Leah's hand.

Vera pulled back the curtain of hair from Leah's face.

'I'm betting this makes things difficult at 'ome when she needs to see to 'er kiddie, right?' Vera said to Daisy, who nodded and met Leah's eyes. Vera let go the fall of hair and sighed.

Daisy said, 'It took you a long time to tell Vera why your man was in prison an' we both admire your honesty about it. Now we need to know who did this.'

Leah had already told Vera that Jem was in Parkhurst serving a three-year sentence for involvement in a fight that ended in the death of a man in Uttoxeter. The place was swimming with American servicemen from the nearby base at Marchington. The Vietnam war was at its height and the television in the bar of the Green Man had been showing the news. Many of the Americans were on their way back to Vietnam, and when some clever dick turned the set off all hell was let loose. Jem waded in when he was punched in the face, and before the military police arrived a man lay on the cobbles in the back yard, bleeding to death from a knife wound. Jem carried a knife that had got lost in the scuffle. Despite swearing the death had nothing to do with him, he was committed.

Vera was also aware Jem had protected Roy Kemp from Don McCloud and was in the hospital wing for his trouble.

Leah held her silence.

'All right, love, if you don't want to tell, I won't bleedin' force you,' said Daisy.

Vera looked at Daisy and shrugged before going over to the small cupboard and taking out a box containing an assortment of bandages, scissors, plasters and ointments. When she came back she dumped the lot on Daisy's paperwork. At the vanity sink in the corner she wet some cotton wool.

With Daisy hovering, Vera motioned towards the small brown bottle she'd put by the sink and said, 'This'll do the trick. Put out your hand.'

Amazingly, she had no resistance from Leah. As the poisonous matter was cleaned away, the circles of skin showed pink and raw.

Tipping a few drops of the brown liquid on to another piece of cotton wool, Vera said, 'This is gonna 'urt. Shout out if you wants.' Only the narrowing of Leah's eyes and the mouth turned inwards to a thin line betrayed her pain.

'Good girl,' said Vera, throwing the cotton wool into the sink and then washing her hands with the see-through brown oval of Pear's soap. 'Your Jem would kill the bleeder who did this.'

'Well he ain't 'ere, is he?'

'But it won't be long before he's out,' said Daisy.

Ignoring Leah's sullen tone, Vera pushed Leah on to the office chair then perched herself on the corner of the desk. She let her gaze drift over the girl, from her thonged sandals to the patchwork skirt that clung softly against her bare legs and then up to the white embroidered blouse that accentuated the swell of her breasts.

'Sorry about the iodine,' she said. 'Got to make sure there ain't going to be no permanent infection. Don't want no germs lurkin', do we?'

Normally the bar girls wore short skirts and low-cut blouses but Leah had made it plain from the outset that she would never wear any clothing that would entice the men to leer at her. Both Vera and Daisy admired her spirit.

'It 'urts.' Leah was peering at her brown-stained hand.

'Of course it bleedin' hurts,' Vera said. 'Everythin' has to get worse before it gets better.'

Daisy said, 'Why don't you dress it an' then Leah can go home for the rest of the morning?'

Leah glared at her. 'I can't afford to take time off. I did clean it meself, you know,' she said, 'but I can't wash up one-'anded, can I, an' dirty water from the glasses an' ashtrays ain't done it no good. We should 'ave a washin''-up machine in this place.'

'We got washing-up machines, only we calls 'em barmaids. Put out yer 'and.' Vera wound a bandage then cut the gauze, tied a knot at Leah's wrist, and said, 'Well you can't work like that. But if you was to give me a hint as to 'ow this came about, I might not dock your wages.'

Vera knew Daisy wouldn't have let her cut Leah's wages anyway but the girl didn't know that.

'Pictures.'

'I like a good film meself,' said Vera. ''Specially that actor John Garfield—'

'Shut up, Vera,' said Daisy.

'Not pictures, *pictures*. Can I go and get me bag?'

Vera nodded and Leah left the office. All the girls kept their handbags beneath the bar where they would be safe. It wasn't long before Leah came back with her patchwork drawstring bag.

'I've been told not to talk to anyone,' she said. 'I slipped them in 'ere because I was scared if I left them at home my little girl or the old lady who looks after her might come across them.' She set two crumpled images face down on the desk in front of Vera. 'You won't like what you're goin' to see.'

Vera snatched up the photos, passing one immediately to Daisy. She stared at the grainy image.

Vera blinked, not sure if what she was looking at was real. As it dawned on her the photo *was* genuine she had to swallow back her vomit.

It was a child, a baby girl, lying on its back with its legs wide open for the camera.

'Fuckin' hell,' said Vera, staring intently.

She gripped the photo, almost piercing it with her long red nails. Her neck and back were clammy with revulsion.

That the child was dead was confirmed by the gash across the tiny neck.

'This is a murdered baby!' Vera let the photograph flutter to the desk. 'No more than three months old!'

The words came out, but so too came the bile. She stumbled across to the sink and heaved up a brown mess of tea.

After a while she wiped her mouth, straightened up and looked at Leah, and at Daisy who held the photograph as though it was a bit of dogshit.

'This is sick,' said Daisy. 'Where's that other photo?'

This time the photograph showed a nude woman lying across a sofa. Her eyes were wide open. She had long, light-coloured hair patched with dark that after a moment or two Vera realised was blood. There was a gaping wound across her neck. Two round darkened patches showed where her breasts had been sliced from her body. Vera thrust the photo at Leah.

'Who would do something like this?'

Vera saw the pain in Leah's eyes as she took back both photos, slipped them in her bag and drew the string closed.

Questions were rolling around in Vera's brain. What had these dreadful images to do with Leah? Who were these poor dead people and what terrible fate had befallen them?

The silence in the room was thunderous.

Finally, Leah spoke in a hushed voice.

'I been with Jem since I was fourteen. Knowed as soon as I saw 'im he was the one. He fought at fairs all over the country, and we 'ad a good life together. The only thing missing was a babby, but it's hard on the road livin' 'and to mouth or from one fight to the next. Jem, he's a lot older than me, never really learned to read or write because he was never in one place long enough to go to school ...'

Leah looked hard at Vera to see if she was shocked but her face showed only understanding.

Vera said, 'Lots of people had little or no education because the war messed everything up. Not bein' able to read or write ain't nothing to be ashamed of. Go on, ducks.'

'Jem's as sharp as a barrer-load of monkeys and he ain't afraid of hard work neither.'

'But now you got a little girl,' put in Daisy.

'Jem reckoned our child needed a proper 'ome, not sleeping under hedges or in a van or makeshift tent. Worst thing we ever did, leavin' the road. Cooped up inside a brick house like a chicken in a run. I knowed it was slowly killing Jem but he wouldn't give in. Wanted our little girl to learn geography and science an' such at school when she got older. I said where better to learn such things than on the road. If the seasons don't tell it all it ain't worth knowin'.'

Leah felt the tears rising, remembering how Jem would catch rain in a bowl for her to wash her hair. 'Better than any of that new-fangled shampoo stuff, Leah,' he'd say. Lovely and shiny, like conkers, her hair was then. She sniffed.

Vera said, 'Cor, bugger me, she don't say a word 'ardly all the time she works 'ere and now she's got a bleedin' book comin' out 'er mouth, chapter by chapter!'

Leah smiled bravely. 'Nan, the old lady who lives in the flat above me in Beach Street, looks after my kiddie while I work, an' this bar work is all the money I got coming in.'

Leah thought of the time she was on the same boat as Daisy going to the island to visit their men. She had longed to go up to Daisy and ask if she could sit with her, but her shame stopped her and the worry of what she'd find when she got to the hospital wing at Parkhurst.

There was a knock on the office door.

'Come in!' Vera yelled.

'The draymen're 'ere,' said Jim.

'You see to them. No short measures, mind. I'll keep me eye on the bar and Leah, you stay in 'ere with Daisy.'

Vera swept out behind Jimmy in a cloud of Californian Poppy.

Daisy smiled at Leah. 'Her bark's worse than 'er bite, you know.'

Leah nodded. 'I been given them photographs as a frightener and they've done that all right. Oh, Daisy, I'm scared.'

'Hush.' Daisy bent and put her arms around her. 'I do know what you mean,' she whispered. There was something in Daisy's voice that told Leah she really did know about fear.

The door opened and Vera clicked in again on her high heels.

'Janice and Marie 'ave turned up now, so you can carry on. Where did we get to?'

Leah took a deep breath. 'We settled 'ere and at first it was all right but then Jem lost his job on the ferry boats. They'd sussed he was a gypsy and they didn't trust him. Then he got a job on a building site but that only lasted a bit longer than the ferry boat job. No work for thieving Romanies! But we don't steal!'

'Don't take on,' Daisy said.

Leah shuddered. 'I don't know what I would 'ave done if you two 'adn't given me a job. You trusted me!'

'Let's get back to the photographs,' said Daisy.

'Jem sent me a visiting order an' I was saving up and getting nowhere fast. Nan didn't have no money neither but she told me about the club man who came round selling bedding and crockery. He would also lend money.' Leah saw Vera raise her eyebrows.

'Nan said she knowed people who paid 'im back weekly.'

'Nan's the woman who looks after your kiddie, right?'

Leah nodded. She could see Vera and Daisy understood how important Nan was to herself and her child.

Vera asked, 'So the clubman called round?'

Leah nodded her head. 'His van was always down Beach Street. I took some sheets off 'im and matching pillow cases, candy-striped ones. I got a melamine tea set, you know one of them unbreakable ones? An' a carriage clock. He said he'd call round for the first payment next week. It all seemed so easy, Vera.'

Leah looked at Daisy. 'I didn't want the clock, but I knowed if I pawned it I'd get enough money on it to visit Jem. It was lovely to feel his arms around me again.'

'Anyway, the following week I 'ad the clubman's money ready and a bit extra because I'd made a few tips, knowing it would look good when I could 'ave a loan.' Leah closed her eyes, remembering. 'The payments were small, to be spread over twenty weeks, 'e said. But if I wanted real money I 'ad to take a certain amount of goods to qualify for the extra credit rating – that's what 'e called it, extra credit rating. I should 'ave realised nothin' is ever that easy.'

Vera said, 'What was 'e like, this bloke?'

'He was 'appy-go-lucky and very helpful. It was almost as if 'e *wanted* me to buy stuff off him. He kept saying things like, "For only a bit extra every week you could have that radio or that towel bale." One week 'e suggested I spread the payments over two years. That made the weekly payments even lower.' Leah looked straight into Daisy's green, long-lashed eyes. 'I thought 'e was the answer to me prayers.'

'We'd have lent you the money to visit your Jem …'

Leah's heart went out to Vera's kindness.

'I'd only been working 'ere five minutes. How could I ask for favours? You was the only one I'd told Jem was in prison and I was ashamed enough as it was …'

Daisy said gently, 'So you kept buyin'?'

'I was amazed at how much I could 'ave on tick. I got a lovely little pushchair for me baby girl an' a playpen an' all for such a piddling amount each week. Then one week 'e said I could borrow actual money. I told him ten pounds would see me right. I made 'im a cup of tea and as he sat talkin' to me he opened 'is wallet and took out four five-pound notes.

'"It's a different account," he said, "I can only do the lowest amount which is twenty, will it do?" Vera, I thought I'd died and gone to 'eaven when he said he wouldn't be wantin' any payments until the end of the month. He said he was goin' away for a week so I could 'ave a free week as well.'

'That bastard knew what he was gettin' you into all right. It's the oldest trick in the book.'

'I was too blind to see it. Anyway, when 'e came a couple of weeks later I 'ad me money ready. Seventy-five pence, Vera. That's all 'e wanted for all that stuff. Then 'e said it would be two quid a week for the cash I'd borrowed. I couldn't believe it. I didn't 'ave any of the twenty pounds left because I'd gone over to the island to see my man. I'd bought the little one new clothes and put food in the cupboard and bought meself a few pretties from the market.'

'Jesus Christ,' said Daisy. 'What did 'e say when you said you didn't 'ave enough to pay 'im?'

'Two pounds a week for twenty weeks he said was the goin' repayment for cash.'

'That's fuckin' twice as much!' Vera looked as

though she was ready to explode. 'One hundred per cent fuckin' interest!'

'He said to leave it 'til next week. The next week I 'ad two pounds ready and seventy-five pence for the goods. He knocked on the door and I opened it and 'e asked me for four pounds seventy-five. I didn't argue, I just gave him all the money I 'ad but I was still fifty pence short so I 'ad to borrow that off Nan. This time I didn't make him any tea.'

'You was square then, with your repayments, like,' Vera said, nodding at her.

Leah shook her head. She thought of her fear while waiting for him to call the following week, worrying about the repayments that seemed to be spiralling out of her control. Fear that hadn't gone away.

'I 'ad to pay four pounds the next week. When I asked why, he said it was the interest. One hundred per cent interest if I missed a payment. I said I'd paid him the four pounds last week and he said that was for the missed payment but it made me late for the next payment. And if I wanted to be up to date and get back to the original two pounds a week I 'ad to pay him six pounds that week. I didn't 'ave it.'

'Fuckin' hell,' Daisy exclaimed, disgust in her tone.

'How was you going to keep all them payments up?' Vera asked.

Leah was beginning to think she shouldn't have burdened either of them with her troubles. She fought hard to keep back the tears.

'Vera, don't ask. You pay me wages, and you let us girls take cash instead of the drinks that the customers buy us. You trusts us to put bottle tops in a glass underneath the counter to show 'ow many drinks we've been bought. That can mount up to quite a bit at the end of a shift.'

Vera nodded. 'So you saved your tips for 'im as well?'

'I *had* to. The following week came and I still didn't have all the money. I remember cryin' and him tellin' me there was a way out of it. If I wanted to take out another loan to pay off the first loan the weekly payments would go down. The first loan and the excess would be cleared and I'd even 'ave some money left over. Fifty pence a week he said a new loan would cost me. One 'undred pounds I'd be borrowing.'

Daisy gave a long low whistle.

'I ain't never seen a hundred pounds since when Jem used to fight and sometimes the winnings poured in. Honest, all I wanted to do was get out of debt. I asked 'im again and 'e said it was true, fifty pence a week and seventy-five pence for the goods. It would be a new loan to be paid back over a much longer period.'

Daisy said, 'So you accepted the loan?'

'I knowed I'd be paying back that money until Jem came out, but one pound and twenty-five pence I was sure I could manage. He 'anded me twelve pounds. Said it was what I 'ad coming to me, left over from takin' out the new loan and takin' off all I owed in arrears.'

82

'That don't seem a lot to me,' said Daisy.

'Well, it seemed a fortune to me. He said the rest of the 'undred pounds had cleared the outstanding loan and 'is fees for arranging things. Well, I'll tell you, I slept easy that night for the first time in ages. I knowed as long as I kept my job here, hopefully I could keep my 'ead above water.'

Leah was startled by the telephone's insistent ring. Daisy's face had gone suddenly pale. Vera leaned across the desk and picked up the handset, her perfume moving with her.

'Where are you now, Angel? I expected you back early this mornin'. You and your fuckin' shoppin'! Just get on that bleedin' train.' Leah saw Vera nod at Daisy and it was as if Daisy was a balloon that had all the air suddenly let out of it. Deflated, yes, that's the word, she thought. Daisy had been so on edge lately.

'Sorry about that,' Vera said. 'It was only Angel sayin' she's on 'er way 'ome. I don't know what's the matter with the silly bitch, she's a bundle of nerves just lately. Anyway, that ain't nothin' to do with you. You carry on.'

'Well, the next week he pocketed the money, an' then he told me 'is boss had decided I was a bad risk and wasn't goin' to allow me to pay the two accounts separately no more. I asked 'im what he meant an' he said the balance of the goods I'd 'ad, the pushchair, the beddin' and such, was goin' to be combined with the loan an' instead of me payin' it all back over two years I 'ad to pay the lot, the goods and the loan, at twenty-five quid a week until it was paid.'

'Fuckin' 'ell,' exploded Vera.

'You poor cow,' said Daisy.

'I told 'im I couldn't do it. He sat there, Vera, as though 'e didn't give a shit. He was even smiling!'

Leah felt the tears rising again. 'You just don't know 'ow I felt. I was trapped.' Her voice faltered. 'Then he said … he said there was a way out. I'd 'ave gone along with almost anything 'e said because I kept thinkin' of how I'd let Jem down. How when 'e came out there'd be this huge debt hangin' around our necks. I was dead scared Jem might do somethin' silly.'

'So what did you say?'

'I said, "I got no money to pay you an' I ain't bein' taken in by your new loans. If you wants your fuckin' money you'll 'ave to take me to court for it!"'

'You didn't mean that!'

'I did, Vera, but then 'e started laughin' at me. Just stood there an' laughed. I think I was more frightened than ever by 'is 'orrible laughter. I seemed to shrivel up to nothin' an' then I found out why he was laughin' at me. He told me not only would I get a prison sentence for non-payment of debt, but almost certainly my baby would be taken into care. And I'd still 'ave to pay the debt when I got out!'

'The bastard,' said Vera. 'But I'm not so sure he ain't right.'

Daisy chimed in. 'Well, if there wasn't no one to

look after your kiddie they might very well take her away. From what you've said, that Nan person don't sound as if she's able to look after a little one full time ...'

Leah shook her head. 'Much as Nan loves Katie an' can manage for a few days, she ain't in any fit state to do it permanently.'

Daisy asked, 'So?'

'He came up with what seemed at the time to be a solution. He said I could work off the money by 'aving some photographer friend of his take some glamour photos of me. He said top-shelf magazines were big business and I 'ad just the kind of looks that men went for. In no time at all, 'e said, I'd be free of debt.'

The sigh seemed to rock Vera's body. 'Oh, my love, you never took 'im at 'is word?'

'He was dead serious. I was petrified, Vera. He's up close to me sayin' all this stuff an' my innocent babe is asleep in the next room. I pushed 'im away an' told 'im to get out. I didn't think 'e'd go but 'e did.'

Even now it made her tremble, remembering his vile breath warm on her face and his scary laugh as he went out of the door.

'What about the police? Didn't you think to go to them for 'elp?'

'Police? You can't be serious, Vera. I'm a gypsy with 'er bloke in prison. In other words, I'm scum. It might be 1972 but women still don't count for much an' a gypsy woman even less. The police needs proof an' I got no payment book an' nothing in writin' to show 'ow much money I've borrowed or paid back.' She saw Vera's horrified face and said, 'Yeah, I know I've been stupid.'

Daisy asked, 'No club card?'

Leah shook her head. 'I don't 'ave an address or even a proper name for the clubman. All I know is 'is name's Simon an' he's been scaring the shit out of me. An' you got to be posh an' with money for the coppers to take notice.' She paused. 'The thing is, I daren't take these photos to the coppers without bein' scared they'll try to pin somethin' on Jem, what with 'im due out soon … An' I don't want Jem knowin' I couldn't cope. And they're keepin' tabs on me.'

'Tabs? What you mean?' Daisy asked.

'When Simon came back he told me they were watching my place an' would keep on doin' so until I agreed to go to this bloke's house at Ann's Hill an' 'ave some photos taken. If I didn't agree, my Jem might just get 'imself hurt in prison.'

She heard Daisy take a huge breath.

'Simon said he'd give me one day to make up me mind. He promised I didn't 'ave to strip off or anythin' like that. I'd be doin' art shots.' She laughed, bitterly. 'Bastard!'

'So, 'ow did 'e know all about you, Leah? About Jem bein' inside?'

'I guess, Daisy, he made it 'is business to find out. I never told 'im a dicky bird about meself. It was the worst twenty-four hours of me life. You know 'ow

I am. I don't like showin' meself off. No one 'cept me 'usband an' the doctor 'as ever seen me without clothes. But I said I'd do it, thinkin' – believin' – it would all end there. Nan thought I was comin' to work so she was all right to look after Katie. I got on the bus. In Brougham Street I found the number of the 'ouse. The door was opened by a scruffy bloke who looked and smelled as though 'e never washed.

'John Pullinger, 'e said 'is name was. He showed me into this dingy front room of this terraced 'ouse where there was a camera on a tripod an' cardboard boxes full of what looked like dressin'-up clothes. There was a big beach ball in the corner. He told me I would be using the beach ball. I would 'old the ball up in front of me, an' when the film was developed it would look as if I was nude. As long as I didn't 'ave to take all me clothes off I thought perhaps I could do it. I asked 'im who would see these photos an' he said they all went abroad. You can imagine my relief at that. I know my Jem would never buy any of them awful magazines.'

Leah remembered her fear, her shyness. The way her heart thumped against her chest when the bloke told her to get undressed. He said photographers didn't even 'see' naked women because they shot them all the time with a camera. She felt a little better when he turned his back so she could slip out of her skirt and blouse.

'The place stank of stale cabbage, Vera. He went out and come back with a mug of tea. Then 'e told me to comb me 'air. He said 'ow photogenic I was and that the camera would love me. I asked if I could go to the toilet first. It was down the bottom of the garden an' there was no light outside. I 'ad to walk past this middle room where I could see a lot more photographic equipment set round a bed. When I asked 'im about that room he said the Super Eight colour camera was for the film shots. I was doin' glamour photos.'

'So then he took photographs of you?'

Leah nodded. 'I 'ad to stand on this cross on the floor an' turn this way an' that while he snapped me. Then he told me to put a top on from the box. I found a blouse that wasn't too revealing then went into the passage to change. He laughed at me. Then he started snappin' away again. I did the beach ball shot in just me knickers and bra, an' some holdin' an open umbrella in front of me. He said all the top professional nude models worked that way. They weren't really nude at all. All the time I was very careful 'e wouldn't see any more of me than was necessary.

'He made me another cup of that greasy tea an' said I'd done well. The next set of photos 'ad to be done on the bed in the other room.

'I told 'im I was only goin' to do the glamour shots. "What? For all that money? You gotta be joking," he said.

'I was so angry I threw the tea at 'im, grabbed me clothes an' made me escape in me knickers and bra. When I got outside it was pitch black an' raining and at the first alleyway I came to I threw me clothes on. I didn't wait for a bus, I ran all the way down Forton Road, into Mumby Road to the ferry. All I kept thinkin' was what a bloody, bloody fool I was.'

Daisy asked, 'What 'appened next?'

'I didn't see or hear from anyone for a couple of days, then Simon caught me as I was leavin' 'ere. He said I shouldn't have run away because it made things more difficult. Now I'd 'ave to participate in a short film for 'im. "You'll get paid," he said. And that really would be the end of it because the debt would be wiped clean as well.'

Vera asked, 'Did you do the film?'

'Did I fuck!' Leah stuck out her chin. 'Vera, I told 'im I wasn't goin' back to that stinkin' place.'

'I bet he didn't like that,' said Daisy.

'No, he didn't. That's when 'e thrust the photos at me an' said, "If you refuse a simple request, these are some of the stills from movies you an' your little girl might just end up in." I was physically sick when I looked at 'em, but he just laughed at me.' Leah burst into tears but Vera was there before Daisy, putting her arms tight around Leah's body. Gradually Leah's sobs lessened.

'I'm sorry,' she sniffed.

Finally Daisy asked, 'Do you want us to look after the photos?'

'Yes,' said Leah and relief coursed through her.

Vera said, 'They'll be safe with us. You do realise what they are, don't you?'

Leah shook her head.

'They wouldn't take the money, not even if you 'anded them the full amount on a bleedin' golden plate. Porno films are money-spinners. Sex with women, sex with men, sex with animals, sex any way you like. It's a huge business and big, big money. But bigger still are those.' Vera pointed to Leah's bag and the photographs. 'These "stills" as they're called are showin' what could 'appen to you an' your little one if you don't do as you're told. And so far you still ain't mentioned the burns on your 'and.'

'I'm comin' to that now. That day I thought if only I could get indoors I'd be safe. I just wasn't quick enough. As I opened the door he was right behind me. He pushed 'imself into the 'allway an' stood there.

'"I don't 'ave any money for you," I said. I couldn't even throw the bleeder out 'cause Nan had come through, walkin' slowly on that stick she uses, an' I didn't want to alarm her. Nan went out into the garden to get the washin' in. As soon as she'd gone, 'e got 'old of me an' pushed me into me livin' room. He grabbed me an' made sure I couldn't get free. Then he began burnin' me with the lighted fag. Vera, I could smell me own flesh burnin'. I 'eard the skin sizzling. Then he threw me away from 'im an' I fell on the floor. He chucked the envelope at me with the photos in. "Just to remind you," he said. Then he strolled past me, casual as you like, opened the door and walked out.'

'Go home, Leah.' And now there was no mistaking

90

the fear in Daisy's voice. 'Guard your kiddie with your life. Don't come back until your 'and is better. We'll see you all right for money. Who's with Katie now?'

'Nan is, but she promised me she wouldn't answer the door to no one.'

'Thank Christ for that,' Vera said.

'It's the photos, ain't it?' Leah's heart was beating fast. 'That woman and the baby are really dead, ain't they?'

'Of course they're dead, Leah.' Daisy's voice was breaking even as she tried to keep it steady. 'People pay a lot to see vile things.'

CHAPTER 7

Angel picked up her bags with the posh shops' names on them and pushed open the door of the red telephone box, stepping over and away from the piss on the floor. She wrinkled her nose in distaste but another look at her shopping made her feel better. It was one of the perks of the job, she thought, that she could buy expensive clothes instead of market goods. Vera liked to shop in Gosport market, liked the cheap and gaudy stuff. Not Angel, she wanted more out of life.

She walked along looking for the platform for the Portsmouth Harbour train. Waterloo Station was always busy, she thought, catching sight of herself in the cafe window. Good figure and long legs. She knew the blokes inside drinking their teas were watching her.

'Can't afford me,' she whispered to herself and she wanted to giggle. There were all sorts of smells in the station, cigarette smoke, grease and the enticing smell of bacon sarnies escaping from the caff. She was hungry and tempted but she wanted to get home.

She showed her ticket to the guard and boarded the train, picking a place next to a window and dropping her packages on the seat beside her. In an hour and a half she'd be back in Gosport, in Daisychains, and she, Daisy and Vera could talk about what had happened last night.

She picked up a bag and couldn't resist peeking inside. Why was it, she asked herself, that whenever she bought anything she had to take it out and look at it before she got home? She opened the box and fingered the red Scalextric car. Michael would love it. It was a model he wanted and she could imagine him playing with it on the large figure-eight track she'd had set out on a big table in his bedroom at the prefab. God, but she hated that council estate! Bloody prefabricated houses made of asbestos and people still living in them long after the authorities should have rehoused the tenants. One day she'd earn enough to *buy* a house. Yes, she really would. She sighed.

Slipping the car back inside its wrapping she looked at the charcoal and the new sketch book she'd also bought for her son. He really did have a talent for drawing, did that boy. She wondered who he'd inherited it from. Not from her side of the family, she was sure of that. Maybe somebody in Roy's family had been clever at sketching things.

A wave of tiredness crept over her and she yawned. The carriage was filling up now and she took a glance at her gold watch. The train would be going soon.

Angel leaned her head against the back of the seat and closed her eyes.

Sleep had been out of the question last night.

The limousine had picked her up from Daisychains in the evening and the first stop had been Annabel's where she'd met the other girls and the men. Jellybean had been in top form, making the group laugh. Angel hadn't eaten much at the club although the food had been top notch, but she'd drunk a lot of champagne and she knew she'd laughed too loudly at Lamby's jokes.

Afterwards they'd gone back to Norma's flat in Maida Vale and got down to business. A bit of bloody good weed and a few snorts and so to bed.

And a good time was had by all.

Not that she minded threesomes, quite enjoyed them really. Extra money, wasn't it? She liked the sex but it was the after-sex she found boring and that seemed to be the part the men enjoyed, when they could moan about their high-powered jobs or their wives who didn't know what sex was any more or, worse, didn't understand them.

All Lamby could talk about had been bloody gardening. Still, that was better than some of the other blokes who moaned about the state of the world and Ugandan affairs and Asians. Uganda? That was the other side of the world, wasn't it? All Angel was interested in was what was happening to her. Them bloody Conservative ministers were a fuckin' hoot. Some of them so far up their own arses that they didn't see what was going on in the real world. Ted Heath should sack the fucking lot of 'em, randy buggers!

Last night had worried her though. They'd been going at it and she had a strange feeling someone was watching them. Not that she minded the voyeurs – if they got their rocks off watching sex, fair enough, no fucking skin off her nose – but this was weird. She'd even looked in the bloody wardrobe. The feeling hadn't gone away, not even with more champagne and coke. Angel wondered if the white stuff was making her paranoid. Her mouth went suddenly dry at the thought. Lavatory. She must get to the lavatory.

'Excuse me, excuse me.'

Leaving her packages on the seat of the carriage, she stumbled out in search of the toilet, breathing a sigh of relief to see it next to the guard's van and vacant. Once inside she locked the door.

She had the shits well and truly this morning and the back of her hair was wet with sweat. Angel foraged in her bag and took out a small plastic bag. Her eyes lit on her face in the mirror above the filthy washbasin, and she smiled at herself. Apart from an anxious air about her, she looked just the same, a very attractive woman with high, fine cheekbones and white-blonde hair that swung down past her shoulders.

She put the plastic bag against the sliver of hard green soap that looked as though it would never be used again and brought her powder compact out, laying it on the ledge of the sink, beside the bag.

After wiping the mirrored glass with her thumb,

she shook a little of the white powder on to its surface. Using a single-edged razor blade that was tucked behind the powder puff, she chopped the small amount of precious white powder into two lines. This was good stuff, not cut with crap. She shivered: her usual dealer had told her he was having a few problems and might not be able to supply her for a while. Luckily she'd had the money for a nice little stock-up. He'd given her the phone number of a mate of his so she wasn't particularly worried. As long as she wasn't without a snort, that was all she cared about.

When she was satisfied the drug was ready, she extracted a ten-pound note and rolled it. Then she snorted each line.

Within minutes the rush would come that would make her feel much better. Her confidence would return and she'd see clearly how stupid she'd been in thinking someone had been spying on her last night.

Angel remembered the very first time she'd been introduced to cocaine. It was an experience she'd never forget, coinciding as it did with her very first visit to the so-called upper classes and their sex games.

'I've got something that'll give you a bit of confidence,' Sally had said.

'How did … ?' Angel had stared at the reflection in the mirror of the self-assured young woman standing next to her in the bathroom of the flat in Maida Vale.

'It's your first time, isn't it?' Sally said, running her fingers through her glossy bob and not waiting for

Angel to reply. 'Don't worry, Norma told me to look after you. I've been putting on a show for this lot for a while now.'

She had opened up her large handbag and taken out the huge rubber dildo. 'I've got plenty of lubricant, you just relax and enjoy it.'

'It's ... it's not my first time with a woman.' Angel hadn't wanted Sally to think she was *that* inexperienced.

'I know. It's because you're performing in front of men who have active parts in running this country, isn't it?'

Angel had looked at Sally, confidence oozing out of her every pore. The woman really did know how she felt.

'Don't think of them as politicians, think of them as the randy old goats they are!' Sally said, and Angel had laughed as Sally continued. 'All we have to do is take it slow and think of the money!'

Angel had nodded then, attempting to renew her lipstick and swearing when her shaking hand caused it to smudge. Once more Sally was delving into her bag and Angel watched fascinated as she prepared and chopped fine white powder on a large flat mirror then drew it into four two-inch lines.

Sally took a drinking straw and cut two short lengths off, then passed one to Angel.

'You had this before?' Angel shook her head. 'This is my candy and I'm sharing it with you.'

'But I don't take drugs!' She'd thought of Vera and

Daisy and how they were both so dead set against them.

'It's coke and it's practically pure.'

She didn't want to make Sally angry, after all, she was supposed to be getting ready to fuck the woman ...

'I've seen what injecting crap can do ...'

'This ain't crap.' Sally's modulated accent suddenly lapsed. 'I been taking this stuff for ages, do I look like some fuckin' druggie off the streets?' She calmed down and her voice lost its shrill quality. 'Look, you're strung up like an overwound clock, and in case you hadn't noticed, there are two of us doing this little performance. Anything goes wrong, Norma'll come down on me like a ton of bricks. I see you got an attack of the collywobbles an' I'm showing you this is what puts me right up on a high so I can get on with my job and get asked back time and again. I'm not forcing you ...'

Angel had looked at Sally, her satin evening dress clinging to her shapely body, her hair softly framing her pretty face and her eyes, alive, bright.

'No after effects?'

Sally's perfume was muskily enticing as she raised her mascara-lashed eyes heavenwards. 'Do I look as though this is bad for you?'

Angel knew she'd give in. 'Show me,' she said.

Immediately the exhilarating rush hit her Angel knew she could go back in the other room with confidence. Sally put her arm across Angel's shoulders.

'How do you feel?'

'Like I could conquer the world.'

Sally smiled at her. 'The rush won't last forever,' she said, and quickly put away her gear. 'Ready?' she asked.

Angel was already slipping off her beaded bolero. 'I'm ready,' she said. Sally pulled the garment back across her shoulders. 'Let me do that for you, in there.' She nodded towards the room as she opened the door. 'The punters like to see us stripping each other.'

Angel stood unmoving as Sally slipped the beaded jacket from her shoulders. The room smelled of cigar smoke and something sweeter, marijuana, was it? Next came her velvet dress as the zip was lowered and the frock fell to the floor at her feet in soft folds.

Seconds later Angel felt Sally kissing her neck.

When the two of them were naked, Angel slid her tongue back and forth over Sally's skin then moved it in tiny circles over her blackberry-hard nipples. Then Angel pushed Sally down on to the bed, leaned across her and placed her hands between Sally's thighs.

'That's my girl,' Sally whispered …

And now Angel packed her stuff back into her bag and for a moment let her body rock with the swaying rhythm of the train and the clickety-clack of the wheels on the rails.

Good. Yes, she felt good now. She wandered back to the carriage and sat down again and thought of the money she'd be receiving from Vera for her London trip. She knew she had to make sure Vera didn't find out she was taking anything. *No drugs* was still her and Daisy's rule. Well, they wouldn't find out, would they?

Daisy was as sharp as a barrow-load of bleeding monkeys though. Look how she'd acted when, years ago, Angel finally had to tell her she'd need some time off from dancing in Daisychains because of the baby she was expecting. It was almost as if she and Vera already knew she was pregnant, even though she was as slim as a reed until the fifth month when she blossomed like a bleeding spot on the face of a thirteen-year-old boy.

'Who's the father?' Daisy had asked.

'Why, me 'usband, Malkie.' Angel had tried to sound convincing but Daisy had laughed right in her face.

'Try again, Angel. I didn't come up the bleedin' Solent in a bucket, y'know.'

The pair of them had been in Daisy's office at the club, eyeing each other like a pair of cats, both bristling but not wanting to fight. Luckily Vera had come in then and taken charge like she was some small sergeant major.

'Who's the father, Angel?' Daisy had repeated. 'It ain't as if I don't already know, I just want to hear you fuckin' say it.'

'Leave 'er alone, Dais.'

'I ain't gonna smack a fuckin' pregnant woman, am I?'

'I told you, 'er an' Roy' – Vera'd pointed at Angel like she was a bit of cod on a fishmonger's slab – 'spent the night together in a room above the Black Bear pub. That's proof enough, ain't it?'

'How did you know about that?' Angel had been genuinely surprised at Vera's words. She'd tossed back her long hair and pretended she didn't really care if they knew or not.

Vera stuck out her chin defiantly. 'I was in the market and saw you an' 'im leave the place.'

Angel remembered the afternoon she'd picked Roy up when he'd been drinking hard. She didn't know at the time that he was eating his heart out because he thought he'd lost Daisy. To Angel, he was a great-looking bloke with a bit of dosh and she hoped it might lead to something more – and it had. She'd become pregnant. 'I didn't know then that him and Daisy 'ad an understanding.'

'I want to 'ear you say it,' Daisy persisted.

'For fuck's sake! *I slept with Roy Kemp!* He's the father of me unborn kiddie. But I promise you, it was only the once, and when you gave me the job 'ere, Daisy, an' told me to keep away from 'im, I did.'

And then the funniest thing happened: Daisy started laughing. But Angel had seen the tears in her eyes that were nothing to do with her laughing. Though why Daisy should have been unhappy about it all Angel couldn't fathom as there were rumours that she'd taken up with that good-looking detective, Vinnie Endersby.

The rumours about her and Vinnie had been right when Daisy's second boy was born not many months later and he was the spittin' image of him, except the lad had blond hair.

Daisy had been good to Angel, letting her work a few shifts behind the bar with that Leah girl, who was easy to get on with, when she was too big for her scanty dance costumes. When she couldn't work no more, Daisy and Vera still paid her every week. Even came out to the prefab to see her. Never let on to a soul who the father of the baby really was.

When Daisy insisted on it, she'd finally told Roy Kemp she was up the duff. At first he was overjoyed, sending her flowers and stuff, and even buying her a pram, a lovely big navy blue Royale pram with a cream plastic interior and big wheels and little wheels. 'Course Malkie knew the baby wasn't his, but Roy never rubbed it in his face. In fact he never went any-where near the prefab, it was always Daisy and Vera who came.

Those last couple of months of pregnancy were happy, she thought. She felt loved and wanted.

Then when Michael was born and Daisy and Vera visited her in Blake's Maternity Home and they saw what that fuckin' awful drug Thalidomide, prescribed by the doctors to help with her morning sickness, had done, they was fallin' over themselves to help her. The shock for her had been terrible. She hadn't wanted Michael then. Wanted to leave him at Blake's. It had taken a long time before she realised it wasn't his fault that his little legs didn't have proper feet.

What she hadn't bargained on was the continuing coldness of Roy and his mother. She reckoned if she, as Michael's mother, had come around to accepting the little mite's deformities then Roy as his father should recognise the boy as his son, whatever was wrong with the lad. But Roy refused to see the boy.

The big-shot gangster was an out-an'-out bastard!

Violet came only a couple of times, bringing gifts, but then the visits stopped.

Her friend Sonia, who had married an Australian bloke and now lived on a sheep farm in New South Wales with only the sheep and a couple of farm workers and her husband to keep her company, had come over to England especially to see Angel and her baby and told Angel to visit any time she wanted with the boy. Sonia had been entranced with baby Michael. The poor cow couldn't have any kids of her own, one botched abortion had seen to that. And Malkie adored the boy. He couldn't have been more proud of Michael if he was his own flesh and blood.

Angel had gone back to work at Daisychains, and Vera had made herself auntie to the boy. Always popping out to Clayhall to visit and she'd push Michael for miles in the wheelchair that Roy had bought. That was the funny part about it. Roy didn't mind how much money he spent on the little lad, he just wouldn't give him what the boy needed most – a father's love. Luckily, Malkie provided that.

Angel stared out the window. The train was just pulling into Portsmouth Harbour Station. She hoped Daisy was in a better mood. She seemed to have lost all her sparkle since she got back from Greece. Perhaps she was worried about her friend Susie who was about to pop her sprog any day now. Angel's eyes flew down to her shopping bags. She hoped Susie would like the Babygro suits she'd bought – white, of course, to do for a boy or a girl. And now she could see the gates of the dockyard, and the pontoon and ferry boats. In a while she'd be on a ferry and, after the short voyage across the harbour, back in Daisychains.

She gathered her packages about her and looked at her watch, then she sighed as she wondered why, when the chips were down, it was always the women who stuck together and gave each other what little comfort they could.

CHAPTER 8

Roy nodded towards Charles and Violet who were sitting at a table in the visiting room. His mother looked especially pleased to see him, with a smile that reached from ear to ear, but the smile turned to a worried frown as her eyes lit on the razor cut that ran through the top of his left brow and into his hairline.

'It's all right, Ma. You got to remember how long I've been here. Many 'ave come off worse than me.' His eyes met hers and he said in a voice only she could hear, 'He'll be sorry, don't you worry.'

He saw her give a sigh of relief and then Violet's flower perfume with just a hint of vanilla floated across to him as he sat down. She'd been baking this morning and had the smell of fresh cakes about her. He smiled at her, his mother and a cooking stove would always be one in his mind. She was a fantastic cook, scones her speciality, topped with strawberry or raspberry jam that she made herself every summer. It wouldn't be long now and she'd soon be cooking for him again and he couldn't wait.

'How's the gypsy?' asked Charles. Roy had written

and told them of the ruckus that had taken place – not the full story of course, he didn't want the screws knowing – but enough to put Violet's mind at rest when she saw him.

'He's a good bloke,' was all Roy said. Jem was already out of hospital, a little the worse for wear but pleased he'd not lost much remission. 'He's getting out soon an' all.' Charles nodded.

'We come over with Violet Kray,' said Charles, after he'd clasped Roy's hand warmly but been warned off by a glare from the guard. No excessive touching was the rule in Parkhurst, in case drugs or money were exchanged despite the rigorous visitor searches and the sniffer dogs doing their substance checks before visitors were allowed to see prisoners.

Roy smiled to himself. Last week the screws had tumbled to the fact that tennis balls chucked back over the perimeter fence had been filled with cannabis. Not that Roy would get caught out doing anything so blatant. He had other ways of getting stuff into the nick: officers bribed to ignore bulging envelopes, newspapers and magazines treated with drugs even though they came straight from newsagents. Wonderful what money can buy, he thought. He'd got stuff in by having it stuffed in earpieces for radios and inside boxed harmonicas. Musical instruments were allowed, only one per person, and though small they were happily big enough to contain what Roy needed them to contain. There'd been a sudden increase of cons wanting to learn the harmonica lately. Fancy that!

He'd even arranged for rosary beads to be doctored. Amazing what a change of religion could do for a con. Then there was alcohol. There were ways and means to get drunk on illicit stuff brewed inside, or 'hooch' as it was called. Not that Roy bothered to sample drugs or drink inside, that was a mug's game for a bloke who needed to keep his mind razor sharp. Money could be made from inmates, or favours doled out with the substances. Respect counted amongst the cons and the establishment, and that meant doing anything and everything inside to keep his position as a 'name'.

Roy bent forward and kissed his mother's velvety cheek.

'She okay?' he asked, looking across the room to where Reg Kray was sitting, hands clasped together, listening intently to his mother.

'Better now she's got the twins reunited,' said Charles, settling back on his chair.

'Wrote to the Prime Minister,' chimed in Violet. 'If you ask me she was running 'erself into the ground. It's not an easy journey from Southampton then across the ferry to the island then the ride in the prison bus. She always visited her boys equally, don't visit one without the other. Sometimes she went to see both of 'em twice a week, and her Charlie an' all.'

'She ain't gettin' any younger,' said Charles with a knowing look.

'Who is?' Violet patted her blue-rinsed curls.

'Reg is a Cat A prisoner same as me but he's been so bleedin' withdrawn lately,' said Roy. 'It don't do to isolate yourself in 'ere. He told me he can't get his dead wife Frances out of his mind. He'll 'ave a breakdown if he ain't careful.'

Roy was worried about his longtime mate. The thirty-year sentence was hanging over Reg like a double-edged sword. Reg was the twin that most people found easy to talk to, not like Ronnie who was likely to jump off the deep end over nothing at all. But these past few weeks Roy had found it difficult to communicate with him, and the ruck with the nutter Don McCloud hadn't helped.

'Don't let it get to you, son,' said Charles. 'Anyway, you're due 'ome soon. Have you talked to Daisy?'

'Yeah, well, sort of.' For a moment the sight of Daisy's trusting face swam before him. 'She'll do as I ask. Not happily, but it's an offer she ain't in a position to turn down.'

He was a bastard and he knew it, but business came first no matter how much he cared about her. The thing was, he did care about her. In spite of Angel and Vinnie and everything else that had passed between them. There wasn't another woman for him who could hold a candle to Daisy Lane. And if anyone touched so much as a hair of her head, he'd kill the bastard.

His attention was drawn swiftly back to his surroundings by the sound of raised voices in the room. Some woman was shouting at a con who'd risen from his seat and was being held back from slapping her one.

'You fuckin' bastard,' she mouthed off as she lunged

at him, fists at the ready. Quickly she was bundled away, swearing and trying to wriggle from the guard's clutches, and even more quickly the con was marched, swearing, from the room. The episode was over in moments but a sense of gloom had now descended on the room. Even the kids were momentarily quiet.

Then suddenly the high expectations and laughter of cons and visitors and children started up again, and once more the room and its stench of cheap perfumes and body odours was back to normal, the incident presumably forgotten.

'I thought Daisy was dead set against drugs in any form?' Charles turned back to Roy.

'She is.'

'But will she keep things to herself, then?'

Roy stared first at Charles then at his mother, willing her to speak up in Daisy's defence.

'Daisy always keeps her mouth shut,' Violet declared. 'Our business won't go any further.'

Charles nodded. He seemed satisfied. Bit of a liberty really, him questioning my judgement, thought Roy. But then Charles, along with Violet, had personally managed the whole of the London end of business while Roy could only work from the sidelines while he was inside.

Roy could see it was telling on Violet, on both of them really. His mother had lost the sparkle that she'd retained well into her later years. She'd married Charles, her late husband's lifelong friend, to have an easier life and to travel, but so far nothing had come of that. Roy's imprisonment had put the lid on what she'd wanted for her retirement years. The worry about young Michael, Roy's son, hadn't helped much, either.

His mother couldn't stand imperfections in people and the boy wasn't the grandson she'd envisaged. Roy understood that – hadn't she passed those same feelings on to him? He knew how illogical it was. He also knew if he lost a leg, *now*, his mother would look after him. But if he'd been born with a deformity his mother would have abandoned him at birth. That's how she was.

Out of the corner of his eye he could see Reg Kray again across the room. He was talking to two visitors now, a man and a woman, but with a barely discernible lift of a dark eyebrow and a slight turn of his chin he got Roy to follow his gaze. In the far corner a blond man was watching Roy. As Roy's eyes met his, the man gave him the briefest of knowing smiles. Don McCloud.

That smile churned Roy's stomach.

'How's the other stuff going?' Roy turned his thoughts back to his business.

His mother and Charles would know what he was on about. There was no way with all the lip-reading and earwigging that went on in prison visiting rooms that he would ask outright. The place was full of narks.

'I know you don't like it much, son, but it's where the money is now. We can ship the stuff abroad easily.

Nearly as big as drugs, this, Roy,' said Charles. 'Your African chums are gonna love it.'

Roy shrugged. 'Extortion and prostitution don't make as much money as they did. I guess I have to move with the times. Or else there's always some fucking toerag willing to step into my shoes.'

'That's right, son. Daisy coming to meet you?' His mother looked at him anxiously.

He smiled, thinking of Daisy's reply when he'd asked her if she'd be waiting outside on the day he was released.

'Am I fuck!' she'd said. That's what he'd always loved about Daisy. She didn't mince her words.

'I don't reckon so.' He grinned at his mother. 'It don't matter, I'll see 'er soon enough.' He slapped a hand on the tabletop. 'This'll give you a bloody laugh. You'll never guess what that daft bint Vera's done?' He didn't wait for a reply. 'She's only got all me girls in Gosport 'aving regular checkups with that struck-off doctor friend of 'ers and making 'em use fucking condoms! I won't be able to do a bleedin' thing with 'em when I get out! That daft tart is a cleanliness freak!'

Charles started laughing but a poke in his ribs from Violet soon stopped him.

'She's making 'em bring in more money than you ever did, son!'

'True, Mum, very true.' Roy shook his head but he was still grinning.

'You need anything bringing in?'

'Nothing I can't get hold of meself, Mum,' he said.

A buzzer signalled visiting time was at an end. Roy saw Violet's eyes were suddenly moist. He reached across the table and took her hands in his. He felt her two wedding rings, Charles's ring on her wedding finger and the ring given to her by his father, now dead, transferred to her right hand. Charles had told her before he married her that she should wear both rings as the memory of her late husband, his friend, needed to be preserved. And besides, he was aware of how much she had loved the man.

'Don't go on, Mum,' Roy said. 'I don't want to see you unhappy.' He rose and kissed her feathery cheek and smelled again the sweetness of her perfume. Charles got up from his chair but just stood there for a couple of very long seconds. It had never been Charles's way to show too much emotion.

Cons were being driven back under the watchful eyes of the screws. That was something he certainly wouldn't miss when he got out, being stared at all the time.

Roy too turned away, not wanting to see Violet and Charles leave the room. He nodded at the guard and began to walk away.

At his side a man spoke softly, his words only for Roy's ears.

'You was lucky the other time when that gypo took what you 'ad coming to you. You ain't gonna be so lucky next time.'

'Piss off,' whispered Roy. 'I'm out of 'ere soon.'

'In your fuckin' box, tosser,' he returned, then gave Roy a smile which showed large yellowed teeth very nearly the same colour as his hair. McCloud slid ahead of him, hissing, 'After you, I just maybe gets that sweet little blonde what visits you.' Roy used every bit of his inner strength not to lunge after the bastard. Any slip-up now and he'd lose remission. But he'd deal with the cunt.

Back in his cell Roy sat on his bed staring at the blue floor. He gave a long sigh. He didn't want harm coming to Daisy or her kiddies, and who knew what contacts the mad bastard had on the outside? It wasn't enough, that warning he'd got Vinnie to give her that she'd be safer on her home ground, keeping a watch out. There was nothing else for it, he'd just have to get to the loony before McCloud got to him and his again. His hand reached up and he fingered the healing cut that would leave a scar.

Roy Kemp was in control, not some scumbag.

Life inside the prison was governed by the clock, and Roy wondered when and how would be the best time to make sure the mental fucker shut up about getting even for McVitie's death. In the large exercise yard he could go for a run and meet up with the bloke but the place was too public. He couldn't trust anyone to keep quiet if he had a go at him there. There was only one man he could put his trust in, but would he want to help? Jem'd not long got out of the hospital, but keeping watch would be good enough. He didn't need Jem to do anything physical.

Following exercise, cons were banged up until lunch, after which it was a good time to use the showers. Wacko showered then. Like most nuts, he was a creature of habit.

Roy ran a hand through his hair and smiled to himself, an idea forming. Already he was feeling better. He went over to the sink and picked up his spare toothbrush. He'd run his plan through to Jem during evening association when they could sit around and chat.

Roy Kemp slept well that night.

Roy winked at Jem on his way to the sheet-metal shop where he worked mornings, then he went on sweeping the landing. Later, he would be mopping it down.

At a quarter to two Roy saw the blond go in the shower room and four cons come out. One of them looked as though he'd never even had time to wipe himself. Roy gave a low chuckle and fingered the toy he'd painstakingly made. Thank Christ there was always a screw willing to be bribed to stay away. Money always fucking talks, thought Roy again, and once the bribe had been taken the guard knew his life wasn't his own any more. Amazing how many screws sold their souls for cash.

Roy knew he had to be quick, the guards changed duties soon.

Jem stood inside the open doorway of the shower

room. The corridor outside was unusually and eerily quiet. The big man gave one short nod at Roy, who slipped past him into the steamy smell of carbolic soap.

'You fuckin' nutcase,' said Roy, after his boot had found the small of his unsuspecting target's wet back, pinning him against the tiled wall. 'I got a present for you bein' as you like to keep yourself clean. I brought you a new toothbrush.' The words were whispered close as Roy held the blond's wrists tightly behind his back.

With a sharp twist and a shove, Roy sent McCloud sprawling away from the running jets and into the centre of the room where the force felled him to the tiled floor.

Immediately the man sprang to his feet and Roy could smell and feel the bloke's fear, saw his eyes dart about the deserted shower room, looking for an escape route and seeing only Jem in the doorway.

'Ain't nobody 'ere but you an' me an' 'im.' Roy dug in his overall trouser pocket and handed him the toothbrush.

One look at it and the naked man tried to bolt for the doorway and Jem. Jem's facial scar running across the lower part of his face and delivered by this bloke was crusted, partly raw and mauve coloured. Roy fingered his own wound delivered by this pitiful wreck and still painful to the touch.

'No you don't, you fucker!' Roy's foot shot out and the man slithered over it to the slippery floor. 'So you want to sit down to clean your teeth, do you? Don't make no difference to me. You ain't goin' nowhere.' Roy knelt beside him and put the brush into the blond's now pliable hand. The man looked at it. Roy wasn't sure if it was water from the showers still in the man's eyes or if he'd started crying.

'Sorry, I didn't bring no toothpaste,' he said. He lifted the man's wet arm and pushed the gripped toothbrush towards his mouth. There was no resistance now; it was like a child opening its mouth to have the teeth-cleaning ritual over and done with. But then, the bloke knew the alternative: if the child doesn't clean its own teeth the parent gives them a good hard scrub.

'Open wide,' said Roy. 'There's a good boy, you do it.'

The man put the toothbrush into his mouth.

'Scrub hard,' said Roy. For a long second or two, the man's hand didn't move. There was no sound in the shower room except the rush of water flowing from the metal heads on to the slanting tiles then down the gully to the drain.

Then the brush touched his gums.

'Don't bother to scream, ain't no one gonna hear a fuckin' dicky bird with these shower jets running full blast.' The tears in the man's eyes dripped down his cheeks.

'Harder,' said Roy. 'Backwards and forwards, there's a good boy.' The man's eyes were now screwed shut, and his hand faltered. 'Fuckin' harder! I'll tell you when to stop.'

Blood began to form in the man's open mouth and to drip from his chin.

'Faster,' commanded Roy, 'You don't finish 'til I say so.' He wondered why he felt nothing for the man. But then the man *was* nothing. Roy stepped back as blood ran down the toothbrush handle and splashed on the floor.

And still, with his eyes tightly shut, pain seeming to seep from every pore of his face, the man's arm moved back and forth in the teeth-cleaning parody.

'Psst!'

Roy turned and nodded at Jem. He backed out of the room, leaving the man still at his chore.

Once again the eerie silence outside the shower room hit Roy.

'We can't be late for work, boss.' Roy wondered where the word boss had come from and knew he could do a lot worse than put Jem on the payroll when Jem finally got out. 'He all right?'

Roy shrugged. 'Who gives a fuckin' shit?' he said. He looked down at his wet prison overalls. 'You better get to the machine shop and I better get mopping the stairway.'

'This is goin' to make the bastard madder than ever.'

Roy turned to Jem. 'It'll make him think twice about threatening me.'

Cons were emerging from cells now, ready to go about the afternoon work shift. Voices were rising like the line of a song, sung low at first then louder as the music became more forceful.

'We'll be okay,' said Jem. He'd half turned his big body to leave Roy and go about his own business. 'There'll be no loss of remission for either of us this time an' you'll be out in a flicker of an eye. Then it'll be my turn.'

Roy nodded, hoping it would be so. He thought briefly of Daisy and how good it would be to see her. He thought too of Violet and Charles, and of the freedom to go wherever he wanted away from this stinking hole without the fear of that twat in the shower room following. Roy imagined himself sitting in the kitchen at Daisy's house, his feet up on a stool and a cup of tea made by Susie at his elbow. Simple pleasures, he knew, but he missed them like hell.

'When you get out, Jem, come to me. I could use a good bloke like you. And you're right. There won't be no comebacks. No one's going to talk, 'specially not the duty screw, and the other inmates'll only say he's a weird fucker anyway. And McCloud sure ain't goin' talk, is he?' Roy let himself laugh as he looked up into the gypsy's brown face. 'He developed a taste for razor blades when he done me an' you. Only fair he got a mouthful of 'em back again, embedded in that fuckin' toothbrush!'

CHAPTER 9

'Who found her?' DI Endersby asked the police surgeon kneeling on the grass beside the mutilated body. The smell of the dead woman rose to greet him as he bent down.

'Those lads.' Somersville waved his hand towards the lay-by. 'Out here birdnesting.' A police car with what looked like two small boys and a policewoman was parked outside the cordoned area. 'They ran hell for leather to the local pub. Bad business, Vinnie.'

'Can you tell me anything other than the obvious?'

'That she's dead? Only that by the look of her she wasn't killed here.'

She was lying on her back close to a beech tree. 'Animals have had a fine feast,' Vinnie said. 'Bloody way to start a weekend, and worse for this poor soul. Scene-of-crime boys are on their way, Tom.'

'A tent would be better,' said Tom Somersville. 'Stop nosy parkers and the press getting an eyeful. Give the poor lass a bit of privacy. We'll know more after the post-mortem.'

Vinnie tried to attune his senses to the surroundings. A Wickham Woods picnic spot with no immediate access for vehicles and a goodish walk from the car park ... nearest road a winding lane with passing places leading to the village of Wickham. Whoever dumped her knew the area. She'd been hidden beneath a bank of rotted beech leaves. Primroses were in bloom near her body.

There was little doubt she'd been murdered.

As he opened the door of his sand-coloured MG Roadster, the scent of the spring flowers he'd bought at a roadside stall welcomed him with their freshness.

Driving towards Peterfield he thought of the baby a woodcutter had found near Queen Elizabeth Country Park.

Somersville had been with him then as well. The body was in a state of decomposition with larval infestation. Vinnie had attended the autopsy that revealed the female child of around three months had been brutalised, raped and sodomised. As yet they were still working on her identity.

Vinnie shivered. Sometimes he hated his job.

He thought about Roy Kemp and how he'd be out any day now. What little contact Vinnie maintained with Daisy would be drastically cut when Roy was on the scene again. He should have forced her to go away with him years ago. Only that was the trouble, you couldn't force Daisy Lane to do anything. He looked at his watch and then switched on his headlights. He was hungry and was looking forward to a hot meal.

He couldn't put men on surveillance at Daisychains or her house in Western Way on the say-so of a gangster in prison. Finances wouldn't allow it. Besides, police presence at her club would drive the punters away.

Roy was worried for Daisy's sake. He wouldn't have summoned Vinnie to go to Greece otherwise. But Roy's gang would keep a good eye on her and the boys. Roy Kemp. It was always Roy Kemp's orders that were obeyed. Whether Daisy realised it or not, he, Vinnie Endersby, felt well and truly in second place.

It had started to rain now. Long lines of water that splashed his windscreen faster than the wipers could clear them hit the soft top of his sports car like a thousand tiny spears.

At the roundabout he turned off and entered the lane. No lights out here in greenbelt country. Trees cast witchlike shadows until the headlights chased them away. The five-bar gate was open and he drove through and parked on the gravel.

The lights shone invitingly from the large house. He switched off the engine and twisted himself from the car, taking the flowers with him. The porch light came on the moment he stepped towards the front door, key in hand.

'You must be tired,' she said, already opening the door to greet him.

'Daddy!' A small boy threw himself at Vinnie's legs. Vinnie managed laughingly to disentangle himself and press the flowers into his hands.

'Take them inside, lad,' he said.

'Darling, they're beautiful,' the blonde said, reaching up to kiss him. He leaned into her, his mouth sliding down to her neck, to the hollow he so loved, and savoured the clean, fresh, expensive scent of her.

'Hello, Clare,' he murmured.

'Go away, you daft bugger,' said Susie. 'If you don't set off soon you'll be driving that bloody car up there in the dark! As it is the rain is pissin' down.'

She reluctantly pushed Si away and lay back against the pillows.

He said, 'I shouldn't really leave you. Your face looks all strained.' She could see the concern in his eyes.

'Your face'll be bloody red in a minute when I slaps you one!'

He drew back and turned to pick up his dark jacket. He was wearing a suit for the special occasion. He looks so smart, thought Susie.

'I don't 'ave to go, Suze. Not with the baby so close an' all . . .'

'You do 'ave to go! It's the anniversary of our Meggie's death an' we ain't missed a year yet. Anyway, your mum's expecting you to pick 'er up, ain't she?'

'I don't like to leave you . . .'

'The baby ain't due for two weeks an' you're only supposed to be stayin' overnight at that bed an' breakfast in Devon.'

His face crumpled like she really had slapped him

and immediately Susie put her hand out and touched his cheek.

'I knows you loves me.' He brightened. She looked into his earnest eyes. 'An' I loves you to bits,' she said. 'You won't forget to take that posy of little daisies for Meggie, will you? I made it up specially.'

Susie's heart ached, remembering how she'd named her little girl Marguerite after the tall daisies. It had been in honour of Daisy who was and always would be Susie's best friend. Marguerite had become shortened to Meggie. When Si and Susie had lived in Devon, Meggie had died in a horrific lorry accident. Every year the two of them visited her grave, but this year Susie wouldn't risk travelling because of the baby so Si was taking his mother instead.

Her husband shook his head. 'Pity there ain't no big daisies out yet,' he said.

'You says that every year,' Susie said, then, 'Give us another big smackeroo, then get yourself off.'

'Sure you'll be all right?'

''Course. Pregnant women gets all sorts of twinges, it don't mean nothing,' she chided. She dragged him to her, breathing in his warm pepperminty smell as their lips touched. God, how she loved this man, she thought. He wasn't clever, he wasn't particularly good-looking, not with his freckly face and white freckly body, but by Christ, she thought, she loved every inch of him. She loved his kindness, his compassion and, especially, the way his red hair wouldn't stay down flat but stuck up on his crown like a bleeding cock's comb.

'Now bugger off,' she said firmly.

At the bedroom door he turned and blew her a kiss.

She listened to his footsteps after he shouted goodbyes to Daisy, Vera and the boys, to the small silence as he picked up his overnight bag and the flowers, and then she heard the front door slam and the engine of his mate's car burst into life. Susie listened until the sound of the car was swallowed up in traffic noises on Western Way, then she reached for the romance book lent her by Vera.

After twisting about to get comfortable and reading a page or two she closed her eyes and listened to the wind. The branches from the willow tree were slashing wetly against the window. She was going to get up later but a little nap would be nice, she decided.

'You always take 'is part! It's not fair!'

'Get down 'ere this fuckin' minute!' Vera was in fighting mode, thought Susie, yawning and struggling once more to a sitting position. The sound of running footsteps went past and then a door slammed. Another pair of footsteps quickly followed accompanied by, 'You little bleeder, you're goin' to come down an' say sorry if it's the last thing I make you do!'

'It don't matter,' called Daisy from below. 'I'm wiping it all up now.'

'More fuckin' fool you then, I'd make the little sod clear it up 'imself. Open this bleedin' door!' Vera was banging on a door that Susie could only imagine was Jamie's bedroom and the little sod had obviously shot the bolt so she couldn't get at him. Susie heaved herself to the edge of the bed and her feet with their swollen ankles felt for her comfy slippers. She swept up her dressing gown and slipped it on. Pulling her door open she was confronted by a very angry Vera.

'Little sod! You know what he did when he found he couldn't win at Monopoly?'

'How the fuck would I know? I was tryin' to get a bit of kip until your shouting woke me up!' Susie looked down to the bottom of the stairs where young Eddie was gazing up at the pair of them. His face was chalk white and there were yellowed stains on his white shirt. Soon he was joined by Daisy who had splash marks on her black silk shirt.

'Leave 'im, Vera. I'll sort 'im out tomorrow morning.'

'Hrmfft,' said Vera. 'Like you was goin' to sort 'im out when he started that fire in the garden shed the other week.'

'Don't bring that up, love. He didn't know what he was doin' was wrong.' Daisy gave Vera a smile that melted Susie's heart. Unfortunately it didn't do much for Vera as she stomped down the stairs. 'Comin' down, Suze?' Vera called after her.

Susie raised her eyes to Daisy who shrugged and said, 'Go an' put the kettle on, sweetheart,' to Eddie, who began walking down the hallway to the kitchen.

It took Susie a while to move her bulk downstairs

and she was glad Si wasn't around to see how painful it was for her to walk along to the kitchen where she plopped down on to a chair next to the boy.

'Jesus, I don't remember bein' as big as this the first time around,' she said. Eddie had taken off his shirt and thrown it on the bench and was sitting at the kitchen table fitting jigsaw pieces into place. The brightly coloured picture of the Spitfire plane in flight over the English countryside looked complicated to Susie. She ruffled Eddie's hair and he turned from his task and grinned at her then went back to his puzzle.

Daisy was setting out cups and saucers on the draining board. Vera was staring through the window.

'It's dark, Vera, surely you can't see nothin' out there?' Susie said.

'Leave her be. She's simmering down,' said Daisy, rattling spoons.

Vera turned and faced them. 'I'm tellin' you you're goin' to 'ave big trouble with that boy. Mark my bleedin' words!'

Susie demanded, 'Is someone goin' to tell me what's 'appened?'

She saw Daisy's mouth was set in a thin line. Susie looked at Vera.

'He pissed over the Monopoly board!'

'He *what*?'

Vera's face was like thunder. 'Jamie took out his willy an' he pissed all over the board while we was playing because he was losin' the bleedin' game. It splashed all over the place, including Eddie's shirt and Daisy's blouse.'

At the sink, Daisy put her hand to her mouth to stifle the giggles that had started.

'Don't you laugh, missy!'

'He's a kid,' said Daisy. This seemed to inflame Vera even more. Susie didn't know what to think. She couldn't imagine the lad doing such a thing. But actually she could, couldn't she? Only last week she'd hauled him away from kicking out at Kibbles, just because the cat was sleeping on his football boots that had been newly cleaned and were lying on the hall floor.

'He's a bloody heathen.' Vera was determined to have the last word, even though the crisis was past. 'Deserves a bloody good 'iding!'

'You give it to 'im then,' said Daisy. 'I won't. I treat both boys the same ...'

'Perhaps that's the trouble,' muttered Vera. 'You can't see that one needs a clout a bit more often.'

'I'll talk to 'im in the mornin'. He won't come out of his room now ...'

'No, he won't,' said Vera. 'Not even to use the bleedin' lavatory. He'll piss the bed again ...'

'Come and sit down, Vera,' said Susie. 'It's no good gettin' yourself upset. Little boys do wet the bed, you know.'

'Yes,' said Daisy, carrying two cups and saucers to the table and setting them down, one in front of Susie. She began stirring her own tea before she bent towards Eddie. 'Go an' get the other drinks, love. I poured out some orange Corona for you, and if you stands on the stool you can get down the Bourbon biscuits.'

Eddie groaned but he did it willingly. Of the two boys, Eddie was, Susie thought, the easiest to love. She could never quite fathom what was going on in Jamie's head, nor in Eddie's if it came to it. He was just like his father had been, a lot going on behind that pretty face.

'Auntie Vera, here's your tea.' Then he went back for his own drink.

'Let me get them down for you,' said Vera, getting up and reaching into the top cupboard for the biscuits. 'I don't want you falling an' 'urting yourself.' She brought out the dark treats and set them in front of Susie who began opening the long packet. The first biscuit Susie passed to Eddie.

'Thanks,' he said politely, and Daisy smiled at him. Vera sat down at the table with a sigh that resounded round the room.

'All right?' asked Daisy.

''Course I'm bleedin' all right,' said Vera.

'You got one of your false eyelashes on crooked, did you know?'

''Course I didn't bleedin' know, else I'd 'ave asked you to sort it out for me, wouldn't I?'

Susie watched her friends drink their tea and gradually the charged atmosphere became one of calm again. She couldn't get comfortable and moved about on the kitchen chair. She put her hands beneath her belly and could feel the child large and solid. Susie smiled to herself. The pain that had started in her groin in the early hours of the morning seemed to have moved to the small of her back. She knew what it was. That mattress in their bedroom needed turning. One of the bleeding springs must be coming through. When Si returned she'd get him to flip the bloody thing over.

'I wouldn't mind another cuppa,' she said.

'Me an' all, Suze,' said Daisy. She was watching Eddie's firm strokes as he pressed pieces into place. He'd started with the outside square of the jigsaw and was now filling in the sky. Susie sighed. From Daisy's words it meant it was her turn to make the tea. In the early days of her pregnancy she'd made it clear that she didn't want mollycoddling, but now she sometimes thought it would be nice to be waited on a bit more.

She got up and waddled towards the sink. That stupid niggling pain was creeping right round to the front of her. Picking up the kettle she began refilling it through the spout, but suddenly the pain seemed to engulf her. She gripped the tap to steady herself and turned towards the table.

'Make your own sodding tea!' Susie dropped the kettle and just got the words out before the wave of pain swallowed her up. 'Oh, fuckin' 'ell.'

'You all right?'

'No I ain't!' She glared at Daisy, who was looking

at the kettle's water seeping all over the kitchen's polished floor tiles.

Then Daisy stared at Susie in alarm. 'That fuckin' backache you've been moanin' about is the bleedin' baby coming!'

Susie gripped her belly. 'Ow! Ow! Ow! It's gone all rigid! Ow!' She held her breath. 'Oh, it's easing now.' She puffed air out, her cheeks feeling too big and round for her small face. Thank God the pain was slipping away and she was able to breathe more easily.

Vera had calmly picked up the kettle and was looking at the dent in it.

'Well, I never,' she said. 'That baby'll be 'ere within the next few hours, you mark my words.'

Daisy pulled Susie back to a chair. 'Sit there a minute.' Then she was down on her knees mopping up the water. 'Don't want no accidents with someone slippin' up on that.' Then, after squeezing the cloth into the sink and rinsing it, 'Thus sayeth the bleedin' oracle according to Vera. We got to time the pains. Babies don't appear by magic.'

But Susie saw the broad smile that passed between them. She eased her bulk on the small seat.

Eddie's eyes were wide. 'It is the baby, isn't it?'

'Yes, her baby's goin' to be born, my love, but you got nothin' to worry about. Women always 'ave to scream an' shout a lot,' Daisy said.

He stared at Susie. 'Can I help?'

Daisy cupped his chin with her hand. 'You can go

upstairs, have a wash, clean your teeth and pop yourself into bed. If Jamie comes in an' asks you can tell him he's got to stay out of the way – both of you 'ave to stay out of the way. That's the best way to 'elp.'

Susie said, 'Give us a kiss?'

Eddie slid from the chair and went to all three of them for kisses.

'I'll be up in a minute,' said Daisy as she watched him open the kitchen door.

As he left the room, Susie said, 'Just me bleedin' luck Si's gone down to Devon.'

'Don't you go thinking about that now,' said Vera. 'I knows you wants to keep thoughts of that little girl alive in your heart but you got to be ready for the living as well.'

Daisy got up from the table and went and washed her hands at the sink. 'I'm off upstairs to tuck the boys in,' she said. 'When I get down I'm phoning Daisychains. Got to get someone to stand in for us tonight.' She came and stood in front of Susie. 'Who's goin' to be a mummy then?' she said, and left the room.

From the wireless, Vera and Susie heard the announcer say, 'The Duke of Windsor was buried today at Frogmore near where he played as a child. The Duke, as Edward VIII, gave up the throne to marry Wallis Simpson ...'

'That's so sad, ain't it, Vera?'

'He really loved her, Suze. But I can't be 'avin' all this news of death an' buryin', you got a new life

131

inside you.' She turned the knob and the announcer's voice was cut off in mid-sentence.

'They do say when someone dies a baby is born,' said Susie.

'For fuck's sake shut up,' said Vera. 'You're givin' me the willies.'

'No I ain't,' said Susie. She started to laugh. 'Sounds as though young Jamie did that while you was playin' Monopoly.'

Vera glared at her and plonked a newly washed cup and saucer on the table so hard the tea slopped. Susie could see a ghost of a smile forming on Vera's lips.

'Little turd,' she said.

'Funny how I fell with Meggie straight away yet it's taken years for me to become pregnant again, ain't it?'

'Just fancy! A June baby. What's meant to be will be,' said Vera.

'What is?' Daisy asked, coming back into the kitchen. 'They're all right.' She nodded upwards. 'More excited than worried, I think. Jamie's unlocked his door – *and* he's been to the lavatory.' She threw this remark at Vera, who sniffed but set down Daisy's tea in front of her.

'Owowow! I don't want to be a bother but it bleedin' 'urts ...' Susie felt tears fill her eyes. She gripped on to Vera's hands and tried to hold her breath.

'We got plenty of time to get to Blake's Maternity Home,' said Vera.

'I don't think so,' Daisy argued. 'By the time I

phone for a bleedin' taxi and it gets 'ere she could have had it. Go and phone Blake's and let 'em know she's on 'er way.'

Susie gritted her teeth as another wave of pain took over.

'Hold on to me, love,' said Daisy and Susie grabbed hold of her, trying not to let her nails dig into Daisy's flesh.

'I want Si,' she yelled.

'He's done his bit,' shouted back Vera. 'An' he ain't here so you'll 'ave to make do with us.'

A sudden whoosh of water streamed down Susie's legs to puddle at her feet, making her pink slippers all soggy. 'Me waters 'ave broke!'

'For fuck's sake, I just wiped up the other mess you made!' Daisy yelled. 'Vera, go up and bring down her case what she's been packing and unpacking for the last six months. Get 'er coat as well ...'

'Bloody dogsbody,' muttered Vera, stomping off again.

Daisy smiled at Susie. They both knew Vera was over the moon about the coming birth. She'd even had a go at knitting some white bootees that had one foot bigger than the other.

'OWWW!'

'Vera, bleedin' 'urry,' shouted Daisy.

'I can't go out like this, whatever will people think?' Susie was talking through the intense pain and gritted teeth. 'What will Si say about me goin' out in me nightie? OWOWOW!'

'Si ain't here, an you're gonna be spending a lot of time in your nightie, so it don't matter a fuck, does it?'

'Here, slip this coat on.' Vera put Susie's coat across her shoulders and Susie could see the small brown case ready in the hallway. Blake's had given her a list and the case contained all the stuff she'd been told to bring. She smiled as she thought of the baby gowns with their long white ties and the tiny vests with their side ribbons. She'd even got some of those stretchy all-in-one suits with poppers. Angel had bought her those, all the way from London.

'If I ain't going in the taxi, 'ow am I getting there?'

Vera looked at her and shrugged. They both looked at Daisy.

'In me MG.'

'Fuckin' 'ell,' said Vera 'She ain't gonna get in there!'

''Course she will.' The look on Daisy's face told Susie she'd better not argue.

Another attack of pain stopped Susie from saying anything of any sense. She felt the belt of her coat being tied over her bump and then she was propelled towards the front door, Vera carrying her case.

Outside, the throaty roar of Daisy's two-seater told her the engine had been started, and Daisy had the flame-coloured car's door open for her.

'Get 'er in,' yelled Daisy, 'and thank Christ that the rain and wind's dropped.'

'I don't think I can …' Susie said.

'Oh yes you bloody will,' said Vera. 'Try putting your big bum in first then I'll shove your legs in.'

Susie never thought her huge bulk would fold into the black leather interior, but it did. Susie eased herself forward, yelling again as another contraction started.

'Put the suitcase in the boot, Vera!'

'Jesus Christ, do I 'ave to do everything?' There was a pause, then, 'There ain't no room for me to come to the maternity 'ospital!'

'No there ain't. And you 'ave to see to the boys an' everythin' ...'

'OWOWOW!'

'Shut up,' said Vera and Daisy together and they both laughed as though Susie wasn't there. Vera shut the car door and Daisy took off down the driveway.

Susie was shrieking with pain again.

'You can't 'ave that kiddie in 'ere, there ain't enough room! Squeeze your legs shut!'

Susie tried to will the pain away. Travelling to hospital in this tiny car wasn't what she'd envisaged. 'I don't know what Si would think if he could see me now,' she gasped.

'Well, 'e couldn't get you to the bleedin' hospital any quicker on his motorbike, could he?'

Susie saw the funny side of that and started laughing.

She watched Military Road disappear, then Daisy drove across by Fort Brockhurst and into Elson.

'It's like a big hard potato!' Susie said holding on to her stomach. 'Vera will get 'old of Si, won't she?'

''Course she will. And then he'll drive like the clappers to get back 'ere for you. You know how much he wants this baby and how much he loves you.'

'OWWW!'

'Hang on, girl, we're 'ere now.'

Susie opened her eyes to see the large building of the maternity home. The entrance was lit up and there was a nurse and a porter hovering on the steps.

Hardly had Daisy stopped the car when the porter rushed over with a wheelchair. Susie felt strong hands unravelling her from the interior of the car.

'Get her into the delivery room, quick …' somebody said, and Susie heard a woman shouting obscenities and screaming at the top of her voice. She suddenly realised it was her. And she didn't care.

She was rolled on to a bed. A bed that smelled sweet and clean and starched and …

'Fuckin' 'ell!'

'Pant, dear, don't push …' Susie didn't give a fuck.

'Daisy!'

'I'm 'ere.'

'Si! I wants Si. Where are you, you bastard!'

'One more push. There's a good girl.'

'Daisy!'

'It's a girl!'

And Susie heard the cry of her child. She forgot the pain. Forgot everything except the plump lump they were laying on her stomach. They were fiddling with the umbilical cord.

'Is my baby all right, Daisy?'

'Yes, darling, of course she is.' Daisy's hand was in hers and suddenly Susie felt very tired and very happy. She eyed the bloody and waxy scrap with red hair plastered to its head, and then the baby girl opened her eyes and stared at her. Susie was enslaved.

'Give her to me.'

The nurse lifted the baby and Susie let go of Daisy's hand and took her child into her arms. She touched her tiny hands then put her finger into her daughter's palm and it was gripped immediately.

'We need to clean her up and check her ...' Nurses were bustling about the bed.

Panic overwhelmed Susie.

'Why? What's the matter with 'er?' She thought suddenly of Angel's boy and what the drug Thalidomide had done. She hadn't taken any tablets though ...

'Nothing, sweetheart, it's just usual practice. She needs weighing, cleaning ...'

'She's gorgeous. Got that lovely red 'air of Si's. What you callin' her, our Suze?'

But another wave of total exhaustion took Susie and she closed her eyes without replying. Her heart was so full of happiness she felt she would burst.

'She *is* lovely, ain't she, Daisy?' she whispered.

'Absolutely,' came the reply. 'But what you goin' to call her, Suze?'

Her answer was slow and clear.

'Joy. Because that's what she's gonna give me and Si.'

*

Daisy walked down the corridor. The old building smelled of disinfectant and she wondered why all hospitals smelled the same.

She'd been allowed to use the trolley phone to try and locate Vera who wasn't at home in Western Way. Glo, the manageress of Vera's massage parlour and a good friend to Daisy and Vera, had volunteered to stay at the house overnight. The boys were asleep and everything was taken care of, Glo assured Daisy, who thought Glo must have a cold or something because she kept sniffing. Daisy hoped the boys wouldn't go down with it. Glo asked about Susie and Daisy told her the good news then said goodbye.

Flowers, she'd bring in some flowers tomorrow, she thought. And where was that Vera? She walked on down the corridor. As she rounded the corner by the main door she caught Vera getting out of a taxi.

One look at Vera's distraught face told her something was wrong.

'What's the matter with you? She's 'ad a little girl and you could look a bit more bleedin 'appy about it …' She peered at Vera's face in the lamplight. Vera had no make-up on.

Vera without make-up!

'What's the matter, Vera?'

'I was still at the house when the police came.'

'Police? What do you mean?' But Vera just stared at her. 'WHAT?'

'Si's dead!'

Now it was Daisy's turn to stare. A coldness stole

over her as Vera said, 'A car jumped the lights just outside Southampton.'

'Oh my God …'

Vera put her arms around Daisy and cried into her hair. Daisy pushed her away and stared at her again. Vera seemed to have aged ten years.

'They never stood a chance, Si an' 'is mum. Just like that, dead.'

Daisy felt like the world was collapsing around her, as Vera carried on talking.

'I came 'ere straight away, telling 'em I'd sort it out because Si's wife was in labour. The coppers came to Suze first before they was goin' to Queen's Road to break the news to the rest of the family. We got to go to the cop shop tomorrow, Dais.'

Daisy couldn't move, couldn't speak. It was like she'd been turned to stone. With an effort she managed to stir herself.

'We can't tell 'er tonight. Let her 'ave 'er happiness with Joy until the morning.'

'Joy?'

Daisy nodded. 'That's what she's calling the babe.'

Vera rolled the name around on her tongue. 'Joy. That's nice. Only that poor little bleeder Suze ain't goin' to have much joy when she gets the bad news, is she, Dais?'

CHAPTER 10

'He really 'as gone, 'asn't he, Dais?'

Daisy gave a big sigh and smoothed back the blonde hair from Susie's face. 'Yes,' she said, staring into her friend's blue, blue eyes, now swollen with tears. 'Si's dead an' it's good that you're accepting that fact.'

She thought about plumping up the pillows at the back of Susie's head on the iron hospital bed, but decided against it. Susie's gaze held hers. 'You won't leave me, will you?'

'Of course I won't. I'm stayin' by your side, stuck to you like a bleedin' stamp on a letter for as long as you need me 'ere.'

'He wanted our baby so much ...' Susie looked down at her child.

'I know 'e did.' Daisy squeezed her hand. It hadn't been easy for Susie accepting the news of Si's death, and Daisy was finding it hard to believe herself.

'We was good together, me an' Si,' Susie said.

'None better.'

Thank you, God, she thought, for bringing Susie

back to the land of the sane. Earlier, Daisy hadn't cared how long she'd had to sit in the antiseptic-smelling room, praying that when Susie woke she'd be herself again. Hours before Susie had been like a mad thing – screaming, shouting, her eyes wild as she'd run up and down the ward, with the other mothers in the maternity wing gawping and gossiping at the sight of her distress.

Daisy had demanded Susie be moved, and as soon as she'd been caught and the needle had gone in, she'd been carried out by a beefy nurse and set up in the single room.

'Mind your own fuckin' businesses,' Daisy had yelled into the ward. ''Ave a bit of compassion.' A strange hush descended when she'd gone back to gather up Susie's belongings.

'Daisy, I wants 'im buried with Meggie.'

'Look, sweetheart, you should think about this later ...'

'No! I need to think about it *now*. When I gets out of this place I'll 'ave this little one to look after ...' Her eyes began swimming with tears again and Daisy tightened her grip on Susie's hand. Susie sighed. 'I wants to concentrate all me thoughts on 'er an' I won't be able to do that unless I got all me grievin' done. I wants to feed Joy meself an' me milk's gonna dry up if I don't pull meself together ...'

Daisy was amazed at her logic. 'You ain't goin' to get out of 'ere in less than a fortnight. Because the birth was quick, you've 'ad to 'ave some nasty tears stitched.'

'I do know that. Will you arrange the funeral for me?' Susie's voice was little more than a whisper. 'Soon as possible?'

Daisy thought of the mangled mess the crash had made of the cars and bodies. She'd been praying that her friend wouldn't want to see Si's body. Susie's words broke into her thoughts. 'I'd rather remember him as he was, Daisy.'

'You sure about this? You really ain't 'ad time for any of this to properly sink in yet, what with givin' birth an' all.'

'Yes, I 'ave, Daisy. Truly, I 'ave.' She gave a tiny smile. 'You know, I got this picture in me mind of Si. The first day I met 'im I was in the caff in North Street an' this delivery boy comes in with the food order from the World's Stores. His face was so covered in freckles you couldn't get a pin in between 'em and he was all arms an' gangly legs an' his red hair was the brightest colour I'd ever seen. He looked at me an' somethin' deep down inside told me he would never 'urt me.'

'He never did, did he?'

Daisy knew that as a child Susie had been abused by her mother's boyfriend. It was no wonder she mistrusted all males.

'Nah,' said Susie. 'I practically 'ad to beg 'im for a kiss.'

Daisy and Susie laughed, but the laugh was short-lived. 'If it 'adn't been for you an' your Eddie sortin' it out, me an' Si would never have been able to marry. Eddie Lane was a bugger, Daisy, but he was good to us. Remember our wedding?'

Daisy nodded. How could she ever forget?

'We was skint in them days, really skint.' Susie looked down at her child like she was telling the infant the story. 'We didn't find out until later that Eddie had forced local pubs to donate beer and spirits. Threatened 'em with violence if they didn't give willingly.' She gave a smile, remembering. 'Them decorations in the Co-op Hall, Daisy. Red, green and white they was.'

'Well, the decorations was really Christmas ones that a Portsmouth pub 'ad been forced to 'and over. Eddie didn't realise what colours they was until his blokes 'ad put 'em up. Your Si's face was a picture when he copped eyes on 'em!'

'But didn't Si look 'andsome, Dais?'

'Sure did, Suze. An' 'is dad nearly 'ad a fit when he realised your Auntie Vera was the prossie he'd been doin' every Thursday for years …'

'… An' Vera just took it all in 'er stride an' walked up the road arm in arm with Si's mum an' dad an' no one was ever the wiser … An' Si just held on to me, like he was never gonna let me go.' Susie's voice dropped to a whisper again. 'That's my Si. That's 'ow I wants to remember 'im. Not in a satin box with bleedin' make-up on to 'old 'im together. Will you sort it? Please, Daisy?'

Daisy let go of her hand and leaned across and stroked her cheek.

She nodded. 'I will.' Then she said, 'Your in-laws might want somethin' completely different for Si's mum ...'

'They'll have 'er down in Ann's Hill Cemetery,' said Susie. 'There's others in their family buried there. But my Si needs to be watchin' over our Meggie.'

Daisy thought back to Susie and Si's first child. Meggie was buried in a churchyard overlooking the sea down in Devon. That had been a road accident and now Si and his mother had been killed the same way, going to visit Meggie's grave on the anniversary of Meggie's death. It was hard to believe.

'Yes, love,' said Daisy. 'Si'll look after her.'

'You must buy a posy of flowers on behalf of Joy as well,' Susie said, smoothing the folds of the sleeping baby's shawl. Daisy was about to agree when a nurse entered the room with a hard swish of her starched skirts.

'I think you should go now, Mrs Lane. Let the patient get some rest. And we need to get the baby back to the nursery.'

'No! I want her to stay!'

'They got rules, Suze,' Daisy said, though she couldn't believe the nurse really meant it. Couldn't she see how agitated she was making Susie?

'Sod the rules, you said you wouldn't leave me ...' Susie's voice was rising.

'Suze, you're getting yourself into a right state ...'

The nurse approached the bed ready to scoop up the child. Daisy saw how white Susie's knuckles were, gripping her daughter, and knew she wouldn't give up her baby without a fight. The nurse's stern face looked like a bag of nails, thought Daisy.

'Half an hour won't make much difference, surely?' Daisy coaxed.

'There's rules,' insisted the nurse.

Daisy envisaged another screaming session, which would mean another needle for Susie. The young woman's nerves were shredded enough already, she needed kindness, not fucking rules, Daisy thought.

'You!' Daisy said to the nurse. 'Outside!' And even she was amazed when the nurse did as she was told. In the corridor, with the door to Susie's room closed, Daisy faced the woman.

'That poor cow 'as just lost 'er 'usband. She's got no one 'cept 'er baby an' me and I'm stayin' right beside 'er. I'll watch 'er sleep of her own accord, without you lot stickin' bleedin' needles in her arm. I won't let 'er roll on the baby, nor nothin'. When Susie's sound asleep I'll put the little one in its cot. Now if you wants to be fuckin' heartless an' turn me out or take 'er baby away, I'll kick up so much bleedin' fuss you'll 'ave to give me the needle as well!'

'But—'

Daisy put her finger up to make a point.

'Four hours I reckon. You come into that room in four hours an' the baby can go back to the nursery an' I'll be ready to leave an' that's a bleedin' promise!'

Without waiting for an answer, Daisy opened the door to Susie's room and went back in, leaving the nurse outside.

Daylight was seeping through the curtains when Daisy opened her eyes. She was still lying full length on the narrow bed with Susie's head on her chest and her arm flung across Daisy's body.

Daisy remembered earlier watching Susie hug the red-haired baby to her swollen breast. The child had sucked hungrily. At the side of the bed, in the canvas cot, the infant slept soundly.

The door was being opened slowly. The nurse from the previous evening looked warily into the room. Her tired face broke into a half smile when she saw them.

'Everything all right, Mrs Lane?'

'Everythin's fine.' Daisy grinned back at her. 'Sorry about last night. I was a bit out of order, and – er – and thank you.'

'Think nothing of it, Mrs Lane.' The nurse's smile grew. 'Tea trolley's on its way, dear.'

CHAPTER 11

'Poor cow can't even go to her own 'usband's funeral,' said Vera.

'I always thought they put stitches in what melted away, Vera, not bloody great staples.' Daisy had her eyes on Marie stripping for the customers on the parquet floor of Daisychains. 'Suze wants 'im and Meggie to be together.'

Music was blaring from the speakers, Nilsson singing 'Without You'. That's a funny song to strip to, thought Daisy. It was early morning and the place smelled of polish and stale smoke.

Vera pushed her half-eaten slice of toast on the plate to the centre of the bar counter and reached for her make-up bag beneath the counter. She propped the small round mirror against a beer bottle. She'd already spread panstick over her face and well down her neck. Now she stretched the skin beneath her chin. Daisy watched her, mesmerised.

'My neck's getting more like a bleedin' chicken's neck every day, Daisy.'

'Be thankful it ain't your face what's baggy then.'

Vera grinned at her, showing her small white teeth. Daisy knew Vera never forgot to clean her teeth three times a day and it was rare for her to go to bed without cleaning off all her make-up. Cleanliness is next to godliness, she would say.

'That girl's good.'

Twenty-year-old Marie was using her long brown hair to good effect, letting it sweep the floor as she bent from the waist and swayed back and forth, running a black feather boa suggestively between her legs. She was down to a black sequinned G-string. She straightened up, tossed the boa around her neck like a scarf and stuck her thumbs in the elastic of the G-string, pulling the flimsy material away from her crotch then letting it snap back against her creamy skin. There were only a dozen or so men sitting in the bar but not one let his eyes stray from her.

'She's a bloody tease, that one,' said Vera. 'I knew 'er dad …'

Marie dragged the waistline down then turned and bent right over so that she could wiggle the G-string about while her arse was practically in one bloke's face. Daisy saw him colour up and she laughed.

'They love it, don't they?'

Now Marie stood upright, showing off her well-shaped heavy breasts, and then, dancing nimbly on her five-inch heels, she chose another punter and leaned into him, grabbing his head and rubbing her breasts in his face. The men started cheering. The bloke made to touch her but she pulled back and shook a finger at him while miming 'no'. The men were laughing. Back in the centre of the small stage area Marie pulled first one string at the side of her G-string then the other and let it fall to the floor. Naked, and holding high the feather boa, she turned, bent over, and spread her legs wide, showing her hairless crotch and again using her hair to best advantage as it swung across the floor like a dark sweeping brush.

'I wish I could do that,' Vera said, as the money, mostly notes, was thrown and fell about the floor. 'She's so supple. Of course in me younger days I could put me legs anywhere as well.'

'She'll bring in the morning punters all right, when the word gets about,' said Daisy. She looked at Vera's wistful face, still staring at the girl as she blew kisses to the men and picked up her tips and clothing. 'What's the matter with you, you daft ol' tart. If that girl is still flauntin' it when she's your age, I'll be surprised. You're a diamond, Vera. Anyway, 'ow come you're puttin' on your slap in 'ere? It's not like you.'

'If you remember rightly, I 'ad to get up at the crack of dawn, get the bus and come down 'ere to sign for the beer deliveries, then I 'ad to sort out Heavenly Bodies. You was still in bed when I bleedin' left!'

Daisy remembered how very near to tears she'd been. Si's death and how Susie would cope weighed heavily on her mind, and how she'd got the boys off to school without murdering them this morning she didn't know. Their constant bickering got on her nerves.

'Mum, he touched my spoon.'

'Have this one then, Jamie.' She'd given him a clean spoon out of the drawer. As soon as it was on the table Eddie made a grab for it and licked it. Jamie lunged at his brother. It'd been like a madhouse.

'Oh, for God's sake,' shouted Daisy. 'Give me a bit of bleedin' peace.'

'Sorry, Mum,' said Jamie with a look that would melt butter. His beautiful whisky-coloured eyes met hers and her heart softened. No matter what these two got up to she'd forgive them.

'It's Eddie you should be saying sorry to.'

'Sorry, Ed.'

Eddie glared at him then he grinned. 'Sorry, Jamie.' Daisy knew Eddie would never bear a grudge. If he did it would have to be about something that really hurt his feelings. After breakfast Eddie had gone to the cupboard beneath the sink and taken out a tin of Kit-E-Kat and opened it, using the electric can opener. Kibbles had appeared as if by magic and Eddie had fed him, afterwards tickling him behind the ears, and Daisy had listened as the cat purred loudly.

Eddie would make sure Jamie was all right at school, that he crossed the roads properly, and Daisy counted her blessings that the older boy looked after his brother so well.

'Help me with me eyelashes, Dais?' Daisy was brought back to the present by Vera's plea. 'You always make such a good job of getting 'em to stay on.'

Daisy clattered her stool back and went to the other side of the bar.

'Give us one then.' She took the spidery object from Vera's red talons. Holding it carefully by the lashes she squeezed glue from a tiny tube on the side to go closest to Vera's skin. 'Close your bleedin' eyes. I can't do it with you staring up at me, can I?' Daisy pressed the caterpillar-like lashes on Vera's lid and touched them into place. Then she proceeded to do the same with the second set of lashes. She noticed the grey hair at Vera's dark hair roots and a well of tenderness rose in her for her friend.

'There,' she said. 'Open your eyes and look at me.' Vera opened her eyes wide and blinked a couple of times.

'Do they look all right, Dais?'

'Lovely,' said Daisy, dropping a kiss on Vera's head. Vera grinned up at her then immediately put a hand up to touch her lashes. Daisy slapped the probing fingers away. 'That's you all over, ain't it? Can't take me bleedin' word for it, you got to touch.'

For a second they glared at each other, then Vera smiled and Daisy felt like crying.

'What's the matter, girly?' asked Vera softly.

'Perhaps I'm not thinkin' straight, but d'you reckon Si's death has anythin' to do with this bloke in prison? His threats?'

'You think this bloke planned the accident to hurt *you*?'

Daisy knew then she was letting her imagination

get the better of her. Putting her fears into words had shown her how silly, how paranoid, she was becoming. She shook her head. 'I'm being daft, ain't I?'

Vera put her arm across Daisy's shoulders, giving her the comfort she needed.

'Yes, bloody daft. Si's death was an accident.'

Daisy left Vera fingering the blue eye shadow on her eyelids and went into the office. She stared out of the window at the ferry boat which had just docked, spilling passengers to spread like ants towards the taxi rank and the bus terminal. A watery sun was trying to shine through the grey clouds.

She saw Angel trotting past the taxi rank and over the road towards the club. Daisy guessed she'd just come off the ferry. Angel's pretty face was marred by a frown and she was oblivious to the stares from men as her blonde hair was tossed this way and that by the wind and she hugged herself into her shortie raincoat. Bloody June, thought Daisy, and it's still cool enough to wear coats. She waved as Angel caught sight of her and the girl nodded her head in recognition, then her eyes moved towards something or someone. She had a curious frown on her face before she glanced away again and continued on her trek towards the club. Daisy saw Angel stop and exchange a few words with Alec and drop some money in his tin. She turned to her desk and flicked through a pile of paperwork. She put a couple of bills on the spike to remind her to send off cheques later in the morning, then she went out, closing the door behind her, and returned to the bar, thinking that Si's death had affected them all.

In the bar, Angel had taken off her coat and slung it across a stool next to the one she was sitting on. Her nylon-clad legs were crossed at the knee and her short black skirt had ridden up. She was talking to Vera and Vera didn't look happy.

'But I got two things on me mind, Vera. I'm not happy with the way things are going …'

'You like the money, though?'

'Yes.'

'You sure you didn't know Norma's husband Colin Levy might be involved in the drugs business?'

'He's a pimp, so what? I don't care what else he's into, that ain't my concern.'

Daisy thought Angel protested a bit too bleeding much when Vera asked her about drugs.

'So what is it?'

'Films. He makes films and tapes.'

'Of you? If that's so I want more bleedin' money an' so do you!'

'It ain't about the money, Vera, or the heroin or the coke he dishes out. These men I'm fuckin' are cabinet ministers.'

'I only hires you out to the bleedin' upper crust …'

'But the films are bein' made without the blokes knowin'. Through peepholes an' such. They're in positions of trust, these men …'

'Bit late for you to start getting all moral-minded,

missy. My advice to you is to keep your nose out of it. Ignore anythin' you see, be like those fuckin' monkeys, see nothin', 'ear nothin', say nothin'!'

'But I can smell trouble brewing an' I don't want to be involved in it. And I don't want my Michael to find out what I do for a living. Me dancin' is fine. Anything else, no!'

'I'm sure you and me an' Daisy'll weather any problems.'

'If Roy was out I could ask him to put out a few feelers and see what's going on.'

'Well, he ain't, not yet, Angel, nearly but not quite.'

'Daisy, you could 'ave a word with Vinnie?'

'The thing is, Vinnie don't talk to me about police stuff and I don't ask. Anyway, you know I ain't seen Vinnie for a while. There's some problem with his father-in-law, up in Liss where 'is boy an' Clare is livin'.'

'I only suggested.'

'Well don't. Besides, that's London police work. Vinnie's supposed to be down 'ere. Not that I see much of him. Working on some strange vice case he don't want to talk about. Mind, there's plenty of vice round 'ere. Anyway, what upset you as you came across the road from the ferry?'

Angel screwed up her face, trying to remember. 'Oh,' she said. 'It was some bloke was peering in the window. I watched but he lost interest and wandered off.'

Daisy looked at Vera, her heart beating fast and fingers of fear running up her spine.

'Probably a new punter and he was scared to come in. Some blokes are, you know.' Vera twisted a curl of hair. 'What did he look like?'

'Nothin' out of the ordinary, short, thickset, a bit mean-looking. If you ain't listening to me I've 'ad enough of this.' Angel stood up and slipped into her coat and swept out of the club.

'Touchy, ain't she?' Vera sighed and picked up her lipstick. Daisy walked over to the bar window and watched Angel run across the tarmac and get on the Haslar bus which was just leaving. Not so much touchy as twitchy thought Daisy, she looked like she had a cold coming on with that runny nose. She was obviously going to Clayhall to see Michael.

'She's only warnin' you, Vera.'

Vera swept her make-up into her bag.

'She's worrying about nothin' at this stage,' she said. 'I'm tellin' you, everything's under control!'

Leah was back at work and she seemed fine. More than fine. She was quite chirpy these days.

'Leah's old man comes out soon after Roy, don't he?'

'I think so.' Vera was now checking the till for change. The new barmaid had said they were out of ten-pence pieces. Good thing Leah's bloke was coming home, thought Daisy. If there *was* any funny business still going on he'd make sure no harm came to her or the kiddie.

'Has she come back to you about, about … ?'

'No.'

'Well then, Vera. If and when she does, we'll be ready, won't we? But since her old man is in for murder, I think anyone will think twice about approaching her again, don't you?'

'If you says so, Dais, if you says so.' Daisy was tapping her nails on the bar top. 'What's the matter with you?'

Daisy took a deep breath. 'We got watered-down booze, sex on tap, gambling, and backhanders going out left, right and centre to Vinnie's superiors so we don't get ourselves closed down. On top of that I got drug dealers practically sitting on me bleedin' door-step.' Daisy pointed through the window to where a dark-haired bloke in trainers and a leather jacket was handing over a small package to another bloke on a bike who passed back some notes.

'Look at that, broad fuckin' daylight an' he knows he ain't gonna get copped by the law. It worries me sick thinking some little kids is goin' to get 'ooked. And then there's that loony who thinks he's Jack "The Hat" McVitie's son, who just might send someone to sort me and mine. Not to mention a fuckin' death in the family.' Daisy couldn't help herself, the tears came thick and fast.

Vera was round the bar in a flash. Her arms went

round Daisy's shoulders and Daisy could feel the warmth from Vera's body pressed against her.

'Don't take on so, Dais.'

Daisy sniffed. She let Vera's words soothe her, then she wiped her face with the back of her hand.

'Vera, I'm so sick of it all. All I wanted was a club we could run the way *we* wanted. Not with all the fucking hassle Roy's landed me in, and the last time I saw 'im he was mutterin' about somethin' else he wanted me to do. He dangles the bleedin' club and Vinnie in front of me like a fuckin' carrot on a bit of string tempting a donkey. I'm sorry. I guess I've just about 'ad it up to 'ere.' Daisy put her hand beneath her chin. 'It ain't easy, is it, Vera?'

'Come on, ducky, don't let it get you down.'

'And I never thought Roy would do the dirty on me with Angel and get her up the duff, did I?' Daisy remembered Vera telling her ages ago the blonde was trouble.

'You can't go broodin' on that, not when you got Vinnie's kiddie. Come on, be fair, Dais.'

Daisy stared into Vera's eyes. 'All I ever wanted was someone to love me like his life depends on it. Vinnie's the only bloke I know who's bleedin' honest. He also knows 'ow much Eddie Lane meant to me.'

'And that's it in a bleedin' nutshell, ain't it? Eddie Lane left an 'ole in your 'eart no other man will ever fill.'

'A woman can love many men in a lifetime, Vera.'
'Yeah, but there's only one who's really special, an' your Eddie casts a long shadow.'

CHAPTER 12

Angel stepped off the bus opposite the Fighting Cocks pub at Clayhall and headed down the wide pathway made of concrete slabs to her mother's prefab.

Her mother had been dead for two years now. She'd finally drunk herself into her grave but the prefab would always, in Angel's mind, be her mother's home, even though Malkie, when Angel had married him to give her child a surname, had taken over the tenancy from the council.

The wire-netting fences dividing the prefabricated houses were hung about with old crisp packets and trapped sweet wrappers. Dandelions and daisies splashed bright colour where the grass wasn't brown from dog's piss.

Some of the inhabitants looked after their squat dwellings. Here and there would be neat gardens and sparkling windows with white net curtains, and white washing blowing on the high lines round in the back gardens. But there were also gardens filled with junk – broken bedsteads and sagging sofas, and discarded prams with their wheels buckled or long ago taken off to make go-karts.

Angel stared around her with distaste. She now lived in a flat in North Street, sharing it with a couple of Vera's other high earners. The flat was kept clean and bright, the furniture polished, all due to Vera and her fetish for cleanliness. If it wasn't for Michael she wouldn't return to the grey prefabs at all. And, of course, she didn't have to explain her little coke habit to anyone in the privacy of her own room at the flat, did she?

As her feet in their high heels stepped daintily around a pile of dog shit, she thought back to when she'd first met Roy Kemp, Michael's father.

He'd been drunk, sitting with his head in his hands on a seat opposite the public toilets near Gosport ferry and worrying about the disappearance of Daisy Lane.

It was Angel's first day back in Gosport and she was running away from a London club manager who thought he owned her and her body. It was time to cut her losses, she'd thought, and get home to her alcoholic mother who she'd been supporting while pretending to be a solicitor's secretary.

She smiled to herself, remembering that she'd bought Roy Kemp more drink, then paid for a night's lodging for the pair of them at the Black Bear in North Street.

Trouble was that Angel had fallen in love with Roy Kemp immediately she'd set eyes on him. And he?

She was only a one-night stand for him, but that one night had left her pregnant.

She hadn't known then that Roy Kemp was a London face and a mate of the Krays. All she saw was the expensive suit, Italian shoes and a wallet full of money. And what was she? A bleeding Gosport girl with an alkie mother who was the laughing stock of Clayhall.

Angel didn't feel at all guilty about trading on her body and looks to get a job as an exotic dancer at Daisy Lane's place. After all, as any Gosport girl knew, you got to use what you got to get on in this world.

What she hadn't reckoned on was never being able to take Daisy Lane's place in Roy Kemp's affection.

Even though she had his son.

And Daisy? Her relationship with the gangster was a sort of love and hate affair, always blowing hot and cold, and then icy cold when she'd discovered Angel in Roy's life and drugs on the menu down at Daisychains. But if Angel cared to admit it to herself, it was the drugs that practically killed their love, not the affair, if you could call it that.

Whatever Daisy Lane did, whoever she ran to, and at the moment it seemed to be that detective bloke with the funny-coloured eyes, Roy Kemp would never let her go. Silly cow couldn't see it though.

Angel would just love to be in Daisy's shoes. She'd let Roy have his bits on the side and she'd close her eyes to the way his money was made. And just think, coke on tap!

The world wasn't a nice place and Daisy had no hope of changing it. Couldn't she see that?

'Yoo! Hoo!' Angel called as she opened the door to the kitchen, noticing a wooden ramp covering the step. She heard the sound of Michael's wheelchair coming from the living room. His face split into a big grin and her heart melted at the sight of him.

'Mum,' he cried. She bent down and enveloped her son. His arms went round her. Strong arms that didn't quite make up for his stunted legs and non-existent feet, covered now by a checked blanket.

'I ain't 'alf missed you,' she said. And Angel meant it. Nothing would have given her greater pleasure than to be with him, in a house of their own, just the two of them. Roy sometimes gave her money but she needed more, and that meant turning tricks and dancing if she wanted to put a bit by for Michael's future.

There didn't seem to be a snowball's chance in hell of Roy Kemp thinking ahead for his own son, not when the only kid he ever talked about was Eddie Lane's bastard.

'We'll go for a walk along the sea wall if you like,' she said. She looked round the spotless kitchen. It had never been so clean when her mother had been alive. Malkie was a good man. She could smell Omo washing powder. Her husband obviously had a white wash boil on the go.

'Yeah, that'd be great,' her son said. 'Dad's built me a ramp so I can get in and out of the prefab on me own now. Did you see it? I don't need to be carried in and out any more or bumped down in the chair.'

She nodded and ruffled his dark hair. He was a good-looking kid, she thought, and she wasn't thinking that just because he was her boy. She imagined Roy had probably looked like Michael when he was young. She couldn't believe Michael was coming up for seven now.

She often wondered if Roy blamed her for taking the tablets. After all, she'd wanted to work in Daisychains and earn money so much she hadn't checked the Asmaval tablets she'd been given to stop her continuous sickness and help her sleep during her pregnancy. She didn't know about Thalidomide then. But why would she?

After Michael had been born and she'd realised the extent and effect of the drug's damage on other children, she thanked God his deformity wasn't worse. Michael *was* one of the lucky ones and Angel loved him to bits. When she discovered Thalidomide was supposed to have been taken off the market in 1961, at first she blamed her doctor, then she blamed herself. She'd read there was talk of compensation. She wasn't holding her breath. Michael was her child and her responsibility and as long as she could earn money she would. Any way she could.

'This is a nice surprise,' sang out Malkie. He loped into the kitchen carrying a model car.

'It's mended now, Michael,' he said. He handed the car to the boy who immediately began examining it, then Malkie kissed Angel on the cheek. He went straight towards the electric kettle and plugged it in. 'I expect you could do with a cuppa? Why don't you go into the living room and I'll bring it in. Want a bit of cake? I made a Victoria sponge.'

'Tea, yes. Cake, no.'

Michael swung his chair round and she followed him into the long room that looked out over the back garden. Malkie's vegetable patch was doing well and the lawned area had been recently cut. She sat down in one of the armchairs. This place bore no resemblance to how it had been when her mother was alive. She looked at Michael's bookcase where reading matter appropriate to his age and much thumbed rubbed shoulders with classics like *Black Beauty* and *Treasure Island*. Books he'd grow into, she thought. The room smelled of polish.

Malkie took Michael to school and brought him home again. Mrs Dune, his head teacher, said her son was above the usual rate of intelligence for his age. Angel worried though that Michael needed something more in his life. She'd seen the look on his face, watching the local lads kicking a football about in the street.

Malkie came in with a tray of tea and Angel wondered if her husband would ever manage to get clothes that fitted his lanky form. His arms were too long for his sleeves and his legs were too long for his trousers. Not that Malkie worried about the way he looked. He cared only for Michael and her. He even gave up his job as a night porter in a Portsmouth hotel to look after the boy. He'd die a thousand deaths if he knew everything Angel got up to. She'd told him she was a dancer and that was all he needed to know. He was well aware Michael wasn't his. There weren't many men who'd ask a girl to marry them knowing she was carrying another bloke's child.

'You look tired,' he said, handing her a cup and saucer.

'Thanks. I 'ave to go back to London tonight,' she said, relieved when he didn't ask what for or why. She took a sip of her tea. 'I only popped in to see you both. A flyin' visit.' Too late she saw her words had wounded them both, Michael especially. 'I came 'specially to take you out,' she said to him.

'Is it all right if we go down to the beach and look for fossils and shells?'

She nodded, glad he looked happier now.

'We'll all go,' Malkie said, pushing his fingers through his straw-blond hair, which immediately fell down again on to his forehead. He turned to the boy. 'Go and put a warm jumper on. It'll be cold and windy down by the bay.'

As Michael left the room, Malkie turned to Angel. 'I knew you'd come today. It's the anniversary of your mum's death. Have you been to the cemetery?'

Angel shook her head. She felt guilt steal over her as she remembered how her mother had died. Fuelled by drink, she had choked to death on her own vomit. Malkie, who frequently popped in and who lived across the path with his own mother, had found her.

'I think sometimes it's better if I remember how she was when she was young and 'appy, before Dad left home,' she said, putting down her tea. She opened her clutch bag and took out some notes. Standing up, she tucked the money behind a black and white spotted dog ornament on the mantelpiece. As she turned she saw the blush appearing on Malkie's face but he didn't say anything. She knew it embarrassed him to have to take her money. 'There's extra there. I've 'ad a good week. I'd like it if you got some flowers for me mum.'

She didn't sit down again because she heard the scrape of the wheelchair, then Michael rolled back into the living room, his hair all slicked down.

'I'm ready,' he said. Angel chugged back the rest of her tea and waited while Malkie took his jacket from the back of a chair.

'Will we get out without your mum coming over?' Angel said with a smile. Malkie's mother lived opposite and Angel knew she wasn't called Mouth Almighty by the inhabitants of the prefabs for nothing.

'She's probably making notes on the time you arrived and the time you're goin' to leave,' he said. He didn't mean it in a nasty way, Angel knew that. Nosy as his mother was, she had a heart of gold and pitched in and helped when she could. Angel tucked her new gold bracelet further up her long sleeve.

It'd been a present. A pink gold rose between white gold leaves and held together by yellow gold bars.

Probably cost a fortune, she thought. Harry, the cabinet minister who'd given it to her, liked to buy her gifts after she'd performed for him. The first time she'd met him had been at a party at a Marlborough Court flat. Vera had hired her out to Glamour International.

Harry liked his sex with a woman who knew her way around so Angel had collected some nice jewellery. Harry wasn't a mean man. Rough, yes, mean, no.

It was the key parties she disliked most and they were all the rage. The men threw keys into a bowl at Norma's flat and when all the girls had finally arrived, each girl picked one. The keys opened pre-booked hotel bedrooms and the owners of the keys took pot luck with the girls.

'You sure you're all right, Angel, love?' Malkie pulled her round to face him. His anxious eyes searched her face.

Angel knew her nose was running. She put up a hand and wiped it.

Her heart was beating fast and her mouth was dry. She licked her lips, feeling the familiar sweating dampening the back of her neck.

'Just tired. Wait there for me, I need the lavatory.'

Once in the safety of the bathroom she locked the door and opened her handbag. From the slit in the lining she removed the small packet and set about chopping and dividing the white powder into two three-inch lines on her mirror.

Moments later, her jangled nerves settled and her confidence restored, she reapplied her lipstick, smiled at herself and pulled the chain as though she really had used the toilet.

Back in the kitchen Malkie turned the handle and pulled the door open then stood well back to let Michael through first.

'Watch me, Mum!' Michael sailed down the ramp and on to the concrete path. He braked the chair, then turned and waited for Angel's reaction. She gave him what she knew he needed, the biggest smile she could muster, then she clapped her hands together. Then she stepped down on to the path herself and put her arms around him, burying her face in his hair.

'Clever, clever boy!' She hoped he didn't feel the tears she was trying to stifle. 'Lock the door, Malkie,' she said briskly. 'C'mon, let's go to the beach.'

CHAPTER 13

'What's the matter with you, Leah? You look like you've lost a fiver and found a quid.' Leah continued pulling the pint of Brickwood's Best bitter for the customer waiting at the bar of Daisychains. 'You don't 'alf look rough, girl,' said Vera.

'Bad night with my little 'un. She's been wakin' up, screaming. Nightmares, I reckon.' Leah set the pint with the overflowing head on the beer mat and took the money proffered.

'Tell us about it,' said Daisy, looking up from the pile of invoices she was sorting through while sat at the bar with a lemonade by her elbow. 'Young Joy 'as us lot up an' down all night as well. Still, tiny babies don't know about clocks, do they?'

Leah smiled.

'You keep the change, dear,' the man said. Leah pulled her fingers away from his clammy hand that still tried to cling to hers after the transaction was finished.

'Thanks, sir,' she said politely, staring at the layer of sweat on his top lip. She tried to ignore the white matter clinging to the inside corners of his eyes. He made her want to throw up. Why did blokes all think they were God's gift to women? Then he returned her smile, showing what looked like bits of nuts trapped in his false teeth. At least, she thanked God, the nasty little sod didn't belong to her. Fancy having to go home to that after her shift here!

Leah turned away and gazed at Vera. She loved the little woman in her dated ruffles that showed the swell of her breasts, and the tight black skirts and high heels that accentuated her neat figure. Leah decided Vera only needed a long black feather boa strung around her neck and she'd look exactly what she was, a brothel madam.

Vera gave her a smile. 'You sure you're all right?'

Leah nodded.

'I'll be in the office if you needs me, Leah. Daisy? You 'eard what I said?' Daisy looked up and nodded, then went back to her invoices, chewing the end of a pencil.

Leah wasn't telling the truth.

After her shift at Daisychains yesterday she'd gone to the house in Brougham Street. John Pullinger, when she'd pressed him, reckoned two more porno films and her debt would be cleared.

She'd never got over her distaste at being fucked in every orifice by different men. Making the skin flicks gave her nightmares, so no wonder Katie was unsettled. She also despised the spotty youth she'd most regularly been paired with. He had the stamina and prick of a horse but the intelligence of a bus ticket.

They'd never had a conversation. When she first met him she felt she should at least get to know him, and he her. But it was clear the bloke had only two things on his mind, his motorbike and the size of his prick.

He wore leathers, including a head mask with a zip for the mouth and eyeholes, and she wore whatever was passed to her when she arrived at the house. It was usually ripped or cut off her anyway during filming. His screen name was Monster.

Her screen name was Red. Not that she felt anything like a Red, but she did what she was told, was handed some cash at the end of a session and went home to her kiddie and Nan and scrubbed herself red raw at the kitchen sink with a scrubbing brush and TCP.

Usually the cash in her hand was enough to buy food or a treat for Katie. She knew the balance of the money went towards paying off her loan, but somehow the couple of films she'd been promised were all that was needed had increased in number.

Leah knew there were girls who liked the work and were proud of their bodies being seen and being used. These girls saw the films as some kind of stepping stone to legitimate films on the real silver screen. Not Leah. For her it was a case of get to the house, take off her clothes, get on the bed and get it over with.

'A brown ale? Mann's or New Forest brown?' She smiled at the customer.

The man in the long grey overcoat smiled back and leaned across the bar to study the bottles.

When he'd made his choice, Leah turned and took a bottle off the shelf then, using the opener set in the wood of the bar, listened as the metal cap fell in the plastic container. With a fluid movement she deftly upended the bottle and poured the drink into a glass with the minimum of foam head forming.

'Done that before, haven't you, luv?'

'A few times,' Leah replied.

'And one for yourself?'

'Thank you,' said Leah. 'I'll 'ave a grapefruit juice.'

She took the man's money and gave him the change, then removed a bottle of juice from the shelf and put it at the back of the half-oval-shaped wooden board used for cutting lemons. Later, she'd put the drink back and fish out a bottle top to put by her stack of tops that represented drinks bought for her by customers and which Vera allowed her girls to change into cash at the end of their shifts.

Leah began washing glasses. She was counting the days to Jem's release now. She wanted a completely fresh start for the pair of them and their little girl. They'd leave Gosport and go back on the road and Jem had willingly agreed to this. She thought of their last prison conversation when he'd smiled into her eyes and she'd felt like crying as she saw how much he loved her.

'Gosport's not been kind, Leah. All I need do is earn some money and we'll be off,' he promised.

That was his plan. He was the man and the bread-winner. When they were away from the town and in the countryside they'd find their own kind of people once more, travellers. They'd be happy, then.

And all the time that Leah was fucking and being fucked, she held on to this dream and it kept her sane.

Could she live with herself afterwards?

She'd been assured that the films were sold abroad, so it was hardly likely Jem would ever see one. She'd certainly never breathe a word to him of what she'd been forced into because it would break his heart.

Vera was out of the office, bustling about putting change in the till. Leah thanked God that Vera and Daisy hadn't referred to the photographs again. Now she felt ashamed she'd broken down and told them everything. It hadn't taken Leah long to realise the photographs were the lever to get her to participate in the sex films. She'd even begun to think the pictures were faked in some way. She was assured that if she did the films, all the interest would be frozen.

One thing was for sure, she was definitely happier now the debt *was* being paid off. She was even happier the next film was going to be her last one.

'I 'opes you gets a bit of shut-eye tonight then, Leah.' Vera slammed the till drawer shut and threw the blue bank bag beneath the bar. Then she put her hands on her hips and stood looking at her. Leah nod-ded and gave her what she thought was a reassuring smile. 'You fancy coming for a walk round the market when your shift is over? I'll treat you to something nice.'

Leah always wondered why with the money Vera was making she preferred to buy cheap clothes from the stalls.

'You never asked *me*,' said Daisy, looking up.

'Because you never bloody wants to come, that's why!'

'Thanks all the same, Vera, but I'll take a rain check if you don't mind,' said Leah. 'You ever figured to splash out on clothes from Fleur's or Chantelle's, 'stead of off the traders?'

Both these shops proclaimed that they sold exclusive designs, and she knew Daisy often bought clothes from them.

'Leah, you are funny. Having a bit of dosh in me pocket and in the bank don't make me want to chuck it about. I like the stallholders. They was good to me when I 'ad nothin', an' often let me 'ave clothes really cheap or for a few favours ...' She winked rapidly to make sure Leah knew what she meant. 'Our Daisy's different. She's 'ad a bleedin' 'ard life an' her Eddie showed her a bit of money could make all the difference. She likes these new-fangled fashions, clumpy-'eeled shoes and short skirts up to 'er arse an' them big droopy 'ats. Mind you, them 'ats is only what Bette Davis an' Joan Crawford used to wear in them old films.' She pushed a stray strand of dark hair off her forehead. 'I do tell 'er she should bin that bleedin' MG and get 'erself a car the kids can get in as well. I saw a nice K-registered yellow Cortina estate the other day in that garage near Brockhurst. When I told 'er about it she said—'

'I said if you likes it so much you bleedin' buy it then!' Daisy interrupted. 'The bus'll do for me boys, it was good enough for me!'

Then Vera, frowning, stared hard out of the bar window towards the taxi rank. Vera's scent wafted towards Leah. 'Alec ain't there today,' she said.

Leah's gaze followed Vera's pointing finger and saw the patch of paving stones outside the blokes' urinals was empty.

Usually Alec was squatting on the pavement amidst his drawings. Faces, country scenes, animals, ferry boat scenes – he could draw anything and everything, and he did. Leah thought the likeness of the Prime Minister, Edward Heath, was especially good. People chucked money in an old biscuit tin for the scruffy individual who could have been any age but had talent at his fingertips.

'I reckon Alec must have been quite an artist until the drink got 'old of 'im,' said Leah.

'Wonder why he's not 'ere?' Vera seemed genuinely worried. 'It's a nice day, 'e *should* be 'ere.'

'Don't take on,' said Daisy.

'Well, it'll save you giving 'im an 'andout like you do most days,' said Leah. She saw Vera's lips clamp together in a thin line. Vera hated anyone to think she was a soft touch.

'So you've seen me then?'

'Can't 'elp it, can I? Not when I'm facin' the window that looks across towards the ferry, can I?'

Vera sniffed. 'S'pose not,' she said. 'I never really know what to do for the best. If I give 'im money I reckon 'e spends it on booze, yet I feel mean if I don't give 'im somethin' 'cause he might go 'ungry. He never asks me for nothin'. Sometimes I get the chef 'ere to do 'im a nice steak an' I takes that over to 'im between some bread.' Vera shrugged. 'He don't 'alf wolf it down. I knew his father, see, an' 'is mother. Sometimes I feel he only lives for his chalks and to draw on that bleedin' bit of pavement.'

'He wasn't there yesterday, neither.'

'Wasn't he?'

Leah knew Vera had been at home yesterday with the boys who'd had a day off school and Daisy had gone up to London to see Roy's mum and Charles. Normally Susie would have looked after Jamie and Eddie but she wasn't coping too well. She wouldn't let her baby out of her sight since her husband's death had knocked all the stuffing out of her. Vera cocked her head on one side like a cheeky Gosport sparrow. 'You sure?'

'As sure as I'm standin' 'ere polishin' glasses.' Leah could see Vera was worried.

'Did you know about this, Dais?'

'How could I, if I wasn't 'ere neither?'

Vera took a bottle of orange squash from the back of the bar and poured some into a tumbler, adding water from a jug on the counter. She took a swallow then asked Leah if she wanted a drink.

Leah shook her head and said, 'If I do, I got plenty of bottle tops.'

'Alec ain't that old, you know,' Vera said. 'Only a few years older than you, Daisy.'

Leah gasped. She was certain the bloke was an old man. Not only did he have a matted discoloured beard but his lank hair was quite grey. He even shuffled about like an old man but then, she thought, drink can age a person beyond all recognition.

'He's the son of a councillor who 'elped me get me licence for Heavenly Bodies,' went on Vera. 'His wife died and the poor bloke went to pieces. He brought that boy up by 'imself, nice house they 'ad at Elson. But Alec's dad could never cope well without Shirley. Then the lad got in with some rough lot.'

'Drugs?' Daisy fingered her invoices into a neat pile and sat back, stretching.

'A bit of cannabis, that's all. I don't think 'e got into the 'ard stuff. Drink was more in 'is line. When his dad committed suicide, Alec lost it for a while an' who could fuckin' blame 'im? At one time 'e took an overdose 'imself but luckily the neighbours found 'im. He went on livin' in the same 'ouse because it was bought and paid for but he don't have no purpose in life no more 'cept for 'is drawin'.'

'Can't no one 'elp him?' Daisy asked but got no answer.

Leah watched Vera as she continued staring out of

the window, deep in thought. Then Leah had to move along the bar and serve another customer who was busily tapping on the counter with a coin to get her attention. God, how she hated that, she thought.

'I'm coming,' she called.

'If you says 'e wasn't there yesterday,' said Vera when Leah came back, 'I might take a trip up to Elson and check 'e's all right.'

'You're a good woman, Vera.'

'Yeah, so I've been told.' Vera grinned at Leah. 'An' because I'm so fuckin' good I'm going to ask you one last time if there's been any comeback about those awful photos?'

Leah knew Vera was bound to ask this question some time or other.

She shook her head.

Vera stared at her. 'Did they just stop botherin' you?'

Leah nodded.

'Sure?'

'They can't get blood out of a stone, can they?'

'S'pose not,' agreed Vera. 'But stuff like that ain't nice an' I reckon it must be goin' on local like. Otherwise there wouldn't be no point in letting you see the photos. After all, the debt collection scam is local, ain't it?'

'How should I know? Anyway, my Jem comes out soon and no one's goin' to mess with me then, are they?'

She wasn't going to tell Vera that she was up for a

filmed threesome tonight. It would be over then, she thought happily. All over, debt paid in full.

Leah fiddled with the long string of jet beads at her neck. Who would ever guess that she, a barmaid who wouldn't even wear a low-cut top, would be fucking people she never knew just to clear a debt started by accepting goods from a bleeding door-to-door clubman?

Vera said, 'I've been doin' a bit of diggin' about them photos.'

Her words chilled Leah to the bone.

'You ain't told no one about me?'

''Course not, you silly bitch. But there's big business in these films an' someone local *'as* got in on the act.'

The hairs on the back of Leah's neck suddenly stood up. 'How do you know this?'

'I got me contacts, girl. I don't know as much as I'd like to yet, but I thank God Roy's 'ome at the weekend. He'll soon put a stop to anythin' on his patch what offends 'im.'

'Vera?'

'Yeah?'

'So you reckon that girl and that baby really was dead?' The sickness was rising in Leah's stomach. 'I'm beginning to think those pictures had been doctored to look like that. Just to frighten me.'

'And did they scare the shit out of you?'

'You know they did.'

Vera nodded as if to say 'I told you so'. Then, as a

customer approached the bar, she said, 'I'll serve this one, Leah.' Vera gave a huge smile to the balding man across the bar. ''Allo, Tommy, 'ow's tricks?'

The man winked at Vera. 'You were the best trick I ever turned, Vera.'

Leah walked along the bar, leaving them to their conversation. At least those awful photos weren't connected to the films *she* was making. Hers were sex romps.

'Leah,' called Vera.

She turned back.

'I'd never thought I'd see the day when I'd be glad to see that bastard Roy Kemp gettin' out of Parkhurst. I forgot to tell you we're 'aving a bit of a do 'ere for 'im on Sunday, to celebrate his 'omecomin'. You'll 'ave to work that night, that's if you don't mind. He'll be going straight to London from the island on the Friday but 'e won't waste time, 'e'll want to check on his assets – an' see Daisy of course.' She waved her hand towards Daisy who raised her eyes heavenwards before putting her empty glass down. Vera clapped her hand to her mouth. 'What a bloody fool I am. Your ol' man comes out soon as well, don't he? 'Ere,' she said, nudging Leah on the arm. 'You 'aven't been getting up to any mischief with any blokes, 'ave you, Miss Prim an' Proper?'

Leah shook her head. Her heart was beating so hard she was sure Vera would hear it.

'Don't look so scared, girl, I'm only teasin' you. I know what a straight-laced lot you gypsies are. Bit like swans, your lot. You takes a man and mates with 'im for life, don't you?'

'I love Jem and he loves me,' said Leah, her voice a whisper. And all the time she was thinking how if Jem even had an inkling about the films, he'd kill her.

'Good for you, girl. There's many that would like to stay faithful to one man, I'm sure.'

Vera turned towards the bottles of spirits left in readiness to refill the optics. She clutched a bottle.

'Put this whisky against my name, Leah. Gloria's comin' in to give you an 'and later. We won't be long. We're going along to see Alec. If he's poorly, this should cheer the bugger up.'

CHAPTER 14

Vera rattled the letter box of the house in Richmond Grove. Daisy saw that what had once been a decently laid-out front garden with a lawn and ornamental bushes had now turned into a jungle. She took a deep breath of the scent from a flourishing white rose scrambling over the fence. Rubbish had blown in from the road and an old mattress had been dumped just inside the gate. Vera now pushed open the letter box in the scarred front door, bent down and yelled, 'Open this bleedin' door. I knows you're in there, Alec Thomas.'

Vera knew nothing of the sort, thought Daisy. But if the bloke was inside she figured it might shake him up a bit. Vera stepped back and eyed the paint-peeled bay window. Daisy noted a yellowed net curtain with a hole in it sagging on a stretched wire. It was closed, as were the rest of the front curtains.

Vera shouted again. 'Open the fuckin' door!'

'I don't see why I 'ad to come 'ere with you,' grumbled Daisy.

'Because if you was worried about someone I'd 'ave to traipse along with you, wouldn't I?'

'Point taken.'

'Come on, pretend we're leaving.'

Daisy knew better than to argue. They walked back down the path as though they were going and Vera turned quickly, just in time to catch the movement at a top window. 'You bugger,' she cried. She pulled the bottle of whisky from her handbag and waved it about. 'I knew the bleeder was there,' she said. Then she walked back to the front door, knocked politely and waited. Daisy followed. This time the door opened.

'Works every bleedin' time,' Vera said, her knee firmly wedged against the wood. 'Folks who don't answer doors just can't resist 'avin' a peek to see who it was, Dais.'

The few inches of open door showed a bit of blood-stained face and a black eye. Daisy wrinkled her nose and made a face at Vera.

'Jesus fuckin' Christ, I can smell 'im from 'ere!' The door opened wider and Vera nearly fell back off the step. Daisy almost exploded. 'Whoever did that to you?'

Her heart went out to him. The blackened eye was staring at her but the other eye was a mauve swollen slit. His nose was twice the normal size and blood seemed to have dripped from it unchecked down his filthy jumper.

Alec made a grab for the bottle.

'Not so fuckin' fast,' Vera yelled, swinging it out of his reach. 'We wants a few answers first.'

Taking a deep breath, Vera pushed past him and

marched inside. Daisy followed, holding her breath. She hadn't been wrong in her assumption that the place would be a stinking tip. She walked on down the hall and into the kitchen. It had a sink full of scummy water in which were stacked filthy pots, some with mouse droppings in them, a cooker that was thick with grease and rancid food left in burned saucepans. Unable to hold her breath any longer, she let it out in a great gasp.

'Jesus, don't you know what fuckin' soap an' water is?' She whirled round to where Alec had followed and was standing watching them, his eyes full of fear. His mouth was open and Daisy saw he still had his own teeth even if they weren't too clean.

'You got set upon again, didn't you? I tol' you it would 'appen if you didn't stop gettin' pissed out of your bleedin' skull all the time.' Vera bent forward, looked up and examined his face, tucking a lock of greasy hair away from one eye. As her hand went near him he flinched. 'You can stop that an' all, I ain't gonna hurt you.' Alec swallowed, his Adam's apple bobbed up and down and he looked relieved. 'You should 'ave the windows open, get a bit of fresh air in 'ere,' Vera said.

Daisy saw the mountain of empty whisky bottles in the corner and wrinkled her nose in disgust. Then, ignoring the filthy dishes in the sink, she turned the tap full on and let it run.

'Don't suppose you got 'ot water, but if not it don't matter.'

Vera, leaving the whisky on the draining board, foraged behind a curtain beneath the sink and came out with an enamelled dog bowl that she rinsed the dust from. Then she poked about in the drawers of the wooden table and sideboard until she found a tea towel that looked as thin as a net curtain but was surprisingly clean.

'You don't do a lot of wipin' up, I see,' Vera said to Alec.

'What are you doing …'

'Oh! It talks, does it?' Vera said. She pulled out a grey-topped plastic stool from the table and on closer examination decided it was actually white but crusted with dirt. 'Sit!' she commanded. Daisy turned from the sink, caught Vera's eye and sighed.

Obediently Alec sat down. Dampening the tea towel in the water-filled dog bowl, Vera began carefully sponging the blood and dirt from the wounds on his face. He winced as she touched open cuts.

Daisy asked, 'Who did that?'

'I don't know. Some kids. The oldest wasn't more than sixteen.'

Daisy was once more reminded of Alec's soft and cultured voice. It held none of the clipped Gosport slangy tones that she and Vera shared. Then she remembered. Alec had not only gone to the local grammar school but he'd also been to university. Of course, Daisy herself had attended the local grammar, only she'd left to get married at sixteen to that waster Kenny Lane. Daisy hadn't gone on to higher education to lose her Gosport accent. Her education had been gained from the streets.

Alec, she knew from Vera, had come back home when his mother had died.

'An' I s'pose you just let a bunch of kids 'it you?' Daisy tutted.

He shrugged. 'What could I do?'

'You could start by bein' a bleedin' man again an' givin' up that shit!' Vera motioned towards the whisky.

'You brought it.'

'Don't mean to say I'm goin' to give it to you, though.' Vera looked into his face. 'You know you could be a good-lookin' bloke if you tidied yourself up a bit. Your father ...'

'I know all about you and my father.'

Daisy heard the anger in his voice.

Vera said, 'That's all right then, ain't it?'

Daisy rinsed out the bowl and cloth and after refilling it with water handed it back to Vera.

Vera said to Alec, 'I ain't finished yet, so sit still. Your dad weren't nobody's fool. He only came to me because your mum was ill. An' I'll tell you somethin' for nothin', your mum was a mate of mine ...' Daisy saw Alec's eyes widen with horror. Vera laughed, a great cackle. 'Oh, I don't mean she was a prossie!' Vera slapped him none too gently around the ear that didn't have blood covering it. 'I mean I knew her well enough to call 'er a true mate an' when she got ill but was still walkin' around town, she comes up to me an' she says, "My Stan been comin' to see you regularly?" Well, Alec, I thought she was goin' to blow a gasket, but she gives me an 'ug an' says, "I know 'e's all right with you, Vera. You can give 'im what I can't an' I knows you won't be makin' no demands on 'im, an' I thank you for that." Well, you could 'ave knocked me down with a feather. Anyway, 'e came every week after that but when I found out 'e was taking time off work to look after your mum an' money was tight in your 'ouse, I did 'im for free for ol' times' sake.'

Daisy grinned at Alec. He started to laugh then and went on laughing until Vera said, 'Keep bloody still. How can I clean you up if you won't bleedin' keep still?' Alec pushed her hand away, stood up and faced her.

'How come you've never told me this before?' he asked.

'We ain't never not seen you sittin' outside the bleedin' urinals before, 'ave we? You ever thought of goin' into St James' over in Portsmouth?'

Daisy could see her words had shocked Alec, but she knew he wasn't stupid and she wondered if the thought hadn't crossed his own mind at some time or other.

'I'm not a mental case!'

'Never said you was,' said Vera, 'but you knows St James' got a place to dry you out. You ought to try it. You're sober enough now, ain't you?'

He held out a hand to show them it was shaking. 'Not really. I've drunk everything I had indoors and I was too scared to go out in case those kids …'

He looked towards the amber liquid.

'If you ain't brave enough to venture out to the offie for more booze an' you ain't got none indoors, then I reckon it shows you can go without it, if you wants,' said Daisy. He looked at her then turned away. She was sure she'd hit a raw nerve there.

Another thought struck her. This house belonged to him. He hadn't sold it for money for drink so he hadn't fallen that far down the pit, not yet he hadn't. And if it had anything to do with her and Vera he wouldn't be falling any deeper. Daisy watched as Vera moved the bottle further along the draining board.

'What's the point of me giving up the drink? You don't know what it's like to be me,' he said.

Vera was frowning at him. Daisy could see his words made her angry. Cheeky bloody self-centred upstart, she thought. And then she realised why Vera had been so insistent she, Daisy, come along to Alec's house. Thinking about him would take her mind off her own problems. But what right had this man to reckon she didn't *have* any problems?

'You know fuck all about what I knows or I don't! An' if you didn't get sozzled so much the fuckin' kids wouldn't take the piss out of you.'

Alec was taken aback at her outburst.

'The whisky gives me peace and for a while blots out the uselessness of my existence.'

'For fuck's sake, that's bloody rubbish talk, that is! What about your chalk paintings?'

What a waste, Daisy thought, an educated bloke so depressed with life he was bloody wasting it.

Vera asked, 'Don't you think you're bein' selfish?'

'I haven't anyone else to worry about,' Alec said, 'so I can be whatever I like.'

Daisy knew they were making him angry but she didn't care. Any emotion was better than his awful apathy. She said, 'There's many would cut off an arm or leg to be able to do 'alf what you can.'

Vera picked up the bowl. 'I'm dumpin' this lot in the sink, it can join the other stinkin' shit you got lyin' around 'ere.'

Daisy was glad about that. After rinsing the stuff in the sink, the bowl of filthy matter and the offending cloth was making her feel sick just looking at it.

'At least your face, 'ead an' neck are clean enough for the gouged skin to heal,' said Vera.

He looked sheepish now, Daisy thought. His eyes met hers. 'Do you really like my drawings?' he asked.

It was an honest question. 'Said so, didn't I? Vera likes 'em an' all.' Vera nodded.

'Want to see some more?' His face had suddenly lit up. She *knew* he cared about his art.

'Only if you says thank you, Vera, for cleanin' me up.'

And then Alec laughed. It was a deep laugh, a proper bloke's laugh, Daisy decided.

'Thank you,' he said. Only he wasn't laughing when he said it and Daisy knew he meant it. 'Come with me.'

Alec walked ahead of her and Vera. Daisy saw he wasn't so much shuffling as limping.

'What's the matter with your leg?'

'Nothing.'

'You ain't a very good liar,' said Vera. 'Let me look?'

He sighed, bent down and rolled up a trouser leg.

Daisy gasped. 'You silly bleeder, you needs a doctor for that!' She could see an open wound that was infected. 'If that gets worse you could get blood poisoning.'

'Stupid sod!' Vera chimed in.

He shrugged and let the material fall again. 'These are all I care about, come on up.' He began to climb the stairs.

'A bit of carpet wouldn't go amiss on 'ere,' grumbled Vera, puffing.

The wooden banister rail felt sticky. Daisy shuddered. 'I reckon you makes enough for chalks an' that's about it from your pitch down the ferry. Where's the money come from to keep this 'ouse on an' buy booze?'

'You're nosy. Mum was well insured.'

He opened the door to a bedroom and stepped inside, urging them to follow. What Daisy saw took her breath away.

Drawings were pinned to every available surface. Canvases were stacked against the walls. A pile of drawings sat on the table. Charcoal sketches and watercolours were lying on a bed that was covered by a red silk coverlet. Daisy gasped again: apart from the jam jars containing brushes, boxes of chalks, paint-stained rags and tubes of paint strewn about, the room was clean. So clean and free from filth that it looked as though this room didn't belong in the house.

'Would you look at this, Vera,' she exclaimed.

Vibrant colours on the canvases formed flowers so real she almost wanted to reach out and smell them. Muted shades conveyed portraits and sketches of people she recognised who regularly used the ferry and came into Daisychains. She was enthralled by a watercolour of a ferry boat, the boatman's face full of concentration as he looped rope over bollards. For once in her life she was speechless. She heard Vera take a deep breath. Daisy was busy savouring the smells of paint, oil and charcoal and something like turpentine. Clean brushes were stacked like sheaves of corn in jars. A covered easel stood near the partly open window. Daisy knew this room and all its contents were loved. She could tell that by the atmosphere of comfort and familiarity the room exuded.

Alec was watching her carefully. Vera moved to-wards the table.

'Can I look through these?' she asked, and Alec just shrugged.

An idea was forming in Daisy's brain, one that could be beneficial for the both of them. Daisy prided herself on knowing a good thing when she saw it.

Carefully she fingered the drawings on the table, looking at each of them in turn.

'This is Angel! And Derek, one of our bouncers.' She dropped the sketches. 'They surely never sat for you? I'd 'ave known if that was so. An' to the best of me bleedin' knowledge you ain't never been inside the club!'

His greasy hair flopped around his face. 'I do a few lines and my memory does the rest.' He looked up, embarrassed.

Across the room Vera was rattling drawings.

'Here's me!' She studied the sketch carefully. 'You got it wrong!' A hand went to her face. 'You never put me scar in.' She dropped the sketch and pulled back her hair to show him and Daisy the long silvery line, a relic of a Stanley knife attack.

'I knew about the scar because it's ancient history, Vera, but it doesn't show and doesn't need to be emphasised. When you smile, the line of your determined chin, that wicked glint in your eyes shows the true you.'

Vera didn't know what to make of all that so she said, 'I think you're givin' me the old flannel,' but Daisy knew she liked his words. Then she began rootling through pictures again.

'It's you!' Vera said to Daisy excitedly.

Alec crossed the room and tried to take the drawing away from Vera. 'It's my Daisy looking through the top window of the gambling den. Daisy with her serious face on,' she exclaimed. 'It's you staring with your Joan Collins eyes for something you can't find. She can smile, y'know.'

Daisy had hold of the drawing now. It was a good likeness. She could feel Alec's gaze on her but when she looked at him he quickly turned away.

Alec moved to take some other sketches on the far side of the table but Vera was quicker.

'That's more like my Daisy,' she said, handing it to her. Daisy liked this sketch better. In it she was throwing back her head and laughing.

'What you workin' on now?' Vera asked and, without waiting for his reply, moved over to the easel and carefully lifted the covering. 'Why, this is you an' all, again,' she said to Daisy, who moved to the easel. The painting was vibrant with life, showing her eyes sparkling with happiness, and yet there was a serenity about her, and Alec had captured it all.

'It's not finished yet,' he said gruffly, taking the cloth from her hand and letting it fall to cover the oil painting once more. He was embarrassed, Daisy realised, though he had no cause to be if he could paint and draw like this ...

Vera spoke. 'You ain't no fuckin' drunk if you can do work like this! No! I knows what's up with you. You drinks when you loses your get up an' go.' She waved an arm around the room. 'This is what keeps you alive an' stops you killin' yourself.' Alec opened his mouth but Vera said, 'No! Let me finish. I think there's times when you gets so lonely and depressed that even all this talent won't satisfy what you needs an' then you drinks to find what ain't *never* been found at the bottom of a bleedin' bottle. Am I right? Or am I right?'

Alec didn't move, didn't speak. Daisy felt his eyes on her but for some reason she couldn't look at him.

'I knew it,' Vera said. 'I fuckin' knew it.' Then, 'Do you like kids?'

Daisy, surprised at Vera's words, saw his mouth open and his eyes widen as he stepped back from her like she was on fire. 'I am *not* a kiddie fiddler!'

Vera started laughing. 'I didn't put that very well, did I? What I meant was do you get on all right with children?'

'I've a teaching certificate, if that's what you mean. I taught English Literature, Drama, Art and Maths at a junior school in Oxford. I *know* children.' Confusion covered his face.

Daisy was struck dumb but she felt the excitement rising in Vera who said, 'I got an idea you're just cryin' out to climb from that bleedin' bottle. Am I right again?' Alec's eyes left Vera and he bowed his head, shuffled his feet and looked at the floorboards. Daisy's heart went out to him.

'Come on,' Vera yelled, stomping towards the bedroom door. 'I'm goin' to get you so fuckin' busy you won't 'ave time to get depressed. Come on, you two!'

Down in the kitchen, Vera took hold of the whisky bottle and unscrewed the top. Staring at Alec, she saw beads of sweat had appeared on his freshly washed forehead.

'Now watch,' she said. 'Both of you.' Then she tipped the golden liquid down the filthy sink.

CHAPTER 15

'Losing your mate, then?'

Jem replied a dutiful, 'Yes, sir,' to the screw. After all, this guard was one of the better ones. Jem had never heard of this one giving any of the cons a kicking.

'For the rest of your sentence you'll be looking over your shoulder making sure that McCloud ain't on your tail.'

'I should 'ave ripped out that bastard's throat when I 'ad the chance. I'm keepin' me nose clean now. It's too close to me release date, sir, for me to think about that tosser.'

The cell door shut with a bang and Jem was on his own.

Would he ever get the stench of sweat and stale air out of his nostrils, he wondered. He thought longingly of wide open spaces and the breeze on his face. He supposed the other cons felt the same. Though most cons were more worried about the screws and the other cons than they were about being shut away. The solitude didn't worry him at all. Being shut inside was another matter.

Thank Christ it wouldn't be for much longer.

Then he'd be back with his Leah. She was a good sort, his wife. He'd missed her. Now there was the kiddie to think about he'd make sure he didn't have to come back to a place like this ever again.

Thanks to Roy Kemp's lady, Daisy Lane, his Leah had a good job at Daisychains. Only it wasn't right she should be working in a bar. He didn't like the thought of other men ogling her. But he trusted his woman.

She'd been a bit on the quiet side the last time she'd visited.

'Katie kept me up last night,' she'd said.

He'd guessed that accounted for the dark circles beneath her eyes.

It wouldn't be long before he'd be able to put a bit of money on the table from a few fist fights. He'd kept himself in trim in the nick, so that wouldn't be a problem. He ran his hand over the weals on his face that were the reminder of his stepping in to take the punishment McCloud had tried to mete out to Roy Kemp.

Jesus, but he hated that fucker McCloud.

It was funny the way Kemp was forced to take that kind of shit from cons in prison. They all wanted to try their luck with a face. Kemp had adapted to life in prison but it didn't mean he liked it. Imprisonment wasn't natural, Jem thought, not to a bloke like Roy Kemp and not for himself.

There were times he wished he could read books.

That would be almost as good as watching films, he thought. Roy Kemp read continuously. Every time the screws opened Kemp's door he was asking to visit the library. He was a good bloke, Kemp was. That was one of the reasons Jem had tried to stop that fucker McCloud from doing him.

And he'd take up the offer of a job from Roy when he got out.

'Fuck!' The light had gone off. The switches were controlled from the outside, and although it was never completely dark in prison the lights wouldn't be switched on again until six in the morning.

He thought he heard light scrabbling. Parkhurst was infested with cockroaches. They came in under the doors. Locks didn't keep them bastards out. They'd climb the walls and walk on the ceilings and drop on your face in the night.

His mind went back again to Leah and her gorgeous mane of red hair.

God, but he loved that bitch.

''Course I'm gonna be all right, Vera.'

Susie finished pegging out the last of the terry-towelling nappies, then stood back in the warm sun and admired their bright whiteness. Joy was asleep in her pram and as she bent over into the milky-smelling coolness to check she was all right, she felt the tears surge again.

She heard the front door slam, which meant Vera had finally gone down to Heavenly Bodies to check on her girls and that she was now, at last, alone in the house.

Susie sat down on the edge of the pond, put her head in her hands and cried. And went on crying until she felt her chest ache with all the sobbing she allowed herself to do. Then she took a deep breath and wiped her face on the bottom of her frilled pinny.

Her eyes fell on the rose bush Si had planted last autumn. Blooms large as breakfast cups and still glistening here and there with morning dew bobbed down at her. She breathed deeply of their sweetness.

'We were all right together, weren't we, Si?'

It felt so good to be able to talk to Si without either Vera or Daisy rushing, worrying, to her side.

She could feel the heat of the sun on her face as she turned and looked towards the shed and the new hasp that had been the last job Si had undertaken.

'I 'ad to keep on moanin' at you to fix that, didn't I?'

In her mind's eye she could see his cheeky grin as he'd said, 'Who's goin' to come round the back of the house an' steal a few ol' rusty tools?'

'It ain't the tools, you daft oaf,' she'd said. 'It's them bottles of oil and cans of weedkiller. I don't want our baby crawlin' in there an' poisonin' itself.'

So finally he'd fixed the door lock.

She sighed. 'Well, love, I suppose you knows your family kicked up a fuss? Said it wasn't right I sent you down to Devon. Vera 'ad a right barney with your brother. *You* know I was right though, don't you?

'An' you don't 'ave to worry about me. With Vera an' Daisy's help I'm gettin' stronger every day.' Susie thought for a moment. 'Oh, yes, I'm goin' to bring your little girl up to love you just as much as I do. Oh, Si, we 'ad such a lot of 'appiness, didn't we? Thank you, darling.' She smiled towards the glistening blooms. 'Kiss Meggie for me.'

A light breeze took some petals from the rose bush and blew them in her direction and Susie caught one. Examining its velvet softness, she raised it to her lips and smiled again. 'I knew you'd understand,' she said.

'You know, I don't think I'll ever change from using Omo washing powder.' Daisy was at the sink rinsing out Eddie's football shorts. 'It gets out all the grass stains, Vera, an' it smells nice an' fresh an' clean.'

'What are you?' Vera asked. 'A bleedin' advert for the washing powder firm?'

Daisy turned and looked at Vera, who was soaking her feet in a bowl of water. Her fluffy mules were on the floor next to a packet of salt, half of which she'd poured into the bowl along with the hot water. Kibbles was stretched over her lap, his great paws hanging limply down Vera's bare legs. Vera popped a Cadbury's Milk Tray Turkish Delight from the box into her mouth and then offered the blue box to Daisy.

'Go on, 'ave one, Dais.' She shook the cardboard and the chocolates rattled.

Daisy shook her head. 'You've ate all the cream ones.'

Still chewing, Vera shrugged then said, 'I got my doctor friend to look at Alec's leg an' it wasn't as bad as it first looked. An' 'e's all set up to go voluntary to St James' to be dried out.'

'The doctor?' Daisy knew the man had been struck off and liked a drink.

'No, you silly cow, Alec.'

'Oh! An' you reckon afterwards Alec'll keep off the booze?' Daisy wrung the shorts until the cold water no longer dripped from them.

'Sure I do.' Vera ran her fingers through the cat's mackerel-coloured fur, looked at the clumps of hairs on her hands, twisted them in her fingers and threw them on the parquet floor. 'I also reckon you was right the punters down the club will pay to have their women's faces sketched by 'im.'

'Not the villains?'

''Course not the villains. It's low profiles for them, but certainly the girlies they're with. We'll get the 'ostesses to ask the blokes if they want to make a gift of a drawin' for their females, the same way they gets the men to buy 'em drinks. I reckon we'll be on to a winner. It'll give Alec a new lease of life.'

'Yeah, in a fuckin' bar when the poor sod's an alkie. I don't know whether to 'ang these shorts out on the line tonight or put 'em in the bathroom to dry.'

'When does he need 'em?'

'Tomorrow.'

'The forecast's rain. If you're goin' to worry about a pair of bleedin' shorts, better dry 'em inside.' Vera popped another chocolate in her mouth and spoke in a muffled voice. 'Could be the makin' of Alec. We also need to 'ave a word with Angel.'

Distracted, Daisy ran her damp hands through her hair. She'd thought a lot about the bloke who reckoned he was Jack McVitie's son and who had vowed to come after Roy Kemp's nearest and dearest himself or send someone else to do his dirty work. She had not forgotten Vinnie and Roy's warnings but she'd decided there wasn't any point in putting her life on hold for something that might or might not happen.

'Alec can teach young Michael how to draw properly. That kid 'as a gift what shouldn't be wasted. For a little tiddler he ain't 'alf talented.'

'I 'ope Alec cleans himself up a bit then, Vera.'

Daisy watched Vera cooing at Kibbles. She'd started the cat purring and the sound almost eclipsed the soft music from the radio.

'You'll be surprised at the change in 'im.'

'You reckon? I'm surprised they got 'im in there on a programme so quickly, Vera.'

A guilty look stole over her friend's face. 'One of the doctors on the medical team there pulled a few strings for me.'

'Why would 'e do that?' The penny dropped and Daisy smiled at Vera. 'I get it. Don't tell me the doctor used to be one of your clients?'

'Oh, no, Daisy. Not 'im, but his dad used to come around and what 'e liked to do was—'

'I don't want to 'ear it, you ol' tart! Let's just 'ope Alec stays off the booze. What was you sayin' about our Angel?'

'I think Angel's puttin' stuff up 'er nose.'

Daisy sighed, then stared hard at Vera. 'She wouldn't dare – would she? She knows 'ow we feel about that shit.'

'We'll see,' said Vera, 'but I'm guessing I'm right.'

'I'm sayin' nothin', but if she is, we got a problem because it's 'er money what keeps 'er kiddie an' Malkie an' that prefab.'

She stood gazing about her kitchen. She liked the large room, the hub of the house that reflected her character with its cheerful yellow gingham curtains and wallpaper covered with patterns of bright kitchen utensils. Then there were Vera's cat ornaments on the top shelf of the dresser, drawings the boys had done stuck on the wallpaper with dressmaking pins, Joy's baby clothes airing on the pulley line and the table covered with bits of this and that in readiness for the morning. Tidy it wasn't, a home it was.

As if reading her mind, Vera said, 'Ain't it nice to 'ave a bit of peace an' quiet?'

'Susie's asleep and so are the boys. I ain't goin' up to the bathroom yet in case I wake Joy.'

'That's good. Suze needs all the rest she can get. Si's death's on 'er mind all the time. I wish we could do somethin' more to 'elp 'er.'

'She's all right, Vera. It's natural for 'er to grieve in 'er own way. It's early days yet, and she ain't just mopin' about, she's gettin' on with things. Work's the best therapy for our Suze.'

'Sometimes you can be very 'ard, Dais.'

'Cruel to be kind, Vera. Anyway,' she mumbled, 'I need 'er to 'elp me plan his lordship's 'omecomin' party. Roy an' 'is family is comin' down to Gosport.'

Daisy glanced at Vera and realised with a jolt that her friend was beginning to show her age. Grey roots were visible beyond the black dye, and lines had formed on her cheeks and around her mouth. Daisy's heart constricted. Vera must have realised Daisy was staring at her for she looked up and treated Daisy to a huge smile that lit up her face and made Daisy see Vera was still a very desirable woman. Daisy bent forward and stroked Kibbles. His body was warm and comforting to the touch.

'Do you realise how old my little man is, Dais?'

Vera's question was completely serious. Daisy knew Vera had obviously given some thought to the old cat. He wasn't as nimble at leaping after garden leaves as he used to be, though he still followed Eddie all over the place just like a small grey dog.

'Don't be thinkin' daft thoughts. He's got years in 'im yet, the bleedin' fleabag.'

Daisy left the kitchen, taking Eddie's shorts with her. Upstairs in the bathroom she hung them over the shower rail, then she went back downstairs. As she walked into the kitchen, she heard a lusty wail.

Vera looked at her and smiled. The cry didn't last long and down the stairs came Susie in her pink dressing gown, barefoot and with the little one clutched tightly to her breast.

'No rest for the wicked,' Susie said. She still had the excess weight about her, Daisy thought, despite pining for her dead husband and not eating.

Susie dumped Joy in Vera's lap, making Kibbles flee for his life. 'Get off, cat,' she said. 'You've 'ad your turn.'

'She's wet,' said Vera.

'An' 'ungry. I got to do a bottle.'

Kibbles had decamped to a kitchen stool where he was eyeing the proceedings with disdain.

'Such a lot to learn, my sweet,' Vera said to the bundle. Daisy watched Susie clattering about, levelling off milk powder and taking a fresh bottle from the Milton sterilising unit.

'Shame your milk dried up,' Daisy said. The shock of Si's death had done that, she reckoned.

'It don't really matter,' said Susie. 'I never would 'ave been able to fiddle about makin' sure she 'ad enough. At least with a bottle I can see what goes inside 'er, can't I?' Susie still had the bloom of motherhood on her, her blonde curls bouncing around her pink and white cheeks. She picked up a terrycloth nappy and began to fold it. 'I been thinking about this party for Roy,' she said. 'I could make 'im a lemon cake. He likes my lemon cakes.'

Vera prised her finger from Joy's palm and looked

over at Daisy and winked. A warm glow was rising in Daisy's heart. Thank God her moaning had done some good. At last Susie was thinking about something else besides the loss of her husband, terrible though it was. Daisy grinned and winked back at Vera, knowing exactly what the older woman was thinking.

Daisy picked up a muslin square and sat down.

'Give us that baby,' Daisy said, breathing in the warm talcum powder and milky smell of Joy as Vera handed her over.

'I know you two been worryin' about me,' said Susie, turning towards them. Her voice was small, like she'd been doing a lot of thinking about the words she was going to say, thought Daisy. 'But you don't 'ave to worry no more. I reckon I was very lucky to 'ave 'ad a decent bloke like my Si to love me as much as he did. I got to stop thinking it ain't fair he was took away from me, but 'ow bleedin' fortunate it is I got a piece of 'im left in our little girl Joy.'

'Bless you, Suze,' said Vera.

'You're one of the bravest people I know,' said Daisy, turning her face away and hoping neither of them would see her tears.

CHAPTER 16

Roy stretched out his long legs and looked round Daisy's kitchen. As always, it was spotlessly clean, with remnants of family life spread about. An ironing board was set up, the iron upended on its asbestos mat and a pile of freshly ironed clothes folded neatly on top of the board. The radio was playing the new number one record 'Telegram Sam' by that ridiculously baby-faced lad. What was his name? Sounded more like a prehistoric monster than a pop star's name, T.Rex, that was it. Vera's cat was sprawled, snoring, on top of the dresser, one leg hanging down. This was a happy room, he thought. A lot had gone on in this kitchen, but the overall sense of peace remained. Indeed, a lot had happened in this house, what with Daisy's fluctuating finances, but the woman had managed to hold on to her home.

'Eddie knew what he was doing when he left you this place,' he said. 'Backing on to Stanley Park like it does, it's exactly the right setting for you.'

'I didn't expect to see you until the weekend,' Daisy said.

He'd been worried about meeting her again. It was one thing her visiting him with a smile stretched on her face because she thought it was the proper thing to do, but to catch her unawares in her own home was another matter.

She was pleased to see him.

She was looking at him now, her eyes searching his face.

'That bastard got you good,' she said. He touched the remains of the wound that had scarred over, then shrugged. Now he was here he didn't know what to say to her. What do you say to a woman you care about who doesn't love you any more? He stared across the room and out of the window.

Susie was pegging terrycloth squares on the rotary line. She'd kept some of the plumpness after the baby's birth and it suited her. There was also a maturity about her that he hadn't noticed before. Probably a lot to do with her husband's death, he thought.

'I wanted to see you, is that so wrong?' He knew his words sounded feeble.

'If you came this afternoon because you thought you'd catch me with Vinnie, you've made a mistake.' She'd put her hands on her hips and her head to one side as though ready for an argument.

He sighed. He thought of Vinnie and how he and the detective were bound together by their actions that rainy night years ago – the night they murdered the boxer Valentine Waite in retribution for the prostitutes he had killed and for keeping Daisy captive, and made the bastard dig his own grave. Daisy knew nothing of this and she never would. She'd have a fit if she discovered his mouldering remains were only a few hundred yards away in a leafy glade.

He digested her words. He knew Vinnie wasn't in Gosport. He'd made it his business to find out where the copper was. And that somewhere was Liss, looking after his other lad, while his ex-wife Clare and her mother were in Guildford, staying near the hospital where Clare's father was undergoing cancer tests.

Roy didn't like the detective but trust was another matter. He trusted Vinnie Endersby. He had to, there was too much at stake on either side.

'I suppose now you're 'ere you'll want a cup of tea?'

'You and your tea,' he laughed. 'What would you do without it?' She smiled at him then, not a forced smile but a genuine one, and he felt the stirrings of lust in his loins.

Daisy started to move past him to get to the kettle. She was so close he could smell the musk of her body mixed with her perfume and the scented shampoo from her freshly washed hair. He grabbed at her hand. It was an automatic movement on his part.

She pulled her hand away but she stopped and turned and touched his face, her fingers trailing lightly along the facial scar. He wanted to take her small hand and smother it with kisses.

'It'll heal well.' Her touch was light. She looked away as his eyes met hers but it was too late, he'd seen the distress in those eyes. 'I'll put the kettle on,' she said gruffly.

He let her move away. She wasn't his any more.

He watched as she reached up into the tall cupboard to take down the Bourbon biscuits. She never seemed to alter, he thought. Slim, but curvy in the right places and always, as now, dressed in black. To him she was still the same girl he'd desired back in the sixties and the few tiny lines she'd accumulated around her eyes and mouth only made him more aware that the past had begun to show and he loved her all the more for it.

And now he was going to bargain with her again and he didn't like himself much for it. But it couldn't be helped. He had a business to run, didn't he?

'I hope this visit don't mean you ain't comin' down on Saturday. That woman out there,' she nodded towards Susie, 'has planned a party for you.'

'I'll be here,' he said. 'Is she coping all right?'

Daisy took a mouthful of air and seemed to let it out slowly before she answered. 'How would you cope if you was a woman and your 'usband was killed the same day you gave birth to his daughter, a little girl he'd wanted with all 'is heart?'

He ran his fingers down the crease of his left trouser leg. 'I only asked, Daisy.'

'An' I'm only sayin', Roy, that it's organisin' this bleedin' party for you what's stopped the daft cow from goin' round the bend, so if you an' yours don't turn up I'll personally find you and cut your bleedin' balls off.'

'I'm coming, I'm coming! Keep your bleedin' hair on. Jesus Christ, you've done nothing but moan since I got here. How about "How are you, Roy? Glad you're out of prison. How are you enjoying your freedom?" '

She glared at him before she pulled the plug from the electric kettle and swirled hot water around the teapot to warm it.

'I was going to ask you that,' she said, picking up the tea caddy with the roses on it.

'An' you can get tea bags now,' he said, watching her spooning leaf tea into the pot.

'I know that! But me an' Vera like tea leaves. We don't like them piddly little bags.'

'No, you'd have to use twice as many because you both drink tar not tea.'

She glared at him before jamming the knitted tea cosy over the teapot. ''Ere,' she said, 'you came specially today to talk about bleedin' tea bags, did you? What d'you want?' She had her back to him, rattling cups and saucers and spoons as though her life depended on it. 'You ain't come to tell me no more 'orrible stories about that nutter you was inside with, 'ave you?'

He shook his head. 'Why do you always think I have an ulterior motive?'

She turned and faced him and raised her eyes heavenwards.

'Because you never do nothing unless there's something in it for you, an' I remember what you said to me when I visited you in the nick.'

In the garden Susie was now bending over the small tartan pram and cooing to the baby inside. The woman's pink cheeks glowed with health. The white washing billowed in the warm summer wind. It was one of those days when, after the confines and greyness of prison, colours were brighter than ever and everything seemed fresh and new. He could pick out the fragrance of talcum powder, and of lemon polish on the shining kitchen surfaces.

Yes, he did have an ulterior motive but he was picking his time carefully to suggest it. He thought he had built a few bridges between himself and Daisy this afternoon and he didn't want to spoil it.

'Was your businesses run well enough for you durin' your island break?' she asked. She brushed back some strands of blonde hair that had fallen across her eyes.

'Yes and no.' He thought about the new direction his mother and Charles had decided on taking. He'd see how it panned out. After all, his old lady had always had a good head for business and his money had certainly grown during his enforced holiday. It was the London patch, so nothing to do with the south coast and Daisy's handling of his affairs. 'But I'm not burdening you with my problems today.'

What the fuck did he say that for? Why hadn't he come right out and asked her for the favour he wanted from her? Roy Kemp, he thought, you need your fucking brains testing. Now he'd have to wait for another time.

'Thank Christ for that,' she said. 'The less I know about your business the better, I got enough on me plate as it is.' She poured dark brown liquid into the cups.

'You'll cope, you always do,' he said. Too late he realised it had come out as though he didn't care, when what he meant was, she *would* cope because she was the strongest woman he knew.

His eyes went to the windowsill where photographs of the children sat. Jamie was grinning from one frame, Eddie was caught with a solemn look in another. He nodded towards the pictures. 'No smiles from Eddie?' Absentmindedly he patted his pocket where his wallet was. Inside it was the photo of Daisy and Eddie he'd had in his cell.

'He's like his dad, solemn little bleeder. Sometimes I swear I don't know what goes on in that boy's 'ead.' She pushed a cup of tea towards him then stood, her feet in their black flat pumps firmly planted on the parquet flooring. 'But it's Uncle Roy this, Uncle Roy that. Sometimes I'm sick of the sound of your name.' He laughed then.

'Would you mind if I hung around until he comes home from school? I'd like to see him.'

Daisy shrugged. 'He'd be miffed if he knew you'd been 'ere an' not waited.' She thought for a moment. 'You'd better stop for tea. Suze 'as decided on Eddie's

213

favourite, toad in the 'ole. Yesterday we 'ad egg an' chips because that's what Jamie likes.'

'That'd be good,' he said. 'Look, I'm taking delivery of a new car later today. Would you let Eddie come along with me? I promise to get 'im back early enough.'

A shadow crossed her face.

'Now what's wrong?'

'You 'ave to take both me boys. I can't 'ave no distinctions made between them.'

He sighed. That wasn't what he wanted at all. Jamie was a little sod when Daisy wasn't around. He tried to make his voice as light as possible.

'All right,' he said.

He could see her relax. Then she put her head on one side.

'Why're you getting a new car? What's wrong with the Humber?'

'Nothing's wrong with it. You can have it if you want.' She was probably remembering all the times they'd sat together in the back drinking brandy. Why did women always want to hang on to things? He was as sentimental as the next man but a brand-new Silver Shadow wasn't to be sniffed at. 'I got my image to keep up. Rollers are *the* cars now.'

'I don't want your bleedin' cast-off. What would I do with a huge thing like your Humber? Anyway, 'ow much is this new one gonna cost?'

'Daisy Lane, if you have to ask how much a Rolls Royce costs then you can't afford one. I just thought young Eddie would like to be my very first passenger.'

'Eddie and Jamie.'

'Okay. But your Eddie's a good kid, Daisy.' He was and all, he thought. He loved the boy. 'A quick-witted little bleeder.' His eyes went to Jamie's photo. 'Two good-looking boys. You and Vinnie all right?' He saw her eyes darken.

She sat down on the bench at the kitchen table, fumbled at the packet of biscuits, opened the end then shoved the packet across the table towards him.

'I ain't seen him for a while. His wife's got some problems with her father so Vinnie's up in the country as well.'

Roy stirred his tea and took a mouthful. Its strength nearly made his hair stand on end. He met Daisy's eyes. He knew she was going to ask him a question.

'I gotta know, Roy. When are you goin' to clear out of Daisychains an' take your drug trafficking with you? Your south coast brothels are fine and making more money than before an' all the insurance collections are up to date. The pubs and clubs are well under control with any bother stamped out before it's been started. I've hated every moment but I've stuck to my part of the bargain and I reckon you got to stick to yours.'

Her earnest face stared at him from across the table. He felt a bastard in view of her hatred of the drug scene, but there wasn't any other way.

'Timing ain't right, Daisy. Timing ain't right,' he said.

CHAPTER 17

'So what you're saying is we've got two dead women and a baby and not much else to go on other than one of the women, this Judy Bowles.' Vinnie pointed towards the photographs pinned to the wall in the incident room. 'Told her friend she was going to break into films?'

He didn't like the way Detective Chief Superintendent Thorne was glaring at him as though he was some kind of nasty smell. Thorne's gold-rimmed spectacles had slipped down his long thin nose and he pursed his lips. Vinnie consoled himself with the fact that his boss had a lousy taste in aftershave; Brut was for the likes of Henry Cooper types, not long tall detectives.

Thorne was now staring at Barry Green as though he expected some miracle to occur at the briefing.

Detective Barry Green shifted uneasily and said, 'She left her friend's flat at six thirty that night and wasn't seen again until her friend identified her at the mortuary.'

Baz Green opened a packet of Juicy Fruit and offered Vinnie a stick.

'Dunno why you buy those, you know I like spear-mint flavour.'

'That's why I buy Juicy Fruit, more for me.'

Thorne coughed and pushed his spectacles up on his nose. 'If I can have your attention? The common denominator seems to be that both women were up to their necks in debt ...'

Vinnie asked, 'Not on the game?'

'On the contrary,' Thorne said. His hand strayed towards the photographs. 'The young mother came from a very good family, had a good job in sales until she stopped working shortly before the kiddie was born. Wouldn't ask her parents for help, and they certainly didn't know about the money she owed various people. Seems like she was scared to tell them.'

Vinnie stared at the photographs. Pinned next to the pictures of the dead girls were images of how they'd looked alive. Both were vivacious, beautiful even. He knew he shouldn't let the job get to him but he sighed and felt a stab of pain pierce his heart. To murder these women in the prime of their lives was bad enough, but as his eyes skipped to the picture of the mutilated baby he wondered at the state of men's minds to have sex with such an innocent tiny child.

'Do you think these murders tie in with the girl discovered on heathland in London?'

'It's possible,' Thorne said. 'It's your job to get out there and find out.'

Later, back at his desk in the smallest office in the world, Vinnie reflected that this was a fucking awful case. It seemed all he and the others were doing was running around in circles, and all he was getting from Thorne was 'time is money'. His thoughts were interrupted by the shrill ring of the phone. He picked it up and his spirits rose.

'Hello, Clare,' he said.

Leah covered her sleeping child's shoulders with the patchwork coverlet then bent down and kissed her on her sweat-damp forehead.

'This time next week, Katie sweetheart, your daddy'll be home again. He'll see what a big girl you've grown into.' The child sighed and Leah stood watching her for a moment, glad she'd been able to put her down early for once. The light evenings didn't help when she needed Katie to sleep.

She shrugged herself into her raincoat, left the bedroom and went to the upstairs flat to tell Nan she was leaving for work.

'I shouldn't be too long tonight.' She hated lying to Nan who thought she was going to her bar job at Daisychains, but what else could she do? She could hardly say to the old dear that she was going off to be filmed while some geezer was fucking the living daylights out of her, could she?

'Don't you worry, dearie, I got a nice romance to read while I sit with the little darling.'

Nan foraged through a stack of newspapers and magazines piled on top of her walnut sideboard and found the book she was looking for, showing it to Leah.

'I don't know what I'd 'ave done without all your help,' Leah said.

She knew Nan was lonely and liked to feel useful, as well as the money Leah paid being welcome to supplement her pension.

'I won't be working so much when Jem gets out,' Leah said. What she meant was this evening she'd be performing in the last film she was ever going to make and she was over the moon about it. Then she could get back to working her normal shifts at Daisychains. After tonight she'd be free from debt and ready to make a new start as Jem left Parkhurst. 'Within a few weeks Jem will have earned enough money to get back on the road again. Then it's goodbye Gosport from us.'

Too late, she saw the hurt darken the old woman's eyes. Nan had no family and Leah knew she and Katie had become the centre of her universe. She quickly put her arms around the birdlike body of the woman.

'I'll write, and we'll come back and see you,' she promised. 'Anyway it'll take a while to get a wagon sorted. Did I tell you Roy Kemp has offered Jem a job?'

Nan shook her head and a hairpin slipped from the grey wispy bun and fell to the lino. Leah picked it up and handed it back to her.

'The pay'll be good,' she went on. 'Roy reckons Jem can look out for Daisy. That lag from Parkhurst, you know, the one who reckons he's McVitie's boy, 'as come out of the prison hospital swearing to get even with Roy.'

'An' he's likely to target Daisy Lane?'

Leah shrugged. 'I'm only goin' on what Jem told me. He said Roy reckoned he could take care of 'imself, but he ain't got eyes in the back of 'is head and it ain't no secret that Daisy an' 'er sons are dear to 'is heart.'

'The nasty so-an'-so wants puttin' down if you asks me.'

'Well, Nan, he's had one or two warnings inside to leave Roy an' his family alone but it's only made the bugger more determined to get even.'

'I reckon the man must be out of his head.'

''Course he is. But psychos don't think the same as everyone else, do they? Even psychos in prison can pay someone to get rid of people on the outside. Money talks, Nan.'

'I s'pose you're right, girly. Anyway, I knows you're right. I don't only read romances, you know, I read murder books, and the things you can learn from them, well ...' Leah gave her another cuddle.

'I made you a cheese and Marmite sandwich, Nan. And there's a Vesta curry in a packet if you get really hungry.'

Nan stepped into the corridor, pulling the door closed behind her. She transferred her stick to her other hand.

'Don't you worry about your little one, she's safe with me.'

Leah saw Nan was a bit shaky on her legs tonight.
'Your knees playin' up again?'

'It's nothing. I ain't answering the door to nobody an' you got a key, so me an' Katie'll be snug as a bug in a rug. Now buzz off. A nice cuppa an' that sandwich an' this book what's about an Italian count who falls in love with this schoolteacher ...'

Leah laughed, then bent down and kissed her feathery cheek.

Maybe later she would bring home a couple of bottles of stout and some fish and chips, the old girl would like that. It was almost a certainty she wouldn't bother to cook the Vesta meal even though Leah knew she liked them.

Leah would be celebrating not having to degrade herself any more. Only of course Nan wouldn't know that, she'd think Leah had just finished an early shift at Daisychains.

As she walked towards the front door she caught a glimpse of herself reflected in the hall mirror. Slim build, skirt down to her ankles and a russet-brown wrap over the top of a long-sleeved blouse. Despite the warm weather it could be cold when it got dark. A tangle of amber glass beads hung over her ample breasts almost to her waist; she'd chosen them specially because they were the colour of her eyes. This was her favourite outfit and she was wearing it because within hours she'd be a free woman again.

She opened the door and stepped out, thinking about the van she'd seen for sale at Elson, a comfortable little dwelling with a woodstove and plenty of bed space. But they'd need a horse to pull the van. The caravan was old-fashioned by today's standards but that didn't matter, a bit of a paint-up and it'd do the three of them fine until they could trade it in for something a bit more modern.

Jem was counting the days until he got out of Parkhurst. She'd marvelled he'd been able to keep it together for so long, him liking the open road so much. Of course, he'd kill her if he found out what had happened while he'd been gone. But after tonight, she could put it all behind her and never think about it again. It would be a secret she would take to her grave.

Leah walked across the road past the car ferry to Portsmouth.

Already the evening was busy with people going about their business. It wasn't dark but the lights shone brightly from Daisychains, beckoning in the punters, and she could hear the muffled sound of the music. A smell of anticipation mingled with brine from the sea. Leah stepped on to the platform of the number 3 Provincial bus waiting at its stage, which would take her to Ann's Hill.

The double-decker trundled up Stoke Road, stopping to put down and pick up passengers. It had started to rain and long straight splashes hit the windows. Fag ends littered the floor at her feet and the air in the bus was sweaty and damp. The bus turned right past the War Memorial Hospital and into Ann's Hill Road.

Leah got off the bus at the Wheatsheaf.

Trying to escape the worst of the rain, she held her wrap over her head and kept close to the houses as she ran down Bedford Street and into Brougham Street. She knocked loudly on the paint-flaked door and was quickly shown inside by a thickset balding man she knew only as Herb.

The cloying stench of the place hit her immediately. Herb pulled a piece of folded paper from his pocket and handed it to her. On the sheet torn from the child's exercise book were her lines to learn.

'They ain't difficult,' he said.

Sprawled on the sagging sofa was the lad she often performed with. He looked up without acknowledging her, but then he only ever spoke to her when the cameras were turning. Odd, she thought, that he knew so much about her intimate body parts but they were complete strangers. His sheet of paper was crumpled at his feet and his eyes were unusually bright. She guessed he was on something. The woman sitting next to him smiled at her and tugged her plastic shorty raincoat down over her knees. Leah saw it had once been white but was now grubby, and when the smile faded from the woman's face it went back to looking bored. The plastic buckle on her coat was broken.

'Move!' the woman said. The lad shifted along to make room on the sofa for Leah. The three of them were squashed together like sardines but there weren't any other chairs in the room.

'Thanks,' said Leah, shaking her head as the woman

produced a packet of fags and offered her one. The woman lit up, the smell of the match cutting through the rank air. Leah took the shawl from her head and shook out her hair. A few droplets of rain fell on to her skirt. She noticed the page of scribbled writing lying on the woman's lap.

This, then, was the threesome.

Leah closed her eyes. Soon, she guessed, Sydie, the bloke who was in charge of the camera, would come into the room and tell them to get undressed.

'Me name's Pat,' said the woman.

'Hello,' returned Leah. She didn't offer her name because she didn't want this woman to know anything about her. After tonight it was hardly likely she'd ever see her again or the fuckin' awful lad. But she smiled at the woman, noticing, now that she had time to look at her properly, that she was older than Leah had first thought, her lipstick bleeding into the creases around her mouth.

A movement at her side caused her to turn. The youth was taking a small tin from his trouser pocket. He popped a pill from it then closed his eyes. Leah was amazed that anyone could swallow tablets without a drink of water. She didn't even want to hazard a guess as to what the pills were.

They sat in silence as the minutes ticked by.

'For fuck's sake,' said Pat. 'I ain't got all the time in the world to waste even if they 'ave!' She pulled herself up and stormed into the hall, her plastic coat crackling with the movement, and leaving the sickly scent of lilies in her wake.

Leah heard the argument rising, Pat's voice louder than anyone else's with a stream of oaths that seemed to have no end, but it appeared to have done the trick because she came back into the room with a smug look on her face.

'It's us next,' she said. Leah nodded. The youth shifted his stance on the sofa but neither spoke nor opened his eyes.

'We're ready now,' called Sydie, coming into the room and glaring at Pat. Leah rose, closely followed by the lad. She looked in disgust at the man, who always seemed to be wearing the same clothes, grey flannel trousers and a collarless shirt stained at the armpits.

In the room where the camera was set up were two men, one focusing the camera, the other drinking from a chipped mug. He put the mug down on a plastic-topped coffee table covered with ring marks and said, 'Get your kit off, ladies and gent.'

Leah, trembling, put her wrap on the only available upright chair and began to unbutton her blouse and skirt. The youth was struggling out of his dirty jeans and discoloured underpants and wriggling into his leather gear. Around his waist was a belt with two sheaths containing a long knife and a smaller one. Pat slipped out of her coat, showing a black skirt and black polo-necked jumper which she allowed to fall to the floor before picking them up and throwing them over the back of the chair.

Pat was soon on the bed that seemed to take up all the space in the small room. She was now naked and trying to fasten a black sequinned mask which barely covered her eyes. Her pendulous breasts were hanging like two exotic fruits, their dark nipples like huge blackberries on her white skin.

After wriggling out of her white cotton bra and knickers Leah too climbed on to the bed. The grey-white sheet was slippery and Leah recognised the feel of rubber sheeting beneath it, rather like the one she used on Katie's cot to save the mattress from becoming too badly soiled.

There were three men in the room now and Pullinger whispered something to Sydie then took over behind the camera. The overhead shadeless bulb was switched off.

'Go for it!' was the cry from Pullinger and Pat reached for Leah.

Leah's eyes adjusted to the harshness of the artificial lighting's brightness and there was no sound except heavy breathing and the humming from the camera.

Pat's hands began to smooth Leah's hot skin. The musky lily smell of her reached Leah and she mentally thanked God this would be the very last time she would ever give over her body.

She slid down to taste the moistness of Pat's cunt while Pat twisted around so that her mouth could seek Leah's cunt. Pat's tongue was probing, teasing, tantalising.

At least that was the impression Leah and Pat had to give according to their lines.

And then Pat sat back while Leah lay motionless until Pat's mouth found her nipple. Pat sucked forcibly for effect while her hands outlined the curves of Leah's body. Then her fingers snaked down to first stroke, and then open, the folds of velvet skin. As she pushed her fingers into Leah's wetness Leah raised her knees so the camera could catch the effect of Pat's probing.

And then Leah drew Pat down on the filthy bed until they were lying breast to breast and Leah could feel the heat of her body. Pat kissed her, her tongue moving deep and certain in her mouth while she cupped Leah's breasts and began kneading her soft flesh. Her hips were moving against Leah's, tantalisingly rubbing her skin with firm pressure. Pat moved to lie full length upon Leah and her pelvis, hot, seemed to sink into Leah's as she put one leg across Leah's legs. Leah could feel her heart beating in time with Pat's.

'I like your breasts,' Pat said for the sake of the camera.

'Yours are fantastic,' replied Leah, as she'd been primed.

They were belly against belly.

Leah's hands brushed Pat's body, exploring her skin, then Leah pushed Pat away from her and Pat lay back on the bed while Leah's mouth explored Pat's cunt. With her head thrust back, as per the script, Pat moaned and cried theatrically as her body arched and quivered and bucked.

Leah's tongue flickered, probed and licked until Pat's screams seemed to echo throughout the room. Both their bodies were glistening with sweat as the youth joined them in his leather vest, belt and head-gear. Below the waist he was naked, his huge cock sticking out like a flagpole. As Pat continued to scream in her mock orgasm the boy grasped a handful of Leah's hair, pulling her and her face away from Pat's cunt and leaving Pat quivering. Leah was thrown on to her back. She could feel the youth's prick tickling her thigh as he bent over her.

'Come on, whore, fuck me,' he said, the sound muffled and menacing through the unzipped mouth of his mask. A thought flashed through Leah's brain that she was the only one without a mask but in a moment it was gone as she remembered her lines.

'Yes, I'll fuck you,' Leah replied. She was lying beneath him now and Pat was on the other side of the bed. She ran her hands over his shoulders and felt his body taut with the weight of holding himself above her to best advantage for the camera.

She raised her cunt towards him and grabbed hold of his hard, small arse.

'You've got the best arse I've ever touched,' she said. His hips were skinny and his cock jutting at her was rock hard. Leah rubbed herself against his prick that was wet with his own juice. And then he rammed, taking her cunt that sucked him in and Leah faked screams of delight. He was going deeper and deeper with each hard thrust. 'You fuck me so well,' shouted Leah. He laughed, a grating, hateful sound.

Pat was back on the scene now. Leah could feel the weight of her as her face pushed in the boy's arse. Over his shoulder Leah could see Pat's small pink tongue flicking around the rim of his arsehole, which Pat had stretched apart with her hands. He was groaning, for the camera or for himself Leah didn't know and didn't care. All she wanted was for the stink of sex and body fluids to go away and for it all to be over.

She saw the camera taking in Pat's raised arse and panning down to Pat's mouth over the boy's body, to his hand on Leah's breast and the pumping action of his huge cock with the musty bollock scent of his balls as they slapped against Leah's arse.

'I want some too,' shouted Pat, pulling him slowly off Leah so the camera could see the full length of his shining prick as it emerged from Leah's cunt.

He scrambled across to Pat and then shoved the whole of him in her mouth. He pressed into her throat, forcing his prick deeper down.

'Get it down you, whore,' he cried.

Pat rolled her face into his shining wet pubic hair.

And now he was playing with Leah's arse, sticking a finger in and turning it around. He was laughing.

Leah was screaming because she had been told to at this point.

'More, more.'

'I'm coming, you bitches,' he cried, and at the very

moment he was about to shoot his load, Pat pulled her mouth away so his huge tool projected high into the air, releasing a mess of milky white cum, which flew everywhere. Then he threw himself down on the bed and lay there, while both of the women licked up the spattered cum like hungry dogs.

Leah's tongue lapped at the dirty bedspread, and all she could hear was the whirring sound of the camera running and the movement on the bed behind her of Pat's tongue licking and the youth breathing heavily as he rose, sated.

Once more her hair was pulled back and she winced as she felt roots tugged from her scalp. Her body was hauled backwards from behind. His hand slid around to grab a breast and squeeze it. He hurt her and she screamed. He let her breast go loose.

'Fucking shut up, whore,' he said.

And then there was another pain – something sharp and piercing beneath the flesh of her breast. She could see blood, red and metallic-smelling. Her brain at first denied what she saw.

Her breast had been sliced through.

She looked to Pat but the woman was pressed against the bedpost, her hand across her mouth, her eyes wild.

Leah screamed and yanked her head away from his grip, leaving hair in his fist as she twisted to face him, but he hit her hard. Her jaw didn't register the pain at first but her head was thrown back. Slowly, pain seeped up from her chest to match the ache emanating from her jaw. She couldn't see his face because the leather mask concealed most of it, but there were slits for his eyes. His pupils were enormous.

And now the liquid ran down her body and on to the sheet. She touched its red slipperiness. It was wet and warm and her breast hung, swinging limply.

The knife was still in his hand. She tried to push him away but the point now pierced her throat and then she heard the grate of its sharpness on bone, as it filleted her skin downwards towards the bottom of her ribcage and onwards to the softness of her belly.

Blood filled her mouth and she began to choke. He pushed her on to her back. The knife traced a pattern in her stomach. There was the stench of stale uncooked meat in the air.

Her eyes were clouding but she could see him straddling her, holding high something that looked like a long, thin, bloody sausage.

Leah could hardly breathe. Her mouth and her nose were filling with her own blood. There was a pounding in her ears, in her head, and the pain was exquisite as the milky film slowly covered her sight.

The youth laughed at the bloody mass in his hand. Leah closed her eyes and tried to swallow back the blood in her mouth, all the while knowing it was useless.

CHAPTER 18

'I 'ate to say it, Angel, but you're very nearly as good at your job as I used to be.' Angel smiled at Vera – it wasn't often she got compliments. 'You'll 'ave a fair bit of dosh coming to you this month with tonight's London trip.'

Angel finished putting on the last touches of red lipstick and snapped her compact shut. 'I could do with it,' she said. 'I wish the car would 'urry up an' get here.'

On the seat beside her was her small overnight case containing her form-fitting evening dress, mink stole, shoes and her own sexy underwear. Angel didn't like borrowing stuff from Mrs Levy that her other girls wore. *She* might be on loan but she preferred to wear her own gear.

The noise in the bar of Daisychains was deafening. There was a stag party of business blokes in and they were already three sheets to the wind. She moved towards the open doorway that faced the harbour and the bus terminus. Big Paul was on duty tonight. Angel looked at him then nodded towards her case.

She didn't want it to disappear.

'I'll keep an eye on it. Okay, Angel?'

He then smiled at Vera who had appeared at her side. 'The stink of fags and beer is getting on me tits tonight,' Angel said. He nodded knowingly. For some reason Angel was extra nervy tonight.

Vera said, 'The car'll come when it's ready.'

Angel thought the older woman sounded just a little wistful. Her days of high-class prostitution were behind her now, but that didn't mean Vera couldn't still command good money for her services, if she'd a mind to. Angel coughed, putting her hand to her mouth and nose and turning away. The scent of Vera's Californian Poppy was powerful.

Angel had good reason to be thankful to Vera, for not only did the small woman show concern for Angel herself but also for her boy. Michael called her Auntie Vera. And Auntie Vera had introduced her boy to Alec.

Alec had changed now he was off the sauce. Him and her Michael had become firm friends and the boy was learning how to draw properly at last, and what was more, Alec reckoned he was talented. He also liked mathematics, which was something Angel had always hated at school. Not only that, but Michael, with his new friend's help, had discovered he liked reading. Alec reckoned he'd never had such an apt pupil, not even when he was teaching in school. Angel felt extremely proud of her boy.

Alec and Malkie also got on well. Alec's house at

Elson was now painted up inside and out. The two men had done wonders while the lad was at school. And Angel had to admit Alec was a good-looking bloke now he was cleaned up. Not that *he* realised it. He still had a fair way to go to get all his confidence back.

Vera had her hands on her hips and was watching the people wandering around the ferry and the bus terminus.

'My Michael can't wait to get 'ome from school so Alec can take him down to the sea to sketch the ships.'

'Yeah, well it's given Alec a focus in 'is life an' all. Evening, Mr Colehill.' They both smiled at the councillor who stepped from the taxi in a cloud of Brut and made straight for the carpeted stairs up to the gambling den. Angel watched the taxi driver raise his eyes heavenwards as he stared at the meagre tip before he drove off down Mumby Road.

Vera pointed across the road. 'Is that Daisy and Mr Big 'imself?'

Angel peered through the crush of people coming across the Ferry Gardens from the boat.

'Sure is,' she said. The sight of Roy gave her a sudden jolt like a kick in her guts. She so wished she didn't care about the bloke. She might be the mother of his son, but while he was inside there was no way she could have put herself through the misery of visiting him.

'Roy wanted to go over Portsmouth to check on

a couple of boozers and a club of 'is in Elm Grove an' Daisy went with 'im. Roy wasn't 'appy with the bankings from the club,' said Vera.

'Thought Daisy'd made it clear if there was any bother on the premises, even a small fight, she was goin' to replace staff.'

'She did. They knows which side their bread's buttered. Where else do they get such bleedin' good wages?'

'So what is it, then?'

'Roy keeps his thoughts to 'imself but I reckons someone's been doin' a bit of what Eddie Lane was good at.'

'Not movin' in and siphonin' off money?' Angel was appalled. Then she relaxed – whatever it was, it didn't seem to be affecting Roy's relationship with Daisy.

Angel could see the small blonde was laughing and looking up at Roy. She's like a doll, thought Angel. A smartly dressed doll with yellow chin-length hair dressed in a black trouser suit. Roy was looking down at Daisy while he was talking to her. Angel could see by the way his body leaned towards her that he was glad to be in her company. A sharp pain ran through her heart. Daisy didn't need Roy Kemp but she could have him any time she wanted with just a word or a snap of her fingers.

Mustn't get sad, she told herself. She'd just done herself a couple of lines in the Ladies and it was too soon for her to start feeling maudlin. She stared at the couple as they drew closer. That's when she saw the man. It was the same bloke she'd seen peering in the office window. He was walking close behind the couple as they strolled oblivious towards Daisychains.

She half expected the man to elbow his way through the crush of people to get to the bus terminus as quickly as he could and board a waiting bus.

He didn't, the man was still behind them.

Fear grabbed at her heart.

There was something wrong.

He was following them. And then it was as if she *knew* what was about to happen. *The man meant to harm Daisy.*

Vera was still chattering to her as Angel rushed from the club. A taxi swept past her with only inches to spare as she ran across the busy road and into the throng of people.

Daisy and Roy were still chatting as they came towards the bus terminus.

Angel was close enough now to see the man raise both hands behind Daisy's back. *He was going to push her into the road.* He'd seen the Provincial double-decker driven at a fair speed coming from the High Street!

Angel threw herself, diving sideways-on at Daisy, falling to the tarmac as she caught Daisy a wallop across the hips that sent her knocking into Roy. Roy had fallen to his knees, swearing, caught off guard and off balance.

There was a united gasp from the people around them.

Angel twisted herself round in time to see the man who with his full force had been about to push Daisy into the path of the bus shoot forward as his hands met only air.

Angel knew it wasn't possible, but it was as though the world had changed to slow motion as the man fell into the path of the bus then disappeared beneath its huge front wheels. And then pandemonium broke out.

With a screech of brakes the green bus shuddered to a halt. The crowd was screaming as one, as disentangling herself from Daisy, Angel staggered to her feet pulling Daisy up with her.

'Roy!' Angel's voice was almost lost in the crush of people craning forward to see what the commotion was about. Angel shouted, 'Move it!' He scrambled to his feet needing no second bidding.

'Never saw 'im coming!' The conductor had fled from his platform and was now repeating the words over and over. The driver had jumped from his cab, his face chalk white, and he looked ready to throw up as he surveyed the crushed, still body beneath the bus.

Angel took a last look at the blood pooling from the broken figure.

Her eyes met Roy's. He had hold of Daisy, clearly stunned. Angel thanked God that Roy had managed to push a path from the throng so they were able to get across the road.

Vera's face was pasty white and her arms went around Daisy. Angel was shaking like a leaf and there were strange aches where she had used muscles her body didn't normally use. Roy pushed her inside the club's doorway.

'Sit down,' he said. Angel found she was planted on exactly the same chair that she'd left before all the commotion had happened. She saw, too, her car had arrived, the driver waiting to take her to London.

Shakily, she raised a hand to him. He waved and she mimed for him to wait for her. He nodded and turned his attention towards the accident across the road.

Vera asked, 'What the fuck 'appened?' She wouldn't let go of Daisy.

Roy said, 'Angel just saved Daisy's life.' He opened the door to the office. 'Let's get out of the way of the punters.'

Customers were gawping through windows.

'Take me case in. I'll get drinks,' said Angel. She picked up her shoulder bag and made for the bar. 'Put these down to staff,' she said. Her voice didn't sound as though it belonged to her. She nodded at the barmaid while she poured brandy from the optics into glasses. She was shivering so much the alcohol was slopping around. 'Find us a tray, Jeannie,' she begged, her mouth dry like a burnt fuse. She downed one of the drinks. 'Take these others into the office, I need a wee.'

In the staff toilet she locked herself in a cubicle,

slipped her handbag from her shoulder, dropped the seat and sat down. She clutched her hands together to try to still the shaking. She took several deep breaths, feeling the brandy work a little magic, and when she felt composed enough, got out her compact, carefully lifting out the legitimate solid block of face powder to get at the white powder in the screw of paper and the single-edged razor blade beneath.

Afterwards she began to feel more like herself again. She checked her nose for tell-tale white remnants and put the makings away.

Then she leaned sideways, her head against the cold wooden wall of the lavatory. Angel closed her eyes and thought of what she had just done. She'd allowed a man to fall to his death beneath a bus so she could save the woman loved by the father of her child. She gave a huge sigh. The coke was kicking in now, dulling the pains in her body and in her knee where she'd fallen to the paving stones. Pity it didn't kill the ache in her heart, she thought.

That bloke in prison, that McCloud, had no doubt got that lowlife to follow Daisy, looking for an opportunity to hurt her. Jesus, the bloke must have been off his rocker to try anything with Roy stuck to her like glue, she thought. Daisy could have been pushed to her death or maimed for life. The bloke might have slipped away with Roy none the wiser. Except that Roy would know McCloud had fulfilled his promise.

Angel knew she'd have nightmares from now on. Over and over she'd see him lurch into the path of the bus, sliding beneath the wheels. She'd see and hear the break of his bones and the dark red of his blood spurting and spreading on the tarmac road.

And why had she even contemplated saving Daisy Lane?

Because Roy Kemp loved her.

Angel realised she had probably performed one of the most unselfish acts of her life.

She'd try not to think about any of it at the moment, she had a job to do. Outside, her car was waiting. She sighed, rose, and looked down. Her stockings were wrecked. Bloody good job she always carried a spare pair.

After a while she opened the cubicle door, went over to the floor-length mirror and checked herself. She washed her face and dried it on the roller towel. After brushing her long hair and shaking it to fluff it up again she refreshed her lipstick. She nodded to herself. The coke had kicked in well now and she was ready to go out and face them all. She remembered she had to get hold of some more of the white stuff – she'd given it a bit of a bashing just lately. Bloody good job she was earning, wasn't it?

In the office Roy was sitting on the corner of the table. She could see Vera watching everyone, her eyes darting from one to the other. Daisy sat like a miniature of herself, caved in and staring at nothing.

Roy said, 'You saved her life. I saw his hands come up but before I had time to register what the bastard was up to, you'd pushed her to safety.'

Angel shrugged.

Vera opened her mouth but obviously thought better of it.

Angel said to Roy, 'I hope that really was the bloke your matey in prison said was goin' to do for you or yours. If not, I've just sent an innocent bloke to his death.'

Vera said, 'Who else would want to harm Daisy?'

'I told you before I seen him 'anging around,' Angel said. 'He's the one was looking in the office window one time.'

'I don't know what to say ...' Daisy had found her voice at last.

'Say fuck all then,' said Angel. 'I ain't never really been able to thank you for all you've done for Michael.'

Daisy heaved herself from her seat and made her way towards Angel. Angel stepped back then bent down and picked up her overnight case, using it as a shield between her and Daisy.

'If you're goin' to do somethin' stupid like throw your arms around me, I'd rather you didn't.' She knew her voice had a brittle edge to it. Daisy stopped in her tracks, nodded then smiled at her.

'I understand,' she said.

'I'm losing money,' Angel announced. She couldn't ignore the catch in her voice and she really didn't want to start getting emotional now.

'You can't go like this,' Vera said. 'Look at the state of you. You've started shiverin' again.'

241

'I'll tidy meself up in the car,' Angel said, then tried for a joke to lessen the tension. 'Give the driver a bit of an eyeful when I change me stockings.'

Roy turned his eyes on her and she felt her resolve weaken when he asked in a soft voice, 'Are you hurt, Angel?'

Angel had a sudden memory of his concern for her once before, when they'd just finished making love in the bedroom of the Black Bear ... She pushed the memory away. He didn't care for her, not like that, the way she wanted him to.

'Stop fussin', I'm fine,' she said.

Vera smiled. 'That's my girl.'

Angel steeled herself to walk swiftly out of the office. She badly needed to be on her own. She'd try not to think too much about what had happened in the last half hour but she knew bloody well it would stay with her while she was being driven to London.

She'd try to concentrate on what she was supposed to be doing. Tonight she was fucking Lord Jellicoe. Angel wasn't surprised he was a real lord.

First they'd have dinner, then they'd go to Annabel's. Angel liked dancing at Annabel's, there were always famous faces there. Then it would be back to his flat in Mayfair.

'Let's go,' she said to the driver, who was still craning his neck at the crowd. An ambulance and the police were there now.

'Nasty business that,' said the driver. He started the engine.

Angel thought about Daisy. It had never entered her mind not to rush forward and try to save her. With Daisy out of the way, Roy might possibly have turned to her for comfort, but she couldn't kid herself it would have been the real thing.

'There ain't nothing like a death to make you realise how precious life is,' said Angel.

Satisfied that whatever she did in the privacy of the back seat of the Mercedes would remain private, she settled into the softness of the leather, opened her bag and took out her compact.

CHAPTER 19

'You sure you're all right, Daisy?'

'I'm fine, Roy, really I am. A few grazes from the paving stones, that's all.'

'Want another brandy?' asked Vera.

'Don't you bleedin' start an' all, Vera! No, I don't want another brandy.'

Vera looked a bit huffy at that and Daisy was immediately ashamed that she'd spoken sharply to her. All Daisy could think about was that she was lucky to be alive and she owed her life to Angel.

The music from the club was loud and she was glad the door was shut fast against the smell of beer and cigarette smoke.

'I need to teach that bastard who planned this a lesson.' Roy's face was like granite.

Here we go again, thought Daisy. Why did blokes always have to work on the eye-for-an-eye principle?

Vera must have been thinking the same thing for she said, 'He's dead. Ain't that fuckin' punishment enough?'

'Not the monkey, Vera, the bleedin' organ grinder.

That cunt McCloud, in prison on the Isle of Wight.'

'How you goin' to do that when you're outside an' he's inside?'

Roy looked at Daisy thoughtfully. He ran his fingers through his hair then said, 'I'll think of something. Jem'd do it like a shot but I don't want nothing to hinder his comin' out. All he could talk about was seeing his wife and kiddie.'

'I'd like to see her an' all,' Vera said. 'The little cow hasn't been into work. I thought her bloke 'ad come out already and she was spendin' time with 'im. I got Sally to cover her shifts. But if you're sure her Jem don't get out 'til next week, what's she up to? It ain't like her to let me down ...'

'She's probably scrubbin' the flat out from top to bottom,' said Daisy. 'Making it all nice for 'er man.'

'It's possible,' said Vera, but she looked peeved as she said, 'She still could let me know, though.' She turned to Roy. 'Who will you get from inside to teach a lesson to that bloke who reckons he's McVitie's son?'

Daisy looked into Roy's slate-coloured eyes. It wasn't hard for her to guess who that someone would be.

'Reggie'll be only too pleased to sort the bleeder out,' said Roy. 'He'll find someone to make it look like a nice little accident.' He put out a hand and stroked Daisy's arm. 'I got a feelin' there's more goin' on here than meets the eye. Don't you go thinking you're safe – not just yet.'

'What do you mean? That bloke's dead!' Daisy sighed. 'Oh, Roy, don't you ever get fed up wantin' to 'urt people?' And then her nerves felt as though they were being pushed through a cheese grater and she was gripping her hands together so tightly that her fingernails were hurting her palms. She opened her hands, surprised to see the indents in her skin filled with blood. She looked at them as though they didn't belong to her, and then it hit her: a man had tried to *kill* her. *A man who didn't even know her.* And now that man lay dead beneath a bus and still Roy was talking about killing!

She'd had enough of all the vicious talk. She made to rise from her seat, and promptly stumbled.

'Hey up,' said Vera making a grab for her, just a little too late. Roy already had hold of Daisy.

'Fancy that,' said Daisy. 'I come over all faint. Well I never.'

'It's bound to tell on you, Daisy. Short break, that's what you need,' said Roy. His arms around her felt comforting. 'I don't want you to be on your own and that's the truth.'

'Don't be bloody stupid,' Daisy said, twisting away from him. 'That was just a little after effect.' She didn't want to worry that someone else *still* might want to harm her or her children.

'You could 'ave somethin' there, Roy,' said Vera, who was giving Daisy a right old-fashioned look. 'She could do with a bit more sunshine.'

'Silly cow,' said Daisy. 'It's bleedin' summer 'ere.'

'Where's your tan then?'

There she goes again, thought Daisy. Just like Vera to want to prove a point, but Daisy could see the worry in her eyes.

'I 'ad one when I got back from Greece but I been too busy to lie around in the sun, ain't I? Stayin' close to Suze an' the baby – as well as doin' all your dirty work,' Daisy added to Roy.

Ignoring the taunt, Roy said, 'That's why I'd like to take you away. Only for a couple of days.'

No one spoke. It was like Roy's words were floating in the air somewhere between the three of them. Daisy's voice came as a surprise even to herself.

'Where?'

She'd probably never have asked if she hadn't known Vinnie wasn't coming back to Gosport for a while. Vinnie had explained Clare's dad was in a really bad way.

'Africa. Kenya to be exact.'

'Oh, Dais!' Vera said. 'How can you refuse? It's lovely there.'

'How do you know? You ain't been there!'

'I seen it on the films. All them wild animals.'

Daisy gave her what she hoped was a withering look to shut her up. She was beginning to feel a little more in charge of herself now, and she knew Vera would start on about bloody Tarzan or Clark Gable an' Joan Crawford an' one of their films set in the tropics if she let her go rabbiting on.

'I got this place to look after. And what about me

boys? An' Suze? She ain't really properly over losing Si yet.'

'No excuse,' said Vera. 'I'm all right 'ere, an' now the punters got a whiff that Roy's out there won't be no bother. Anyway, what we got bouncers for? Suze'll cope fine, she's a strong little cow. And if at 'ome we can't manage between us to look after two little boys, and a baby girl and a cat, then there must be somethin' wrong with us. Roy didn't say an 'oliday, so it ain't gonna be for all that long, is it?'

Daisy was looking at Roy. He had a strange smile on his face.

'Just a couple of days. What about it, Daisy?' She knew without a doubt that Roy would have some ulterior motive for wanting her to go to Kenya with him, but surely there wasn't anything for her to worry about, was there? Perhaps when he came back he'd move the drug dealing out of Daisychains.

She glared at him. If he thought by taking her away he was going to get inside her knickers, he had another think coming. She might not have seen much of Vinnie since those few happy days they'd spent together on Kos but there was no way she was going to hurt him.

'No funny business? I ain't sleepin' with you!'

Roy laughed. It was so good to hear that lovely deep rumble of his, it immediately made her feel much better.

Africa! She'd never in her wildest dreams ever thought she'd visit a country so far away. She remembered when she was a little girl sitting in the front row of the class at St John's Infants' School. Pinned to the wall right opposite her desk was a map of Africa with the Congo River running through it. She could see it all in her mind's eye now. The land was all coloured yellow and brown to show how hot it was there.

'Where in Kenya?' She remembered Africa was a huge place.

'Mombasa. But we'll stay on the coast beside the sea.' Little curls of excitement began to stir Daisy's imagination.

'Will it be 'ot?'

Roy had a smile on his face that stretched from ear to ear.

'About three times as hot as it is 'ere.'

'And no funny business?'

'No funny business,' he promised.

'If you was goin' to take me, you could get up to all the funny business you wanted,' said Vera. 'I wouldn't mind at all!'

Daisy ignored Vera.

'When?' Daisy asked. Then she remembered the dreadful accident at Heathrow still fresh in everyone's minds. 'What if the plane crashes like that BEA Trident what crashed in Staines just takin' off from Heathrow? One hundred and eighteen people were killed …'

'Stop it, Daisy. You're safer on a plane than you are crossing the road.'

Daisy looked at Roy. His words went straight to her heart. Outside on the road a man had died. No one spoke. The office was heavy with gloom.

'I 'eard talk of a takeover goin' on with Roy Kemp's manor. That little cunt McCloud knows more'n he's lettin' on. Get it out of 'im before you finishes 'im.' Reg Kray leaned across the billiard table to take a shot with his cue. Expensive cologne rose from his silk shirt which accentuated his muscular body. 'No skin off my nose, mate. But it's got to be clean an' quick.'

Jem said, 'I'm pretty sure Roy knows nothin' …'

'Get it out of McCloud. Them bastards don't send love letters.' Reg cued the ball into the pocket.

Now it was Jem's turn and he messed up his shot purposely.

Recreation from six until nine gave the cons time to unwind. Some were watching *Coronation Street*, the rest were lazing about, chatting, playing ping-pong or board games. The room was noisy and the place smelled of farts.

There wasn't much point in *not* letting Reg Kray win the game, after all he wanted to keep on the right side of the big man, didn't he?

He also needed to get even with the little blond fucker for the decorative scars he now had on his face. It wouldn't seem right letting Reg or Ron do his dirty work for him. Besides, if *he* did the job for Roy Kemp, then it would go some part of the way to paying him back for the work he'd be giving him when he left this stinking place on Friday.

'It'll be clean,' he said. Music was playing, that little American kid Donny Osmond singing 'Puppy Love'. 'What d'you reckon to that twat?' Jem asked.

'Little fucker won't last,' said Reggie. 'Not like Frank Sinatra. Now he's a proper singer.'

Jem nodded agreement.

He knew the gangster was not well. He was being prescribed Stelazine for mental disorders and Librium for his anxiety. His bouts of paranoia had escalated and being locked up didn't help at all. There'd also been rumours about splitting the twins up again. Ron had only just been allowed back into the Special Security block from the hospital.

A fight had broken out between Ron and another prisoner and the guards were finding it increasingly difficult to keep Ron calm. Despite his brother's outbursts, Reg did have a stabilising influence on his twin. The authorities had made a brave decision in transferring Ron to Parkhurst so he could be with his brother.

Jem knew Reg was finding it difficult to keep his nose clean. It was hard to command respect when every threat, every challenge, every insult from another con had to be carefully assessed and sorted, otherwise his prison position became threatened. Every bugger wanted to have a go at a well-known face, wanted a piece of him. No wonder Reggie suffered from anxiety.

Jem had already made his preparations. He'd planned exactly how he was going to get some information and pay the bastard McCloud back. And he certainly didn't want the aggro of getting copped for it – his freedom was too precious and too near. All he'd needed was Reggie Kray's go-ahead, and he'd got that.

Jem was all psyched up anyway because normally he'd have received a letter from Leah today. He'd decided her letter had most probably been held back. The prison authorities checked all incoming and outgoing mail in case anything in the letters needed to be banned. Tomorrow, he consoled himself, he'd be bound to hear from her. She'd never once missed replying, though how she deciphered his scrawl he'd never know. He'd got one of the screws to write her address on the envelope, him not being too clever with the reading and writing. He couldn't wait to see her and little Katie.

No, he wouldn't make a mess of offing that blond shit McCloud.

He patted his top pocket and looked around the recreation room. The bastard was still playing cards. Ah well, he could wait. Sooner or later the scumbag would need to take a piss, and then …

Minutes later McCloud pushed himself away from the table and made his way to the lavatory. At a discreet distance Jem followed, knowing no one would be taking the slightest bit of notice. Screws really only perked up when there was aggro, and the recreation period was going as sweet as a nut tonight.

Jem was right behind him as the man pushed open a cubicle door. Quick as a flash Jem grabbed the man's mouth from behind. He wished the cubicle doors weren't just half doors but it couldn't be helped, he'd just have to do the deed quickly.

'Don't try squealing,' he warned, his fingers digging into McCloud's cheeks. The bloke let his body go limp. McCloud had spent a good while in the hospital wing after his 'accidental' toothbrush incident and Jem knew he still couldn't swallow or eat properly. Jem's hands were like plates of meat, big and heavy, and he was well used to bare-knuckle fighting and setting up heavy fairground equipment. The pressure on McCloud's fragile mouth would be painful and this would be to Jem's advantage. 'There's a good lad,' he said. 'Your daddy Jack would be pleased with you, that's if McVitie really was your daddy.' The man gave a feeble try at struggling but Jem continued holding his jaw in a grip like steel. 'Your little plan to get rid of Roy Kemp's lady didn't work. Your mate's copped it. An' I got a grievance about the scars you left me with.' Jem could see the fear in McCloud's eyes. 'First you need to tell me who reckons they've balls enough to invade Roy's territory.'

A further squeeze and Jem saw tears drip from the man's eyes, eyes that were like a rabbit's caught in headlights. He released his grip long enough to hear the answer.

'There's no one else. Fuck you ...'

With white knuckles Jem's grip returned harder than ever.

Pain shot through McCloud's eyes.

'Tell me an' I'll go easy on you. You don't need no more 'ospital treatment.'

White spittle was forming at the corners of McCloud's mauve damaged lips. Jem used his finger-nails to scrape the tender skin that was so fragile it broke, letting red blood seep on to his hands.

McCloud groaned. 'Maxi brothers. Gaetano's come over from Italy, he reckons he owes Roy for destroying his kid brother ...'

Jem didn't want to hear any more. Roy had told him how he'd sorted the brothers for the fruit-machine scams the boys had tried to pull on Roy's equipment a few years back.

'If you been working for them fuckin' Eyeties you bin battin' on the wrong wicket, scum,' he said. Before McCloud could move Jem had him in a one-handed bloodied vice-like grip.

Fumbling in his pocket he slipped the object into the man's ear. With one sharp slap the deed was done.

Jem felt the man sag against him after a cry that started in the back of McCloud's throat but never became more than a strangled moan. He held him firmly to stop him slipping.

'Don't pass out on me now, lad, I haven't finished yet.'

He turned McCloud round so that he was facing

him. Wide staring eyes met his. 'Close your mouth, mate, you look like a drooling idiot. I need to give you a matching pair, one of anything is no good, is it?'

He had no resistance from McCloud as he repeated the exercise, this time on the other side of his head.

'If you get out of this, it'll be a dead cert you won't be thinking up any more ways to hurt people, an' you certainly won't be any use to the Maxis.'

When the job was done he lowered the man to the seat and propped him against the cistern. The glazed-eyed McCloud was very pliable.

If he could get back into the recreation room without anyone seeing him, he was home and dry. He opened the door and slipped out. Certain no one had paid him the slightest bit of attention, he went over to a solitary red-haired lifer sitting at a table. There was a set of draughts in front of him. Jem sat down and looked around. Reggie Kray caught his eye and Jem gave him just the slightest of nods then looked away. It didn't do to look blokes straight in the eye here.

'I'll give you a game, Dave,' he said. The man treated him to a gap-toothed grin. Dave was a little hard of hearing so he had to raise his voice. Jem thought about the man he'd left in the lavatory. He'd be a bit hard of hearing as well, that's if he ever recovered from having a couple of biros banged through his ears and up into his brain.

'Want to be whites, Dave?' he asked, setting out the pieces.

CHAPTER 20

'She's so good,' Daisy said, reluctantly passing the sleeping child back to Susie. Daisy had made a huge wave in Joy's hair.

'You used to lick your fingers and smooth the boys' hair in curls like that. That would 'ave made Si smile.' Susie's eyes grew misty.

'Don't you go dwellin' on that,' Daisy said. The last thing she needed was Susie in floods of tears today of all days. The main bar of Daisychains was decked out with streamers and a big placard saying 'Welcome Home Roy'. For once the place smelled of vanilla and fish paste and almond icing from the spread set out along the bar, the aromas of fags and stale beer banished by Susie's frantic polishing.

'Don't worry, Dais. I'm learnin' to live with the fact that Si ain't gonna suddenly walk in the front door. I got a lot to be thankful for. Especially a good friend like you.'

Susie nuzzled into the soft folds of Joy's hand-knitted shawl.

Daisy put her arm around Susie's shoulder. She knew she shouldn't be so hard on the girl, but hard work was the only way to stop dwelling on the bad stuff. 'Shut up, you daft tart, you'll make *me* cry!'

'You'll wake 'er up then,' said Susie, grinning. The scent of 4711 eau de Cologne, Susie's favourite, wafted above the talcum powder smell of Joy.

'That ain't true,' Daisy said. 'That child would sleep through a bomb blast an' then open her eyes, smiling.'

'Well, she's sleeping through this racket all right.' Music blared throughout the bar. Susie said, 'Roy looks good.'

Across the room Roy was chatting to Alec. There were no punters today as it was a private party. Roy had a pint on the bar, Alec a glass of lemonade. He was showing Roy some of Michael's sketches, and Daisy could tell by Roy's body language that he really was interested. It was a start to creating a bridge to Michael, she thought, and silently blessed Alec.

'When don't the bastard look good?' Daisy said. Almost as if he could tell he was being discussed, Roy looked towards them, giving Daisy a smile and Susie an exaggerated wink. Susie dimpled up and went a deeper pink than her usual healthy colour.

'He's been preoccupied since he's been out of the nick,' said Daisy. 'Got something that's worryin' him but he ain't said nothing an' I don't want to ask. That bloke what tried to fuckin' murder me was scary enough. I don't want to find out there's even more stuff for me to worry about.' She saw Susie was still gazing at Roy.

'You ain't 'alf lucky to 'ave two gorgeous men after you.'

Daisy puffed out her cheeks and let the air blow from them slowly.

'One I don't see enough of and the other's more a friend an' always will be. An' I need to keep me bleedin' eyes on Roy because I never know what stunts he's goin' to pull next.'

Susie didn't look convinced.

'You look pretty today,' Daisy said. Susie's blonde curls shone and her red top was exactly the same shade of red as the roses on her ankle-length skirt. 'You don't 'alf love your rose prints, don't you, girl?'

Susie grinned back at her and said, 'A bit more colour on you wouldn't be bad.'

Daisy looked down at her tailored black trouser suit. Under the jacket she had on a black silk sleeveless top.

'I feel all right in black. I always think bright colours make me stand out and I don't want to stand out. I like meltin' into the shadows.' Daisy had said that so many times she really believed it.

'You couldn't melt anywhere if you tried. Anyway, you wears black because your Eddie liked to see you in black ...'

'An' that an' all,' said Daisy. No flies on our Susie, she thought. She looked across at Roy who was still watching her.

'Bastard!' she mouthed at him, and he threw back his head and laughed.

'Daisy!' exclaimed Susie accusingly. 'I do wish you wouldn't swear so much! And certainly not around the kiddies!'

'Get off your 'igh 'orse, our Suze,' Daisy replied, but she wasn't cross. She looked closely at Joy. 'Anyway, that little one's still fast asleep.'

'I forgot,' Susie said. 'Vera's in the office an' she told me to tell you she wants a chat.'

'For Christ's sake this is a party, she shouldn't even be in the bleedin' office.'

Daisy walked around the edge of the floor so as not to disturb the few brave souls who were dancing. The floor space was mostly taken up with a line of Roy's London mates who, along with Violet Kray and Roy's mother and Charles, were heavily into the palais glide.

She pushed open the office door and was met by Vera sitting at the desk with the telephone in her hands.

'Won't be a moment, I'm just sorting the beer order.' Vera finished the call. 'Business still 'as to go on, Dais, don't it?' she said.

'You didn't get me in 'ere to talk about work, did you?'

Vera shook her head. She had dyed her roots the evening before and her hair shone. She had on a new orange frilled blouse and a black skirt, her waist nipped in tightly by a wide black patent belt that matched her patent high heels. Daisy smiled at her fondly.

259

'No, but I'm worried about Leah. She knew I wanted her in today.'

'I told you, I bet her hubby's already out an' she's tucked up in bed with 'im,' said Daisy. 'You can't blame her for that, can you? Poor bloke must be dyin' to get his hands on his pretty wife.'

Vera gave a huge sigh. 'I'm sure Jem ain't out yet. I did go round to Beach Street. The lights was on so someone was in.'

'Did you knock on the door?'

'I did,' said Vera. 'I suppose Leah could 'ave been asleep.'

Daisy was thoughtful. 'Pity she ain't got no telephone, ain't it? Wouldn't seem so bad phonin' 'er. Anyway, 'ave we got cover for 'er bar work?'

Vera nodded then said, 'I might pop back again later.'

'You do that if it makes you feel better, but stop worryin' about her, you know how happy she's been lately. An' you get out of 'ere an' come an' 'ave a drink an' a chat with some of our guests. Suze 'as worked her socks off to make today go with a swing. Don't let 'er see you ain't enjoyin' it, Vera.'

Just then the door burst open and Daisy's two sons fell into the office.

'Mum, Mum, Uncle Roy says to ask you if we can go and play football over on the Ferry Gardens. Can we, can we?'

It was Eddie doing all the talking as usual, egged on by Jamie, she realised.

'Them gardens got Keep Off The Grass signs all over the place.'

'Aw, Mum!'

'Who else is goin'?'

'Mac the barman, Saul, Mick.' He was reeling off the names of the men who worked in Daisychains. 'An' Alec's takin' Michael an' some of the ladies from Auntie Vera's place have offered to be in goal … Pleeease!'

'Let 'em go,' said Vera.

'Oh, bloody go on then,' said Daisy, 'but mind that bleedin' road!'

The two boys turned and ran off before she could change her mind. Daisy caught the door before it slammed.

'I need a drink,' she said.

'Pity Vinnie couldn't be 'ere as well,' said Vera.

'He couldn't get the time off.'

There seemed to be a mass exodus of people and kids leaving the place.

'I said, pity Vinnie couldn't be 'ere.'

Daisy rounded on her friend. 'I 'eard you. And I told you. You want a drink or not?' Vera shook her head. Out of the window Daisy could see Roy holding back a tide of kids to make sure they crossed the road safely.

'I guess it's because he spends so much time at his father-in-law's place,' Vera said.

'I'm not even goin' to reply to that nasty remark,' said Daisy. 'He *has* got another son, you know.' A lump suddenly rose in her throat to see Roy now pushing the wheelchair containing his boy, while Alec walked alongside.

Daisy turned away. You could never tell what people would do next. She thought about the time Vinnie surprised her in Greece and how their lovemaking had been so sweet and passionate on the flower-filled hillside at Kefalos.

'You and Vinnie ain't so different,' Vera said.

'How come you always seem to tune into my thoughts? I was just thinkin' about 'im. Sometimes I reckon you're an' ol' witch in disguise.'

'We 'ave just been talkin' about 'im, Dais. Anyway, I only got to look at your face to know what's goin' through your 'ead.'

Daisy shrugged. 'So you reckon me an' Vinnie's the same?'

'No, I said you two are alike.'

'What d'you mean?'

'The pull of 'is wife is stronger than 'is love for you.'

Daisy frowned. 'If I didn't know you was me friend I'd 'ave parted your 'ead for sayin' that.'

'I speak as I find.'

'Vinnie knows how much I love Eddie.' As her words tumbled from her lips she realised what she'd said. She looked at Vera who was staring at her with a strange expression on her face.

'I think you just worked it out, missy. You *still* love

him. An' no bloke likes to be second best. Not even to a dead man.'

'So what you saying? That Clare is less complicated?'

Vera nodded. 'I'm not sayin' he even realises it himself. But when you've shared a life with someone, 'ad a kiddie with them, sometimes it's easier to slip back into the old routine and forgive mistakes than it is to fight every step of the way with someone new, knowing you'll always be an also-ran.'

'But me an' Vinnie, we got a child …'

'But you ran to Vinnie when Roy upset you. Vinnie knows he ain't just second best but *third* bleedin' best.'

Daisy thought about the night she'd first slept with Vinnie in his house at Alverstoke.

'I'd left Daisychains in the rain an' I was cryin' because Roy hadn't taken any notice of me when I said I didn't want no drugs in this place.'

And Vinnie had picked up the pieces, she thought. Vera was nodding her head as though to say I told you so.

'But Vinnie loves me, he said so.'

'He probably does, Dais, in his own way. An' just 'ow many times do you tell 'im you love 'im?'

Daisy remembered their exact words after their lovemaking in Greece.

He'd said, '*I love you, Daisy*,' and she'd replied, '*I know you do*.'

Daisy shook her head.

'Give blokes enough rope and they 'angs them-selves,' said Vera.

'So what you're sayin' is I've kept 'im at arm's length so long, wanting this club clear of drugs an' tryin' to make money for me boys' future, I've been storin' up trouble for meself? Is that it, Vera? Is that what I've done?'

'What you askin' me for, Dais, when you just put it in a nutshell?'

'Oh, fuck,' said Daisy. 'Fuck, fuck, fuck!' Vera opened her mouth to speak but Daisy said, 'Shut up. Sometimes you get on me bleedin' wick. I'm goin' to watch the football, you comin'?'

The sunlight hit Daisy as they emerged into the afternoon air. Squeals and shouts of pleasure echoed from the football players. Vera's girls were tackling the 'boys'' team. Little Michael was waving his arms frantically and yelling for Alec to score a goal. Roy was weaving up and down between two piles of coats that were makeshift goalposts. He had his sleeves rolled up and there was a huge black mark on the knees of his Savile Row suit trousers. Bri tackled him and they both went down laughing, while Summer ran with the ball only for it to be stolen by Alec. Glo was holding baby Joy and Susie was running on the grass yelling for Alec to pass her the 'fuckin' ball'.

Vera grabbed hold of Daisy's arm as they walked across the road.

'I wasn't 'avin' a go at you, Dais. I just don't want you to get 'urt.'

'I know, Vera, I know. If you don't know what goes on in blokes' heads by now, no one does.'

'Well, I've 'ad more men than you've 'ad 'ot dinners, Dais.'

'An' you still manages to twist them round your little finger.'

Someone had scored a goal and the shouting was tremendous.

'You do realise, Daisy, that playin' ball games on a Sunday on the Ferry Gardens is punishable by a fine, if we're caught?' Daisy twisted her head and looked at Vera's triumphant look.

'In that case you'll 'ave to use some of your many charms on your old clients at the Town Hall or the local nick, and sort that out an' all, won't you, Vera me ol' tart!'

CHAPTER 21

'Fuckin' 'ell,' said Daisy. 'This is 'ot!' She lifted her face towards the sun and sighed contentedly. Even the slight breeze was warm.

'I promised you sunshine and sunshine you shall have, my princess.' The driver, assisted by Roy, hauled both cases into the large black car's boot, then Roy climbed into the back seat with Daisy. He addressed the driver as soon as the man got in,

'Do you have your orders?' The driver turned.

'Yes, sir.' Roy smiled at him. The car began to move away from Port Reitz Airport. Daisy's eyes were glued to the windows and already the back of her neck was running with perspiration.

'There's a lot of building work goin' on,' she said.

'The airport is expanding to accommodate much larger aeroplanes, Daisy. The government has visualised the profit to be made from tourism.'

She nodded knowingly. 'That's already 'appened in Spain, hasn't it?'

Strange trees with peculiar blooms caught her eye. 'Africa is so ... different,' she said. The further the car was travelling from the airport the busier the road was becoming. There were no pavements and the dirt road was pitted. Everyone seemed to be driving fast and bumping about and all the ancient dusty vehicles were packed with people.

She watched with fascination as the women, with their brightly patterned dresses and matching head-scarves, some clutching the hands of tiny children, walked with filled cane baskets perched tall. 'The women walk with such poise. They don't slouch along like we do.'

'Probably because they carry 'eavy burdens on their heads from an early age. Correct posture's important,' said Roy. He'd taken off his jacket and rolled up his shirtsleeves.

'Can't we 'ave the windows open?' Daisy moaned. 'There's not much bleedin' air in this car.'

'Better not. This is a poor country. There's no pub-lic assistance or 'andouts from the government here. People work or die. And if there's no work they'll steal. You can't blame 'em, can you, when they've got families to support? So, when the driver has to pause in a traffic snarl-up, we don't want no one reaching into the car and making a grab for your bracelet or your 'andbag, do we?'

Daisy looked at her wrist where the wide gold band rested. She shuddered, and said, 'You mean someone might steal from me while *you're* 'ere?'

'Of course.' Roy laughed. 'We don't want to put temptation in people's way. It ain't them what's corrupt, Daisy, it's the government. Here the rich get richer and the poor get sod all!'

Daisy pressed her nose to the window, watching the crowds of people. The road was lined with shacks hung about with dusty clothes, and barrows whose owners were selling food – mostly exotic fruit the like she'd never seen before. She was entranced, but she was also tired. It had been a long flight.

She'd slept on the plane coming over and hadn't realised she was so worn out. Once she'd woken up and the interior lighting had been turned right down. All around her people were sleeping in their seats and she saw that Roy had placed a blanket around her to keep her warm.

He had been asleep beside her, his mouth slightly open, and she could see the little chip in his front tooth where he'd fallen in the street as a child. His head was held upright by the cushioned head rest, and she'd watched him for a few seconds with a special kind of warmth stealing over her. He was one of those blokes who grew better-looking the older they got. The grey at his temples and the remains of prison pallor didn't disguise the fact that he could still turn women's heads. For a while she'd listened to the plane's engines, then, overcome with drowsiness, she'd snuggled down again at his side.

She was determined to enjoy this break, even more so now Roy had assured her she was safer with him at her side. The man who claimed he was McVitie's son had been well and truly sorted, so Roy had told her.

He touched her arm.

'See the prison behind the trees?' He pointed to a large building near the water's edge. 'There's reported to be thousands of prisoners inside there. We might think we get treated bad inside in England but it's much harder over 'ere.'

Daisy glanced away quickly, not wanting to think about anyone being locked up in such a gloomy-looking place.

'Is this Mombasa?' Daisy reckoned they'd travelled about ten miles from the airport. She always judged distances by the mileage from Gosport to Fareham, which was about five miles.

'Sure is. Over a million people live 'ere. It's an island.'

She marvelled at the swell of the population. Away from the main road, she saw shacks with tin roofs – obviously living accommodation – where men sat or squatted, chatting or dozing outside them. She saw blocks of flats, but with their broken windows and bits of dirty curtains hanging outside where the wind had caught them, they were unlike any in Gosport. The sight of poverty was everywhere, and she didn't think she'd ever seen so many people in one place before.

'Are we staying 'ere?' Everything was new and exciting, and also a little scary.

They passed a huge hoarding advertising Eno's for upset stomachs, then another poster proclaiming Omo to be the perfect washing powder.

'No,' replied Roy. 'The Adventurer Hotel on the

beach will be our 'ome, but soon we'll be passing through the posh part of Mombasa to get there. Nyali is a bit like Alverstoke, that's where the moneyed people live. Tonight we're coming back to Nyali to have dinner with some people I'd like you to meet.'

Daisy pressed his hand as a response and wondered when he'd mention the real reason he'd come to Kenya. Who were these people? Why were they having dinner together?

They turned off the main road after passing a huge marketplace where men and women were milling around ramshackle carts laden with furniture, old clothes, bananas, coconuts and piles of shoes.

'Bloody market traders gets everywhere,' laughed Daisy. 'It's just like bleedin' Gosport High Street.'

Soon they were on a narrower road that seemed to have been carved through scrubland. The sides were lined with colourful flowering bushes, but yet again the driver had to steer away from the large potholes. Then suddenly they were in a different kind of residential area.

'Jesus Christ!' Daisy exclaimed.

The houses were enormous! Set back from the highway, they were inside huge fenced-off areas, with guards at the closed gates. Long driveways led through well-tended gardens, planted with abundant trees and flowers, to dwellings that made her own home seem like a shed.

'Makes Alverstoke look a bit bleedin' scruffy,' she said. Then, 'Did you order this car?' She'd asked this because the vehicle was new and very clean, not at all like the other cars she'd seen on the road. She'd been amazed that some of the wrecks were even drivable.

'No, it was provided for me ... for us.'

'Oh.'

The driver had been silent for most of the journey but when they reached a secluded lane he turned into it, saying in perfect English, 'Not too far now, sir. I hope you will be comfortable here.'

Daisy liked the look of the large hotel set in grounds full of flowering shrubs and palm trees, with a huge lake at the end of the drive. The driver slowed at the gate and after winding down the window and speaking to the guard dressed in a uniform complete with gun, the barrier was lifted and they were allowed through.

The hotel façade was in the Art Deco style. Daisy immediately wondered if the rooms would be so grand. The car pulled to a halt outside the foyer and the driver leapt out and opened the doors for Daisy and Roy. Almost simultaneously, porters came from the hotel to take the luggage.

Roy felt for Daisy's hand again and together they climbed the marbled steps and entered the hotel. Roy took some money from his wallet, tipped the porters and looked around for the driver. He spoke briefly to him, glanced at his watch and then the man left.

The desk clerk gave Roy a key and called a waiting porter to take the cases and show them the way to their rooms.

When Roy opened the door for her and Daisy stepped inside the large room, she was practically struck dumb. White walls and cane furniture and, on a cane table, a huge bouquet of flowers filled the room with its scent. There was also a large balcony that Daisy immediately ran to and leaned over.

'It's bleedin' lovely,' she said. She took deep breaths of the warm air. 'There's even chairs out here for us to sit in the sun. An' look at that pool!' She pointed down to the lawns shaded with palm trees where sun loungers were placed around a huge pool. 'Jesus, will you look at that! Them's real monkeys jumpin' about in them trees ... listen to 'em chattering away to each other. Oh, Roy, this is so exciting. An' there's a bar with a thatched roof at the side of the pool. I could really get to like it 'ere.'

She went back into the room and stood for a moment looking around at the pristine whiteness. 'Where's the bleedin' beds?'

Roy was smiling at her, like he was indulging a child, she thought. He pointed to a door that was only partly open.

'This is a suite, Daisy. The bathroom is over there, the bedroom through there.' He waved towards another door. Tiredness forgotten, she ran over and pushed the door, revealing a large bedroom, also painted white.

'That's a bloody double bed. I thought I told you no funny business?'

She turned to him, her hands on her hips. He was

still smiling. She looked back at the bed. It was a very nice one, she thought. White curtains matched the thin white bed cover, and there was a dressing table with a seat, wall lights, a wardrobe and another balcony!

'I didn't book the accommodation, Daisy.'

'Who did?' She saw there were more flowers, this time on the small table on the balcony.

'The man or men we're going to see tonight.'

'Did you tell 'em we was married?' She turned to face him.

'No. It … didn't come up.' He said the words slowly, as if he was wanting to get something off his chest. 'But they do think you're my permanent partner.'

She hadn't the heart to be angry. She could see the lines of tiredness on his face, the worry in his eyes.

'This is all about what you was tryin' to tell me when you was in prison, ain't it?' His face was set in stone, she thought. She gave a huge sigh and stood quite still, her eyes never leaving his. 'This is somethin' to do with drugs, ain't it, and you knew if you asked me outright I'd never agree to come with you. Is that right?' She waited while he digested her words.

He ran his fingers through his hair, then, without removing his gaze from her, he said, 'You got it in one. Respectability is what I'm showing to them and I'm about to clinch a deal – I hope. These are family men. *Rich* family men. They've made it their business to find out about you and 'ow while I was away you took over my businesses, working side by side with Charles and my mother.'

'That part's true – not that I got you new deals, not like Charles – but what about Vinnie? Where does 'e come in?'

'He don't. You've never pushed that affair out into the open. You've concealed it so he can keep 'is job. My friends associate you with *me*. I'm grateful, Daisy.'

She let his words sink in. It seemed as though the past was knitting up before her eyes, each stitch helping Roy complete the pattern. His pattern.

'An' my boys?' She didn't even wait for his answer. 'You let these people believe they belong to you.'

'I never once suggested—'

'You didn't 'ave to, did you? My Eddie worships you …'

'And it's no secret *I love him*, Daisy.'

She sank down on the bed. It was too hot to think standing up. All kinds of questions were running around in her head, but she already knew the answers were staring her in the face.

'Why on earth didn't I twig it before? When he's old enough you want 'im to take up where you leave off, don't you?'

'Eddie'll never want for a thing, Daisy. Not with me behind 'im.'

She wasn't sure whether she wanted to lunge at him and rake her nails down his face for taking it upon himself to decide her beloved son's prospects, or be happy he cared enough about her to secure her boy's future. Even if that future was on the wrong side of the law!

'An' what if it's not what he wants?'

'Then he goes 'is own way. But I'll make sure I'm there for him.'

'He's nearly ten years old, Roy, that's all. Anything can happen.'

'One step at a time, Daisy. My first step is dinner tonight with new friends and you on me arm.'

She looked at Roy for a long time.

And Eddie? Whatever path he took when he was older *would* be his decision. Yes, her son loved Roy, but he also had her sense of fairness and justice, *and* he had a legacy coming to him to spend when he was of age. The money she'd put in trust for him when he was a baby would enable her son to choose his own lifestyle. No, she had no worries there.

And Jamie? Daisychains, and the money she could make when it belonged solely to her and Vera, would be his legacy, drug free. And she'd give every waking moment to making sure her second son would be as secure as her first. She mulled over Roy's words. But what about Roy's own son? Where did he come in all this?

'Michael? What does he get out of it?'

A shadow passed across Roy's face.

'I was wrong about 'im, Daisy. The boy can't walk but he makes up for it in other ways. I been talking to Alec and the lad not only 'as a talent for drawing, but since Alec's been helping him with his school work he's discovered the little tyke's a genius with figures.'

'I told you you should put your prejudices behind you and look at the real child, didn't I?'

He nodded. 'Your Vera was right an' all. She told me I should spend time with 'im, and I've been taking her advice. It'll take a while to build a good relationship between us but I'll 'ave a go. I'd like to think he won't want for anything all the time I'm around. And later, when he's older, a business like mine needs a bloke good with money and figures ...' He sighed. 'Malkie treats 'im like his own and the kid loves the bloke. He's got security and that's what counts at present. An' I 'ave to admit that Angel is a good mum.'

Daisy liked it that Roy could now give his own child some of the love he deserved. He wasn't such a bad bloke after all, she thought, he does look after the people he cares about. That thought brought her back to the present.

'Is there any danger to me 'ere?'

Roy bent forward and took one of her hands in his.

'Do you seriously think I'd let any 'arm come to you?'

There was a faint smile hovering on his lips. He knows he's got me, she thought. The bastard! Daisy pushed his hand away.

'Well, I ain't even goin' to ask what you're up to, Roy Kemp!' There was a sudden look of surprise on his face that made her want to laugh. She stomped

past him and back into the living room of the apart-
ment, aware he was following close behind, and began
hauling her suitcase into the bedroom. 'If we're only
'ere for a few days I'm bloody well goin' to lay by that
pool and get brown. You can do what you like!'

Roy started to laugh at the same time as taking the
case from her and then putting it down on the metal
suitcase table.

'Daisy, do as you please. You always do. At least I
know when you're with me you're safe.'

'An' what about that? I wouldn't be bleedin' safe in
there with you!' She pointed towards the double bed.

'If you don't want to sleep in that with me I'll sleep
on two chairs pushed together.' She narrowed her eyes
at him.

'Fair enough,' she said as he walked away. 'I think I
can just about 'andle bein' nice to you when there are
people around.' She began fiddling with the key to her
case. The next thing she saw was a large red trumpet-
shaped flower being offered to her by Roy.

'For you, Daisy. You're one in a million.'

His hand touched her fingers as she took the
sweet-smelling flower. Something like an electric jolt
ran through her. That same remembered feeling she'd
had in the past when he'd smiled or held her. Don't
be silly, girl, she told herself; don't get on that old
merry-go-round again with him, it hurts too much.
Besides, how would Vinnie feel? A nasty little thought
ran through her mind that Vinnie was too busy worrying about his bleeding wife! You can stop that an' all,

she told herself. It doesn't become you, Daisy Lane, to think nasty thoughts. Karma always has a way of turning the tables against you.

With the flower in her hand, she left the suitcase and the nearness of him and went out on to the balcony. She placed her flower in the vase where the other blooms were, and called back at Roy, 'Don't Africa smell lovely?' She took a couple of deep breaths then looked into the bedroom at the net tied above the bed. He saw her looking at it.

'Mosquito net,' he said.

'I know that,' she said. 'I ain't bleedin' stupid! Anyway, I got some pills off Vera's doctor mate.'

'Good,' he said, 'I don't want you falling ill, do I?'

He disappeared, only to return with his suitcase which he slung on to the bed.

'Don't put your suitcase that side. You'll get that cover all grubby. I want that side of the bed!'

Roy rocked back on his heels. A grin split his face.

'So I do get a side?'

'Might do,' she said grudgingly. 'But I meant what I said.' He lifted the case and set it on the floor, then creased his brows and gave a laugh that rumbled from deep within him.

'I know,' he said. 'No funny business.'

CHAPTER 22

Daisy glanced in the hotel room's full-length mirror, deciding she looked pretty good in a black dress that clung in all the right places. The sun had worked its magic, bringing a glow to her cheeks, and her skin tingled deliciously. She was also aware of the praise – and the lust – in Roy's eyes.

The same driver met them in the foyer, and as Daisy walked down the steps to get in the car she was surprised to feel a similar warmth to the one she'd experienced during the day, as though night and day held no difference in temperature. A myriad of noises met her ears: frogs croaking, the hum of grasshoppers, but above all it was the heat she loved with a new-found passion. Fleetingly she remembered the cold, cold winters Vera and herself had experienced in Gosport when Bert's Cafe was their home and how they'd sat around the open door of the oven to keep warm. No problems like that here, she thought!

Again there was the rigmarole of the guards opening and closing the gate. This time the journey didn't take so long.

The house, at the end of a long drive, again with a guard at the gated entrance, was like something she'd only ever seen in films. Daisy squeezed Roy's hand. Panic was now stealing over her, but Roy seemed to know exactly how she was feeling.

'It'll be fine,' he said. 'Don't worry.'

They were shown into a high-ceilinged hallway that was almost as large as the lobby of the hotel they'd just left. White marble made the place feel cool and flowers were everywhere, throwing out their sweet fresh scent. Red velvet sofas and armchairs gave the area a comfortable feel.

Three men came to meet them, shaking first Roy's hand and then hers. They were very tall, wore suits, and their African-accented English was impeccable. But the word 'Hujambo' was strange to her ears. Daisy realised it was the Kenyan greeting.

One of the men took her arm and guided her towards a room where the door was ajar. Inside, she was welcomed by three women who immediately rose from their seats and put her at ease with their broad smiles and questions about her health, the plane trip and how she was coping with the heat. The men, including Roy, had disappeared.

'Come. Sit down and talk to us,' said one. Daisy discovered her name was Adam, which she reckoned was a strange name for a woman.

'We have English names and our own tribal names,' Adam confided. Daisy thought she had the whitest teeth she'd ever seen, and the straightest! Sofia and

Mabel were the other two women. All three had the most beautifully manicured and long painted nails that Daisy had ever seen. Vera would be green with envy, she thought.

She allowed herself to be led to a silk sofa where she made herself comfortable and was promptly handed a glass of iced water that tasted like nectar.

Daisy looked about her. She knew when Vera asked her what the house was like all she'd be able to say would be 'like something out of one of them posh magazines, only bleedin' posher!' Silk wallpaper, glass chandeliers, and the whole place smelling of musk and flowers. Through a huge window that ran the length of the room, she could see manicured lawns under the subdued lighting, and a swimming pool surrounded by loungers and tables and umbrellas.

After a while she realised the house was Adam's and she was married to the tallest of the Kenyan men, Paul. Sofia and Mabel were the wives of the other two men. All three men had been partners for a long time, and that was the limit of the women's discussion of their husband's business interests. It didn't take long for Daisy to realise that men and women's roles were clearly defined, with the women definitely taking a back seat, but it was a shock when she asked about the beautifully laid table for four at the far end of the room and was told by Adam, 'We don't eat with the men. Mostly the men eat with other men. We usually eat with our children.' Mabel was surprised to hear that everyone ate together at mealtimes in England.

All three women were dressed in brightly coloured silks that accentuated their burnished skins. Against their exotic looks and beaded and braided hair, Daisy felt like one of the drab sparrows hopping about on the Ferry Gardens.

Swahili was their first language, explained Adam.

Daisy, who had warmed to her straight away, asked, 'How come your English is better than mine?'

'We have been taught English in school,' Sofia replied. 'Shall we eat? Or would you prefer to wait?'

The four women sat around the highly polished table, laid with glittering tableware and damask napkins, and were waited on by servants. Daisy ate small portions of the food and found it delicious, even though she had absolutely no idea what she was eating. She was happy to drink iced water after it was explained that alcohol was not on the menu but if she, as a guest, wanted wine it could be provided. Roy had already told her that for many Kenyans their religious beliefs forbade alcohol.

The women asked Daisy questions about her family and about Roy and she was completely honest with her replies. She had known him for years, she had worked with him, she was extremely fond of his mother and visited her frequently. She also said a little prayer that she wasn't asked any question where she might have to bend the truth. Daisy hated liars and remembered her mother telling her, 'You can believe a thief but never a liar.' She was also well aware that whatever information she gave might be relayed to the men and could affect Roy's chances of a deal with them. She remembered the old saying, 'The head that shares the pillow shares the secrets.'

Daisy learned that 'sisi ni marafiki' meant 'we are friends'. And by the time it got to the girly giggly stage near the end of the meal, she felt they really were her new friends.

'Would you like to see my children?'

'I wouldn't like to wake them, Adam,' Daisy replied.

'They sleep like logs,' Adam said, rising from the table and beckoning Daisy to follow through a door at the far end of the room.

A wide marble staircase led to the bedrooms. Daisy glanced into the rooms as she was hurried towards the nursery. She reckoned all her bedrooms could fit easily into just one of these luxurious rooms.

At the end of the softly lit hallway Adam listened outside the slightly open door then turned to Daisy and put a finger to her lips.

Daisy tiptoed inside, careful not to tread on the scattered toys, to where either side of the spacious children's room was a bed. Each bed had a red coverlet. Each bed contained a small child. On the wall was a picture of a group of smiling children of assorted ages standing in front of a building. It's a school photograph, Daisy thought, until she realised Adam's children were too young for school.

A little girl in white pyjamas was sprawled across one bed. Clutched in her arms was a gnawed cloth monkey. The toy was scruffy. Daisy looked at Adam, who shrugged.

'It's her favourite toy,' she whispered. 'I can't even prise it away from her to wash it.' Daisy knew exactly what Adam meant and suddenly she felt very close to this woman who had a different religion, lived in a different country, but was so like her in being protective of her family.

In the other bed, tangled in the covers, was a little boy. She guessed he was the youngest.

'How old?'

Adam waved towards the boy. 'Paulie is two.' She motioned towards the other bed. 'Sarah is three.'

Daisy smiled at her. 'Beautiful,' she said. Just then the little girl moved in her sleep. 'Quick,' whispered Daisy, indicating to Adam that they should leave the room. She didn't want to wake the sleeping children.

Adam pulled the door to behind them.

Downstairs, the remains of the meal was being cleared away by a servant and Adam and Daisy joined Mabel and Sofia, who were sitting at a candlelit table by the pool drinking fruit juices.

Daisy remembered the photograph in the children's room.

'Who are they?' she asked. 'They looked so happy.'

'We call the children our second family,' said Adam. 'It is an orphanage the six of us support. My husband grew up poor in Mombasa and vowed to put something back into the community so we had the home built.'

'Each child goes to school and will have help supporting them when they reach the age of eighteen to find work,' said Mabel.

'We also provide health assistance because often the children who arrive are ill or infirm,' Sofia explained.

'And fun. Fun is important,' said Adam. 'Some of the little ones have never laughed. Life has already dealt them the worst blows. So we visit animal parks, have parties and trips to the beach with plenty of ice creams – and we make sure the people who work with the children are not corrupt in any way. There is much corruption in Kenya,' she added, a frown crossing her face.

Daisy didn't know what to say. She thought of those smiling children in the photograph. These women wanted for nothing themselves and were determined to share. Finally she said, 'You are very kind people.'

'No, Daisy,' Adam said, taking her hand. 'Each of us had unfortunate upbringings. We were lucky to have married men who are determined to make money and allow us to use the money as we wish. Perhaps one day when we meet again we will tell you how the harshness of life in Africa affected each one of us here.' She shrugged. 'When you come again, you must stay for longer and meet our other family. We are the fortunate ones to be able to do this.'

Daisy took in her words. She was about to say she'd love to visit the children when Paul came out of the house and whispered in Adam's ear.

Roy followed behind Paul and he was smiling from

ear to ear. A warmth stole through her as his eyes sought hers. That one shared momentary look reminded her of the bond between them, the unbreakable thread of caring and sharing that would never go away.

It was time for them to go, for Daisy to hug her new friends and leave their hospitality. Goodbye, 'kwaheri', Daisy, she was told. She caught the words 'ashanti' and 'biashara nzuri' which, once alone in the car with Roy, he explained meant thank you and good business.

Back at the hotel, relaxing on a big squashy sofa in the bar with a brandy and lime in her hand, Daisy asked, 'D'you think it went well?'

Roy had his long legs stretched out in front of him and a smile still on his face.

'Very, very well.'

'Was I all right?'

'You passed the test with flying colours.'

She wanted to tell him about the orphanage, how she had bonded with Adam, Sofia and Mabel, but his words made her think. 'What d'you mean by that?'

'Women here don't as a rule run businesses. My new friends were impressed that a little thing like you could look after an operation like mine while I was incapacitated.'

'Now you and I put up a united front, is that it?'

He nodded. 'Family is special here, Dais, a bit like the Sicilian Mafia and the way their relatives care for each other. These men didn't want to include me in

286

any of their deals unless I could persuade them I was dependable enough to take on the responsibility.'

Here we go again, she thought. 'But I don't want to be included in your dirty deals ...' He leaned forward and gently touched her cheek.

'You don't 'ave to be. Not again. I'm only sorry I couldn't have prevented the tragedy at Gosport's ferry terminus. You must know I couldn't bear it if anything happened to you, Daisy.' She saw the concern in his eyes. 'But that's in the past, done and dusted.' He put his hand to his inside pocket and pulled out a long brown envelope. Daisy could see the London solicitor's name on it.

'What's this?' He'd taken the brandy glass from her hand and replaced it with the sealed package.

'Open it.'

Her heart was beating fast but she did as he asked. After she read through the pages she began to cry.

'You kept your promise, you kept your promise!' She was looking at him with new eyes and the tears began to roll down her cheeks. She couldn't hold back and threw herself at him, holding him close, breathing him in.

'Daisy, Daisy,' he laughed, trying to disentangle himself. 'Don't spill my drink, it's the first I've 'ad all night.' He put down his brandy, took a handkerchief from his pocket and tried to wipe her cheeks but she grabbed the hanky from him and wiped her eyes herself.

'Oh, Roy,' she said. 'The club is really, finally

mine? Well, mine an' Vera's? No more drugs in Daisy-chains?'

'I'm bowing out of *your* club,' he said. He waved towards the waiter who immediately came over.

'More drinks,' he said. 'Large ones,' then to Daisy, 'Would you rather have champagne? I guess you'd like to celebrate.' She shook her head.

'I don't want an 'angover. I just want another very large brandy.'

The waiter left and Daisy said thoughtfully, 'Does this mean you an' me won't ever see each other again?'

'Do you want *not* to see me?'

Daisy sighed. 'Look, you toerag, I came 'ere with you so's you'd give me no more bleedin' excuses for not letting me have your share of the club. I've fulfilled my part of the bargain. An' now you've fulfilled yours. You'll go on with your criminal activities whether I'm around or not.' She looked at him shyly. 'I don't think I want you out of my life altogether.'

There. She'd said it, told him she wanted him. Her heart was beating fast.

'An' why's that?' He had that infuriating grin on his face again. Daisy didn't know whether she wanted to smack him or kiss him. She took a deep breath.

'Because my Eddie bleedin' worships the ground you walk on. He's lost one dad and I don't want him to lose another one!' It was the truth. Eddie *did* love Roy.

Roy bent forward and kissed her on the nose.

'Just call and I'll come, Daisy. I love you, you silly cow!'

'An' in my own way, I love you, Roy.' She stared into his slate-grey eyes. He pushed back the waves of hair that had fallen to his forehead.

Her words had come out automatically. But she realised she'd told him the truth.

After all they'd been through together, the good times and the bad, she honestly couldn't imagine him not being there beside her.

'Listen,' he said, breaking the gaze between them, and the intimacy of the moment was gone.

It was, thought Daisy, almost as if Roy had decided he wanted the conversation to go no further lest she say or do something she might back out of later. She was surprised that she felt hurt. Then Roy spoke.

'I've done what I came to do and it's worked out to my advantage. But what I'd really like to do is bring you back here again so I can take you on a safari to see the wild animals. Eddie, Jamie, and Michael as well, if you like?'

'I'd love that,' she said. Her heart swam with delight that he'd included his own son. He wasn't the hard man he pretended to be, but hadn't she always known that?

The waiter deposited two huge brandies on the small table.

'To us,' Roy said, picking one up and passing it to her.

Daisy clicked her glass with Roy's and took a sip of her drink.

Despite her great happiness a huge wave of tiredness overtook her and she put her other hand to her mouth to stifle the yawn.

'It's been quite a day, Daisy,' he said. 'You must be tired. You ready for your bed?'

She stood up. 'I think I'm too excited to sleep now I got Daisychains to meself.' She gave him a big grin. 'Thank you, Roy, you don't know how 'appy you've made me.' She thought for a moment then said, 'Can I laze around tomorrow by the pool? I think I could just about manage that.'

He began to laugh. That deep throaty sound she liked so much. She realised, what with the overnight plane travel, the short nap in the sun, the strain of the dinner and now the alcohol, she was almost dead on her feet. She kicked off her high heels and found herself facing his broad chest.

'Come on, little girl,' he said. 'Bed for you.'

She slurred, 'An' where are you goin' to sleep?'

'With you, Daisy,' Roy said. 'Where else but with you?'

Daisy looked up and narrowed her eyes at him. She could smell his cologne and almost taste the maleness of him. That old fascinating tingle of anticipation began to travel from her loins through her body.

Then she whispered, more to remind herself than him, 'No bloody funny business, Roy Kemp!'

CHAPTER 23

'Who took the bleedin' photos?' Daisy drummed her fingers on the desk top.

Her voice was raised above the deafening music of T.Rex's 'Metal Guru' issuing into the office from the club's smoky bar. She could see Angel, who was slumped on a chair opposite the desk, was upset; her mascara had run and her eyes were red-rimmed with weeping.

Daisy's sharp eyes had also taken in the telltale grains of white powder clinging to Angel's nostrils.

'The first photos was taken by Norma's old man. Then I think it might have been some photographer from the *News of the World.*' Angel's body heaved with another loud sniff.

Vera, perched on the corner of the desk, had slitty eyes like a cat's and her voice was sharp. 'You bleedin' think?'

'Well, Norma's husband said he was goin' to show the world what she was up to with her girls and the ministers of the cabinet. There's pictures of me an' him in bed. Oh, whatever shall I do? He's the junior defence minister, a lord for Christ's sake, an' I'll be named in the papers and Michael will find out what I've been doing for a living. I don't want my boy to be ashamed of me.'

Daisy continued drumming her fingers and her nails made sharp clicking sounds. She tried to think, but instead pictures of Vinnie came into her mind.

He'd told her he was looking into a bit of business in the area and expected to be in Gosport until it was sorted. Daisy had been around him long enough to know he'd only tell her what he wanted her to know so she hadn't pressed him for details. What she was cross about was that she'd asked him if he wanted to come along to Western Way and see the boys and he'd said no, he had too much work on. She couldn't quite take that in. Fancy him being apart from his own son and then not being bothered about seeing him when he had the chance. But blokes were funny creatures, she thought.

And why oh why hadn't she and Vera taken more notice ages ago when Angel had been trying to tell them she thought there was something funny going on in London with that Levy woman? Well, she knew why, didn't she? Both she and Vera had mistakenly put Angel's fears down to the paranoia that cocaine brought.

Vera now said, 'Calm down, Angel. What *exactly* were you doin' in bed with your so-called Lamby?'

'We were, we were … Oh, Vera …' Angel had started bawling again.

'Stop it!' Vera took a handkerchief from her sleeve and passed it to the girl across the table, who sniffed again then blew into it noisily. 'What was supposedly goin' on in that bed?'

'There might 'ave been three of us, Vera ... you know ... doin' stuff to each other, and smoking a bit of weed.'

Vera tried hard not to laugh. She looked across at Daisy then she put her hand across her mouth. 'Well, that won't do the silly sod much good, will it? Not when it becomes public knowledge.'

'Edward Heath has ordered a Security Commission enquiry into Lamby's affairs and into the leader of the House of Lords.'

Daisy asked, 'Who told you this?'

'Lamby.'

Vera whistled. 'This is going to be a big scandal, then. A lot of heads is goin' to roll. How did it all start to unravel at the seams then?'

'I don't want one of the heads that'll roll to be mine,' wailed Angel and began sobbing even louder.

Vera got up and went round the desk. Grabbing Angel's shoulders, she shook her until the girl's blonde hair flew about her face like a fluttering curtain.

'Stop bein' so fuckin' dramatic! We need to know what's 'appened. Start from the bleedin' beginnin'.'

Vera let go and once more took up her perch on the desk in front of Angel, who looked at her with frightened watery eyes.

'Apparently there was some police raid on a porno

shop in Soho. They found a notebook what was in code. All names and addresses, the coppers worked out. This earl, what's the leader of the Lords, was the only name what wasn't coded. The sex shop belongs to Norma's husband, an' they'd 'ad a bit of a fallin' out, her an' him, an' he was supposed to have gone abroad to buy drugs, so Norma reckoned. He let slip that Lamby was a regular punter at the sex romps his wife provided. Norma's old man's been taking photos, see, so Lamby couldn't say he had nothin' to do with it. I told you both a long time ago I thought somethin' was goin' on ...' Angel's eyes closed, she gave a huge shoulder-rising sigh and then started crying afresh. She opened her eyes just in time to see Vera lean towards her and raise a hand. Angel shrank back.

'Cryin' ain't goin' to solve a fuckin' thing! Don't make me slap you one!' Daisy could see Vera was pleased when her words had the desired effect and Angel's tears stopped.

'What are the police doin' about this?' Daisy asked.

'Edward Heath has got MI5 involved because there's police officers in up to their necks as well,' Angel sniffed.

Vera shook her head. 'Jesus fuckin' Christ! This is goin' to rock the country when – if – it all comes out!'

'I know, Vera. Of course, it ain't *all* out in the open yet—'

Vera cut Angel off. 'Maybe it'll be hushed up. With

294

so many top names involved, the government won't want to look as though their dicks can't be kept in their trousers. Then there's the country's security and stuff. That'll be questioned – the 'eads what shares pillows shares secrets.'

Daisy thought for a moment as she surveyed the cowed girl. This was Angel, the dancer she'd thought was as hard as nails. The Gosport girl who'd used her looks and body and fucked her way to the top of her profession.

She hadn't liked Angel at all when she'd first met her. The bitch had caused a lot of trouble by sleeping with Roy Kemp and producing his kiddie. Daisy had made sure Angel kept her job, not only because she was a skilled dancer but also because Daisy needed to make sure young Michael didn't want for anything. The turnaround had been that Angel really loved her Thalidomide kiddie. And Angel had saved Daisy's life so she would be eternally in Angel's debt for that. Daisy had to get her thinking cap on, and fast, not only because Michael's welfare bonded Angel, Daisy and Vera.

If Angel didn't care so much about her boy and what he might think of his mother in years to come, Daisy knew Vera would be relishing this scandal and thinking how famous she would be if and when the news finally broke. With her name linked to cabinet ministers, Angel could then command the highest of fees, she'd be another Christine Keeler.

Vera said, 'You could be famous, Angel,' but that

just sent Angel into more floods of tears. The hanky was now sodden wet.

'I don't want that. I don't want Michael to hate me. I don't want the other kids taunting 'im that I'm a fuckin' call girl.'

Vera leaned forward and put her arms around the girl. 'It's not goin' to come out straight away, but when it does the press'll think up a bleedin' good title for it. "Sex Scandal Ministers" or "Peeping Tom" something or other.'

Angel pulled back and looked at her with horror.

Daisy said, 'They got to find out who you are first, 'aven't they?'

Angel blew her nose again. She made to hand back the cotton square but Vera said, 'Nah, you keep it, love. What else was you photographed doing, can you remember?'

Angel blushed, and Vera laughed.

'How can you blush? What you gets up to with those bleedin' ministers is what I pays you to do.'

Angel was folding pleats into her skirt where there weren't any. After a long telling silence she whispered, 'Coke. There might 'ave been other drugs involved.' She raised her voice. 'But I wasn't interested in syringes and stuff. Oh, Vera, there's supposed to be about fifteen photographs.'

Daisy took a deep breath and exhaled slowly. 'I think we need a cup of tea to talk this over, don't you?' She slid off the table and went and plugged in the electric kettle.

'Trouble is, Angel,' she said, 'because these men are lords, leaders of the country, it ain't goin' to go away.' Daisy tried to think. 'You sure it's the *News of the World*?'

Angel nodded. 'Yes, I'm sure.'

'That paper'll be like a dog with a bone. They like to get to the nitty gritty.' Daisy rinsed out the teapot then took a cloth and began wiping two mugs that had been standing on the draining board. She looked at Angel and saw her face was chalk white. That reminded her.

'Sticking that shit up your nose all this bleedin' time ain't the fuckin' answer, either.'

Vera gasped.

Angel's jaw dropped. 'What ... what d'you mean?'

'Come off it, Angel. I didn't come up the Solent in a bleedin' bucket. You're sniffin' up your profits like the stuff's goin' out of circulation, ain't you?'

Angel pressed her lips together but that, Daisy noticed, didn't stop her hands from shaking. Angel's secret wasn't a secret any longer.

Vera said, 'Your little habit isn't goin' to disappear by itself any more than this shit will. It'll be like the bleedin' Profumo scandal all over again. I got to think.' Vera handed a mug of thick brown tea to Angel, who grabbed it and began drinking noisily, her shaking hands making it slop over the rim.

Daisy stared at the beaten girl and her heart went out to her. She put her hand on Angel's hair, feeling its fine silkiness. Silly, silly girl, she thought. If she keeps sticking that crap in her body, her hair'll be like straw.

'Leave it with us,' Vera said at last.

'You ain't gonna tell anyone about all this, are you?' Vera shook her head.

Daisy thought she'd never seen anyone so unhappy as this girl before her.

'Do your Michael and that Malkie still think you're a dancer?'

Angel nodded. 'An' if Alec knows what I gets up to in London he ain't never breathed a word ...'

'He's a good bloke, Alec is. I think he's got a bit of a thing for our Daisy 'ere.'

'Shut up,' Daisy said. Alec had certainly pulled out all the stops since Vera had got him on that alcoholics' programme over in Portsmouth. He dressed well, he'd put on weight and she'd had many enquiries about him from lonely women. He was an asset to the club as well, drawing sketches of the punters' women and selling them.

Angel was still talking and Daisy tuned in to her again.

'... But you and Daisy both know lots of influential people, Vera. Can't they help me?'

'Sure I do, lovey,' replied Vera, 'but they're all local people. The little favours I can call in won't be any bleedin' 'elp at all.'

Daisy knew she had to do something. Perhaps one of the first steps to take would be to get Angel clean again. If she was off the drugs at least she'd be able to think straight. All the time Angel had been in the office she'd been either shivering or crying and Daisy just wanted the old cocky Angel back again, the woman who'd been so self-assured she'd bowled the blokes over with her slinky dancing. An idea was forming in Daisy's mind ... well, she could only ask Angel, couldn't she?

"'Ow about if Vera 'as a word with 'er ol' mate Doctor Dillinger, see if he can't 'elp you ease up on that crap you're sniffin'?' She stared first at Angel then at Vera, who nodded in agreement. 'At least then you'll still 'ave a job.' Daisy could see Angel was going to protest.

Vera chimed in. 'We can't 'ave a no drugs rule an' agree to you goin' on usin'. Surely you can see that?'

'I can do it on me own if I wants to.' Angel's mouth was now a thin hard line and she looked as though she really meant what she said, thought Daisy. Only her shaking hands were betraying her.

'You're only doin' what all drunks and druggies do. Pretending you can 'andle the substances, an' not realising the substances is 'andling you.'

Angel let her gaze fall to the carpet. Then in a tiny voice, she said, 'You'd help me?'

'Of course,' Vera said. 'Me an' Daisy won't want to lose you, you silly girl.'

Angel began nodding her head. 'Thank you,' she said.

'Doc Dillinger might be able to pull a few strings and get you in St James'. Look 'ow it worked for

Alec. I know 'is problem was the booze but you got an addiction, just the same as he 'as.'

Angel suddenly clasped Vera to her. Vera wasn't one for sudden bursts of affection. Daisy knew Vera would feel hot and embarrassed. Vera pulled away.

'Look, like I said, leave it all with us,' she said.

'Go 'ome an' spend a bit of time with that little boy of yours,' Daisy said. A thought crossed her mind. 'Alec said him an' Malkie took the lad fishing off the sea wall. The little bugger caught a cod. Big enough to gut and eat, it was.'

Angel gave a sudden smile. Daisy had forgotten how utterly beautiful the woman was when she smiled. Angel sniffed, then said, 'You better not spread that about, Daisy. Not with the cod war hotting up.'

'Yeah, that might be in the *Evening News* an' all, Angel. "Seven-year-old flouting laws by taking cod from Solent waters."'

Angel gave a half-hearted laugh.

'Now piss off,' said Vera. 'I got some thinking to do. And we're a barmaid short because that Leah ain't shown 'er face.'

'You mean the girl with that gorgeous red 'air?'

Vera nodded. 'That's the one. Her old man came 'ome from prison an' couldn't find hide nor hair of her.'

'Ain't she got a little girl?'

'Yes,' Daisy sighed. 'The babysitter's an' ol' lady. Old Nan can't walk far. She's all right indoors but she can't cope with cobbles an' pavements. She uses a stick, see, and it took her all 'er strength to get the kiddie an' herself over to us to see if we knew where Leah was just before Jem got out.'

'Is the little girl all right?'

'She's fine. Especially now she's got 'er daddy home. Roy's given him a job, you know?' Vera confided. 'He's not a bad bloke, this Jem. I 'ad to tell 'im off though, the bugger 'as a nasty 'abit of cleanin' his nails with a bloody flick knife. Fair gives me the shits that does. I told 'im not to do it in 'ere. The punters don't like seein' that. Mind you, 'e's out of his mind with worry about Leah.'

Daisy didn't add that she too was worried about the girl. It wasn't like Leah to leave the kiddie. And Daisy knew how much she'd been looking forward to her old man's release from Parkhurst. She'd asked Vera to put out feelers asking her girls if they'd seen or heard anything of Leah, but so far no one was saying a dickybird.

'Vera, do you think she's all right?'

That's a bleeding daft question, thought Daisy. Still, it showed Angel was thinking about someone else instead of herself.

'How should I bleedin' know? I ain't no fuckin' oracle, am I? If it was anyone except Leah I'd have thought she'd run off with some bloke, but Leah ain't like that,' said Vera. 'She idolises her 'usband.'

Another thought struck Daisy. 'I know you didn't know 'er very well, but you 'aven't 'eard anything about her an' local debt collectors and nasty photos?' she asked Angel.

Angel shook her head. Here we go again, thought Daisy as she saw the tears well up in Angel's eyes.

'The only nasty photos I know about are those taken of me,' she said.

CHAPTER 24

Vinnie pulled out a stray dandelion that had dared to invade the tarmac of the tennis court and threw it down where it could shrivel and die in the hot sun.

'Race you to the house, Dad!'

'I don't think so, Jack.' He wiped the beads of sweat from his forehead. 'Playing tennis with you is enough exercise for one afternoon.' He thought how not so long ago he'd have willingly taken his son up on the offer. Might even have won. Now he knew his limitations, especially when the heat of the day was against him. 'I'll put away the racquets if you'll go in and organise a couple of drinks.'

He watched his boy run easily across the expanse of lawn towards the house, the labrador running beside him. This was a delightful place, he thought, an ideal home for his boy to have matured into a typical middle-class lad with expectations.

When and how did his eldest son grow so tall? Vinnie knew he'd missed a great deal of the boy's younger years while he was chasing his career. But it wasn't only that, was it, he chided himself. He'd had to wait to enter his son's life again on the say-so of Clare.

He knew he'd been a fool to let her dictate his visitation rights, but everything comes to him who waits, and now it had. Why? Because he knew Clare better than she knew herself. All the pleading in the world hadn't stopped the affair she'd embarked on but he'd banked on the fact that she'd get bored – and he'd been right. Now Vinnie was back in her life again and he relished it.

Reaching the summerhouse, it was almost as if thinking about Clare had conjured her up, for he heard her voice calling him.

He waved at her slight figure. She was miming a telephone call, her blonde hair rising and falling across her pretty face in the slight breeze.

Vinnie hurried towards the French doors, open to catch the summer warmth.

'Thank you, darling,' he said, taking the phone from her. The scent of her perfume was in his nostrils. He put his ear to the receiver.

'Are you goin' to call me "darling" as well?' Vinnie knew the voice and he shuddered. He put his fingers across the mouthpiece.

'Business,' he said softly. He watched the sway of Clare's hips in the thin cotton dress as she walked from the room. When she'd closed the door, he said, immediately regretting the words as they left his mouth, 'How did you get this number?'

'No secrets between us, Vinnie. I don't need to be a bleedin' detective to keep tabs on you.'

He sighed. 'Okay, what do you want, Roy?'

'Meet me at the end of the lane. Now.'

The line had gone dead.

'Bastard,' Vinnie said to the receiver. Roy Kemp had hung up on him.

Upstairs he changed from his tennis shorts into a pair of slacks. The bastard can wait on me, he decided. Downstairs in the kitchen Clare was putting the finishing touches to a salad. He kissed the back of her neck and said, 'I won't be long.'

She turned. 'How long? Don't forget we're going to see Dad.'

He looked into her pale blue eyes and smiled.

'Not long. I'll be back in plenty of time to make visiting hours at the hospital.' Picking up an apple from the bowl on the worktop he bit into it, savouring its freshness. 'I promise,' he said, through a mouthful of the fragrant fruit.

Outside in the sunshine he rounded the front of the house and opened the five-bar gate, closing it behind him. He didn't need the dog following him.

The narrow lane with its tall hedges of beech was cool and it wasn't long before he spotted the Silver Shadow tucked into a passing place as far as its bulk would allow. He could just about make out Roy Kemp sitting in the driver's seat. He was alone. Opening the door, Roy got out and started walking towards Vinnie. He'd done a fair bit of working out in prison, decided Vinnie. His weight was evenly distributed and his walk a swagger that implied the world owed him. There was a grin on Roy's face. Vinnie noted the gold cufflinks and the immaculate lightweight dark suit. Too bloody hot for a suit, thought Vinnie, but on Roy Kemp it looked just right.

'If you'd been any longer I'd 'ave come and got you. And I know you wouldn't 'ave liked that.' Vinnie saw the slight chip in the whiteness of Roy's front tooth. Roy pushed back the lock of hair that fell across his forehead. 'Come on, let's walk,' he said, not waiting for Vinnie to refuse.

The spicy clean scent of Roy's cologne only reminded Vinnie he hadn't showered after the hectic game of tennis.

He fell into step with Roy. Twigs broke beneath their shoes and Roy stopped only once to allow a couple of cyclists safe journey down the narrow lane. Roy paused at a gate that heralded the entrance to a field, and Vinnie watched in silence as he lifted the rusted chain that held the gate shut.

The field had been turned over to grass and a felled tree made as good a place as any for them both to sit.

'I got a proposition,' said Roy. His long legs were stretched out in front of him and he was staring hard into Vinnie's face.

'So?'

Roy's eyes narrowed. 'I'm gonna give you a lift up in your career. You're goin' to arrest some very nasty blokes.'

Vinnie pursed his lips then asked, 'How d'you reckon on doing that? And more to the point, why would you do anything for me?'

'First you agree this goes no further than between you and me?'

Vinnie lifted his hand and ran his fingers across his chin, feeling the slight stubble.

'What is this? Another binding secret?'

Roy shrugged. 'You could look at it like that. Beneficial to you, beneficial to me. You know I don't give out freebies.'

'What if I don't want to play?'

Roy bent forward and slapped Vinnie on the knee. 'You will, me ol' son, you will. I know you got bodies of mutilated women pilin' up all over the countryside. A kiddie as well. Be quite a feather in your cap when *you* sort it – with my help that is.'

Vinnie's mind raced ahead. The bastard knew how he wanted promotion. How much he wanted – no, *needed* – to show Clare he could provide her and the boy with the middle-class lifestyle she was used to. But he wasn't going to give Roy Kemp the satisfaction of asking him how he'd discovered Clare was back in his life. The bastard had only been out a matter of weeks so he hadn't let the grass grow under his feet, had he? And what did he know about the mutilated girls?

'What do you want, Roy?'

Only he knew already what Roy wanted. He just needed to hear him say it. A ladybird had landed on Vinnie's slacks and he lightly brushed it away.

'Daisy's got her club and I'm out of it,' Roy said. 'I made her a promise I'd leave the way clear for you and her ...' He sat back on the uncomfortable trunk. 'Only I got a feeling, a very strong feeling, that you've let 'er down. I ain't gonna be the one to tell 'er you an' your missus is getting all cosy again. I'm disappointed in you, Vinnie. I really thought you were more of a man than to leave poor Daisy 'anging around like a spare prick at a fuckin' wedding.'

Vinnie stared at him. The gangster's steel-grey eyes were boring into him. 'You want to give me information that'll clear up the mutilated girls' murders and in exchange I tell Daisy it's over between me and her?'

Vinnie already knew what his answer would be. How could it be otherwise?

'Got it in one, copper.'

He had to test Roy. 'It'll break her heart.'

'If you don't tell her, I'll break your fucking neck ...'

Vinnie gave a long drawn out sigh. 'I wasn't going to keep her hanging on a string. I'll pick a good time.'

'No! You'll do it sooner.'

'But what about Jamie?'

'For fuck's sake, Vinnie. I ain't gonna stop you seeing your lad, but Daisy deserves a bit of honesty from you.'

Roy Kemp's tone held malice. He was the only

bloke Vinnie knew who could threaten with a soft voice.

'You'll do what I want, Vinnie, because what I got's worth a lot to you. I want you in Gosport next week …'

'He wants you to what?'

'You got cloth ears or somethin', Vera?' Without waiting for an answer Daisy threw her head forward and bending at the waist began to brush her hair vigorously. Through the fall of her hair she saw Vera's red fluffy high-heeled mules plant themselves in front of her. After a while she stopped brushing and her eyes followed Vera's black-nyloned legs, up past her black silk dressing gown to her disbelieving pansticked face. Daisy stood eye to eye with Vera and shook her hair so that it settled into its fringed bob.

'You ain't goin'?'

'Don't look so surprised, Vera. He's sendin' a car. Him and me are meeting two of the three blokes I met in Kenya.' Daisy lifted the blonde hairs from her brush, and deposited them in the rubbish bin attached by a string to the inside of the kitchen cupboard door beneath the sink.

'What they want over 'ere?'

'Roy's done a drugs deal with them an' they're buying kinky films off 'im.'

Vera sniffed disapprovingly. 'He's kept that close to 'is chest. I didn't know he was into porno.'

Daisy turned towards Vera. 'Neither did he until

Charles told 'im. It was one of them new directions Charles an' his mother set up while he was in Parkhurst.'

'How does 'e feel about that?' Vera sat down heavily on the bench at the scrubbed table. Daisy could see the swathe of grey at her roots. For once her eyelashes were absent and, apart from the tan panstick, making her look as though she'd been on an exotic beach holiday, her face was devoid of make-up.

'It's money, Vera. What's not good for him to feel about making money?'

'At least you know where you stand with Roy.'

'What's that supposed to mean?' Daisy pulled out a chair and sat opposite her.

'Ever since you two 'ave known each other, he's looked out for you, an' whatever big show he puts on in public, he always comes back to you – even if he does exploit you.'

Daisy said, 'I don't want no bleedin' bloke to always *come back* to me. I want a man I can look up to. I don't care what side of the law he's on as long as he's kind to me an' mine and loves me.'

Vera got up, holding the small of her back as though it pained her, and moved towards the kettle, turning and nodding to Daisy as a way of asking if she fancied a cuppa.

'Yes, please,' Daisy said, then, 'What d'you mean, he exploits me?'

There was a smug look on Vera's face.

'He took you away so it would look good for 'im

and to curry favour with them blokes. Am I right or am I right?'

'Don't you say another word, Vera, just fuckin' don't!'

'See? I'm right. I don't blame 'im though, because he wouldn't let any 'arm come to you.' Vera plugged in the kettle. 'I'll tell you what won me over again with him: the way he was with Michael at the party. You know he's been out to the prefab several times since then? An' he took the lad, on 'is own, mind, to the funfair at Clarence Pier in Southsea. That kiddie 'ad a whale of a time.'

'I didn't know that, Vera.' It pleased Daisy no end that at last Roy had taken to his son. She watched as Vera reached up into a cupboard and took down a packet of Bourbon biscuits. She could just fancy a bit of chocolate. 'I did think the day of the party there was hope that Roy'd accept him.'

'I think he 'as, Dais. Your Roy don't ever do anything he don't mean, an' I reckon he had a lot of time inside to think about his boy. That overture is the first of many, mark my words.'

Daisy nodded. Vera had put the biscuits on the table and Daisy was busy tearing off the packaging. She felt Vera's eyes boring into her. 'You don't reckon I should go tonight, do you?'

'How d'you make that out?'

'The way when you ain't talking your mouth is all screwed up like a cat's arse!'

'Fuckin' sure you shouldn't go. I thought you was against drugs an' all that?'

'You know I am, but the drugs deal's done an' dusted. This is mucky films. You of all people should realise sex is only business. I know what I'm doing.'

Vera pulled out a kitchen chair, which scraped on the parquet flooring, and sat herself down again. Daisy sighed. Vera was about to give her a lecture.

'Hasn't it occurred to you 'e could be usin' you again?'

'We all use each other, Vera.' The words were said too quickly. 'But since me an' you got sole control of the club now, how *can* he use me? All I'm doin' is 'avin' an evenin' off to meet a couple of African blokes whose wives I got on famously with. Anyway, you know I'll be safe with Roy, which is the real reason he wants me with 'im tonight. I don't think watchin' a few mucky films is goin' to corrupt me, do you? Look on it as one last favour I'm doin' to show me an' 'im is solid, so he can do future business with his new friends. Vinnie's comin' to pick me up, Roy said. I really do believe he meant it that I could 'ave my Vinnie as well as the club.'

Vera stared deep into Daisy's eyes. So deep that Daisy gave an involuntary shiver. She tried changing the subject.

'You sorted out anythin' for Angel yet? I'll be honest with you, she's like a wet blanket, forever sniffing, and as for 'aving a decent conversation with her, well it's like she's got bleedin' ants crawlin' all over 'er the way she twitches.'

Vera gave a huge sigh. The kettle was boiling so she got up and started clattering mugs about. 'She's startin' a programme. Doc Dillinger's still got mates an' she's jumped the queue for St James' Hospital.'

'Thank Christ for that. She can't dance properly. She's so highly strung all the time it's gettin' on my nerves. I told 'er she can take a bit of time off an' we'll pay 'er. Now she's not goin' up to London, fuck knows where she's getting 'old of the stuff though.'

'We done our best so far, Dais. Can't do no more'n that. What about all this government stuff? Did you 'ave a word with Roy?'

'Put it like this, Vera, he laughed like a drain an' said they was all at it! He said he'd chatted with the 'ome secretary, some bloke called Carr, who reckoned it wasn't a bleedin' crime for any of 'em to 'ave mistresses an' there ain't no real proof about the drugs as yet. But I think Roy's as keen as Angel for the wraps to be kept on this story for young Michael's sake. I know he'll do what he can, pulling in a few favours 'ere an' there.'

Vera shook her head. 'That's if he stays out of prison long enough. Just supposin' Roy's out of the picture again. Who's going to look after his business?'

'His mother and Charles.'

'Grow up, Dais. They don't want it any more, you knows that. Now Violet's married, 'er and Charles wants to fuck off to be on their own to – where is it?

313

– Bognor Regis or some place, where they can join all the other old codgers sitting in the rain in them shelters drinking tea out of flasks and eating chips. You knows Violet don't want no more dealings with Roy's firm. She wants to take it easy.'

Vera had hit the nail on the head. Violet did want out of the business. but rather than let her friend have the upper hand Daisy said, 'That's just your suspicious mind. Anyway, who says Roy'll go back inside?'

Vera was stirring the tea in the pot. 'I bet the Kray brothers thought the same thing until almost all of their so-called friends squealed on them when the time came. You can't bank on Roy stayin' out of clink, Dais.'

After a while Daisy said, 'He won't go back inside.' But Vera had planted a seed of doubt. 'Look, you silly ol' tart. He confessed the reason he took me to Africa was to show the Kenyans he had a sort of family business. Anyway, I already tol' you all of this …'

There was a knowing grin on Vera's face that Daisy wanted to smack right off.

'You think it's possible he might be grooming me?' Now she'd put Vera's thoughts into words, she didn't like the sound of them.

'You reckon these Kenyans would do business with just anyone if Roy wasn't there?' Vera smoothed the knitted tea cosy down on the tea pot.

Daisy shook her head. 'Not likely. This ain't just a tinpot operation.'

'Well, you think about it. Roy can't trade from

inside, not with his mum and Charles out of the way, so you'll be next in line to take over. Especially as his contacts know you ain't just a pretty face.'

'He couldn't make me do anythin' I didn't want to do.'

'You sure of that? An' why's he inviting a bleedin' detective to a showin' of mucky films?'

'I don't know, do I? Why are you bein' so nasty? Why don't you just pour out that bleedin' tea before I eat all these sodding biscuits?' She looked at the ravaged packet and the crumbs scattered on the table.

'Because whatever 'appens to you, Daisy, if it hurts you, it hurts me.' Vera plonked a mug of tea down in front of her. Daisy held on to her hand, feeling its warmth. Touched by Vera's words she smiled up at her. Vera shook her hand away and in a gruff voice asked, 'What time is Roy sending a car for you?'

'Nine. Vinnie's showing up just before.'

'You got plenty of time then to think about what I've said. Where you goin'? I 'ope it ain't Daisychains.'

'Steady up, Vera. There's a pub called the Alma. It's at the bottom of Alma Street along Forton Road, opposite Hutfield's Garage and not far from the Criterion cinema.'

Vera had been looking perplexed but Daisy knew as soon as she mentioned the picture palace that Vera would get her bearings, and now she nodded knowingly.

'The owner of the pub has turned over the big meetin' room upstairs to Roy.'

Vera sat down on the bench again. 'Last time I saw Vinnie in Gosport he was lookin' like a lost sheep with a right moody expression on 'is mush.'

'Roy reckoned his new friends might be impressed to see a detective there,' said Daisy. 'It would show Roy had the police in his pocket. He'd tell 'em Vinnie an' 'im 'ad history together.'

Vera laughed, showing her small white teeth. 'Yeah, that 'istory is you.'

'I'll ignore your bleedin' sarcasm. Anyway, it's a way of seein' Vinnie. I expect he's up to 'is neck in work.'

'If you say so, missy. I'm surprised that either of them likes the thought of you sitting an' watching mucky films though.'

'Don't be so daft, Vera. It really ain't nothin' but pretend, is it? An' Roy says if I'm with 'im tonight no one's likely to harm me while he's doin' the deal.' She picked up her mug of tea and drank it back. She could see Vera wasn't listening, she'd caught sight of Kibbles sitting on the window box outside the kitchen window. Daisy had planted yellow pansies to last through the autumn and Kibbles had flattened them. She was just about to say something but Vera beat her to it by going to the window and letting him in. Daisy watched his four paws trample the blooms.

Vera cooed, 'My boy, where you been since tea time?'

'One of these bleedin' days that cat's gonna answer you back and you'll get the fright of your life.'

*

'I didn't expect you to get here so early, Vinnie.' Daisy threw herself at him as soon as he stepped into the hall, taking deep breaths of his pine-scented cologne, mixed with the smells of coal tar soap and minty toothpaste. He managed to hold her in a sort of one-armed embrace while he laid two parcels on the hall table. Her eyes took in his flowered shirt with long pointy collar tips and a pair of flared trousers topped by a leather bomber jacket. He looked quite comfortable out of his usual blue shirt and suit that was police issue.

She put her face up to be kissed, closing her eyes and expecting him to nuzzle into her, but he pecked her cheek lightly. They so needed to spend more time together, to talk, to get back into their warm, loving relationship, she thought. She stepped back, her eyes meeting his.

'Can you stay tonight?'

'I can't, I'm on early turns.' Daisy saw what she wanted to see, an honesty that intimate knowledge of him had brought her. She pushed her disappointment out of sight. She knew the one thing all men hated was a woman who went on and on about needing to be loved. Nagging was the word that sprang to mind.

'Fair enough,' she said. For a moment Daisy felt awkward, even embarrassed. Then she asked, 'You want to peep in on Jamie?'

He'd hardly had time to reply before she watched him take the stairs two at a time. She was glad she'd left the hall light on for it meant that he wouldn't wake Jamie as he pushed open the bedroom door. He'd look in on Eddie as well. She liked it that he never showed any favouritism with her boys. Her eyes flew towards the two packages he'd left on the hall table. She knew they'd contain presents for the boys and they'd be chuffed to bits in the morning when they opened them.

Vinnie always seemed to have a knack of buying the right kind of toys. But then, she thought, he had plenty of practice with his Jack. How old was Jack now? About her Eddie's age, wasn't he? No, he was a couple of years older, which made him around eleven, twelve or so.

Vinnie came down the stairs with a smile on his face.

'Two peaceful boys,' he said. 'You're doin' a grand job, Daisy.' Then, 'Someone's splashing about in the bathroom.'

'Vera. She's dying her roots. Though why she can't properly wash off the dye in the sink after she's finished I don't know. She uses the shower for that then she 'as a bleedin' bath. The whole bathroom looks like a bloody bomb 'as 'it it. I told her I ain't cleanin' it up, not tonight I'm not. She'll 'ave to sort it out 'erself in the morning. Our Vera is as clean as freshly fallen snow but by God she can make a mess when she wants!'

He smiled. 'Where's Suze and the baby?'

'Nosy, aren't you? Oh, I forgot, you're a bloody copper.' She laughed at her own joke. 'Suze has gone down to visit Si's sisters at Queen's Road and she's stayin' overnight. That's one of the perks about hiring a manager for Daisychains, no need for us both to be down there all the time. It's Vera what's stayin' in with the boys tonight.'

It seemed as though he was digesting the information. Then his beautiful different-coloured eyes seemed to twinkle at her and he said, 'Did I tell you you look nice?'

'Thank you.' Daisy knew she was going red. She never could take a compliment. She'd taken care with her make-up and was wearing a simple long-sleeved black wool dress. Her only jewellery was the gold bangle.

To hide her embarrassment she walked over to the newly acquired television set and switched it off. The signature music to *Coronation Street* died. Vera loved the programme. She said Elsie Tanner reminded her of herself. Daisy couldn't see it but she wasn't going to argue with Vera.

'Not much of an outing for you an' me, a scruffy pub.' She was thinking of the luxurious home she and Roy had been invited to in Nyali.

'Makes sense, Daisy.' Vinnie sat down on one of the kitchen chairs, his long legs stretched out in front of him. 'Roy can't go anywhere without everyone knowing who he is. That's the price of having a known face.'

'I suppose so,' she said, looking around the room for her clutch bag.

'I gather it's a business merger of some kind? Drugs for him, films for them?'

Daisy bristled. She knew it was just Vinnie's way but he always asked searching questions. 'I don't really know and I don't much care. At least with 'im out of Daisychains, you and me can breathe more easily. We might even get to spend a bit more time together.'

'True.' Daisy thought his answer could have had a bit more enthusiasm to it.

'What did Roy tell you about why he wanted you to be there, Daisy? At the pub tonight, I mean?'

She sighed. She didn't want to tell him she was looking forward to chatting to the Africans and sending her love back to their wives, to Adam in particular. 'Because it looks better for 'im an' it's safer for me. The Kenyans treated me well in Mombasa. Besides, it's no skin off my nose to 'elp him out. Especially now I got the papers to prove Daisychains belongs to me an' Vera. Anyway, why are *you* coming?'

'Why wouldn't I, Daisy?' Frown lines suddenly appeared in his forehead and he asked, 'By the way, do you know anything about money-lending?'

Daisy couldn't lie to save her life. 'One of our girls 'ad got herself into trouble with a door-to-door salesman and now she's run off.'

She saw she now had Vinnie's full attention. He'd probably be tapping Roy for information. Her heart took a dive. She'd hoped he'd come tonight just to be with her. She remembered the photographs in the safe at Daisychains that Leah had asked her and Vera to look after. A shiver ran through her. Did they have any bearing on Leah's disappearance? And if she gave them to Vinnie, would he think Roy had anything to do with whatever was going on?

She suddenly felt fiercely protective of the gangster. Daisy snatched her handbag off the bread bin where she'd left it earlier. 'Money-lendin' ain't nothin' to do with Roy.'

'To be honest, Daisy, you don't know what Roy's taken on lately. But, like you, I'm pretty certain he isn't involved. Though I might take you up on your offer to come back here afterwards. Why haven't you talked to me about this missing girl before?' He ran his hands through his curly hair.

So, she thought, he couldn't find the time to stay the night with *her* but he might come back to talk to Vera about some scam. She had only one answer to that, didn't she?

'Because I *never* bloody sees you, do I?'

She expected him to come back at her with a smart reply. Instead he was looking at her with a sad expression on his face.

Sudden fear surrounded Daisy's heart. She asked quickly, 'What is it? What's the matter?'

Vinnie gave a huge sigh that seemed to take all the air from his body.

'We can't go on like this, Daisy. Pretending everything's all right when we both know it's not.'

Daisy felt as though she was rooted to the spot.

'What are you sayin' … ?'

'I'm saying I'm weak. I couldn't go on waiting around any longer for you to love me.'

'I do ...' Daisy couldn't get her words out because he'd placed his fingers across her mouth. Her heart was hammering against her chest nineteen to the dozen.

'No. You don't love me. You *needed* me. Eddie Lane rules your heart and always will. He's dead an' you won't let 'im lie down, Daisy.'

Daisy pulled his hand away from her face.

'You knew ...' Then she stopped talking and stared at him. How could she have been so blind? This wasn't about *her*. It was about *him*.

'You've been sleepin' with Clare, 'aven't you?'

But she didn't need for him to answer her, she could see it in his eyes. That 'it wasn't my fault', little-boy look.

'She *is* my wife ...'

'An' I got your little boy ...'

He took a step towards her and held out his arms.

'Don't touch me. I need to think.' She turned and walked from the hallway into the kitchen and sat down heavily on the bench. Then she put her elbows on the table and rested her head in her hands.

Did she want to scream at him? Did she want to beg him to stay with her? The answer was no – to both those questions. She thought of his words. Yes, she *would* always love Eddie Lane. But in her heart there would always be a place for him, Vinnie Endersby. But the bastard had been right all the time. *She didn't love him.* Maybe she never had.

She could sense his presence at her side.

'Daisy … I …'

'Jamie'll be all right with me, you know,' she said, looking up at him, not letting him finish his sentence. Vinnie looked as though the end of the world had come and suddenly Daisy wanted to laugh. But she treated him to only the tiniest of smiles. In all fairness, she'd not thought about Vinnie at all when she'd tumbled into bed with Roy. Her heart wasn't broken by Vinnie's revelations, it was her pride that was dented. And that blasted Vera had been right all the time! 'What I mean is, you can see 'im whenever you wants,' she said.

His face broke into a smile that split his face from ear to ear.

Briefly she wondered if she should tell him about sleeping with Roy in Mombasa, but quickly decided against it. Scoring points off each other wasn't the right way to end a relationship.

Daisy stood up. She was standing very close to him, this man she'd borne a child with. Jamie would be the link between them, always. Daisy could feel his nearness, smell the maleness of him. It was right he should go back to the woman he really loved. She put her arms around his neck and laid her head on his chest.

'I did try,' she said.

Vinnie bent his head down and kissed the top of her head.

'We both did, Dais. We both did.'

The silence that followed was broken by the letter box rattling.

'That could be the car to take us to the Alma,' she said.

CHAPTER 25

Daisy had always liked the Alma. It was a friendly little place, full of regulars playing dominoes and darts and drinking pints rather than cocktails. Not that she and Vinny were shown through the main bar. No, the driver of the black Mercedes pushed open the side door then left them to climb the uncarpeted stairs. Up above it was reasonably quiet, with muted music drifting up from the jukebox below.

To Daisy's surprise, Roy was already sitting at a table on which were two half-drunk pints of beer, one presumably for the man behind the projector, a scruffy-looking individual Daisy hadn't seen before, and the other for Jem. Roy had his usual glass of brandy but she could see he'd hardly touched it. There were two glasses of orange juice next to the brandy. These drinks belonged, Daisy supposed, to the African guests, who sat stiff-backed on the upright chairs. Daisy beamed towards Paul, who smiled a greeting back at her and said, 'Hujambo, Daisy.'

'We've been waiting for you two. Today I've been giving my friends here' – Roy waved towards the two expensively suited men – 'a tour of some of my south coast enterprises.' He looked pleased with himself as he came towards her and put his arms around her, kissing her on the cheek. The two Kenyans seemed to like that, she thought. Roy introduced Vinnie to them and Daisy was amused to see them pumping Vinnie's arm like he was a long-lost relative. She marvelled at how enthusiastically he responded.

'Jem, please go down and get drinks for Daisy and Vinnie.' Jem nodded at Roy and put his knife away in his inside pocket. He'd been casually leaning against the wall playing with it. 'I asked for sandwiches as well, but nothing too heavy as we're going on to Poppy's later.' Roy mentioned one of his Southsea clubs that served excellent food.

Daisy had to admit Roy looked tasty tonight. His hair was curling on to his jacket collar and he wore a sober-coloured suit like the Kenyans.

Momentarily she was reminded of how it had been when their affair had just begun. The quick glances, the intimate smiles, the way her heart had fluttered when he'd entered a room. And then she thought of the scenes with Vinnie before they'd left for the Alma and was proud of the way they'd both been civilised about ending their relationship – although the 'end' hadn't really sunk in yet. Daisy knew she'd cry when she was alone later. It was a shame you couldn't turn your feelings about men on and off like a tap, she thought. Life would be much more simple that way.

She wondered when the rot had really set in

between her and Roy. Was it really just his affair with Angel? Or was it when she couldn't bear him to touch her after Valentine Waite had kept her locked up and had abused her? After that she'd not only lost interest in Roy but in herself as well. Or was it when Roy had flatly refused to have anything to do with his son? Daisy couldn't even bring herself to understand his feelings on that score, since it wasn't the kiddie's fault he was a Thalidomide child. Happily, though, Roy now seemed to be on a path towards accepting Michael.

So was that how all relationships progressed, that gradual pulling away from each other until nothing remained?

Could she really let her relationship with Roy disintegrate?

The answer to that was quite simple: she didn't want him controlling her but she didn't want him out of her life.

Her thoughts were interrupted as the door opened and Jem returned with a tray of drinks and a huge pile of sandwiches, topped by another plate. He set the tray on the table and Daisy picked up the glass of brandy and lime that she guessed was her drink.

'Thanks,' she whispered to him, and asked, 'How you coping with the little one? Katie?'

'Not too well,' Jem said. 'I've got my sister looking after her at the moment. Old Nan can't do any more than her best and the travelling folk are down near Eastleigh. It's for the best 'til I get meself sorted out and my wife comes home again.'

Daisy wished she hadn't asked. Jem seemed to have caved in on himself. And no wonder, thought Daisy, he loved the very bones of Leah. She went over to Roy and asked, 'What's it to be then? *Gone with the Wind* and ice creams during the interval?'

He glared at her. 'If we're all ready,' he announced, but the general chit-chat didn't die away.

Roy waved towards the rear of the room where the scruffy man leaned at the side of the tall projector. At the opposite end of the room where Daisy stood a large silver screen hung on the wall. Below it, lying on the floor, was its packaging, a long metal tube. The man at the projector, Daisy noticed, wasn't joining in with the chatting. Then Roy said, 'No, *Gone with the Wind*'s too long. That bloke Pullinger, running the projector, makes much shorter films. He'll also be making a packet for his bosses if my friends like what they see tonight. You can choose the film.'

Daisy eyed the boxes of spool cans.

'I'm not really an authority on mucky films.'

'You'll have to close your eyes, then, instead of watching. My friends will want to know they're getting their money's worth.'

'And if the goods are up to scratch you'll get your goods?' Roy nodded.

'I suppose it's no good me askin' how you'll get all this stuff shifted abroad?'

'You don't need to know, Daisy. Goods in, goods out, it's not your problem.'

She shrugged. 'You are so right. It's not my

problem, but …' She whispered low so that no one else could possibly hear. 'If you're tryin' to screw me over, Roy Kemp, I'll bleedin' swing for you.'

His eyes opened wide. She'd remembered Vera's words of warning but the look on his face told her he had no idea what she was talking about. Or maybe he was just too clever for her? She shrugged off his arm and went over to the box of films and knelt down staring at the titles. 'Lost Virgins', 'Bare Cheek', 'Done to a Turn', 'Red's Glory'. Daisy tipped back the brandy and swallowed, leaving her glass on the floor beside the box. Randomly she picked a film and took it back to Roy. Did these films always have to have such crappy titles, she wondered. She handed the cold canister to Roy.

'This one,' she said. He didn't even glance at the title but took it to the back of the room and handed it to the man called Pullinger then returned to her side. Daisy was well aware of his cologne, male and musky. She sat down on a nearby chair.

Pullinger opened the canister and began carefully setting the spool. When it was done he called, 'I'm ready when you are.' Daisy shivered; there was something about the bloke that gave her the creeps.

Jem turned down the lights, the projector whirred into life and the film began.

Daisy was struck dumb by what she saw. She watched the screen couple fuck tirelessly from every conceivable angle and orifice until she got bored. Jesus Christ, she thought, in and out, grunt and groan, what's so special about watching? Surely it must be much better to be *doing* it. Perhaps she'd hit the nail on the head there. Some men *couldn't* do it. Some men had no hope of ever loving a woman. This wasn't love though, was it? It was only sex. But she knew there was all kinds of sex. And thank God for that, else she and Vera would have been out of business a long time ago.

She studied the couple's faces and neither seemed to be really enjoying it. They pretended they were having a wonderful time but it was all so false. She knew couples watched films like these to get themselves in the mood for lovemaking. She shuddered. Surely a woman, or a bloke come to that, must wonder if their partner was imagining having sex with the person they'd just seen on the screen? Daisy reckoned the day she'd have to resort to watching mucky films to fancy the bloke she was supposed to be having sex with, she shouldn't be having sex with him at all!

But men and women, not only in England, but in other countries too, would buy these films and it was simply a business to Roy.

In turn she studied the men's faces in the room. Their eyes seemed glued to the screen, all but two men. Roy was watching her. She shrugged her shoulders and raised her eyes heavenwards, and as she did so, she caught Vinnie staring at Roy.

Men were so transparent, she thought. The others were totally involved in the writhings of the big-breasted blonde and the enormously endowed bloke on the screen. Then she smiled to herself. She wished Vera was here. She'd have a right laugh.

Eventually the film ended.

Again it was alcohol all round, except for the guests who asked for water, and after some discussion it was agreed another film should be shown.

Daisy again chose the film, this time 'Soldier's Revenge', and settled down for another boring time.

A whirring sound announced the film's start. No titles or credits.

It started with a woman sitting on a bed. She had her back to the camera. Her blonde hair tumbled down her back. Daisy thought it was quite obviously a wig which stopped short at her perfectly rounded buttocks. The woman rose, bending forward, and the camera zoomed in on her arse and fanny. Daisy saw her wrists and ankles were tied. She could move but not away from the bed. Then the camera panned to the doorway to a blond man wearing what looked like an officer's uniform, except without trousers. Instead, he wore a wide belt which held a whip and a curved knife. His erect prick was as big as the long knife.

Daisy looked around the room. All eyes were on the flickering screen. She suddenly began to feel quite ill at ease and left her seat without, she hoped, disturbing the men's views.

When she reached Roy's side she whispered, 'In the space of an hour I've seen more tits and fannies than I've ever seen down the club.'

'Sshh!' he whispered back to her.

'I bet Vera's seen bigger pricks than that,' Daisy said. 'Does this turn you on?'

Roy looked away from the screen, smiled and said, 'No, I like skinny blondes with big green eyes and an annoying habit of not keeping their gobs shut when I'm trying to sell goods I ain't never set eyes on before. I also like to keep that skinny blonde where I can keep an eye on her.'

'Oh.'

She sat down again and watched the screen. She actually thought it was quite clever how the girl was screaming and screaming, but it was her arse and fanny with the knotted leather whip slicing into her skin that was filling the screen. In fact the blood from the whiplashes looked quite real, she decided. The man threw aside the whip and was now scoring deep lines with the knife on her flesh that quickly filled with blood. The man then draped himself across her bloodied back and began fucking the girl up the arse while she spoke dirty to him.

Daisy watched the two Kenyans talking quietly together.

She whispered to Roy, 'What d'you think?'

'They're biting,' he said. 'Go and get another film before this one finishes.'

'Do I 'ave to? These don't do nothin' for me,' she said.

One look at his frowning face and she went back to the box of films.

The two men had paused in their conversation.

Paul stared at Roy and nodded. Daisy thought she'd be glad when tonight was over. Vinnie was looking at her strangely, and she would have felt happier if he didn't seem so glum. After all, he'd got her say-so to go back with his wife, hadn't he?

She delved into the box and picked out another canister, 'Red's Glory'. The smell of cigar and cigarette smoke hung in the air. Daisy gave the film to Roy, who passed it to the projectionist.

While the bloke was setting up the machine, Daisy whispered to Jem who was now standing next to her, 'I'm fed up with all this.' Roy came back and slipped a hand on her shoulder. She could feel the heat of him through her woollen dress.

Again the print was grainy. All six men seemed enthralled by the action, which began with two women on a bed. One was in her thirties, guessed Daisy, the other with magnificent hair was lying with her back to the camera. On screen a man entered the room.

Daisy felt Jem's body stiffen beside her. She herself gave an intake of breath as she watched the long-haired woman pretending to enjoy sex with the older woman, and then with the man, who was wearing a zippered mask.

It seemed as though Daisy's heart had stopped beating and her mouth went suddenly dry. She *knew* this woman! Jem was staring at the screen, unable to take his eyes from the degrading scenes. Daisy opened her mouth to speak but only a strangled sort of sound emerged. She poked her elbow into Roy's side and as he looked down, his forehead was creased as though he was wondering what the hell was the matter with her. Jem had begun stepping from one foot to the other. He was breathing fast. Daisy looked away and sought Vinnie's face across the room. He was watching both her and Jem. She could tell Vinnie knew something was very wrong.

Only the whirring sound of the projector broke the silence.

Daisy sensed Jem's pain as he watched the woman being first manhandled, fucked, then grabbed by her hair. She was obviously taken aback by what was happening to her. No one could be this good an actress, thought Daisy.

Now there was real fear on the woman's face as she realised her breast had been cut. The men in the room gasped but were unable to tear their eyes from the screen.

The back of Daisy's neck was damp with cold fear. Surely this unspeakable filmed action couldn't be real?

But Daisy knew it was.

She watched the projectionist's face. He actually seemed pleased by the reactions from the men in the room. Daisy wasn't sure whether she felt more sick looking at him or at the woman being gutted on film.

Roy's face had gone white. Even in the semi-darkness she could see that for a man who rarely betrayed emotion to outsiders, he was disturbed.

The camera had caught every moment of the woman's slow and bloody death.

From downstairs Nilsson's 'Without You' floated up from the jukebox. It was the only sound in the room now that the projector had finished running. The small audience sat motionless.

Daisy looked at Jem. His eyes glittered with tears and the pain scored his face. He began fumbling in his inside pocket.

A low growl seemed to grow and erupt from his throat as he roughly pushed Daisy aside and lunged towards Roy, his knife in his hand.

'Bastard, fucking bastard!'

Daisy fell to the floor. The silence in the room turned into an uproar. She scrambled aside, pulling herself to the relative safety of the wall, and heard the projector tumble over on the wooden floor. Vinnie ran towards her and the two struggling men. The glint of the knife made her turn towards the three men wrestling for possession of the weapon. The box containing the canisters of film was kicked over and the cans clattered and rolled about the wooden floor.

A movement, a slamming of the door, told Daisy that the projectionist, Pullinger, had slipped from the room and was running down the stairs, his shoes echoing on the bare boards. The Kenyans were huddled together, their faces immobile.

Everything seemed to happen so fast. And all the while the three men were struggling, oaths and shouts adding to the confusion.

And then through the gloom she saw Roy had managed to disentangle himself and with the aid of a chair, heave himself to his feet.

Daisy was hugging her knees, trembling, but when Roy moved so did she. And as she scrambled up she saw Vinnie roll away from the figure on the floor. Roy put out his hand and helped Vinnie to his feet.

Wordlessly Daisy flew across the room, her arms falling helplessly to her sides as she halted and looked down at the prone figure.

Then Paul switched on the electric light and the room was illuminated.

Daisy spoke first, her voice clear as a bell's chimes cutting through the sweat and metallic stench of blood pooling beneath Jem's body. 'He's dead, isn't he?'

Roy's suit was blood-spattered and creased, his hair a waving mass that he ran one hand through while using the other to gather her to him. 'Vinnie killed him to save my life,' he said. Daisy noticed his hands were shaking. So the bastard did get scared, did he? Her eyes locked on to his. Thank God he was all right, she thought.

Patches of blood covered Vinnie's dishevelled and torn clothing. He let the knife fall from his hand. It clattered to the floor at his feet. His eyes were still on the body.

'You have a problem,' said Paul in his precise English. Both Kenyans stepped forwards and surveyed the dead man. 'I don't think we want to be involved.'

Daisy said to Vinnie, 'Are you all right?' She could see he wasn't badly hurt, any more than Roy was.

He nodded. But his beautiful eyes looked like they were made of glass, washed by the sea, totally lifeless.

Daisy thought quickly. It made good sense to get out of here fast, before the owner of the place came up to see what all the noise was about. If he caught a glimpse of the man on the floor …

'Give me your car keys an' where *is* the fuckin' thing?'

Roy reacted immediately, taking them from his pocket, and without even questioning her intentions said, 'Top of Alma Street.'

'Did you know Leah was goin' to be killed in that film?' Daisy's voice was soft and cold. It mattered very much to her that Roy *didn't* know.

'I swear I didn't.'

And Daisy knew he was telling the truth.

She turned and walked towards the Kenyans. Daisy had never felt more clear-headed or in control.

'You two, you got all your belongings?'

Paul and his partner nodded.

'Come with me. You'll be safe, I promise. These two will clear things up.' She turned towards Roy. It was as if that special bond between them needed no words.

She could trust him to get rid of the body without ruining Vinnie's police career. Getting rid of people was second nature to Roy.

And Vinnie? He'd just killed a man. But in his

career it probably wasn't the first time nor was it likely to be the last.

She sprang into action.

'C'mon!' she said. The two Kenyans followed her down the stairs, through the door and out on to Alma Street. 'This way.' She led them briskly past the terraced houses that ended in a clearing at the top of the street where cars were parked.

The night had a chill to it and the sky was threaded with stars. Daisy saw the bulk of the huge new Rolls Royce Silver Shadow. She thought lovingly of her tiny MG as she unlocked the door. It's a bloody big bastard you got to drive here, Dais, she told herself.

'Don't worry about tonight,' she said, with a calm she didn't know she had. 'It was just a hiccup. Roy'll fix it. Get inside.'

'I don't understand why the man went berserk,' said Paul, when he was settled in the vast expanse of the back seat. Daisy wasn't about to tell him the reason.

Daisy turned the engine over. Her mouth had gone dry. She carefully reversed so she could turn the monster then drive down Alma Street, past the pub where nothing looked out of place at all.

Despite concentrating on her driving she decided the most important job for her was to keep these men happy. If this deal didn't go through perhaps Roy might come back at her with some claim on the club, and she'd have no security for Jamie's future. And that was what she wanted above all – both her boys to have money behind them when they came of age.

Daisy felt the strength of the engine beneath her hands. She wished she'd had the sense to alter the driver's seat as her legs had to stretch full out to reach the pedals. Damn that bloody lanky Roy Kemp, she thought. But she was doing fine and the beast didn't rattle like her little car.

She took a deep breath of the interior's leather, feeling happier now she had everything under control.

'We're goin' to my house. I met your family so now you can meet mine. I'll introduce you to my mate Vera, you'll like her. I reckon we could all do with a cup of tea.'

CHAPTER 26

Roy looked down at Jem's body.

'I suppose I ought to thank you,' he said. 'I ain't gonna ask you why you saved my bacon. I don't suppose you know yourself why you did it.'

Vinnie took a deep breath and blew the air out slowly. 'You can owe me one, you fucker.'

Roy shrugged. 'You go down an' have a word with the landlord. Spin him a yarn and grease his palm.' He took out his wallet and without counting peeled off some notes and handed them to Vinnie. 'If he don't see or hear anything he can't say nothing, can he?'

Roy watched him disappear and heard his footsteps descend the stairs. He went over to the curtains and pulled one off its wire. Back at the body he lifted it to a sitting position, took off Jem's bloodied coat and replaced it with his own suit jacket. He'd concealed the wound that had now stopped bleeding.

Using the liquid from the remaining beer glasses that hadn't been overturned, a jug of tap water and the curtain, he cleaned up the floorboards.

'Regular little Mary Jane cleaning maid, ain't you?'

Roy raised his head and looked at Vinnie who'd come into the room.

'Rule one, get rid of evidence.'

Vinnie handed him a large brandy which Roy drank back in one go, relishing first its aroma then its heat as it eased its way down his throat. He handed the empty glass back to Vinnie.

'He okay down there?'

Vinnie nodded. 'He ain't going to go against *you*, is he?'

'Rule two,' said Roy with a slight grin. 'If you ever call me Mary Jane again I'll spoil your good looks, copper. Rule three is to get rid of the body.'

'Any ideas?'

'Go an' call a taxi.'

'What for?'

'In case you've forgotten, mate, I gave my car keys to Daisy and I sent a car to pick you both up so we got no bleedin' transport.'

'So we're gettin' rid of a body by fucking taxi?!'

'That's right. We'll put 'im in the middle, walk him downstairs, an' tell the cab driver he's not well an' we're taking 'im 'ome.'

Roy could see Vinnie thought he'd gone mad.

'But he's *not* not well, he's fuckin' *dead*!'

'The cab driver won't know that.'

'I suppose you've got a nice grave all thought out.'

'Haven't I always? Without much in the way of identification on 'im, and if it's a fair while before 'is bones are found, I reckon we'll get away with it, don't you?'

Vinny sniffed. 'So when his body comes to light there's a fair betting I'll be heading up the team to find the murder victim's killer – which is me.'

'Well,' said Roy, 'If you ain't clever enough to work out something to get yourself off the bleedin' 'ook by that time, you ain't the detective I thought you were.'

Vinnie gave him a look that would wither fresh flowers before turning on his heels and going downstairs again.

Using Jem's coat, Roy put a bit of a polish on the floorboards, then started gathering up the broken glass. He looked at Jem, lying there peaceful, like he was asleep.

'I'm so sorry, pal,' he said. 'I never expected this to happen. I 'ad no idea about your missus. You was a fucking good mate to me inside.' He felt a lump rise in his throat. He tried to swallow it away as Vinnie returned.

Vinnie went straight over to the canisters in the boxes.

'I don't even know if the missing girls and that kiddie are in those films.'

'How many dead girls d'you want, for Christ's sake? That was Jem's wife on that fucking screen an' before you ask I swear on my mother's life I didn't know she'd been killed. Missing, yes. I'd never set eyes on the bint.'

'Is that why Jem went for you? He thought *you'd* had his missus killed?'

'It's the only reason I can come up with, Vinnie. This ain't no tinpot operation. The fucking Maxi brothers headed up by Gaetano Maxi moved in on my manor while I was inside. It wasn't until I got out I discovered those fuckin' Eyeties financed these films with *my* money, what they creamed off my clubs, and my wonderful father-in-law Charles made a deal to buy them! That's really takin' the piss, that is!'

'So you're into buying porno and snuff movies?'

'That bugger Charles reckoned I would be.' Roy gave a sigh that seemed to rock his body. 'I gotta get 'im put out to grass before he ruins me.'

'You'd kill your own granny for money, you bastard.'

'I'm into drugs, they're the universal currency, you sad copper, not killing young girls or bleedin' grannies. And I really gotta hand it to Gaetano Maxi. Setting me up. He knew the Kenyans would buy off me but they wouldn't touch a gang they'd had no dealings with.'

'So that's why you got the Africans over here.'

'I had to go all the way else the brothers would've smelt a rat. The Kenyans wanted to see some of the stock *I* was buying as a middleman. I wanted you 'ere so when you recognised the girls in the films *you* could put the bastard Maxis away legitimately. Get the fuckers out of me 'air without me resorting to violence. I get my manor back to myself, you get the fucking murderers.'

'The police need to catch them first!'

'That little projectionist ain't got far. I had a couple of my blokes staked out round his gaff. He'll squeal like a stuck pig.' He stared hard at Vinnie. 'You said anything to Daisy yet? I didn't save her from coming to harm from Gaetano Maxi just for *you* to piss 'er about.'

'I still don't see why she had to sit through this shit.'

'She's safer by my side. I couldn't take the chance with me 'ere that the Maxis might have decided it was a good time to move in on 'er down the club or at her 'ome.'

'Thought of everything, didn't you?' Roy couldn't ignore the sarcasm in Vinnie's voice, but he didn't retaliate. Instead, he said quietly, 'I been too long away, Vinnie. Even you took advantage of my good nature.'

He saw Vinnie look away from him but he heard him say softly, 'She knows.'

'And?'

Vinnie turned and faced him. 'Don't make me spell it out. She knows about me and Clare. Leave it at that.'

Roy nodded, then looked around the room. Satisfied that between them they'd cleared away any sign of a fight, he went over to the projector and set it on its legs then looked towards the boxes of films.

'They're yours to use as evidence,' he said. 'But I'm confiscating one boxload.'

'Thought you only dealt in drugs?'

'These are a present for my African friends. What with making copies they'll be quids in. A nice little sweetener, I reckon. No doubt you'll discover many more films when you pick up the Maxis.' Roy heard footsteps on the stairs and Vinnie opened the door a few inches to hear what the pub owner wanted. The taxi had arrived.

'Let's get this poor bastard to his resting place,' said Roy, going over to Jem's body. 'Then you can proceed with your own investigations.'

Roy knocked loudly on Daisy's front door and when it was opened snapped, 'I 'ad to take a bloody taxi to get 'ere! And why is my car out on the road?'

Daisy shrugged, and stepped aside for Roy to enter the hallway of her home. He inhaled the comforting smell that family living exuded. Her eyes were very bright, so he knew she'd been crying. She was wearing her old off-white dressing gown, tied loosely around her middle.

What he didn't know was what to say to her. She'd shown she had guts all right in taking charge the way she had earlier. For Christ's sake, she'd just seen a bloke knifed. And one of her bar girls murdered on the screen. A lesser woman would have been a mass of shredded nerves.

She said without emotion, 'I couldn't back the

bloody thing in me driveway. Your car keys are on the kitchen table.' He followed her down the hall and into the kitchen. The pad of Daisy's bare feet on the parquet floor was music to his ears. She said, 'I didn't want you goin' on at me just because I might have scratched it!'

'You *haven't?*'

'No, I fuckin' 'aven't! An' where's your jacket?'

'Put to a better use, Daisy. Where is everyone?' He'd seen that the only body beside Daisy and himself was that bloody fat cat of Vera's, asleep on the bench. Without thinking he put out a hand and scratched it behind its ear. 'Hello, puss,' he said.

'They're out,' said Daisy, going over to the kettle. He watched as she plugged it in. 'My kids are asleep upstairs, so I get to mind 'em.'

She looked scrubbed and clean and the ends of her hair were wet. She was never as tough as she liked people to think she was. He knew this woman through and through and he'd give anything for her to care about him the way she once had. And he'd noticed that it was him she'd run to first in that room above the Alma, not that pretty boy of a copper. He went to her and put his hands on her shoulders. He could feel her warmth through the thick material.

'Are you all right?'

Green eyes stared back at him. Fuck it, he thought. Is that all I can say when I really want to scoop her up and hold her close? Her nerves must have gone through the shredder with her putting on that grand show of icy calm.

'I am now I've been left on me own an' 'ad a bit of a cry,' she said. 'I suppose you want to know where your men are?'

'I do, but I want to say how sorry I am that you had to be there and go through that … that fucking fiasco.'

'It wasn't a fiasco. It was a death, Roy.' Her voice trembled but she held his gaze. Even without a scrap of make-up and her face all shiny she looked wonderful to him.

'Yes, and if it hadn't been for Vinnie I'd 'ave been the dead man. I need you to believe me, I 'ad no idea that was Jem's wife up there on the screen. I'd never even set eyes on 'er before.'

'At first I couldn't believe you didn't know,' said Daisy, 'but I remembered in all the times I'd visited you in Parkhurst, I'd only ever caught a glimpse of Leah once meself. So it was 'ighly possible *you'd* never seen her at visiting times. An' I know cons don't go flashing pictures of their families about. Anyway, it was pretty obvious, or you'd 'ave turned the bleedin' projector off immediately. It must 'ave been a shock when Jem came at you like that.'

He led her to the pine bench, and for the next few minutes told her all he knew. She sat very still listening to his every word.

'I'd have done the same, Daisy, if it was my woman up there.' I bloody would an' all, he thought.

There was near silence in the room except for the sound of the clock ticking and the cat purring. He looked at Daisy sitting on the edge of her seat and he breathed in the clean soapy smell of her. She pulled her dressing gown across to cover her knees just as the kettle started singing. She made to move.

'Don't bother,' he said. 'If I don't know 'ow to make a pot of tea in your kitchen by now there must be something wrong.'

He rinsed out the teapot while the kettle boiled fast and furious, then he made the tea, thick and strong like Daisy preferred it.

'Did you know Vinnie was looking into the death of a woman and her child? Their bodies turned up in shallow graves in the New Forest. Another woman was found in Wickham Woods. He said some photographs have been going the rounds …'

'Blonde, was she? Baby about three months?'

'How d'you know that?' He turned, holding two mugs, and looked at her in surprise.

'There's photos in our safe down at Daisychains.'

Roy was motionless for a few moments. Then he put the mugs on the table and took the sterilised milk out of the fridge.

'Vinnie don't confide in me. Leastways, not nothin' to do with police business,' she said. 'For Leah it must have started some time ago. She told Vera and me she'd got into debt. When she couldn't pay, the photos were given to 'er as a warning.'

Roy searched in the cutlery drawer for spoons but

he was listening to every word. It seemed to him that in his absence at Her Majesty's pleasure there'd been a lot going on.

'The debt was pushed beyond 'er control ...'

'That's how it works, Dais. This bloke, local bastard, runs a mobile van with household goods and clothing. Low repayments. All very innocent at first, then the squeeze gets put on. It's a front for money-lending. The women are given the chance to pay off their so-called loans, first by appearing in mild porno flicks or photographs and then the stuff gets muckier. Took me a while to put two and two together, beginning with that nutcase who thought he was McVitie's son. I found out from Jem that he was in with the Maxis. Still, it'll be a feather in your detective's cap, nailing the fuckers behind this business.'

'I do believe you 'ad nothing to do with it, Roy. An' he ain't my detective no more.'

He heard her words and stared at her intently. His heart was soaring but it wouldn't do to let Daisy know how happy her words had made him.

'He'll always be your detective, Daisy. To me, at any rate.'

He fetched the teapot and the milk to the table. He knew she didn't take sugar and since being inside he'd given it up as well.

Daisy said, 'So it's possible Leah thought she was clearing her debt by appearing in those films?'

'She didn't tell Vera or you about them?'

'No! When Vera asked her if everything was all

right she said it was. An' you know Vera, she don't only ask the once.'

'That's the clever bit. These scumbags know fucking well the women wouldn't say a word. They'd be that ashamed, poor bitches.'

'D'you think she was aware she could be killed?'

He shook his head. 'Of course not. The women are shown photographs of dead women and kiddies to frighten them into submission, but after a while they doubt the authenticity of the pictures.'

'How much of this did Vinnie know?'

'Not as much as he does now. He only knew the films were coming from this area, but two snuff films were picked up in London, in Soho. Gaetano Maxi didn't want to sell the films in dribs and drabs, he wanted a big deal, and that's 'ow come Charles was approached when I was inside. I can't blame Charles. I don't blame him.'

Roy looked down at his soiled shirt and trousers. He sniffed, not liking Jem's blood on him. Thank Christ this was Gosport, he thought. On his way to Daisy's, the taxi bloke wasn't at all fazed by a dishevelled, blood-spattered man climbing inside his cab. Long ago he used to keep a spare change of clothes in Daisy's wardrobe, but knowing the feisty little bitch like he did, it was possible she'd chucked them out.

'Was it when the films was spotted in London that Vinnie was called in?' He nodded and began pouring out the tea.

An unreal silence filled the kitchen. He decided to ask her.

'You got any of my clothes upstairs?' Her face was uncomprehending. He explained, 'I'd like to clean myself up.'

'Vinnie kills a man an' you want to look smart?'

He gave a huge sigh. 'No, Daisy. I stink of me mate's blood. Vinnie saved my life. I'm in Vinnie's debt.' Another thread to bind him to the detective, he thought. 'I gave Vinnie what he needed to make the arrest of Pullinger and the Maxi brothers. They're probably bein' roped in now.'

'An' Jem's body?'

'We sorted it.'

'How?'

'You don't want to know, Daisy.' He saw her shiver. He wished he could let down his guard, then he'd be able to confide that Jem's death had hit him hard. And he was still smarting from the realisation that Jem could have thought for one moment he'd have anything to do with Leah's death. Daisy's voice took him out of his thoughts.

'Jem's got a kiddie ...'

'The child is as we speak being collected by Jem's sister. Don't worry, it's already been taken care of. They're travellers, fairground folk who've now acquired cash to buy a new ride. They're satisfied with what they've been told and the kiddie'll be loved. The sister's got no little ones of 'er own. I can't take away their grief or the fact that the little girl has lost her daddy but I've done what I think is best.'

He could see by the way she was nodding that she was satisfied with that.

'Will you be brought into it?' He was touched that she worried about him. He answered honestly.

'No. Neither will you. Tonight never happened. Well, not in the way it really did. Pullinger won't dare open his mouth about Vinnie topping Jem, and if he did, who's goin' to believe him?'

She nodded. 'An' Leah's body?'

He sighed. 'Vinnie'll find it – eventually – and others.'

She took a long pull on her tea, put down the cup and asked, 'What do you get out of all this? You don't ever do anythin' for nothing.'

That was more like his Daisy, he thought. By Christ she was smart.

'Daisy, Daisy. How well you know me. I get four things out of tonight. My life. Your safety. My business.'

'And the snuff films?'

'They're big business abroad these days. Many are filmed in Bangkok.'

'I don't think I want to know. I felt sick watchin' that stuff tonight. I'm goin' upstairs to see if my boys are all right.'

Thank Christ for that, he thought, as she swept past him.

It had been said that snuff films were a myth. But

that wasn't the truth. If there was money to be made then someone somewhere made that money …

He and Vinnie had been tying boulders to Jem's body with rope they'd discovered in the small boatyard at the end of Ferrol Road. Roy took a deep breath of the mud-filled air and glanced across to the bank on the far side of Forton Lake. Only blokes with boats ventured in these waters fed by the Solent, and not many of them because the mud held secrets of the old prison hulks moored there long ago. Treacherous waters, these, unless you knew them well.

'So you told Daisy?'

'I did.'

They tipped the body into a rowing boat that was moored on the wooden pontoon and climbed in. 'You can row,' said Roy. 'And don't make no fuckin' noise.'

The moon was hidden by low-slung clouds and the only light came from a lamppost at the bottom of the road. A cat slunk through the netting fence of the yard and hid itself beneath an upturned boat. Roy saw two sharp eyes glaring at him. Vinnie was puffing and panting with the exertion of the oars.

'She's got no room in her heart except for her kids and that small-time crook that was Eddie Lane,' Vinnie gasped.

'I know that. And you knew that when you moved in on her,' said Roy.

'I meant it when I told her to make sure his son

remembers *his* father. That boy thinks too much of you. It's not healthy, you bastard.'

Roy figured they'd come to about the middle of the sea-fed inlet.

'Here will do.'

Vinnie set the oars straight in the rowlocks. 'We ought to say a few words.'

'Like a prayer or something?' Roy looked down at Jem's body. He was a big man and they'd had a hell of a job getting him this far. 'Say it in your mind, copper, we ain't never said no prayers getting rid of people before.'

He saw Vinnie give him an old-fashioned look as they leaned carefully forward and heaved Jem's bulk over the side. The small craft rocked dangerously.

'Mind out,' shouted Vinnie.

Roy's heart was beating furiously. The water lapped more easily around the rowboat now the two of them were seated once more. He looked at the dark place where Jem's body had disappeared. There was little likelihood of it resurfacing. The crabs and bottom feeders would dine well tonight.

'Mind you keep your mouth shut about this,' he said.

'Or what?' Vinnie was wiping his hands down his clothes.

'You know fucking well what. I go down, you go down. Each of us on our toes, eh? Never knowing 'ow the other'll jump.'

'Quite so.' Vinnie pulled the oars out and began

rowing. 'I hear you've been putting it about a bit up in the Smoke since you got out?'

'I been shut up in Parkhurst, so what?'

'You don't like me being in bed with my wife but you shag anything that moves.'

'You kind of forget *I'm* the free agent. *You* were Daisy's bloke.'

'And you want to be in my place?'

'If she'd have me, I make no bones about it. It ain't no guarantee she'll come running to me. That woman's a law unto herself. I 'appen to care whether she's hurting or not, that's all.'

When they reached the pontoon there was still a dark silence between them that continued until Roy retied the boat.

'Give me a head start, then start walking,' he said.

He'd set off and flagged down a taxi in Whitworth Road when the rain came …

Daisy's voice broke into Roy's thoughts.

'You said *four* things.'

He answered, knowing he'd probably get his head bitten off.

'I got you on my side, Daisy. I saw the look on your face when you thought I was 'urt.' She sat down opposite him and opened her mouth to speak, but he leaned over and put his fingers across her lips. 'Let me finish.' He took his hand away. 'You jumped in the deep end and took charge when I hardly knew what was 'appening. You did that because somewhere deep

355

down inside there's still a little bit of you that can't let go.'

Daisy closed her eyes. She was breathing heavily, and he could almost see her mulling things over in her mind. Then she picked up her mug and drank the rest of her tea, cold the way she liked it.

The moment had passed. He cursed inwardly but said as breezily as he could, 'So, you're in alone, smelling of vanilla bath salts. Where's my African friends?'

CHAPTER 27

'You both looks like you lost a fiver and found a quid.'

Vera threw her red jacket over the back of the chair, pulled her pin from her large black hat and taking it from her curls shook her head vigorously.

'I likes that hat but it makes me head ache.' She replaced the pin in the hat for safekeeping.

'There's tea in the pot, if you fancy it,' said Daisy.

'Feel better now, do you?' Vera sniffed at Daisy, who still looked like a bloody wet weekend, but the question was ignored.

'So where are my Africans?' Roy repeated.

Vera set her hat over the radio on the sideboard and said, 'You should thank me, Roy Kemp, for what I've put meself through tonight. And you don't look so 'ot. Ain't you goin' to clean yourself up a bit?' She didn't think she'd ever seen Roy looking like he'd been pulled through a hedge backwards. She sank down on the bench next to Daisy and eased off her high heels. 'Cor, that's better.' Roy stared at her in amazement.

She said to him, 'You reckon I ain't capable of lookin' after a couple of blokes?'

'You're very capable, I'll grant you that.'

'Well, Daisy brought 'em back 'ere and gave 'em a cup of tea. Don't know what we'd do without tea, do you? She made me get meself up—'

'It took 'er bloody ages, Roy, you know what she's like plasterin' her face on,' Daisy chimed in.

'Afterwards I took the pair of 'em down to Daisychains. They said they 'adn't eaten, so we fed 'em and then I got Mike to rig the roulette wheel so they won some dosh. You can pay me back what they won an' all. I ain't a bleedin' charity case. Then we went round to Heavenly Bodies, and though they don't drink no alcohol neither of 'em turned down Kirsty nor Samantha's ministrations. That's when I left. It can't be 'ard for you to believe that two Africans could go off and be wined and dined by me. I'm a slice of English 'ospitality, I am.'

'Are they happy?'

'Really 'appy.' She winked at Daisy. 'They wasn't particularly worried about what happened at the Alma. They're *big* men in Mombasa. I think that might have slipped your mind, Roy Kemp.'

'So where are they now?'

'If they ain't still down at Heavenly Bodies they could have turned in for the night. I arranged for me flat to be sorted for 'em. Gloria didn't mind bunking down the club for once.'

Vera could see he was looking at her with his mouth

open. She never allowed blokes in her flat. Kibbles was the only male ever to have taken up residence. Vera saw him asleep on Roy's knee.

'He likes you, my little man does,' she said. 'What I say is if a bloke likes animals he's kind to women an' all.'

You're letting 'em stay in your flat? Daisy had her wits about her after all, did she?

'They can't stay 'ere, can they? The only bedroom with no one in it tonight is Susie's an' she'd 'ave a fit if she came back unexpectedly to find two huge black men in her bed, wouldn't she?'

Roy began to laugh. Vera knew he would. Then just as suddenly he stopped.

'Did you do all this just to help me?'

'Might 'ave,' Vera said. She stared hard at him. 'But I was keepin' in your good books because I don't want you goin' back on your word about helpin' Angel. Anyway, where's Vinnie?'

'Where else but writing reports and rounding up Pullinger's pals, the Maxi brothers. He sends his regards.' Vera could see Daisy had been crying. 'He said he'll be round tomorrow. Wants to talk to you both.'

'That's because she knows more about Leah than I do,' Daisy said. Vera suddenly remembered and got to her feet. Going round the table she took her handbag off the sideboard. A cloud of Californian Poppy perfume sprang out and she sniffed heartily.

'Bugger,' she said. 'The bleedin' top's come off me scent. Still, it'll make me bag smell nice, won't it?

Look what I got!' She took out a roll of notes as big as her fist. 'I won this tonight.'

Vera looked at Daisy and saw she was frowning.

'It's our bleedin' money, Vera!'

'It *was* our money. It's mine now to spend on clothes down the market. I've kept a tally of exactly 'ow much *you* bleedin' owes us, Roy Kemp.' She foraged in her bag and came out with a sheet of paper that she pushed into his hands.

'Christ! You spent all this? An' what's this "Services Rendered" malarkey?'

Vera shrugged.

'Me and Daisy's runnin' a business an' on that sheet of paper is what we spent on your African mates, including their gambling winnings an' mine. An' my Kirsty and Samantha's fuck money. You want the best, Roy Kemp, you got to pay for it! An' I don't want you sayin' we're all square as you managed to keep it hushed up about our Angel.'

'Would I?' She saw a smile lift the corner of his mouth. He was a handsome bugger, she thought. If only she was ten years younger ... well, perhaps twenty years younger. 'I knows you, an' I ain't just come up the Solent in a bleedin' bucket.'

'You told Angel she's off the hook?'

''Course I 'ave. Can't let the poor cow be miserable about that an' all. She's goin' into St James' on Wednesday. I wanted to make sure she 'ad no bleedin' worries to make her want to stick any more of that muck up her nose.'

'No one told me about you sortin' Angel out.' Vera could see Daisy was a bit put out.

'I was asleep when you got in, wasn't I, an' then I 'ad to take that Paul an' 'is mate out. Nice blokes, ain't they? You know they got pretty little kiddies and lovely wives. I saw photos of them ...'

'I wish you'd get on with it, our Vera.' Daisy had that sour look she got sometimes. Bit like she was sucking lemons.

'It's my fault,' Roy said. 'What with one thing an' another tonight it'd slipped my mind ...'

'Treatin' me like a bloody mushroom, keepin' me in the dark about stuff ...' Daisy was grumbling, but she didn't mean it, Vera knew that.

'I managed to pull in a few favours. Don't forget, Michael's my son an' all.' It warmed the cockles of Vera's heart to hear him say that. She gave a wink to Daisy who, grumbles forgotten, winked back at her.

'I can't do nothin' about that sordid government business getting out,' Roy said, stretching out his long legs. 'I reckon by April or May of next year, 1973 will be remembered as the year the government was blown apart by the sex scandal. Lambton, Jellicoe, Levy, it'll all come out. The story 'as reached Murdoch's press and the lid won't be kept on this. It's goin' to be the London sex scandal that'll shake Heath's regime.'

'But there are photos of our Angel in bed with ...'

'Not any more. The negatives have conveniently disappeared. There are still photos to be used as evidence, but not of Angel.'

'I reckon it's a shame in a way, I could have done with a bit of exposure as 'er madam,' said Vera. She could see Daisy glaring at her. 'Well, you can't deny it would up the profits at Daisychains.' She thought she'd better shut up, they were both glaring at her now.

'I suppose I should thank you for that, an' all?'

Vera smiled inwardly as she saw the look of hope on Roy's face at Daisy's words. He thinks he's in 'ere, she thought.

'Come upstairs with me,' said Daisy, beaming at Roy.

Roy gently lifted down a disgruntled Kibbles to the floor then practically shot to his feet. Daisy got up from the bench and swept out of the kitchen ahead of him with a determined look on her face. Vera heard their soft footsteps on the stair carpet then the click of Daisy's bedroom door closing.

After a while Daisy returned to the kitchen and, taking a bowl from beneath the sink, began to part fill it with hot water. She reached up into the cupboard and took out the salt and sprinkled in a good handful. Bringing it over to Vera she said, 'I'll get you a towel in a minute. Take your bleedin' stockings off and soak your feet.'

'What about Roy?'

'What *about* Roy?'

'What you doin' for 'im, Dais?'

'Oh, that? He asked me earlier if I still 'ad any of 'is

clothes 'ere. I do, an' I showed him where they was so he could 'ave a bleedin' shower.'

'Is that all?'

''Course that's all, you daft tart!'

CHAPTER 28

'You look a right old bag!'

Her jangled nerves would quieten in a while; they always did. Angel leaned against the tiled wall of the Daisychains ladies' toilet, took a few deep breaths, and waited for the rush to kick in. And it did, almost immediately, allowing her the strength to quickly gather up her compact, flush the cut straw down the lavatory and take a last look at her face in the compact's mirror after she'd wiped off the remains of the white powder. 'No, girl, you don't look so bad after all,' she whispered.

In a few days' time she'd be in St James', getting used to being without a snort, so she thought she'd better use up her stash now. In the wall mirror outside she saw how thin she'd become. But hell, who wanted to be fat anyway? A few moments ago she'd been tired but now she was on top of the world and looking forward to seeing her boy.

She opened the door carefully. Vera would do her nut if she caught her using. Angel walked out of the club into the dull drizzle of rain that obscured the view of Portsmouth.

Luckily the bus was waiting at the terminus. She jumped on and went upstairs, seating herself next to a window.

She felt electrified, as though she was wired to some invisible current. She also needed to go to the toilet and hoped she could hold out until she got to the prefab. She'd been having a bit of trouble just lately. Coke did that to her, gave her the shits. She was also thirsty all the time – she'd make a pot of tea when she got to Clayhall.

Michael was out with Malkie, who'd taken the boy to Hill Head to sketch the small boats moored up near the sailing club. Her Michael was a clever little bastard. Got that from his father, no doubt. Angel sighed contentedly.

Who'd have thought Roy would have got her off the hook like that? Of course, Daisy and Vera had a lot to do with it as well and she *had* been working for Vera ... Still, it showed Roy cared about her, didn't it?

'Where to, love?'

'Fighting Cocks.' Angel opened her purse and gave the conductor the right fare. He nodded and gave her a ticket to the pub on the corner at Clayhall where the prefabs were.

She pushed back her long hair. Fuck it! The hit was wearing off already. That was the trouble – the rushes wore off so soon. She wiped her nose. This cold she had didn't help, either. When she wasn't coughing, her nose was running. Next week, once she'd started the programme, she'd be on the way to becoming a decent woman again. She couldn't wait.

Her heart was beating fast. She wondered if the woman sitting next to her could hear it. Don't be stupid, she told herself. You're getting paranoid again.

Michael and Malkie wouldn't be home until four o'clock. Her son would be dead chuffed to see her. It would be a lovely surprise for him to find her there, waiting.

She knew she was going to have a hard time in hospital, but Alec had told her it would be well worth it in the end. She'd be a proper mum again. Camping. That's what she'd do in the summer. Buy a tent and some sleeping bags. Take Michael camping in the New Forest. She could take Daisy's boys as well. They'd have a whale of a time. Maybe, just maybe, Roy might come along . . .

He'd be at the airport now, waving off his African mates. Nice blokes, what she'd seen of them. When she'd asked Vera why they were in Gosport, Vera had tapped the side of her nose and said, 'That's for me to know and you to find out!'

It was still raining when she got off the bus and crossed the road, taking care not to twist her ankles in her high heels on the broken paving stones as she walked down to the prefab where her son lived.

The rain made everything smell fresh and clean.

She knew when the rain stopped the dog shit and thrown-away fish and chip wrappers would still be there, nearly washed away, but not quite.

The kitchen door wasn't locked.

'Hello,' she said to Alec. He was sitting at the kitchen table working on some papers.

'Malkie and Michael are out.' He gave her a lovely smile and got up to greet her. He had lovely manners, she thought.

'I know. I came as a surprise for Michael. You don't mind?'

He laughed, showing white teeth. 'Why should I mind? You've more right here than I have. I'm just working out some maths for Michael to get his teeth into before he goes to bed. I can see him taking it up. Maybe becoming an accountant.'

'Really?'

'Don't look so surprised. He's got it in him.' She preened. 'Why don't you make yourself a cup of tea or something and I'll be with you in a moment as soon as I've finished.'

'I'll just go in the bathroom and dry my hair,' she said. 'That rain's the deadly kind that soaks right in.'

Angel walked through the living room and into the bathroom. The whole place smelled of polish, she thought. Alec was a nice chap. He had a bit of a thing for Daisy, not that Daisy could see it. Everyone else could spot it, but not her.

Angel admired the way Alec had turned his life around. But she was going to do the very same thing, wasn't she? She made it to the bathroom just in time. Bloody stomach cramps she had now, even after getting rid of that lot.

She opened her bag and took out her compact.

She had the new stuff she'd got off the kid in Daisychains.

She wasn't going to buy any more. Didn't have the cash anyway. This was positively the last she'd do.

She was well aware that withdrawal was going to hit her hard. She'd had discussions with Vera's doctor friend and he'd told her she'd be agitated, tired and depressed for a long time after she'd stopped the habit. She'd feel as though all the world was against her. Didn't she feel like that now?

It would be worth it. She could do it. She *would* quit. For Michael's sake she'd do it. In the meantime, where was the harm in using up this last supply?

In the base of her compact lay the screw of paper containing the white powder. On the top of the cistern she piled a small amount then chopped it fine with her blade. A quick snort and then another, and immediately the rush hit her. She put down the toilet pan lid and sat there. This was a rubbish hit. She was coming down already. Her head was woozy, but where was the feeling of wellbeing?

Unsteadily she chopped in the rest of the powder. What did she need to keep any of it back for? She'd be on top of the world for when Michael came home. That'd surprise him.

She had to turn away from the powder as a

coughing fit started. She didn't want to blow any of the precious stuff away, did she? When the coughing subsided it left her with a pain in her chest. Never mind, when the high hit her that'd soon go. She took one line, then the other.

Jesus, but her heart was beating fast. She hadn't had *that* much coke, had she? She was suddenly confused. Had she just had a snort that hadn't hit the spot or what? She must have, there wasn't any left. She didn't remember. Jesus, but her throat was dry.

Angel staggered towards the bath and turned on the tap, taking great gulps of cold water, but she couldn't breathe properly and drink at the same time. It was as though she couldn't get enough air into her lungs. And the pain was cutting her in two. She looked at her hand, which was shaking. She tried to turn the tap off but although her hand was on the metal, it wasn't turning it. Her hand didn't seem to belong to her any more. And now she couldn't lift her arm. What the fuck was happening? This was shitty coke, she thought. That little fucker she got it off must have thinned it with something nasty. No, this couldn't happen, not to her. She was going to St James'.

Her mouth felt funny and her tongue seemed to fill it up. She wanted to cry out to Alec ... it was Alec in the kitchen ... wasn't it?

Angel slid to the floor.

All she'd wanted to do, she thought, was to surprise her Michael.

*

Daisy looked down at the rooftops of the houses in Portchester. They looked tiny, like doll's houses. She remembered sitting in this very same car park, with the same man at her side, after Kenny, her husband, had been cremated. Eddie Lane had been waiting for her in the lounge of the Seagull pub where she'd arranged for refreshments for Kenny's mourners.

That seemed a long time ago. The service for Angel at the crematorium had brought it all back.

'I don't think I'll ever get over the sight of young Michael in his wheelchair saying goodbye to his mother,' said Daisy. 'I'm going to see that sight for-ever in me dreams.'

'He wanted to be there. If I'd stopped him, in years to come he'd've hated me.' Roy put his hand on Daisy's knee. She looked across at him in the driver's seat of the Rolls. He was tired and his face was lined with pain. The new leather interior and his cologne were vying for attention. 'She was a good mother,' he said.

'Who's goin' to look after Michael now?'

'I'm his father, Daisy.'

She nodded. 'I've waited a long time to 'ear you say that.'

'Top-up?' He didn't wait for her to reply but took his hand from her knee and reached into the cabinet built into the dashboard. He poured a generous measure of brandy into the glass in her hand, then added lime juice from another bottle. Daisy watched the swirl of the liquids as the flavours mixed.

She waited until he'd refilled his own glass then said, 'You ain't really goin' into business makin' mucky films, are you?'

'You could easily persuade me not to, Daisy.'

She grinned at him and saw he meant it. Her heart lifted. 'I'm beginning to like this car.' She gazed around the interior. 'I was always drinkin' brandy with you in the back of your old Humber, remember?'

'I remember,' he said. 'And most times we were toastin' each other and thanking God for the good things in our lives.'

Daisy thought about Susie and how even a blind man could see her love for Joy was helping her over the tragic loss of Si. And Vera? Vera was the one constant in Daisy's life that never changed. Alec? He was going back to teaching. Taken a post at St John's School in Forton Road. She knew he'd still be part of Michael's life, and thanked God for it.

'The way things 'ave panned out at least I ain't in fear of me bleedin' life any more,' she said.

'And you got two cracking boys in Eddie and Jamie, Dais.'

'This ain't no celebration, though.'

He swallowed a good mouthful and said, 'I don't know, that copper of yours ain't hanging around you no more, is he?'

Daisy's hand gripped the glass hard and she gave an involuntary intake of breath.

'That was below the belt, even for you, you bastard.' She looked at him. He had a smug grin on his face.

'You knew, didn't you, that he was back with Clare?'

His voice was like melted chocolate, dark and smooth.

'He wasn't any good for you, Daisy. He doesn't understand you like I do.'

'You shit!' Daisy could feel her temper rising. 'You could've warned me what was coming an' you never did.' It was like a black fog had suddenly descended on her and she couldn't shake it off. 'Well, I ain't warning *you* about this!'

She watched her hand swing across as she threw the brandy at him. It seemed to pour from the glass as if in slow motion. Then the glass rolled to the floor.

Daisy stayed in the car just long enough to watch the liquid run through Roy's wavy hair, over his surprised face, and then drip on to his brand-new expensive silk shirt and dark suit.

Opening the door, she swung out her legs and then walked purposefully over the cobbles of the car park and down the road.

There were only a few die-hard leaves hanging on the trees and already it smelled like the depths of winter. The grass was damp where it had recently rained and at the sides of the road very late Michaelmas daisies bloomed purple and blue, but their edges were aged with brown.

She took great gulps of the fresh cold air and it seemed as if every intake of clean air gave her back the confidence she thought she'd lost when Vinnie told her he was going back to his wife.

Fucking men, she thought, more bleeding trouble than they're worth. What did she and Vera need with blokes? Only good for carrying heavy weights, most of them.

Well, she and Vera had Daisychains and they'd make it into a bigger success than it had ever been now that drugs weren't being sold there. She had her boys and she loved the bones of them. She lived in Gosport, the best place on the south coast, where the people were real people, not bleeding cardboard cut-outs.

All that made her a very wealthy woman indeed.

Daisy heard the distinctive purr of the Rolls behind her. It was following her. She walked at an even more leisurely pace, but the car didn't overtake her. Then she began to laugh. Quietly at first, then louder and louder until the tears began to roll down her cheeks. She was still laughing but she couldn't resist stopping and waiting until the big car drew up beside her.

Roy had wiped off most of the brandy but his hair was still wet. She could smell the fruity smell of lime juice on him and his silk shirt was dark with the stickiness. His slate-grey eyes were creased into a smile. There was an upturn to his mouth as he leaned over and opened the door on the passenger side.

'Get in,' he said. 'You contrary bitch.'

'Piss off,' Daisy said.

But she got in anyway.

If you enjoyed *Fatal Cut*,
don't miss

JAIL BAIT

published by Orion in March 2010.
Price £18.99
ISBN: 978-0-7528-9734-9

Here's a taster . . .

CHAPTER 1

Lol, eyes closed, stretched her neck up so she wouldn't have to see his face. He was holding her arms, his spit dribbling from his grunting mouth as he ripped into her.

'You fuckin' love it!' The others were yelling and laughing, watching and waiting as she continued to struggle, the gravel cutting into her flesh. Tears were running down her face. God, how it hurt.

'Lemme go you fuckin' bastard!' Amazingly, he lifted himself from her back and rolled off. For a moment he lay on his side.

Her body raw, Lol moaned, opening her eyes, and made to rise from the dirt. The smell of his sweaty flesh and the horror of what had been done to her forced her to puke, and she tried in vain to wipe her long hair away from the vomit.

'Help me,' she whispered, looking up at them. But now the man was standing and Lol could do no more than watch as he bent and grabbed her by what re-mained of her skirt and blouse, lifted her, and swung his other arm in a stiff arc, hitting her mouth with his clenched fist.

'Anyone else want a go?' he growled before throwing Lol down again as though she was a rag doll.

Someone slapped the man on the back and he laughed then staggered away from her. Lol closed her eyes. No one, nothing could help her now. She lay there, afraid even to moan. From somewhere came the muted sounds of Abba.

'You're cute.' A second man was bending towards her now licking his lips. He mumbled something and shoved a red froth of lace in her broken face. Her panties. The laughter grew. 'You certainly know how to get a bloke all of a quiver, you do.'

'Ma! Come 'ere!'

But Eddie Lane didn't wait for his mother. He could see what looked like a woman struggling with a man in the near darkness of the alley near the tobacconist's shop. He turned from the window and elbowed his way through the drunken crowd celebrating Red Rum's third Aintree Grand National win. Out through Daisychains' brass and wood door, and then he was quickly across the road towards the ferry, narrowly missing being hit by a car and running straight into the small crowd of young thugs.

'Get off 'er!' He yanked at the clothing of a bare-arsed bloke about to give his all to the girl face down on the ground. While the man clutched at his genitals, Eddie hit him. A well aimed punch that lifted the bloke off his feet and sent him staggering back into his group of mates.

Eddie stepped back, his hand sliding to the breast pocket of his leather jacket. He withdrew his knife and pressed the button that locked the blade in the open position. The silence was now palpable.

'Which of you fuckers want this?' Eddie was breathing hard. He was also aware that at nearly seventeen he was probably younger than at least three of the men but he was banking on the blade scaring the shit out of them. He thanked God he was tall, well built, and had had the advantage of growing up on Gosport's tough streets. He stood his ground.

A voice yelled, 'The fucker wouldn't dare …'

'I ain't takin' the bleedin' chance,' said another.

He noted it took less than a blink of an eyelid for the group to clear and for the coward adjusting his clothing to yell back at him from the safe distance of Rennie's Boatyard's entrance along Beach Street,

'Fuckin' freak!'

Eddie breathed a sigh of relief. His heart was beating like a fucking hammer drill. Despite his practised skill with the blade he hadn't had the faintest idea what he would do if the group had called his bluff. He put away the knife and bent down to the girl.

At first she screamed, 'Get off me!' She fell back, rolling on her side, crying and groaning. He stared at the blood in her blonde hair and the cuts on her skin from the sharp gravel. He put out a hand and stroked the side of her face. She flinched as his fingers made contact and struck out at him, sobbing.

'No more!'

Eddie grabbed at both her flailing hands, noticing that several of her long painted nails had been torn away.

'Relax,' he said. Her small heart-shaped face was streaked with mascara and she'd lost one false eyelash. His heart went out to her; his Auntie Vera was always having trouble with her false eyelashes and his mum was forever fixing them. 'I'm not going to hurt you,' he said.

She tried to yank her hands free.

'Relax,' he said again. And then she opened her lids and looked pleadingly up at him with frightened eyes: violet eyes, swimming with tears, pitifully searched his face. He stared at her, past her straight nose below which a very kissable mouth trembled, despite a top lip split in two places, while blood was fast drying into the heavy puffiness already covering one side of her face.

'They've gone,' Eddie said, letting go of her wrists, which felt small and fragile, almost birdlike.

The girl's eyes went right through him as if he were naked. He squirmed beneath her gaze and then he was pushed aside.

'Come out the way, let the dog see the bleedin' rabbit!'

He stepped back and the fierce small woman hunkered down in front of the girl – no mean feat, for Vera was wearing a tight skirt and four-inch heels. A waft of her heavy perfume flew into his nostrils.

'How bad is she hurt, Vera?'

'How the fuck do I know when I ain't looked at 'er yet? Let's get her back to the safety of Daisychains,' she said. 'People are beginning to gawp.'

'If it had been darker you'd not have noticed the bastards as did this,' said Daisy, his mother, who had followed Vera out the club. She put her hand on her son's arm. 'Wouldn't you 'ave thought that at least someone else would have stepped in and stopped this before it got ugly?'

'People are scared of gettin' involved, Daisy. It was lucky for 'er Eddie looked out the window.'

His mother didn't answer Vera, but smoothed back the hair that had fallen across the girl's face. 'You're safe now,' she said, and there was no mistaking the compassion in her voice. Then to Eddie, 'Give us your coat to cover her with, son.'

He slipped out of his leather jacket and handed it to Daisy, who said, 'You'll be getting a reputation like your father 'ad for flashin' that fucking knife about. You know I don't like that thing, even though it served its purpose this time.' She looked down at the girl. 'C'mon, sweetheart, let's get you sorted out.' They pulled the girl gently back into a sitting position and slipped Eddie's jacket around her.

'I ... I'll be ... I'll be all right.'

She was struggling to gather her torn clothing

around herself and there was a gasp from Vera, who was helping her. 'Fuck me!'

'Oh!' Daisy whispered. She turned her head and stared up at Eddie.

'What's the matter, Mum? She's going to be all right, ain't she?'

He couldn't explain but it suddenly mattered very much to him that the girl would be safe and sound.

'We'll do our very best, son. You probably saved her life. Carry her over to Daisychains.' He could determine nothing from his mother's steady gaze until she whispered, 'Only this little girl ain't a she, he's a he!'

CHAPTER 2

'We're losing money every fuckin' day.' Daisy waved the small wad of notes she'd just removed from the till beneath Vera's nose.

'Calm yourself, Dais, you'll give yourself an 'eart attack!'

Vera pushed Daisy's hand away and continued leaning on the bar top. 'What d'yer expect?' She waved a scarlet-nailed hand around Daisychains' near empty bar. 'You wants this place run squeaky clean, so without the pull of drugs the punters goes elsewhere. You can't bloody blame 'em.'

Daisy sighed, folded the notes, and slammed the till drawer shut. She put the notes in her pocket. 'We're goin' under, Vera. Can't afford decent wages no more for top-line girls so we have to make do with scrubbers.' Vera opened her mouth but Daisy stopped her. 'Let me finish. I'd like to smarten the club up a bit, a lick of paint 'ere and there. Maybe that'd liven things up.' She took a deep breath, and smelled only polish and air freshener. At this time of night the club should be reeking of fags and men and the leathery smell of their plump wallets, she thought.

'The outside do look shabby, Dais ...' Vera walked to a table and picked up a lone fag packet that she brought back to the bar and placed on an empty ash-tray.

Daisy stared at Vera's trim small body in her tight black skirt and red frilled silk blouse wafting her trademark perfume about her.

'There just ain't the cash, Vera.' Daisy pointed across the room to where a good-looking man in jeans and flowered shirt was rubbing a table with a yellow duster. 'Even Alec gives us a couple of hours' work a day for free.' Daisy gazed at the man who, feeling her eyes upon him, looked up with a smile that transformed his sad face.

'Only because the school's closed, Daisy, an' he don't 'ave to get up in the mornin's. He can't teach when there ain't no kids there, can he? Thank God teachers get paid during the 'olidays so he don't mind workin' for nothing.' Vera leant forward and whispered, 'He only comes in because he likes you, Dais an' I reckon he needs a bit of company. Lately he's seemed more depressed than usual ...' Vera's eyes fixed on Alec and Daisy could see she was deep in thought, then Vera straightened up and said, 'But if we can't afford to pay staff we certainly can't afford no tins of bleedin' paint.'

'Shut up about the fuckin' paint. And an alcoholic workin' in a pub is enough to make anyone depressed,' said Daisy. She remembered when Alec had been a defeated man, hunched on his patch opposite the club outside the men's urinals. People travelling by bus and ferry boat to Portsmouth chucked coins into a tin for him, if he was lucky. He was a pavement artist of the highest calibre but a drunk as well. He'd had long matted hair and he'd stunk to high heaven.

She and Vera had got him into a special detox programme over in Portsmouth and he'd been clean ever since. More than clean. He'd embraced life and gone back to teaching, but there were times like today when Daisy could almost reach out and touch his loneliness.

Daisy saw Vera's eyes take in the four male customers huddled over their dregs of beer. David Soul was singing 'Don't Give Up On Us Baby' and Daisy wished with all her heart that she wouldn't have to give up on the club she'd fought so hard to keep running. 'I sent the croupiers home, Vera. There's no punters at the gaming tables.'

'But it's not even midnight, Dais.'

Daisy shrugged. 'We used to 'ave such a lot of fun in 'ere, didn't we?' She looked at the clock and her voice was wistful as she added, 'Remember when the Kray twins brought that gangster film star George Raft in 'ere? All our girls were over 'im like a bleedin' rash.'

She saw Vera smile. 'Customers was fallin' over themselves to get in then, but you can't live in the past. Roy was around a lot in them days an' he brought a sort of swagger to the place.'

'What you're sayin' Vera, is the place 'as gone down hill since I made Roy opt out of this club an' take his bleedin' drug deals with 'im.'

Vera shrugged.

'So, it's me own fault, is it? Don't you understand I didn't want my boys, Eddie and Jamie, brought up in a bloody druggie's paradise?'

Vera held her gaze steady.

'You could let me put some money in, Dais?'

'Don't you fuckin' patronise me!' Daisy snapped. She tapped her fingers angrily on the bar top, but she knew that without help of some kind there was no way she could pay the pile of household bills and club invoices she'd hidden at home in a kitchen drawer. It had got to the stage where she didn't even open the envelopes any more, just dumped them in the kitchen cabinet to join the others as soon as the postman delivered them.

But pride wouldn't let her accept Vera's money. Her outburst had caused her friend's face to crumple in on itself like a screwed-up paper bag. Daisy knew the offer was genuine but she also knew the high street massage parlour Vera owned was going through a slump.

Birth control pills had taken away the fear of unwanted pregnancies and women were giving sex away like sweets from a bag. Only the regular johns went to Vera's shop, Heavenly Bodies, now. Nevertheless, Daisy knew she shouldn't have snapped at her friend.

And no way was she going to worry her further

by telling her she suspected some bloke was spying on herself – or on the goings-on in the club. Twice Daisy thought she'd caught a glimpse of the same dark-haired man peeping through the smoked glass windows of Daisychains, but he'd melted away into the shadows before she'd copped a better look at him. It wasn't worth worrying about, she told herself.